I0699711

XELAN'S VERSE

VAST COLLECTIVE BOOK XII

Nicole Hayes

THE VAST COLLECTIVE SERIES

Last of Daylight
By the Pale Moonlight
Asylum in Firelight
Nox's Verse
Glass Chains
Pyrite Prison
Restraining Silver
Korac's Verse
Thirst
Levee
Flood
Xelan's Verse
Cascading Light

CONTENTS

ENTRY ONE
Family, Friends, and The Foundation of Ruination
Page 1

ENTRY TWO
Family Complex
Page 25

ENTRY THREE
The Beginning Of Everything
Page 43

ENTRY FOUR
And The Beginning Of The End
Page 61

ENTRY FIVE
Everything I Wanted
Page 83

ENTRY SIX
And Everything I Lost
Page 113

ENTRY SEVEN
My Progeny Or My People
Page 137

ENTRY EIGHT
Chasing All The Wrong I'd Made
Page 155

ENTRY NINE
Amends For Others
Page 175

ENTRY TEN
My Ultimate Weakness
Page 195

ENTRY ELEVEN
My Brother, The Villain; Myself, The Monster
Page 225

ENTRY TWELVE
Amends For Myself
Page 247

ENTRY THIRTEEN
Alone With Me
Page 263

ENTRY FOURTEEN
Hope In The Light Of Shadow
Page 299

SNEAK PEEK
Page 323

TIME LINE
Page 330

TRIGGER WARNINGS

Please consider my entire series 'Rated R.' These books are meant for readers sixteen years and older. Read with the following triggers in mind:
- Graphic Violence
- Graphic Language
- Graphic Sex Scenes
- Deep Dive into Mental Illness
- Abortion
- Gaslighting
- Domestic Violence
- Threat of Cannibalism
- Battle Scenes
- Colonization
- Genocide

ENTRY ONE

FAMILY, FRIENDS, AND THE FOUNDATION
OF RUINATION

I AM PAX'S FATHER, TAMEKA'S HUSBAND, THE PRINCE OF CINDER, MENTOR TO THE SHADOW, AND A CONCERTED EMPEROR OF IONA PAX. *While you've never thought of me as a monster, there was a time in my life when I'm certain I was one.*

"That's not how the story starts, Superman."

Rayne, are you giggling at me?

When you nod, this four-year-old memory of you grins big enough to show a missing baby tooth while perched precariously on my knee.

Well, then it's only fair if I—Tickle attack!

"No! Hehehe stop!" You kick out with your tiny sneakers and try to wiggle away, but I earned every one of those high-pitched squeals.

I am safer inside this old Divine Booth than I am anywhere else in Iona Pax. Here, I can hide from those I love most. In this custom memory experience, I can talk to you and share the story of my Verse with you. I don't know where you are, Rayne, but I haven't forgotten my promise. I'll never stop looking for you.
But the others...
Now that they've met the monster in me, I fear their judgment. Their hurt, confused expressions. But most of all, I fear their doubt. How could they continue following someone like me when they can't even stand to look in my direction?

"Because you kept too much from them for too long."

Your mother had her hands full with you at this age. At twelve-years-old, the other figment of you borders the ages where blunt honesty comes less from innocence and more from a sudden awareness of the fables told by the adults around you. It's a hard place to dwell.

While I stare at you from across the coffee table in my study, you sit on the floor and write in your notebook, refusing to make eye contact.

It was never my plan to withhold information. The timing was never right. I wanted you to be there.

"We're always here, Superman." Your tiny hand reaches for my face, and I lean down into it, feeling at once whole and lost. "You don't have to look for us anymore."

The older you assures me without an upward glance, "It's okay to be afraid to let go. Hell, I think it makes you normal." This iteration of you is dressed with entirely too much defiance, all black and spiked. Long before the days when I taught you how to take care of yourself, you were already confident in your abilities and your words.

I'm not ready to hear them because both versions of you are correct.

I'm not telling it right.

With a ruffle of your little headband, I bounce my knee once, to your delight, before continuing properly.

Once upon a time, there was a handsome Prince who threw a glamorous party for his friends.

"You'd better have a good fucking reason for hijacking my union night, Traitor Prince."

Was that anyway to refer to an Emperor? Korac was naturally upset with my timing. I didn't blame him, but he usually held such high regard for decorum.

At least Sagan was taking my ill-timed announcement with grace. "If you're ready to tell, I'm ready to listen." She opened a conduit to the stronghold.

Tameka left my side to stand by it. "Who's coming with us?"

"Me!" Pax hopped out of his seat, remembering to bring his straw—It's his current favorite quirk. I adore it. He took up at his mother's side.

Kyle asked, "Will there be more food?"

I stepped into the conduit, turning back to say, "I organized it all. Rooms are arranged, too. I wanted everyone together when I told my Verse—"

"But why did you wait until my wedding night?!" Korac growled out while pinching the bridge of his nose. He really was a sight to see when flustered.

This was so much payback for every smirk he'd given me when Tameka asked a question I wasn't ready to answer. For every snide comment referencing my less than pristine past. Yes. This was deliberate.

"I wish I'd been there to see it." Preteen you is experiencing a mean streak. Your wicked grin belies your pretense of being too cool and absorbed in your writing to listen.

Every time I see you, Rayne, I beam at you because you're so much like me.

We relocated the wedding party to my stronghold, where Tameka, Pax, and I lived under Aria and Torch's guardianship. The two Gargantuan Lyriks took up posts at the entrances to the room, prepared at all times to defend the Imperial family.

I ordered, "Progeny with me. Everyone else is welcome to join as they like. We'll be in my study."

I didn't wait to see if anyone followed. I climbed the synchronized steps up the ravine filled with mementos under glass, a museum of my life.

When I entered the hexagonal room lined with my journals and furnished with black couches, I saw you sitting there. Young and full of purpose, the figment of my memories asked me to deliver you into enemy territory and endanger your life for one sample of my brother's blood. It was the first time you said to me, "I love you, Superman—"

"It always smells of leather in here," Sagan remarked as she followed me inside. Her smile matched the place, warm and haunted.

Did Sagan know? Have you told her? About the day I tried to convince you to hide from it all in here, safe, and how you refused?

Tameka knew. She smoothed one warm hand up my shoulder and kissed my cheek. The soft smile on her beautiful lips spoke volumes of her empathy. I love her for it. She said, "Let's all get comfortable."

Andrew and Lucas filed in, stealing one plush loveseat to themselves. Korac sat in an armchair, and Sagan draped herself in his lap. It was fair given that I'd ruined their wedding night. Kyle and Silence followed, with her peering around the room until her gunmetal eyes located the small fireplace filled with Cascading Light. They remained standing. Tumu and Lamassau were the last to file in, occupying the big couch with the Gargantuan compressed to seven feet of his height. Outside, I could hear the others quietly talk amongst themselves.

Bones said, "I got a caramel cheesecake and one hundred credits that says Xelan's Verse will be the best of the three."

"I'll take that bet," Iuo answered.

Twenty-One raised him, "Two caramel cheesecakes that the original will reign supreme."

Lam hissed on the couch, and Tumu chuckled at him.

When Pehton said, "Three on Korac's," Korac beamed at her.

The General said, "Proceed."

Tameka nudged me.

I guess I'd avoided it enough. "Because I know Rayne and Iona Pax will eventually want to hear this, I'm recording the moment in a perfect hologram. This room and anyone in it will appear in my Verse to her. Come and go as you please. I only ask that you participate while in the room."

Outside, Miy muttered, "Participate?"

Someone shushed her.

Tameka hid a wince as she always did when I mentioned you, Rayne.

She and the others thought I was struggling to grieve you, unaware of all the ways you could return to us.

Korac glared at me with a raised brow. Interested and eager for me to proceed. As much as he abhorred the timing, my General was looking forward to this.

I lifted Tameka's hand and kissed it.

Abashed, Pax cried, "Dad!"

We all melted for a moment at him, hiding his reddened face, then I nodded at one wall of journals. "Tameka, reach for the first. Yes, the highest." I directed her as she followed my request by climbing the ladder and collecting the very first volume. "Read the first line for me."

Tameka smiled at the gathered people before opening it. Then she frowned and read, "Our father is not—*cannot be*—mine." She peered curiously at me.

I nodded, more solemn this time before saying, "As I was telling Sagan months ago when Korac's Verse first aired, these histories steal away whatever sense I've made of my life."

Kyle says, "I don't know. It sounds like you were making perfect sense before."

I held up a finger. "Ah. But there's the issue. I had no confirmation. I was raised under a man I was certain couldn't be my father, but with no evidence to support me or reason to dare doubt my mother. Nox's Verse rocked my foundation."

As I understand it now, it also rocked yours, Rayne.

"Hee." During the telling of my story, a strand of your hair escaped your headband. I tuck it back under for you, and your eyes sparkle with glee.

Back to the tale.

Tameka returned to my side while I stared at the black fire, saying, "Given how much was already explained in the other two Verses, I must deviate from how each of them began. We don't open with my conception. The Shadow and the rest of the empire already know that. Instead, I'll start with my earliest memory."

"**NOCK**. Nock, wake up."

I was Earth-age three. A noise alarmed me in my sleep, and when I realized what it was, I sought my older brother.

"Xelan? What is it?" Nox's deep voice was rough with the edge of sleep as he stirred in his bed. After rubbing them, he peered at me through black eyes.

I remembered they were always so shiny and dark, like onyx. In them, I saw my reflection. Small of frame, the braid my mother had made of my hair was longer than I was tall. Tiny hands fidgeted with the sliver of Elden's nacre around my neck. My face and arms were chubby, like Pax's. Meeting my son for the first time took me back to this exact moment.

While I shared this story, Korac propped an elbow on the arm of the chair and rested his jaw in that hand. Sagan scooted to the edge of his lap, eager to listen. Tameka pulled Pax away from an old sword I'd left on display. The rest of the Shadow in the room waited for me to continue.

It's hard for me to remember Nox like this.

"You loved him." Preteen you states the painful truth with a soft confidence I miss from our quiet conversations. "Of course, you loved your older brother. He protected you from so much."

I forgot how much until I read his Verse.

On that night millions of years ago, I looked into my brother's eyes and knew—I *knew*—even at Earth-age eight, he could help.

"Nock, da yells at ma."

Nox sprung to the edge of his bed and placed both hands on my shoulders. "Tell me. What was she doing?"

I thought it was an odd question even at my tender age, but I answered. "Screaming."

With jerky movements, he picked me up and switched our places—Me in the bed and him, standing at its side. Nox put a finger in my face, saying, "Get under the covers with the blanket over your head. Do not come out until you hear my voice. Understand me, brother mine?"

I didn't understand any of this. "I wanna go wichu."

Nox shook his head. His eyes were so grave as he glanced toward mother's room through the open chamber door. "In the bed, Xelan. I can explain when I return."

What else could I do? I nodded and did as he told me.

On bare feet, Nox padded silently out of the room. When he opened the door to mother's chambers, I heard...

At this point in the telling, Tameka took my hand. Korac looked away from me to stare into the distance, seeing what we both knew was happening.

"How does one forget the sound of muffled screams through a clamped hand?"

For the life of me, Rayne, I wish you'd never had to experience it.

The iteration of you writing at the coffee table shrugs, but little you takes my face in her tiny hands, saying, "Focus, Superman."

Safe under Nox's covers, I heard father shout, "Get the fuck out of here!"

My brother's voice was steady. "*I* wish to stay. *You* may go."

"Heathen, I will not tolerate your intrusion on my union." Heathen. Umbra had always referred to his eldest son as 'Heathen.' It never occurred to me to ask why.

In an even tone, Nox asked, "Mother, do you want father to stay?"

Savis didn't hesitate. "No."

"She has no say—"

A meaty sound interrupted Umbra's protest, followed by a loud grunt. Something heavy hit stone.

All this took place while I hid under the covers. I flinched, clutching the nacre splinter. I wanted to see, but the recollection of Nox's earnest eyes kept me in bed. To the best of my knowledge, someone was struck and fell.

Then came a dragging sound. Father was cursing and groaning.

From the hallway, Nox said, "I tire of you, old man. Leave her, or I take you apart next time. Starting with your most fond appendage."

A whimper sounded next.

"Good. Go back to Amolot."

I can only assume the next sounds I heard were father standing and shuffling away.

Mother's voice came next. "Thank you, my son." By the noise that reached me, I knew she'd kissed his hair.

Nox said, "Thank Xelan. He alerted me."

She sounded…empty as she said, "You boys should never hear such things."

"True words, mother. Why can we not leave? Uncle Vinco's people will protect us." Let me take this moment to remind you that Nox was only eight.

There was so much reason in mother's response, a deeper purpose. "One day, you will understand your place here. Yours and Xelan's. Until then, we endure."

Nox sounded more skeptical as he questioned, "Like your eye? Who will look after you?"

"Karter and Para will tend to my injuries. You return to your brother."

Defeated, Nox said, "Good night, mother."

"Good night, my son." Louder, mother called down the hall, "Good night, Xelan."

I was too confused to respond. What was wrong with my family? Why was father always hurting mother? And why was she always relying on Nox to save her? This was my earliest memory, but echoes of these exact events played through my recollection. This wasn't the first occasion.

Sagan said, "It was hard for her to leave him. You were royalty."

Korac patted her knee.

"No." I had to disagree. "Thanks to Nox's Verse, I can see things more clearly. These were tests. My mother was testing Nox and I."

Korac frowned, asking, "What do you mean?" He loved mother, thankful for all her maternal care during his time on Cinder before her death. His defensiveness was expected, but...

"She threatened to cut off your fingers if you called her 'Lady Savis.' Mother wasn't exactly warm. I believe you used the word 'severe.'"

With ice in his eyes, Korac looked away.

Silence was staring at me, and only then did I realize how insensitive I was being toward her feelings. "I'm sorry. I—"

"No apology is necessary," Silence said, as Kyle put an arm around her. She stared up at me with steel eyes taken straight from my father's gene pool. "My daughter's life was hard, and she survived in her own way. We often fortify ourselves to withstand strife. Why should Savis be any different?"

Fortified. Yes.

"That's it exactly," I said.

Andrew asked, "What happened next?"

Both of your iterations lean forward. The twelve-year-old figment presses, "What happened with Nox?" Even in this Divine Booth experience, you're asking, as if my answer holds a weight I'm not yet privy to. Still, I give into you as I gave into their expectant faces.

Nox returned to the room, closing the door behind him. "I never meant to leave it open. Xelan, were you listening the entire time?"

I pretended to be asleep while contemplating the dysfunction of my family. I was only three...

Tears squeezed from my shut lids before I could stop them, and Nox approached the bed. It dipped with his weight, substantial even at eight. The bed was pushed against the wall. Nox laid down alongside me on the edge and tucked me between him and the solid stone, leaving his back exposed to the door.

Nox said, "Shh, brother mine. Tomorrow will be better. I promise."

"Nox?"

"Hmm?"

How could I express my gratitude for having a brother willing to face my nightmares for me? One who readily stormed into our mother's room and rescued her from father's abuse? Who returned and shared his bed with me? What could I possibly say to that?

"I love you."

"I love you, too, pup. Now sleep and dream of the stars."

Everyone in my study was looking down at the floor. I wondered what they were thinking about. The tragedy of it all? Two brothers torn asunder by different approaches to the same goal? Or were they pitying our miserable childhood—

"They were loving you for turning out so wonderfully, and now they can appreciate Nox's part in that without your shame or defensiveness."

Little Rayne, it always disturbs me when you speak like this. Now that Pax does it occasionally, you'd think I'd grow used to it.

But yes. You're right. You're so right. Now that I think back on it, their faces were sad, but there were smiles beneath *it. Warm, loving ones which make the foundation of all that is Shadow.*

I owe them an apology.

Eventually, Tameka squeezed my hand. Her voice was soft, almost gentle, when she asked, "What would you like to share with us next?"

I didn't want to meet their gazes, but it seemed important to look up and face them. That's when I noticed Pax had climbed onto the couch and fell asleep, stretched across Lamassau's and Tumu's legs. They'd covered him with a duvet and let him snuggle in.

These people are my family.
Speaking of...

I smiled. "I'm sorry I started on such a grim note. Not everything was soured by abuse and schemes. Tameka, will you please turn to page two hundred and eight?" She did, and I continued, "Korac, would you mind reading the next entry?"

Tameka shot me a reassuring smile before handing my journal over to the Iona General, who accepted it with a suspicious glance in my direction.

Kyle chuckled, saying, "I don't know if I'd want to read it either."

Silence nudged him.

Lucas and Andrew shared a knowing look.

Korac looked up at Sagan, still perched on his lap before reading aloud, "Today, Nox and I made a new friend. An Icarean boy with white hair, white skin, and white eyes. His name is Korac, and he is our new brother. Mother said so." He stopped reading for a second to swallow, careful to keep his eyes from meeting anyone else's in the study before continuing. "I added a sample of his blood to the rest of my collection and snitched a few strands of his hair. One day, I hope to use one of those Tritan devices to test his DNA. I am not entirely convinced he is solely Icarean. No other Icarus looks as he does. I am fascinated with his company and look forward to making him more at home here in the Spire. Not only as a guard, but as my brother."

When Korac could read no further, I recited the next entries by heart.

"EXCELLENT, KORAC," I said, while calculating the newest update to his stats. "Your sessions with Karter are paying off. Soon, you might compete with Nox for speed."

Upside-down with his head grappled between the oldest Prince's ankles, our guard asked in a voice squeezed from choking, "What about strength?"

Releasing Korac from the lock, Nox barked out a laugh. No Icarus could match my brother for strength, and I suspected the reduction in Nox's speed was an intentional feign, but to an unknown end. Regardless, the boost to Korac's ego had him holding his chin a little higher as he crawled to his hands and knees.

Progress.

We were in the circle where father and Amolot 'trained.' I was Earth-age ten, Korac was closer to thirteen, and Nox was nearly sixteen. Decades for us, but only a year by Earth standards, had passed since Korac's arrival. Some assassination attempt on Umbra's life had recently failed. As a result, Amolot put the Spire on lock down. For an entire Earth year.

Training and terrorizing the Spire with pranks were the only forms of entertainment open to us.

I needed samples, Korac seemed restless, and even though Nox snuck out occasionally, he'd grown *more* brooding, if that were even possible.

Adventure.

We craved it. Lava boarding in the Ignis Desert wouldn't cut it this time. I knew just the thing.

One hour of flight in Nox's care later…

"Your highness, a village festival?" Korac sounded skeptical until a female strode by with legs nearly as tall as myself. Only his eyes followed her as he straightened the wrap concealing his hair. "Perhaps, I judged too quickly."

Nox gave an amused 'humph' between us.

While I admired the towering bonfires and acrobatics above, I offered out of hand, "I overheard Karter discussing the festival with one of the kitchen hands. I calculate three hours before mother and father notice us missing. Four hours before the Valkyrie are sent to fetch us. So enjoy this while you can."

"What if I object to this, Xelan?" Nox sounded questioning, not scolding. He reasoned, "I am responsible for you."

Taken in by the over stimulation surrounding us, I assured him, "I promise if anything happens to us, everyone will be quite confident I got us into it. No one would ever believe you'd willingly attend a social event, brother."

At the time, I'd dismissed it, but Nox had winced. It lingered as I pressed, "Find a partner to dance with and drink some nectar, liquor, or what have you. I know I am grateful not to be locked inside that tower another moment with…"

None of us needed to remark on Umbra's caged rat behavior. I only wished I could've brought mother with us to the party.

Korac entreated Nox, "Come along, your highness. Let us get drunk and find some entertainment."

In the study of my stronghold, Korac of the present smiled. We all possess such a smile, reminiscing about days gone by. It suited him.

Meanwhile, in my memory, Korac convinced Nox to follow him down the main thoroughfare toward a liquor vendor. I kept up, too young to go off on my own, but desperate to indulge in my curiosities.

The people performing acrobatics, for instance, did so with a balance only inherited to the winged Icari. I required only a sample of their hair to test their genetic chains. Perhaps they were descended from Elden's Coalition.

And this stand beside the alcohol vendor sold roasted kelp on a stick. It smelled divine, but how did it compare to our waning Vittle crops? Genus? Growth habits? I asked, "Nox, did you bring enough currency for—"

He handed me a fistful of coins, and I beamed at him before running to the kelp shack. It tasted like meat. How fascinating. I thanked the man and found my brothers had sat on a log behind me. It was a massive black trunk with tiny mushrooms forming on its south side. I collected a sample while Korac and Nox drank, staring into a bonfire surrounded by dancers of all sizes, genders, and skill.

They were all naked, and the bright flames glowed along their skin.

Flushed, I sat down with my eyes on the ground, eating my kelp and fidgeting with Elden's nacre shard. A pair of bare, bangled feet appeared in my line of sight. I glanced up to find a woman standing in front of Nox. She was built more slender than Karter and softer, like some of mother's nurses. Her black wavy hair cascaded to the back of her knees, beaded and ribboned.

Korac feigned nonchalance as he took a drink to disguise his eyes on her.

Without looking, Nox offered the woman some nectar, and she took a greedy drink of it until the liquor poured from her lips and rivered down her naked skin.

Korac choked on his drink.

"Did not."
"Sh… I'm telling my Verse."

The willowy female offered her hand to Nox.

Let me remind you, he was comparable to the hormonal maturity of a teenage boy on Earth.

Nox finally looked up to meet the woman's pale green eyes and solemnly shook his head.

As the female danced her way back to the fireside, Nox watched her go with something unreadable in his eyes.

That was the first time I took notice of it—My brother's peculiarity. I'd convinced myself he turned her down in my presence and accepted plenty of other offers without detection, but...

To distract myself from the quiet moment, especially with Korac's considering side glances at Nox, I searched for the source of the music. A band played on a stage accompanied by a singer. I watched long enough to see them swap one vocalist for another, but not at random. Each of the singers approached a man at the stage before they were selected. They were volunteering to sing Verses.

I'd found a way to salvage this outing.

I stored my kelp sample, saying, "Drink up, you two. I know how to revive the night." I ran to the stage without seeing if they followed because—

I gave Korac a pointed look in my study.

—They always did.

He chuffed and said, "Yeah. Right into trouble."

"The best kind." I grinned.

Sagan snickered, and Tameka bumped me with her hip. "Now we know where Rayne gets it from."

I beamed at her, prepared to continue—

Korac pointed a finger at me. "No. You do *not* get to finish this story. You're already coming out of it as some angel. I'll tell it."

"Be my guest."

"This crazy son of a respectable Icarean female signed us up to sing two rungs of Vinco's Verse. Have any of you in this room ever read the Coalition member's Verse?"

Heads shook all around. Except Sagan. She just grinned at her husband as he continued to hijack my Verse.

Korac paused to think of a comparison and then announced, "Imagine singing the *Iliad* at a party."

Kyle's eyes went wide, muttering, "That's like twelve *Bohemian Rhapsodies*."

Andrew nearly spat out his drink and choked it down to prevent doing so, while Lucas patted his back.

Tameka looked up at me, asking, "Really, Xelan?" I was still grinning.

"Did you sing it, Superman?"

I grin at you, too, before continuing.

Both of my brothers were drunk on good nectar and rousing music. Before they knew what we were doing, I dragged them onto the stage. There we were. Two princes and their exotic royal guard breaking lockdown to cause trouble.

The music started, and I froze. Hundreds of people stared up at me, and I forgot how Uncle Vinco's Verse opened. My heart went into my throat and choked me.

Korac blinked wide eyes at me.

"That's true, I did. Because I couldn't fathom what the fuck you were thinking—"

"Battle-bred and true,
"I will find my way to you."
The crowd stomped their feet.
"No matter how many oceans I cross—
"The mountains I climb to the sky—"
They clapped in time to the beat.
"I will never forget you.
"Elden swore our victory in Silence,
"And soon I will come home to stay."
Nox sang the opening lines, and by the time Korac and I gained our wits about us to help, hundreds of Icari joined in the harmony.

Sagan asked, "What is it, Korac?"

The Iona General looked lost in the memory. He confessed, "It was the first time I'd heard Nox sing."

At twelve, your curiosity is well-placed, Rayne, but I wish it was for any subject other than Nox. You look up from your notebook to say, "Maybe you're the reason I wanted to sing live."

You pay me a mercy by not asking what's truly on your mind. What was on everyone's mind, apparently.

"Was Nox any good?" Andrew asked the burning question.

Korac's eyes met mine, and a moment passed between us. With so much conflict in my heart, I nodded to grant him permission to answer, thankful he even asked before speaking.

My General said, "Yes. That baritone went a long way toward pleasing the crowd. I hit the tenor notes, and obviously the princeling went for a soprano—"

"Falsetto, more like."

"Sh... I'm telling your Verse."

The moment was a triumph. Millions of years later, Nox mentioned in his Verse that Uncle Vinco's story was his favorite. I don't think I could've chosen a better selection. And he performed. He interacted with the crowd, sweeping his arms and punching at the fighting moments—All of it encouraged Korac and me to perform with him. The battles described in Vinco's Verse never made sense to me, as Elden's time was a golden age. Not to mention there were so many references to the quiet—

"Silence," Kyle corrected.

She patted his leg with a frown—A living, breathing legend.

It occurred to me to ask, "Do you understand it all now?"

The Mother of the galaxy shook her head. Silence's voice was sad as she admitted, "Not entirely. Only what Remorse had said. Elden took my armies meant to invade Enki and scoured the Twelve Worlds looking for me, leaving your mother—my daughter—to be raised by aunts and uncles."

A reflective quiet filled the room until Tameka interrupted, "So, what happened next?"

"Me!" Karter called from the doorway, with Echo in her arms.

Sagan adorably hopped out of Korac's lap to greet her mother-in-law and baby girl while Korac glowed even from behind his mask of composure.

Karter added, "We figured out where the three errant, misbehaving ingrates went and busted up the party—"

Korac barked out a laugh. "Hah!"

Even I smirked at Karter's nonsense.

Para appeared beside her. "That's not exactly what happened…"

During a rousing chorus where the acrobats flipped over our stage, one landed in the crowd next to two familiar faces. I was startled and tripped over my words when I spotted Karter and Para.

"Para, would you like to tell us what you were doing?"

The smallest Valkyrie grinned. "We sang and danced with them, loud as anyone else around us." Her eyes sparkled. "For three hours."

I confessed, "I was a little out of my ten-year-old element when the naked dancers joined us on stage, but I managed."

With a glance at his mother and back at me, Korac said, "Tell them what happened when we arrived at the Spire."

"First, I want to say that Nox flew us everywhere. There's no need to keep repeating this, so I'll only say it once. He did so at the detriment of his fuse. Anytime I mention contact between him and another other than myself, it cost him. But he did it anyway."

Korac bowed with his head.

When we arrived back at the Spire, Umbra, Amolot, and Savis awaited our return. Mother took a signal from Karter—

Karter said, "It was a look to let her know you boys were all right."

—And Savis turned on her heel for her bedchamber, calling, "Nox, with me."

My brother patted my shoulder before following mother to a proper scolding.

Off the hook, Korac and I headed for the kitchens—

Father stepped in our way. "Mongrel, you call yourself 'guard' to the royal Princes, but you let them put themselves at risk."

Korac stared at him with cold eyes—

"Yes, like that."

"This is how I always look, Wingmaster."

"Wingmaster." The preschooler version of you giggles at Korac's use of my name.

I'm quite fond of it, too, Rayne.
Back to the story.

MY PERSONAL GUARD PUT HIMSELF BETWEEN UMBRA AND ME WITH THAT ICY STARE, AND I HATED IT. I hated that Umbra's abuse warranted such defenses for children, and I hated Korac's willingness to risk himself for me. None of this was right.

I tried to diffuse the situation. "I have watched your sessions with Amolot. Neither of you is a challenge for Korac. Let us pass."

What was meant to smother a cinder only ignited the flames. Umbra ordered, "To the training circle. Now."

Diplomacy. I needed more practice in it.

We followed Amolot and father to the veranda with the training circle, and I tried one more time. "Father, is this necessary?"

"Quiet. Your brother may find it his business to protect you from me, but I will have a lesson out of you yet. Watch as I take it out of your mongrel's hide. Amo?"

Umbra's guard joined him.

With the same confidence I saw when he had nearly bested Nox earlier in the day and out on that stage in front of hundreds of Icari—

"You, Korac, my hero stepped into the circle with my father and his burly female."

"Are you blushing?" Pehton asked from the doorway. "No."

Lamassau laughed. "You said that awfully fast, General."

Sagan left Echo's side to drape herself around her husband once more. "Don't worry, I'll vouch for you. Nothing can make Korac blush."

I grinned. "Give me time."

Umbra and Amolot opened their wings. I winced. Korac wasn't in his grappling suit, but before I could say as much, he caught my eye behind his opponents. Unfiltered arrogance lifted his mouth into a smirk.

Korac said, "I meant it as reassuring."

Pure, undiluted arrogance.

Amolot attacked in a flurry of rushing wings, and Umbra all but disappeared—

Reappeared behind Korac, who ducked in time to miss the first blow with a roll which finished in an uppercut into Amolot's jaw.

I heard the bones pop and shatter from across the balcony as blue blood poured from her mouth.

The groaning wench spit up part of her tongue, which Korac had made her bite off—

Umbra wrapped his arms around the younger man's middle, and no matter how many times he tried to roll him off, Umbra's wings helped him maintain the upper hand. Especially as the Icarean King ascended.

"Father, no!" I shrieked before I called, "Nox! Nox, help!"

"Quiet, you little bastard." Umbra shouted at me, as he took my best friend to the sky, certain to send him to a gruesome end while I watched.

No.

"You've been quiet a while now, Superman," you observe, paused in your writing. "Why can't you say what happened next?"

I didn't want to talk about what happened next.

The pre-schooler version of you kicks your little legs as you ask, "Were you this quiet with them?"

Yes.

Your pigtails sway when you tilt your head, assessing me. "What did they do?"

"Tell them, Emperor." Korac sounded...affected but...

You lay your pencil down on your notebook loud enough to catch my attention. "It's not with judgment. He wants you to feel comfortable and safe enough to discuss these things. Do you feel safe with Tameka, Pax, and Sagan? If not, why did you start—"

But I do. I love everyone in that room—

"Then trust them," both versions of you say. You smile. "It's what you'd say to me."

I blacked out. When I came to, Korac was back on the veranda, standing over me. Umbra and Amolot were nowhere in sight.

"My Prince, what do you remember?"

While I considered he'd never called me that before, Korac swept the hair from my face as I blinked up at him and into Li's bloated redness above. What *did* I remember? "I…I do not know…"

Korac glanced around to ensure we were alone before he put his lips right to my ear and muttered, "Tell no one of this. No natural creature could commit such feats, and I fear what the penalty will be for your abnormalities. You ran up the walls of the Spire to the next level, defying all sense and reason. Then you leapt onto Umbra's back while he stared, bewildered and afraid. My Prince, you ripped his pinions off with your teeth. We plummeted, only able to ride him down to the balcony and use his body as a meat shield. You damned near killed him. When Amolot, mostly recovered from her injury, came to her master's aid, you turned…wild eyes on her. They were so dark a blue as to match the depths of sapphires. She took him and fled. Umbra and Amolot will never repeat it, for their defeat was swift and unforgettable. To a child."

I sat up and gripped his arms. "I have to tell Nox—"

"No." Korac shook his head, grave. "No. If anyone learned of this, they would behead you and study your brain. Prince or no. Nox could never save you from such a fate. Better to spare him from the burden of knowing."

I thought about his words for a moment, frowning. Then I asked, "What about your burden?"

Grave, Korac vowed, "I carry any burden my Prince demands. You saved my life."

"Now you mean to save mine."

My guard and best friend gave a single nod, so signature to his nature that it had become a symbol. Confidence. Loyalty. Solidarity. The best soldier.

"Thank you, Korac."

ENTRY TWO

FAMILY COMPLEX

WE TOOK A BREAK FOR PEOPLE TO EAT AND GET SOME ALONE TIME WITH OUR PARTNERS.
Before we regathered in the study, Tameka and I put Pax to sleep. After I tucked his covers up to those red curls, he looked at me with eyes so like my own, asking, "Dad, will you sing to me?"

I glanced over at Tameka across Pax's bed from me. She was radiant. Happy. Her dual thumbs-up was all the encouragement I needed. I lowered the lights and sat on the edge of Pax's bed. He wiggled eagerly to make room. It ruffled his hair in his face, and I brushed it aside as I began to sing.

Para.
Karter.
Korac.
Nox.
The night we all sang together always comes to mind.

Little you presses a small hand to my face.

Preteen you says, "I've only heard you sing once."

It hurts for me to sing because it reminds me of my mother putting me to bed. It reminds me of my brother's habit of singing while performing idle tasks. It reminds me of before.

"One day, will you sing for me again?"

Of course I will, Rayne. One day.

Pax rolled over and fell asleep. Tameka took my hand as we left his room. Outside the door, she pulled me in for a hug. "I'm sorry you felt the need to hide yourself at such a young age."

I basked in her warmth, breathing her in. I'm so lucky.

"Damn straight." The adolescent you smirks, knowing exactly how much your best friend is worth.

"Thank you," I said, squeezing and scratching Tameka's back in a circle. "I'm afraid this isn't going as I'd expected."

Tameka's laughter is a beautiful sound, like if sunshine could resonate a chord. "When does anything go as expected? You're doing great."

Keeping my arm around her shoulders, I guided her out of the tunnel with a deep breath. As I let it out, I asked, "Are you ready for more?"

Tameka beamed at me. "Oh yeah. But you stop the moment you feel exhausted or uncomfortable. We'll all understand."

"Hah! If that were the case, I never would've made it past the opening."

Tameka nudged me playfully, and I kissed her hair as we ascended the synchronized steps.

She did other flirtatious things on the way up, which I'll spare you from knowing, but my smile was more of a smirk when we entered the study with her hand in my back pocket.

Leaning against a wall of shelves, Korac nodded at me as Tameka and I entered. I don't know if it was intentional, but the Iona General chafed his hand down Sagan's arm, notably missing a few ribbons.

What do you think, Rayne—Why are you smirking at me like that?

"Oh, just looking forward to more of this pissing contest between the pair of you."

Well.
I'll endeavor to deliver.

More people filed into my study. Couch space was supplemented with pillows borrowed from around the stronghold. Off to the corner bearing my desk, Caedes sat nestled into a cushion with Pehton between his legs. Karter took the armchair on my right after Sagan and Korac relinquished it to her. She cooed at Echo, dozing in her bassinet beside the chair. Chris and Para snuggled up at her feet, and Karter occasionally scratched through their hair. Tumu and Lamassau kept the couch but nuzzled closer together to let Ross and Jack cuddle at the far end. Kyle and Silence hadn't returned yet for... obvious reasons. Andrew and Lucas claimed the loveseat, with the Progeny stretched out, while the Icarus rubbed his partner's feet. Aria and Torch flanked the door, taking their role far more seriously than I could ever ask, but then I noticed they weren't really here. Their eyes were vacant as they surfed worlds beyond this one.

Voices from the others accumulated in the ravine outside the study, roaming the museum of stolen artifacts. T.A.O., Devis, and Andrius among them were once more in their first home. Lynn and Pablo fell asleep on a pallet outside the door. Matt and Lucy entertained Bethany and their entourage in predatory silence. Iuo, Twenty-One, Miy, and

Bones snooped while Smith lectured on the significance of each piece with unnerving accuracy.

"And this is from Pil. It's the blueprints to the very first dwarf mechsuit."

Bones whispered conspiratorially, "How the hell and why the hell did Xelan get it?"

Smith said, "Ah, but that's why we're here. Is it not?"

Even from the other room, I recognized Miy's incredulous snort. I imagined Twenty-One's silence was his harmless assessment of the schematics.

Once again, I took up to the front of the room with the fireplace behind me. Tameka was at my side, with her trademark optimism rolling off of her in waves of infectious enthusiasm. I am so lucky.

"Before I go onto the Tritan missions on Lacceirus Capra and Monarch 3, are there any burning questions or requests regarding my childhood?" My voice nearly trembled with the offer to invade my personal life, but since I put off sharing my truths with this family I'd worked so hard to build for so long, I could afford to be generous with my revelations. Maybe they wouldn't ask anything too close to revealing the monster in me. Not yet, anyway.

In tradition with Earth schooling, Ross raised her hand. "Yes, Ross?"

She glanced nervously at Korac before meeting my eyes again, wetting her lips to say, "Many Feet was such a big part of both Verses. Is there anything you want to add?"

"You went quiet again, Superman."

I think... I think I'm ashamed.

"There's no need for it."

There I was worried someone might tread too close to my worst secret, and Kyle's younger sister only wanted to hear about my beloved Hellkite.

Your tiny hand takes the fist I'd made and opens it, spreading out your own fingers, so small against my palm. You say, "We love what makes you, you."

I kiss your hair and glimpse the preteen version of staring at me. Your expression is soft and so is your voice as you gently press, "Tell us about Many Feet."

After Many Feet faltered during our journey from Elden's Great House, I retired her, as Nox had stated in his Verse. As Korac learned in his Verse, I allowed my guard's regular visits to her cave, despite my orders to let her rest. Hinted at, but not entirely confirmed, I was still engaging the Hellkite in my experiments.

"Many Feet, how's my girl—Oof!"

The one-ton beast pounced on me as I entered her cave. Her crocodile snout rooted around my person for the north cave mushrooms I'd scavenged as a reward. "No, no, girl. Those are for after. Step off." I was laughing at her eagerness.

Earth-age eleven, my head was full of mischief, and Many Feet would help me test a hypothesis before I committed my next stunt.

Korac said, "Oh, Elden. What did you do to her?"

I think I've developed a wicked streak. Korac's misery made me grin at the room as I painted the rest of the scene.

"Here, girl. Have something to drink." I poured the glowing liquid—

"No fucking way—"

Into a bowl and took notes as she lathed it up. When two minutes passed with no effect, I was certain I'd failed. With a heavy sigh of defeat, I rewarded her with the mushrooms and made my way out of the cave.

I wondered what I should change about the formula. Was it concentrated enough? Should I try another phosphorous component—

A blue glow illuminated the cavern behind me, and I spun to find a most glorious sight. I think I grinned so widely I damaged the muscles in my face.

"Please, no," Korac groaned.

While Sagan consoled him with gentle touches, she beamed at me to continue.

Many Feet wasn't allowed to fly, especially not long distances. But no one said she couldn't bound.

Umbra was entertaining some Tritans and a few representatives from Reipon. Maybe two thousand guests filled the Spire. Korac was off on some mission for father, according to mother. Nox went out hunting, and there was no sign of Karter or Para anywhere in the Spire.

I was totally unsupervised.

"And you called me a handful." You're grinning at me.

As Tameka has already stated, Rayne, you got it from me.

I saddled Many Feet up and loped with her up the stairs and out of the cave. The bottom floor was empty, but activity from the party echoed down the central column of the Spire. I calculated exactly seven minutes of mayhem before someone intervened. With deft hands, I checked my munitions.

Ready.

The screams…

The blinding pandemonium…

People fainted at the sight of the glowing beast and its hooded rider. They ducked and dodged as I fired pepper bombs from my launcher, specifically designed to shoot below the nanite field projectile threshold. Amolot tried to take Many Feet head-on, but my ol' girl pivoted and crashed into the biggest table.

Umbra's table.

Food and drink went everywhere.

Unfortunately, so did the pyrotechnics they'd created for the night's ambience. A three-meter canister contained white flames in a cylindrical spiral. When it fell over, all the magnesium spilled in a napalm flare.

Terrified, I spurred Many Feet to flee to my room where I packed a bag. I was only eleven, and I dreaded my punishment.

Sagan asked Korac, "Why didn't you mention this in your Verse?"

"You're about to find out."

I cried so hard that day. Snot and tears rained down my face, but I couldn't move swiftly enough. Clothes, provisions, research—all of it went into my bag until it brimmed with my privileged belongings—

"My son."

I stopped, but couldn't face my mother. I gripped Elden's nacre shard for strength, asking, "How long before father makes it up here? Five minutes? Three? I won't survive it this time. He will kill me."

Savis put her hands on my shoulders and stood behind me, a small comfort before the end. But when she spoke, I'd never heard her voice quite like in this moment. "I took care of it, Xelan. Not a word of tonight will be spoken. There will be no punishment. Not from him, nor Amolot."

I whirled and stared up at her, my face ruined with my weeping. Astonished, I asked, "How?"

Savis pulled a handkerchief from her shaking wrist and wiped my face, hands gentle and trembling. Mother knelt, putting herself at my height as she said, "With my word. I made Umbra a promise, and now I will make you one.

While I never have agreed with your father's ambitions, his anger upsets my work. I cannot move freely around the Spire while he stews in his constant resentments."

I swallowed a hiccuping sob to ask, "What is the promise, mother?"

Her uncharacteristic tone didn't change as Savis said, "If you place me in the position of gratifying that man again, I will force you to euthanize your precious Many Feet. Do you understand?"

Ross' recoil was much like my reaction in the moment.

To the people listening in the study, I said, "I wish I'd chosen a different entry from my Verse."

Korac surprised me when he said, "No. This is what the Verses are about."

Tameka took my hand and kissed it. Diverting, she asked, "What was the look on Umbra's face when you first rode Many Feet into the banquet?"

I couldn't help but smile. Even Korac smirked, imagining it.

UMBRA WAS SITTING BESIDE MY MOTHER AT THE HEAD TABLE WITH SOME DEAD ANIMAL ROASTED ON A PLATTER. When I first bounded onto the floor, father's eyes doubled in size and he shrieked at the glowing beast. Before he could recognize her, Many Feet had blundered through the party to his table and went straight for the roast. By then, Umbra was hiding behind Savis, who stood as still as an ethereal statue. She'd recognized me long before he did. Perhaps that contributed to his anger.

Andrew barked out a laugh, and the room turned to him. He held up his hands. "Sorry for interrupting. I'm just imagining the *Mad Max* reject hiding behind his infirmed wife."

Ross' smile at the image restored my confidence. I could do this.

"You got this, Superman."

While I waited for Nox and Korac to return, I agonized over telling them. Not telling them. But when Korac glided up the stairs to his room, I glimpsed the grave look of concentration on his face and the unexpected slump to his shoulders. Jaw clenched. Eyes narrowed. Something was wrong.

We know now from Korac's Verse that he'd just discovered Karter and Para had established a society among a colony of slaves, farmed for their nacres to forge Umbra's weapons.

Across the hall from one another, we locked eyes. Each with our own secret we withheld. The first of so many.

I pointed. "Did Nox give you his whip?"

In my study, I said, "Korac, you grinned so openly it took me aback. You said, 'Yes,' with so much reverence. You held it up and asked, 'Have you ever seen anything so beautiful?'"

"Looking at your smile, I thought, yes, I had—"

"Why is Many Feet asleep in my room?"

Korac glanced over my shoulder and I turned to find Nox had returned and stood in his doorway. His eyes landed on me with brotherly knowing. I didn't need to tell Nox I'd gotten into a new level of mischief. The knowledge of it was written all over his face.

But I couldn't rely on my big brother for everything, could I? The deadly look in my mother's eyes and the ice in her voice as she threatened to scar me for life with the murder of my pet...

I stood there in the space between our three rooms, and I cried. Because I couldn't say a word. Because it was all too much. And because the love on their faces, for me and each other, made me want to protect them from the trauma of the night.

In the study, I fell quiet.

Tameka asked Korac, "What happened next?"

He said, "I didn't know why he broke down, but I knew we'd help him. Nox brought the smaller Prince to his side and steered him toward the oldest brother's bedchamber. There we let Xelan cry into Many Feet's hide, while she slumbered. Whatever had happened had tired him out." He met my eyes and added, "You fell asleep swiftly. Like Echo does after warm milk."

When I woke next, I was in Nox's bed. My brothers had taken Many Feet back to the cave and left me breakfast. When I went looking for them, I found mother's chamber door open. I entered without knocking to apologize for the night before only to find Umbra was there, rummaging through her things.

"Where is it? Where is the cursed thing—"

My bare feet padded on the stone, alerting Umbra to my presence.

Father whirled, but something like relief passed over his face when he realized it was me. He sank down on mother's bed and sighed the relief out. His hands hung between his knees, and his head hung off his shoulders. He looked defeated. Especially as he wiped a hand down his face and stared at mother's bedside table. Idly, Umbra opened the drawer in it, seeking what he seemed sure he wouldn't find. "Damn."

"Father?"

For the first time since I could remember, he signaled for me to come to his side without threat or malice.

Of course, I did. I wanted to know what was in his eyes. The steel in them was tempered.

"Xelan, have you ever seen your mother with an instrument? A needle, perhaps?"

I frowned. "No, Da."

At the familiarity, emotions warred over Umbra's expression. A completely foreign warmth battled against the typical wave of disgust. Both passed in an instant as his eyes took in the room once more. He made to wipe his hand down his face again, but it stopped over his eyes. Then came the most unexpected sound.

Umbra squeezed out a sob.

In a broken voice, he asked, surely not to me but perhaps to Elden, "Why does she hasten to leave me?"

I feared where this would lead. While I'd never seen my father vulnerable and my curiosity burned in me, I dreaded the repercussions of such exposure. Would Umbra kill me for simply witnessing this moment of weakness?

With a swift and wet inhale, Umbra collected himself, choking down the emotion, and wiped the tears from his eyes. He gazed down at me, and I nearly fled, but...

"Son, look after your mother. If you see the instrument, take it from her and report it to me. This is a mission for you. Do you understand?"

I nodded, ready to do or say anything to survive the moment.

But Umbra didn't say another word. Didn't kick or hit me. He simply left me in mother's chambers. Alone.

I never saw a needle and never searched her room. I didn't see a point in it aside from indulging father's paranoia. Even after Savis told me on her deathbed that father had poisoned her and Nox did nothing to stop it—Even then, I still didn't make the connection. Didn't want to believe my mother had hated her existence so much that she'd slowly poison herself to death just to spite Umbra—

"You're getting ahead of yourself."

I suppose I am.

In the study, I'd gone quiet again. Tumu stood from the couch and put his arm on my shoulder. It's strange how familiar and comforting two voids could become after you'd spent a million years staring into them for guidance and friendship.

The Gargantuan Tritan hugged me.

Another warmth enveloped my back, and I could tell by her scent that it was Tameka.

While I soaked in their affection, Tumu sighed, "Ahh… The threesome I always wanted—"

The room burst into laughter.

We broke apart quickly, and Tameka swatted Tumu, who cried, "Ow."

"Wait until you get back to the couch," Lamassau threatened.

Tumu winked at me. "Worth it."

You'd put down your pencil, leaned your elbow on the tabletop, and pressed your chin on your fist, enraptured. No preteen is too cool for my story. Your smile says so. "We're so lucky to have them."

Yes, we are.

<hr>

With the mood restored, I asked again, "Is anyone else brave enough to request something from my childhood?"

Sagan said, "I have one."

I smiled at her, always happy to answer her questions. The look she gave Korac beforehand wavered my certainty a bit.

Sagan asked, "What was Nox like as a brother? You've given a few examples, so I'm not exactly looking for a memory. Maybe a summary?"

"Tell us, Superman. What was he like?" You're poised over the coffee table. Those bright eyes are full of so much… *need*. You *need* the answer to this question. You *need* to know what Nox was like from his little brother's perspective.

I wish you needed anything else from me.

The room waited for me to respond, holding a collective breath.

"Sagan?"

Like the young soldier I'd trained, she straightened at my call. "Yes?"

I pointed at the furthest volumes where Tameka had returned the first. "Grab volume three and read the entry on page seventeen."

Sagan's eagerness was infectious, banishing some of my anxieties about the topic. Then she read, "Today, I counted how many times father grabbed my brother by his robes. Eight. Yesterday it was ten. And tomorrow it will likely be more of the same. All day, father pulls Nox by his clothes with hateful words.

"'Come here, heathen.'

"'Look at me when I speak to you.'

"'Never turn your back on me, or do I need to teach you some respect?'"

Still lingering on the ladder, Sagan lowered the tome to peer at me. Her violet eyes were filled with sadness as she said, "This is awful. How old were the two of you here?"

The eyes in the room ping-ponged between us.

I said, "In that entry, I was eight and Nox was fourteen. We know from his Verse that he underwent full Weapon conversion at seven and easily defeated father shortly after. But, knowing Umbra as we do, the King of Cinder still threw his weight around. While Nox rarely rose to the bait and could easily dispense of father with…Korac, how would you describe the look he coined just for Umbra?"

"Embodied retribution."

"Elegantly put."

Sagan smiled at both of us before asking, "So, what happened?"

I gestured with my hand for her to turn the page. "Go to volume six. Page one hundred and twenty."

"Heathen, I forbid you to go!" Umbra shouted at my brother's door.

Nox, who had lingered in the doorway, turned his back on father.

I spied them from a tunnel between our chambers and dreaded the consequences of my brother's actions. Only fidgeting with the splinter of the nacre around my neck kept me silent.

Like always, Umbra reached out and grabbed his son's robes, jerking Nox back into the hall—

Lightning fast, Nox slipped out of them, twisted them around our father's neck, reared back, strangled him.

I hid myself further, as my brother followed our father to the stone floor. The latter gagged and hacked for air. The former was ice cold and so very done—

"Release your father, my son."

I peered at mother, trembling in the hallway after having her sleep disturbed. To my surprise, Nox glared at her and tightened his hold on Umbra's throat.

Nox said, "I grow tired of his hands on me."

"Then stop wearing your robes," Savis offered this as if it made utter sense. Not as if she were excusing Umbra's part in the conflict. "Your father will have no purchase on you."

The next thing Nox said only made sense in hindsight of him discovering her rebellion, her willingness to have me murdered, and Nox usurping Umbra's throne. "Sensible, as always, Lady Savis. Yes. Let me disgrace this family with my lack of decorum to better reflect the savagery contained within these walls." He let Umbra go and never wore a shirt again.

Sagan asked Korac, "Did you know about this?"

Korac took another drink before answering, "I knew before I arrived on Cinder, he'd refused to wear top dress. That he detested fabric on his skin. I tried often to coordinate armor and other such things between the three of us, and I knew not to include a shirt for Nox.

"In fact, the only time I can recall him wearing one..." Korac glanced at me, and I waved him on. "Was when Rayne came to the fortress for their dance, Nox had dressed in a silk shirt I'd tailored to fit him should such an occasion arise. Still, he refused to button it."

Preteen you is staring at your notebook and all the words I can't see from across the room. It's almost as if you're searching them for meaning. After another moment passes, you mutter, "Why did he bother?"

I wince, and the preschooler version of you kisses my cheek. "All better."

If only it were that easy.

Back to my study, Korac requested, "Tell them about your first drunken night."
I wasn't entirely sure why I'd share that one—
He raised a brow at me.
Oh.
Fine.

Nox and Korac raided Umbra's stash of Reipon spirits to get me drunk. I was fourteen. Too young, of course, but... We floated on our backs in some spring we found while caving in Li Mountain. Somehow, the conversation drifted toward our future partners. Ideal attributes and such.

I entertained this theory that Icari sought characteristics in partners, male or female, which best reflected a lack in their present lives. A thirst for something out of reach.

I asked, "What would you seek in someone, Nox?"

My brother splashed me, getting water all over my face. When I glared through soaked lashes like a drowned rat, he caved. "Fine. Fine. I would want someone..." The pause wasn't pensive. It was heavy. A little sad, and now I know why. His voice was so quiet when he said, "Someone kind and brave."

Korac snorted into his bottle. "They'd have to be."

We laughed like hyenas. Unnecessarily loud with the echo, but all in good humor.

When Korac didn't volunteer, I went next. "Someone brilliant and extraordinary."

Korac glanced at me with…something. It prompted me to ask, "What about you?"

He shook his head. Before taking another drink, he said, "Not touching that one."

Nox respected our guard's privacy, but I had a burning need to know, which I didn't fully understand. "What? Someone exceptional? Gorgeous? What is it, Korac?"

Staring at the ceiling, he muttered, "Someone forbidden."

Well, that stopped my prodding. What kind of answer was that?

Korac kissed Sagan before saying, "An accurate one!"

"Twice so."

Astute observation, Rayne. I'm glad someone else caught it.

Karter asked the next question. "In my son's Verse, he asked you to confirm the frequency of Nox's happiness. How often you could remember him smile."

Para patted Karter's leg with an expectant look on her face. A few faces waited for the answer.

I sighed.

"Why, Superman?"

Because I don't want to think of my brother as a tragedy that I should forgive after he was my enemy for so long.

"Can you forgive him?"

Can you?

You don't answer the question. Neither versions of you. Instead, both of you say, "End on a happy note."

I did. I told them the truth. "His smiles weren't common, but if I could get one out of him, *I* felt like the hero. I'd saved my brother with every grin, smirk, or chuckle."

"I'll drink to that," Korac said, as he toasted me.

The entire room toasted.

Stealing smiles from adversity. A trademark of the Shadow.

ENTRY THREE

THE BEGINNING OF EVERYTHING

"Let's move onto Enki's designs, and how I learned what they were up to."
People returned to the study, more so than before, and they brought in blankets for pallets. Snacks arrived, drifting in scents of dips and hors d'oeuvres. Bones offered to top off drinks. By now, everyone was fairly tired and slightly drunk.

I was wide awake and sober. My mind raced with which entries to tell as we steadily marched toward the secrets I feared to unveil.

> Little you poked my nose, and I can't help but smile. In doing so, I know it's sad.
>
> "Don't be sad," you say, unaware, or perhaps perfectly aware, of what you're asking of me.
>
> Preteen you pulls your knees to your chest and hugs them, saying, "We only ask that when you're

sad, you remember to be happy for what you have. That's how we get by."

You have so much. More than you know, Kayne.

"So do you."

Tumu folded his arms and leveled his stare at me. "Not all of Enki was making designs."

I chuckled, waving him off. "Of course not. Just one half of the remainder of your species."

"Fair," Lamassau said.

I said, "I listened to the conversations between my father and the cloaked Tritans around the Spire, but more importantly, I listened to the conversations they had amongst themselves. They treated me like a child, like I wasn't a threat—Almost as if I was one of them."

Tameka said, "What a dangerous mistake to make."

Tumu chuffed.

Korac smirked.

EARTH-AGE TWELVE, I WANDERED AROUND ONE OF FATHER'S POST-CONQUEST BANQUETS. Bored to tears. At twenty years of age, Nox was forced into diplomacy—mingling, to his disgust, with leaders he despised under Umbra's careful scrutiny. Even Korac, at sixteen, took part in polite conversation. By this point, he was training Cinder's troops for combat, poised as Amolot's successor.

Sitting only a few feet from me in my study, Karter beamed at her son. "All my doing."

"The simple truth," Korac agreed, a little in his cups.

Moving on.

One night in particular, I found the Tritan I often caught spying on me and zeroed in on him. A shorter Tritan muttered to him, "The mineral we require... Will the atmospheric disrupter be prepared in time—"

The suspicious Tritan, which father called 'Primary,' waved the other off dismissively. "Yes, yes. The Icari are primed to deploy it. Soon."

There was movement in the crowd, as people parted for Nox like rivers around a mountain, drawing their attention.

The sight prompted the Primary to say, "Perhaps it is time to cut the puppet's strings."

The shorter Tritan sounded skeptical. "And crown that beast the next King?"

His words made me wince, but I kept quiet.

"Yes. Send him and his General. We shall test their mettle."

Within the same week, Korac and Nox went with father to L. Capra and destroyed its atmosphere. At the time, Nox had told me a story of how they saved everyone on the planet, so imagine my dismay when I visited there for the first time and they immediately arrested me for war crimes. Simply because I was an Icarus.

Sagan asked, "Is that how you met Kombuchi?"

I smiled at her. "We're not there yet. Let's return to the sample Nox collected for me."

Korac gave me the comm device he stole from the Tritans, unaware of the riches within, while Nox provided me with the means—the beginnings—of all things Progeny.

For my tenth birthday, the Tritans gifted me a special handheld device for my calculations. I agree with Korac's assumption that it was probably some attempt on Remorse's part toward a paternal connection. Regardless, it was the foundation of my first lab. The comms device Korac provided me combined the missing components I needed for soil analysis.

With everything assembled, I tested the sample from L. Capra and discovered restorative properties in one of the minerals. Applied to the right atomic structure, it generated cells. Like a nacre. Only these cells were brand new.

I kept this to myself, but the next time Nox and Korac were sent out on a mission, I'd demand to go.

I waited two more years. In the meantime, the Lyriks visited the Spire and stayed for an undetermined amount of time. Much to father's delight. I understand from reading the Verses that some strife took place between Gale, Nox, and Korac. For the record, she was nothing but kind to me. I was younger and more handsome—

Korac said, "Fuck you, your imperial majesty."

—So it's understandable that I was easier to get along with, but I also appreciate finally learning their sides of the story. It seemed to be as complex as anything else involved in our twisted pasts.

Little you beams, and preteen you says, "I'm glad it's all coming out in the open now."

Me, too, Rayne.
Onward to Monarch 3, where everything started to unravel.

Andrew raised a hand. "Can I take this one? I always wondered what happened between you and F8."

"Yeah. Why the hell would she ever release you?" Kyle asked as he and Silence reentered the study, settling on a pallet. Both of them glowed.

I asked, "Sagan, do you mind grabbing volume three hundred and ten and handing it over to—Thank you." Still perched on the ladder, she handed my journal to Andrew, who looked at me expectantly. I said, "Page two hundred and thirty-eight. The memory continues into the next volume, but we'll start here."

Andrew found the page and cleared his throat before reading.

NOX WARNED ME TO STAY NEAR THE CONDUIT, BUT OUR SOLDIERS BROKE FORMATIONS IN A PANIC. Drones, insects the size of full-grown Icari, buzzed about and seized our people by the dozen. I knew I was about to break my promise.

I ran to the pulsating hive and found an opening beneath it. The hive was agitated by the activity, and while I desperately wanted to study it, I needed to retrieve—

Umbra flew out of a perfectly cylindrical chute in the 'ground' without a backward glance for the people he'd abandoned. He shouted orders which I ignored to search for—

There!

Korac, Nox, and a garrison of soldiers stood in a pool of fascinating pre-digestive enzymes, surrounded by carnivorous larvae. I yelled, "Nox! Father's called the retreat. However did you get down there?"

Korac cursed as if my intrusion was ill-timed.

While some of the soldiers defended the phalanx from the approaching homo-insects, Nox called, "Xelan, go! Leave us!"

No. There had to be a way. I looked around, searching for sturdy vegetation. Something—

Vines.

The vines looked hardy and capable. Maybe not strong enough to hold Nox, but he could fly out while the others climbed to their escape.

Armed with a plan, I shouted, "I can find a way to get you—"

I cried out when a drone snatched me from behind and carried me off. Although I wriggled and fought, I didn't want to hurt him. I wanted to understand him, and I tried to reason with him. "What is it? What is it you want? I can help! Just let me go! My brothers will aid you—"

The next sound I made wasn't very noble nor heroic. Somewhere between a gulp and a shriek, like I'd swallowed my stomach and squeezed the air out of it in one go. They'd dropped me from a great height when I'd yet to come into my wings. I thought the next sound I'd hear would be an inelegant splat as my bones emptied onto some—

Squelch.

It's interesting to describe the inside of a hive sac. Later, I could compare it to an acid trip dipped in a sticky substance with the viscosity of honey. Light shone from beneath the fluid, reflecting onto the color-changing walls, floors, and ceiling. Green. Purple. Red. The gas was thicker here, hovering over the reproductive mucous. It was sweeter condensed within the heart of the tree, almost cloyingly so—

I finally discovered the source.

A butterfly stood at the highest point. Black and red wings draped off her back like a cape for her matching battle armor. Antennae twitched and sensed more about me than I could ever know of her. Where her drones had needle-nosed mouths, her lips were like all the other females I'd seen thus far. The twenty facets of her insect eyes returned the light in a diamond shimmer, and they were shedding tears.

When she spoke, her voice vibrated in a humming I found distressing. "Leave. Leave now. Spare my people."

I held up my hands in surrender, but the big drone who'd captured me—later, I learned was Seps—forced me to my knees before his queen. This invasion was awful and was never something I wanted. "I apologize on behalf of the Icari. There was some mistake. We will leave immediately."

Their heads tilted this way and that. I overheard their clicking exchange.

"What did he say?"

"Did anyone make out his language?"

Why couldn't they understand me—

Oh.

Of course.

No nacres. No translation.

In full supplication, I kowtowed and stretched my hands out to her until my face was buried in the sweet fog. I closed my eyes and prayed to Elden she'd understand my message.

Reading the entry, Andrew noted, "Like the Icari with Silence." She smiled at him, and I nodded at him to continue reading.

Seps asked, "What do you make of it, your majesty?"

The queen declared, "Peace. Take him back. He will tell the others to spare us."

Yes. I would.

After Seps carried me to the surface, I sought my brothers. I knew Nox and Korac would side with me and we would leave this place unharmed—

Limbs, heads, dismembered torsos littered the once beautiful habitat, transforming the flowers into a battlefield. And ripping apart a drone in the very center was…

"Nox."

Korac blanched at my voice.

Nox turned and said, without apology, "I thought they killed you."

Let me say that it is no excuse. Blind vengeance is not a reason to commit genocide.

Your voice is soft as you say, "I'm not sure I would've done much different. Not in the moment."

That's what scares me, Rayne. You and Nox have a lot in common.

You don't respond to the comment, but you say, "I'd like to think I'd be more like you. I want to be more like you. At least . . . in that instance."

Be yourself, but the best of yourself.

The little version of you gives me a thumbs-up. "Right!"

Nox's Verse covered what occurred while I tried to convince them to stop murdering a beautiful race of people, terrified out of their minds for their survival. Umbra withered the hive with some toxin. Not only would it mean death for the tree, but for the queen and her drones. They were so vulnerable, and Remorse had hired my father to assassinate them. Hired me to collect gas samples for them.

I rushed to climb back into the hive, while my brother and my best friend tried to drag me down. I cried, "I can save them. We just have to save the queen. The rest will survive."

Nox grabbed me by the collar. "No. We have no idea what Umbra did to them. It could kill you, too."

Quick to act, I suggested, "I can give her my blood. It will—"

Nox held me still and pointed out the obvious to me. "She has no nacre. It will never work."

I turned back to watch the thriving heart in the center of a magnificent ecosystem shrivel until it resembled the rotted pit of some fruit. I knew what I had to do. "Then let her have mine! I am worth less than an entire species. Let me do this."

Korac wrapped his arms around me and lifted me physically away.

I wept. "I cannot let them die. Not knowing I had a hand in it."

Nox pointed a finger in my face and ordered, "Stay here." To Korac, he said, "Do not release him." Then he disappeared.

I glanced back at Korac where he held me and asked on a hiccup of a sob, "Why would father do this?"

Korac shook his head. "Your majesty, that does not concern me."

"What does?"

My best friend confessed, "That you would give your life so easily for another's with so little regard for your own—"

"From a fallen soldier." Nox returned, holding out a nacre covered in blue gore. Korac released me, and Nox clasped my hand with it, saying, "Just the nacre. Do not give her your blood. This is more than enough."

I nodded. "Yes. Yes, this should do."

They both let me go inside alone.

Korac chuffed into his drink, "'*Let.*'"

At this point in the story, everyone in the study was on the edge of their seats much like you are now, Rayne. This moment is missing from both Verses. No one but F8 and I know what took place here.

Until now.

The Queen of the hive shrieked in her death throes, withering into nothing. Her gasping screams wounded me. How she shrank back as I approached, bearing an incredible gift in my outstretched hand, broke me.

"Oh, please say you can understand me. Please. We are not part of this!"

I wasn't aware enough of her anatomy to know where a nacre should store within her, so I coaxed it to her lips and begged her to take it. "It will save you. I can save you. Please."

I didn't believe she took it because I was so convincing. The Queen I'd later know as F8 swallowed the nacre because I'd given her little other choice. But to make it go down easier, I coated it with my blood after tearing into my arm with my teeth. It healed nearly instantly, hiding the evidence.

Tumu's eyes widened. "You didn't."

Korac muttered, "I knew it."

Tameka grinned. "It was the right thing to do."

I am so lucky.

Still unsure how she would fare, I left the Queen to her fate and rejoined my brothers outside. As we escaped Monarch 3 back into Enki, I was destined for a new mission, determined and backed by my self-righteous indignation.

On the conduit's threshold, I vowed, "One day." I would return and learn if she survived. Learned if I made any difference.

Until then I let Eminent Lance know in the shrine, "I will take no part in genocide."

Unaware of his double agent status at the time, I fumed when he said, "Of course, Prince Xelan. We sent you with that very notion in mind. We knew you would prevent their demise."

Now I know Lance meant it literally, but then...

I was acutely aware of Korac smirking at me and of Nox gaping as I pressed, "I am no mock leader like my father. Nor am I good soldier like my brother."

You poke me. "You went quiet again."

I was just thinking. In his Verse, this is where Nox referred to me as the rightful leader of Cinder.

In the study, Sagan noticed my reflective silence and gently confirmed, "I think he meant it. At that moment, you were Nox's hero."

Painful confusion made me frown, but I carried on with the story.

I disavowed Cinder from Enki, and to our surprise, Umbra didn't object. He even sent the Lyriks from the Spire. Before the night was over, he suggested an alliance of our better traits. The four of us—Father, Nox, Korac, and I—worked together from that point on to prepare Cinder for independence.

Korac toasted, and the others joined. He said, "To that glorious night."

And yet...
Monarch 3 was the first time I saw my brother as something other than a hero. Something closer to our father. A monster.

You grow quiet, and I wince at the weight of your silence.

Rayne…

I'd startled you out of your thoughts, and you smile to soften your next words. "No. You don't need to explain yourself to me. I understand. What makes me sad is that so did Nox, and… you two never worked it out. He knew how you drew your conclusions. Hell—"

Language.

"—He even agreed with them, but… *Monster?* After all the love between you two—How quickly it distilled into that."

Do you think less of me yet?

"Absolutely not."

You will and perhaps there's justice in that—Ow.

My hand stings where you flicked it with your little fingers as you scold me in the teeniest voice. "Stop that. Nothing can make me not love you."

Preteen you repeats, "Nothing." You search my eyes, push a strand of hair behind your ear, and continue. "They still love you, too. Your Verse is for healing. Right now, a few of your scars are bleeding, but when they seam back together, you'll barely see them. Trust in your family."

That's a tall order.

You poke me in the arm. "Trust."

Yes, ma'am. How could I ever argue with you?

AFTER WITNESSING THE CARNAGE AND UNNECESSARY DESTRUCTION ON MONARCH 3, I BEGAN TO SUSPECT NOX WASN'T ENTIRELY HONEST WITH ME ABOUT WHAT HAD HAPPENED ON L. CAPRA. I began to doubt my brother, and even if his motivations were to spare me the burden of some atrocity, it wouldn't matter. If there was any indication of illegitimacy of his account to me, I would never trust him again.

After climbing down the ladder, Sagan returned to Korac's side. She snuggled close and squeezed his bicep, consoling her husband. My General wouldn't look at the room, choosing, instead, to stare at the floor.

I knew why. The collapse of our trio was hard on all of us, but I think it was especially hard on the boy who'd come from so little. The family he'd found in salvation on Cinder was disintegrating all over again in his recollection of these memories.

The last recollection.

Once I've finished with my Verse, Korac could stifle the sorrow once again. Bury it in the love of his mother, wife, and daughter.

I squeezed Tameka against my side and kissed her temple. She beamed up at me with warmth and affection.

This kind of love is the only way to move forward. That's why I worry about you, Rayne.

Both versions of you perk up. "Why?"

Who do you have to love you in the present and teach you to live for right now rather than linger in the past? With you alone out there, keeping us safe—

Because I know you. That's the only course of action known to my little girl—Sacrificing your happiness to preserve ours. Some would say you inherited it. In the meantime, who looks after you?

You stare at me with those big blue eyes before answering, "I'll be fine. Don't worry about me."

Textbook Rayne Echo Callahan.

In my study, I say to Andrew, "Open the next volume and read from page three hundred and twelve, please."

Andrew opened the next journal and found the page, reading, "'Using the gas sample I collected from Monarch 3 and the soil samples Nox gathered from L. Capra, I was able to restore Vittle nutrients enough to produce supplements. Awful tasting bricks of nourishment, but they were something more than what we had.'"

Korac grimaced. "I can testify to all of those things."

Andrew smiled and pointed at the entry. "There's an archive of notes here for your research on the Vittle crop. Do you mind if we use this for the agricultural museum?"

Filled with pride, I beamed."Of course."

I continued on with the story.

Lost in my desire to revitalize our species, I was completely oblivious to the signs of the oncoming revolt. I never noticed mother's clandestine outings or followed Karter and Para to a mysterious continent full of nacre hosts. Fervent, I only wanted to reproduce our lifeline, and it never occurred to me how many forces were out to divide us.

Until the night the 'merchant' came to dinner, discussing new planets. As if the Icari would ever abandon Cinder.

An hour into the meal, the alarm sounded.

As a quiet settled into the study, I asked Karter, "Would you like to share your point of view? Nox and Korac have covered the evening from our perspective pretty thoroughly."

Karter glanced between the faces in the room before peering down at Para on the floor. The small Valkyrie nodded, and Karter sat straighter in the chair. "Of course. Let's start with the first time Gale approached me. It was on her second visit to the Spire, which was, coincidentally, the night she tried to seduce Nox. I found her afterward in the kitchens. The woman could put some food away."

Caedes humphed, and after everyone peered at him, elaborated. "Lyriks have quite the appetite."

Chuckles and giggles filled the room as Pehton's cheeks blossomed with an orange glow. She nudged him, half-heartedly, before tossing an hors d'oeuvre in her mouth.

Korac muttered, "Women who are never sated are the best—Ow. Baby, don't bruise the goods." He rubbed his bicep where Sagan nudged it.

She grinned with a warning finger in his face. "One more out of you, mister, and I'll—"

"I think we should get back to the Verse," Tameka interrupted. "Karter, if you would continue?"

The Valkyrie beamed and assented with a nod. "Right. I found Gale there eating leftovers, which I came to peruse myself. She asked, 'Hey, you lead the Valkyrie, correct?'"

"I shook my head, saying, 'You mean Amolot.'"

"But Gale insisted, 'No. They call you, Karter, their leader—'"

Para interrupted the story with a little cheer before saying, "Go on."

Karter said, "Gale accused me of having other charges to look after. I knew what she meant, but I wasn't certain who'd tipped her off. Still, I took her to the nacre farm." She lost a little color before continuing, "I'd never seen someone so…affected. At the sight of all those people enslaved for Umbra's weapons, Gale fumed. I mean literally fumed."

Pehton gave a little cheer.

I couldn't help but smile at all my guests—Comfortable, fed, and a little drunk in good company. I'd always pictured the stronghold filled with family. Who knew it would grow into one of this size?

"Gale came by many times, supplying me with technology and tools for the community under my care." Karter adjusted Echo's covers as she told the story, seeming to distract herself for comfort. "Then she came around with the notion to release them. Before long, that turned into schemes to usurp or overthrow Umbra.

"Savis became involved. She wanted little to do with the Lyriki aspect of things, but she trusted me to ally with someone strong enough to eliminate the King of Cinder.

"But then Monarch 3 happened, and you..." Karter gestured at me, "...removed us from Tritan and Lyriki involvement—Tumu, do you know what Gale's orders were?"

Tumu, who was snuggled on the couch with Lamassau, straightened to tell his part of this story. He cleared his throat and rotated his neck, popping out every kink before framing with his hands. He said, "Picture it. Pehton ran the prison half-staff after trading the volition of all the Lyriki Wardens to Razor—"

"Thanks for that, by the way." Miy rolled her eyes, snuggled next to Twenty-One.

Pehton winced.

"—Sorry." Tumu continued, "Triss was helping the Pain Curator establish the Emporium of Exotic Experiences and the Obsidian Palace.

"Gale was storming around Enki, extra upset since discovering Primary Rem had installed another source of nacre ore on Cinder using slaves from around the Vast Collective. Now the puppet Remorse put in charge over the source had gained a backbone thanks to Rem's son. Umbra was poised as a proper threat to Rem's machinations, and a despondent Primary is lethal.

"Gale and Korac uhm... *related*, reminding her of everything she couldn't have as an intergalactic triple agent. Things were looking bleak for our little-known heroine.

She turned to me for help. Smuggling test subjects out of our labs proved to be tricky work, but how could I resist?

"Then the time came, and Remorse ordered her to capture the King and Princes of Cinder plus one impeccably dressed guard."

Korac toasted.

Karter took over from there. "Gale arrived and asked us to besieged the colony to overthrow Umbra. She swore to me that nothing would happen to you three boys. Or your mother."

I glanced over at Korac, who had composed his mask once again. I, better than anyone know, what he hides under it. Regret, confusion, and loss.

The next, I said, "If I hadn't read it myself in his Verse, I would never have believed Nox *understood* me in that moment. I thought he was already so far gone he couldn't recognize right from wrong. Or appreciate how much it broke my heart to watch him murder a woman who we knew virtually nothing about."

The room settled into a quiet, where no one looked at me. Instead, they lived the moment in their minds, each of them questioning what they would do in our place.

When I confessed, "I'm not any better than Nox," it got their attention.

You, Rayne, sit up and give me a questioning look.

I rubbed the back of my neck and sighed, uncomfortable with the next admission. "When I told Nox, 'There is a better way than this. Killing her was unnecessary.' It wasn't a matter of virtues or morals. Although, I can understand how he'd come to that conclusion. I meant it was more pragmatic to keep Gale alive for interrogation and study."

Pehton recoiled.

Korac narrowed his eyes at me.

Sagan looked away. Her eyes—her expression was full of...

"You got quiet again, Superman. What was on Sagan's face?" the twelve-year-old version of you asks.

Revulsion and disappointment. In me.

"No."

No? No. You weren't there, Rayne. You didn't see it... The horror in her sweet eyes. My friend was disgusted with me—

"No. She wasn't. The circumstance was horrifying. It compounded the misunderstanding between you and Nox. Tell me, why were you so quick to think of interrogation?"

Because Gale nearly killed Karter, who protected me from Gale's vocal attack—To save me. Now we know what kind of pressure Gale was under. She needed to keep up appearances to continue saving thousands more lives, but Karter is worth more than millions to me.

"And how many millions could you have saved by interrogating Gale, learning her true motivations, and joining forces with her? How much of this war may have been avoided?"

Do you agree then that Nox was wrong for killing her?

The little version of you boops her forehead to mine, while the preteen you answers, "I understand you both in this instance. But to ask me what I would have done in your place is asking something impossible to answer. I don't know. That was the entire reason Nox wrote his Verse was to show me how uncertain everything was for him. Killing Gale for trying to kill you—especially with her deadly abilities—made sense.

Keeping her alive to understand her motivations also makes sense."

That's what Sagan said.

"Nothing is ever black or white." She faced me again, and there were tears lining her lashes. "Nothing is ever easy."

Tameka stepped between us so I could see the… I was so surprised to find love in her eyes. She pulled me in for an embrace, and I took it, feeling like a thief.

"You don't steal their love. You made it possible."

Oh, Rayne. There's so much worse to come.

Your smirk is unexpected as you say, "That's what all you boys tell me, and so far, I've loved each of you more with every Verse."

Is that you confessing to loving Nox?

You return your gaze back to the notebook and change the subject. "How about you brushing Korac's hair afterward, eh?"

Cute. You and Sagan are so single-minded.

Korac covered it well when he said, "Sometimes a hair brushing is just a hair brushing." There's no need to put Tameka through it again, especially when I have more… exciting encounters to cover.

Both versions of you snicker, which helps soften what comes next.

ENTRY FOUR

AND THE BEGINNING OF THE END

SAGAN POINTED OUT, "WHAT ABOUT WHEN YOU FIRST GOT YOUR WINGS? You'd discovered them by now because the last time you three went lava surfing was earlier in the same day the Lyriks attacked."

I almost winced and tried to recover by dismissing it. "Oh, getting my wings wasn't nearly as fantastical as my brother or dramatic as Korac."

Korac cut through my pretense. "You never told me or Nox how you came by them, either. I don't even think Savis knew."

I STUDIED BIRDS. How they came to fly. When it was the right time, mothers dropped their offspring from the nest, and their children either commanded their instincts enough to soar or... Not.

Li Mountain was the tallest peak on Cinder. Savis spoke of it often as her favorite climbing spot. We—Korac, Nox, and I—had scaled it many times, never aware of our foremother sleeping within. At the equivalence of sixteen,

I climbed to the top, walked to the edge, and jumped off. I was alone, but I knew I could do it—

"No, you didn't." Karter sounded sure of it. Her face was filled with...

"It was awe, Superman, not horror. You're reaching for anguish when there isn't any. She was proud of you. Impressed, even. Everyone in that room was. Look again."

Tameka's eyes sparkled, Korac's brows shot up, Tumu nodded with high regard—

All was as you said. They were impressed. Not eyes glistening with concerned tears. Or face drawn tight in confusion. Or nodding solemnly. Each of them hid smiles beneath their respect.

"That's right. So what happened next?"

I clapped to change the subject. "Let's discuss where we are in the lineup right now. I'm eighteen, Korac is twenty-one, and Nox is twenty-two. Umbra was educating Nox on how to ascend to the throne as King. Mother was... very ill. Korac was sneaking off to meet his friend Ementa on the secret continent of nacre slaves, whose evolution far surpassed ours. Meanwhile, I was in my lab. I was surrounded by Valkyrie sleeping in stasis, while I constantly worked to restore the Icari to something close to standard intelligence, speed, and living without the inclusion of our excessive appetites."

Korac looked pained as he admitted, "I wished I'd taken you to see the cities Ementa's people had made... All that technology..."

My smile was meant to ease him as I shook my head. "I don't hold it against you. I only learned of the secret civilization six months ago, and it's senseless to mourn something which was gone before I could miss it. Especially given how little I'd left the lab or gave you the opportunity to share. Still, every gift you returned with, I kept. With this new contextual lens, I can study them properly as artifacts of a lost people. Thank you."

Iuo muttered, "There's a trace of a blush."

Korac, a little drunk, clicked his tongue and rolled his eyes. Where he couldn't see, Sagan gave Iuo the most adorable wink.

I gestured at the Lamian King Elect. "Since you drew attention to yourself, why don't you read the next entry?"

"Sure thing, Wingmaster." He slipped into his bipedal form and stretched before approaching the ladder. "Which one?"

"Volume three hundred and ten. Pages twenty-one through thirty-six."

Iuo read on.

Nox and I argued that day about how to acquire ore from Thailea. I was certain diplomacy could prevail. Nox seemed positive they wouldn't relinquish even a sample of the precious material from Thailean tombs. Not without a fight.

I struggled to see his side, as was the way with us after Mon3. Every day he slipped further into father's shadow. Every day I lost him more.

Instead of arguing with him further, I focused on Korac, who entered my lab with a feather in his step. I wondered absently who the lucky girl was *this* time? Was I jealous? Why did his usual promiscuity suddenly bother me?

But I knew. Of course, I knew. My heart rate elevated at the sight of him. The very air smelled different when he was around, and I couldn't get enough of it.

I should rectify what was between us immediately.

In the meantime, I used my blood, a sample of Thailean ore, the Mon3 gas, and L. Capra's unstable mineral to create Many Feet II. I'd never seen Korac smile so broadly, and I welcomed sharing the experience with him. But Nox...

"How did you accomplish this?"

As soon as he asked, I knew it wasn't an idle curiosity, and eventually I got the entire truth out of him. Father, Korac, and Nox had selected a planet—Even thinking of it as 'selection' infuriated me.

How could someone choose to steal a planet? Already populated with a sentient race?! And then dare to ask me to help by creating hybrids?!

I told them exactly how I felt. "We will not sacrifice another race for ours, Nox."

A light shone in his black eyes before he said, "And with your help, sacrifice is unnecessary."

I dreaded his proposal, but listened to the entire thing. Create a hybrid race using the biological traits superior in the Icari but absent of their weaknesses. No starvation. No deadly reaction to certain solar radiations.

Earth.

Humans.

Iuo finished the entry and set his black and blue eyes on me. The entire room gazed on. This was such a pivotal point for all the Verses.

It starts with him and ends with her.

You shift which leg you want your weight on, curled on the floor, staring at your notebook. Those black Sharpie painted fingernails push through your hair in a frustrated gesture as you blow the air from your cheeks.

Talk to me, Rayne.

"I think I am 'her.'"

No. Why? Silence has confirmed the saying is older than—

"It feels right, Xelan."

Not superman. This causes me some concern, and I dread your answer to my next question.
Do you think the 'him' they refer to is Nox?

Both versions of you tilt your head, considering. Eventually, little you says, "No." Then preteen you says, "But I don't think it means you either."

Little you notices me shiver from the chill of the lingering question.

Who?
Let's continue.

Sagan spoke up. "This is where you told Korac you thought Nox was becoming a monster like your father."

Her husband gave her a side squeeze.

I nodded. "Yes. At this point in the entry, I'd been working for eight days, ten hours, and forty-eight minutes without sleep."

Tameka went still beside me, and I pressed my hand into her back, comforting her.

Pehton and Sagan didn't seem concerned about it, and I knew what they were tag-teaming me for as the Lyrik confirmed, "And it took some convincing to get you into bed that night. Right?"

I couldn't help it. I stole one out of Korac's playbook and pinched the bridge of my nose, chuckling.

Korac gave me a casual shrug, as if to ask, "Who can blame them?"

Iuo must have read ahead in the journal because he looked up from it and winked at me.

Everyone was against me.

That same night, Korac tried to seduce me for the first time, and I persuaded him to talk until we fell asleep. But the girls all want the details of the flirting and kissing. Well, all of them except Tameka. She looked fine with the abbreviated version.

"Ladies. Please. It was only the first night me and Korac held each other. We spent the entire evening talking about how we would spoil Many Feet II."

Sagan pouted.

Pehton took a sip of her drink, snorting into it, "Sure."

Iuo confirmed, "It's true. The next entry is about Colita, and then..." He went ahead a few volumes, and I wished he hadn't.

The look on his face...

Little you asks, "Is it time?"

Yes, Rayne. It's time.

Korac lowered his gaze and kept it on the floor.

Tameka took my hand and held it with her warmth.

I wished I could hug Pax for this, but I'm glad he wasn't in my study to hear about the day Nox and I sent our parents to Eternity.

"Read, Iuo. Please."

"I'm writing this entry after several days have passed. I couldn't bring myself to write until now.

"When Korac was helping me load Vittle seedlings into the cold frames, Colita came to collect us at mother's behest."

I swallowed, unable to stop the rise of emotions as a close friend read one of the worst moments of my life.

KORAC WENT TO MOTHER'S BEDSIDE FIRST.

While he was in there, Nox stood sentinel at the door. But me? Wearing a rut in the stone, I paced, wringing out the answer to Savis' illness in my hands. Repeatedly, I whispered to Elden's nacre shard, asking for strength. I could do this. I could figure out a last-minute solution to prolong her life. None of my tests on mother had ever produced a disease known to Icarean kind. Instead, it presented as more of an allergic reaction. Any other examinations, she refused, finding them too invasive.

Well, not today. Today, I would—

Korac emerged with tears streaking his composed mask.

I shattered.

Nothing—Not a damned thing—would give me more comfort in that moment than Korac holding me, but Nox was standing right there. I feared my brother's interference with my relationship or jealousy or—

I couldn't turn off the voice in my head that said, *"Don't let him know."*

So, Korac coolly announced, "She wants to see Xelan," and stepped by me, offering only a nod to conceal the pain in his eyes.

I was so completely alone in this, and it was all my fault—

Nox crushed me in an embrace. I mean, 'broke my rib' crushed me. My big brother held me while I cried over a loss I couldn't prevent.

That was it.

I could forgive Nox for all of it. We could move on from Mon3 and Gale, united as brothers once more. All thanks to mother, reuniting us in her last hour.

But when I pulled away, there was an anxiety tightening the corners of Nox's eyes. It had nothing to do with loss. Before I could ask about it, mother weakly called me through the door and I didn't waste another moment.

I sat on the edge of her bed and took her reaching hand in mine. Kissing her paper-white knuckles was like kissing frost, cold and delicate. The drapes filled her room as if they were wraiths preparing to carry her away.

"Mother, let me save you. Let me try another test. Or stasis, even—"

"Your father did this to me."

I believed her instantly, but... "How?"

Savis' voice was so small as she said, "Poison, son. For millennia. Since forever."

White hot rage blinded me and filled my veins with enough warmth to thaw her frozen fingers. I'd never known such fury. "I will kill him for this."

And I meant right at that moment. I stood, but Savis pulled me back. "Wait. Son, do not let your brother stop you."

"Why would Nox stop me—No."

Savis gave the weakest of nods to confirm my budding suspicions.

Not fully aware of it, my fists kept clenching and I was tightening my jaw. I could barely talk through it. "Speak clearly, mother. I want no regrets."

A cobalt tear squeezed from the corners of her iridescent eyes. "He was not accomplice to it, but he knew and did nothing to stop it for fear of your father's retaliation. Please, have mercy on your brother."

I kissed her knuckles and placed her hand gently back to rest on her bed. This would be my last time laying eyes upon her on this plane. I knew it, and I vowed to her, "Before you reach Eternity, you will already be avenged."

"I love you, my son. You are everything I hoped you would be."

I kept my promise. Without more than a look at Nox and a considering glance at Korac, I flew off to find Umbra.

The bastard had stolen my mother, raped her when she was just a girl, and forced her to serve his abuse for her entire life. Savis, the daughter of Elden, deserved a better death. I couldn't give her that, but I could give her the next best thing.

Retribution.

Umbra was in his tower, an empty place he deemed off limits for his time to meditate. Even Amolot wasn't allowed in there. I alighted in the window, intending to barrel into him and skin his murderous hide—

My father was on his knees with his head in his hands. Only then did I notice I was drenched in rain and lightning streaked across the red sky. It was my first storm, and I couldn't give it a second thought. I could only think about my reason for flying here.

"Umbra."

With each of his sobs, lightning branched through the sky. He said into his hands, "She refused me. Even on her deathbed she refused to speak to me—"

I climbed out of the window, accusing, "Because you are without any goodness, you venomous monster. Let her find peace without more of your poison—"

"LEAVE ME!" Tears and spittle sprayed out of Umbra's mouth. Every vein and muscle in his body strained with the shout. Grief was plain on his face. "GO!"

I heard footsteps on the stairs leading to the tower, and I knew it had to be—

Korac appeared in the doorway. I stepped around the mess that was the King of Cinder to tell my best friend to, "Guard the door."

"My Prince, perhaps—"

"It was an order." I closed it on the distress that was naked on Korac's face and hated myself, but I wanted no one to witness this premeditated crime. "Umbra, stand and face me."

He let out a toxic laugh. "So this is it. You would be my executioner. Well go on, *son*. Put me out of my fucking misery, never mind you will lose all the protection I ever afforded you—The blockade I made of my life will dissolve, and then when the shit rolls in, you will come to better understand me, boy." On the final note, he stood and faced me.

It was the first time I'd noticed the wrinkles carving deltas on his face, gathering near his eyes and mouth. His scars, stretched and faded like worn leather, were hidden beneath a thinning black curtain of hair streaked with gray. The King of Cinder had lost weight in recent months, leaving his harnesses to hang loosely from his shoulders and ribs.

Even evil aged.

Knowing this would be quick, I shook my head. "I will *never* understand a monster like you." Faster than he could see, I rushed him, twisted him around, and folded him in half, breaking his back. I nearly broke him in two, but I wanted him to suffer a while in his debilitated state. Letting him fall to the floor, I nudged him with my boot and called him, "Lower than dirt."

The rain stopped.

I paused there in my storytelling to assess the room. Matt surprised me by raising his hand.

"Yes?"

Nothing in his eyes or demeanor gave away the nature of his question. So when he asked, "What was it like killing your own father?" I nearly failed to disguise my initial shock.

People shifted uncomfortably, but some scrutinized my response with unveiled judgment—

"Curiosity. Concern. Love."

Rayne—

"I *know*, Superman. Trust me."

If I remembered correctly, Matt was never concerned with the wellbeing of his parents, unlike the rest of the Shadow who were beside themselves after the Invasion. No, Matt wasn't bothered in the least. So I gathered his question was a personal one, and I endeavored to answer it with some sensitivity and honesty.

"I thought the anger would go away. It didn't. I thought this resentment, threatening to burn a hole through me, would cool and ease—It just kept flaring. All I accomplished in killing Umbra was my mother's agenda and crowning Nox, King of Cinder."

Twenty-One held up his drink in a toast, and I couldn't fathom why. Then Bones mirrored him. Karter. Para. Lucas—All the Icari in the room. Our converted P.O.W. said, "We thank you for delivering us from chaos's reign and into a peace unlike one we'd ever known."

"I'll drink to that," Korac toasted this time with water and met my eyes as he did so. "To Umbra's fall."

Karter held up her drink. "To Lady Savis in Eternity."
Para repeated, "To Lady Savis."

It never occurred to me what the regime changeover from Umbra to Nox was like for the Icarean race. I was caught in the eye of this confusing storm, and my mother's lies only contributed to the debris. To me, Nox stood in Umbra's shadow, and Korac, blinded by hero worship, couldn't see it.

"Now, we've made it to where Nox built his castle, and all of Cinder was relocating to it. There are more trials ahead, but I thought this would be a good place to pause for questions or requests."

Sagan immediately raised her hand, and Elden help me. I knew—I *knew*—what she wanted to ask. It was finally time to get this story out there.

Something on my face gave me away, because Sagan blushed when I called on her. "Yes?"

She maintained eye contact anyway as she persisted. "You know."

Korac looked between us, perplexed before... "No. Oh, no."

Tameka asked, "What?"

I smiled down at her, as I took her hand. "You might not want to stay for this."

Tumu laughed, signifying he'd figured it out at the same moment.

Even Lamassau grinned. "I'm invested."

Again, Tameka asked, "Which memory is this?"

Andrew deduced which one and stood with an exaggerated stretch. "It's a good time to get up and explore the stronghold. Wanna come with, Lucas?"

The golden-eyed Icarus laughed elegantly. "Sure."

I asked Tameka, whose eyes were sparkling with curiosity, "What happened the night of Nox's coronation, according to his Verse?"

I watched Tameka work it out. Primary Rem accosted Nox. Disturbed, Nox went to confide in Korac about it. He found us in the library—

"Oh, my god."

There it was.

Tameka headed for the door. "I'll just go check on Pax. Excuse me."

Caedes and Jack followed Tameka out. In fact, several people left the study until only a handful remained. Tumu and Lamassau refreshed their drinks before returning to the couch. Pehton claimed the loveseat and sat on the edge of it. Korac tried to leave, but Sagan took his hand and whispered something, which convinced him to stay.

The Seamswalker grinned. "Ready when you are, Wingmaster."

Rayne, if you want I can skip this part—

"Keep storytelling, Superman."

Nox's coronation festival beckoned another dance with a certain pale Icarus, but I wanted to secure as many original Verses as possible. My brother likely would never notice with everything moving to the new castle. Even the idea of discussing it with him exhausted me—

"Thievery, your highness?"

There was no mistaking the elegant cadence in Korac's voice from behind me.

Shit.

I froze, mid-reach. "Will you tell on me to Nox?"

Korac stepped further into the library, closing the door behind him. "Will you give me incentive not to?"

Ahh. This. I sagged with relief. This discussion I didn't mind. "Korac, I—"

I turned to find the newly appointed General had stripped to his white silk undershirt and matching pants.

But what caught my breath was the midnight blue ribbon tied in Icarean bridal fashion around his biceps.

I won't lie. I gaped. Open-mouthed. Eyes wide. When I took a deep breath, I smelled a freshness…A coolness I'd never experienced on Cinder.

Korac's lips lifted into a smirk which melted me while he asked, "It makes a statement, does it not?"

"That is…Not. Fair." I shook my head incredulously.

Silver elegance strode to me, casual and languid like a cat. A cat that hungered for his next meal. I pressed my back against the books as Korac stepped into my personal space.

"I beg a moment, Korac. Please practice some reason—"

A finger pressed against my lips. Soft, slender, with perfectly manicured nails. Korac lowered his finger and brought those beautiful pale eyes closer, with only one intention in them. Familiar by now with his attentions, I wondered why I resisted him at all.

"One kiss, your highness," Korac offered. Innocence in his voice. Carnal fire in his eyes.

In my study, Korac scoffed. "Who talks like that?"
"Sh…He's telling his Verse," Sagan admonished.

In the story, I flinched. Korac promised to give me time to think on his proposal. Two weeks ago, he'd told me—in great detail—exactly what he wanted from our relationship. It made me worry over our compatibility. Could I let Korac do those things to me? Could I trust someone so much to let them bind me, gag me, and take me?

Ignoring the tempting smirk, I looked deeper. I looked into those colorless eyes, so close I made out a starburst of gray flecks.

A shadow hid within them.

Doubt. Fear. Hurt.

Not only could I trust Korac enough to do those things to me, but at that moment, I wanted nothing more.

I kissed him.

The future General grabbed my wrists and pinned me to the shelves. Shoved his knees between my legs and ground his hips against mine.

Want... Someone *wanted* me.

An unfamiliar scent married with the crisp smell already dominating the room. Dominating me. Sweet and smoky. Honey and leather. My scent.

The heat from my blush alerted Korac, who pulled slightly away and dropped my wrists. Breathless, my General offered, "If you want to stop at any point—"

I pulled one ribbon on his bicep, tightening it. Hard. "Korac, I know you wore this to tempt me to distraction. Your wicked streak will be the end of me."

The smirk returned with a vengeance, and a promising gleam appeared in his eyes. Silkenly, Korac assured, "Come now, my Prince. I seek not your end, but your undoing."

In my study, Korac barked out a laugh, saying, "I can't believe Nox overheard that."

I know my eyes were glittering because I was grinning so wide. "It's better he fled instead of overhearing what came after."

Pehton snickered into a full-on laugh. "You *can* blush, Korac!"

"Fuck, I need more alcohol for this."

In the recollection, Korac did something unexpected. He dropped to his knees and wrenched my pants off my hips. I blushed once more.

Silver flashed in his gaze as Korac eyed his prize. "We will both thoroughly enjoy it." The last he spoke, uhm... against me.

Back in my study, Sagan snickered. "Now Wingmaster is blushing!"

Yes, well. One does when providing a detailed account of their first time.

My eyes fluttered closed, and my head went back against the books. They ground against me as I turned this way and that. Korac tempted me while the shelves bit into my back. I made far too much noise for Nox to be the only one who spied us.

I let instinct take over and gripped Korac's hair. My eyes rolled back, and I let out a loud groan. The sensation disappeared, and I cried out in disappointment.

Confused, I stared down at the General on his knees.

Korac commanded, "Your highness, hands behind your back until I say so. Do not touch me until I give word."

I shuddered at the ice in his eyes. Yet the vulnerability there—the sorrow—was what moved me to place my hands behind my back. I nodded once to assent.

The reward far surpassed the chore. Korac practiced a wealth of patience as he spent the next hour exploring me. Tongue. Lips. Teeth. Up. Down. In. Out. Around. Before too long, I was whimpering with my knees begging to buckle. The need for release was too great. Sure, I recognized it for what it was. Although a virgin to others, I'd experimented on myself. But this...

Nothing compared to this.

With the loss of my control, I gripped Korac's hair again. In punishment, long nails dug into my thighs until they bled.

I cried out and released the General who stood slowly and backed away. The swelling in his soft gray lips didn't stop him from smirking. Not the daring smirk I had come to like. No. This was a vindictive smile I would come to love.

Sweetly, Korac assured, "One day I will find a bottom who follows my instruction. Until then your training will do."

In the study, Sagan gave a little cheer, prompting chuckles all around.

Back in the story, Korac wrenched me by the arm with unexpected strength and speed. In one fluid motion, the General twisted my arm behind my back and bent me over a table.

I shouted in alarm, "Korac, stop!" Even though he released me, my voice wavered as my heart pounded in my throat. I said, "I am inexperienced, and I want no pain in this. I want you, but not the pain. Not at first." My breath marked the surface of the table where I was pressed against it.

Korac planted his hands on either side of my head and leaned forward until we met eye-to-eye. Midnight to silver. The warmth of his front pressed along my back, revitalizing my waning desire.

The more experienced Icarus purred, "I accept your terms, Xelan. Breathe when I say. At any point, stop me with any word of your choosing. I will not fail you." He prepared me for what would come next.

What word? What word? Something I'd never say in passion. But fun—

"Banana."

Pehton choked on her laughter.

Sagan picked up a pillow to cover the volume of her giggles.

The men remaining in the room quirked an eyebrow each.

In the story, the bark of laughter from behind made me jump. Korac kissed down my spine as if to ease the anxiety. Between kisses, he purred, "As your highness wishes. Breathe, my dear Prince. Let me introduce you to the next chapter of your life." He bent over me completely until his lips brushed my ear. "The best chapter."

Korac delivered on his promise.

When we found paradise together, he met my eyes, and tears had glistened in his. Still, he smirked. Of course, he smirked. "My Prince, look at the state of you."

"Hah! I hope you came prepared."

At the arch of the General's brow, I grinned. "I plan to leave every surface in this library in quite the state. Are you up for the challenge?"

Korac was, in fact, up for the challenge.

Little you says, "Nox was happy for you."

Out of all the revelations in his Verse, that one... Oh, Rayne, it hurts the most. I won't lie to you. I'd give anything to change it—Keeping Korac a secret when everyone knew, anyway. I've never felt so foolish and out of my mind—So utterly **mistaken.**
But I couldn't...
Shake it.
This dread of the worst people in my life knowing and using it against us.

With a gentle push, preteen you states, "You were paranoid." You watch me rake my hands down my face and search every trace of my expression for a reason to be concerned.

I was. And properly so. How could I not be on edge? We were planning to invade another planet, and what with warnings of "Imminent" around the Spire...

You wince a little before asking, "Are you sure it wasn't part of a more internal mindset? The vulnerability had bothered you before you discovered the carvings in the windows. And if you were truly paranoid about Imminent, you would've moved to Nox's Castle with them."

You're right. About all of it. I can guarantee honesty with you, but only in so far as I can be honest with myself.

"Were you honest with the others?"

Everyone returned to my study after a brief break, after I mentioned this would be the last entry before we moved onto the first Icarean migration to Earth. No one looked ready to sleep, but everyone stretched out to relax. It was a heartwarming sight—

All of my family was comfortable and happy. Safe. We'd fought so hard, and this reward was well-earned.

I met all their faces, filled with ease, before I set out to destroy it.

"Only three people in this room read or have listened to the uncensored version of Korac's Verse."

Korac perked up, Sagan tilted her head, and Tameka turned those beautiful green eyes on me with curiosity.

Uncomfortable with the scrutiny, I cleared my throat before continuing with my confession. "I've encountered both versions, and the only difference between the two is the level of privacy Korac and Sagan afforded Rayne... and me."

Now the rest of the Shadow shifted with fresh interest.

"I have episodes of mania and depression similar to bipolar disorder in humans." I couldn't bear to see any reactions or hear any responses, so I barreled through. "They present in periods of extreme focus on work while ignoring anything else—Relationships, responsibilities, and self care. I can't think about or look at anything but my research. Likewise, I experience self-doubt, loss of control, and extreme grief for days—sometimes weeks—at a time. Unable to remove myself from the downward spiral of racing thoughts.

"Given our closeness, you..." I nodded at Korac. "...noticed my complication before I knew I was stricken with it. And I thank you for respecting me enough to withhold it from your public Verse."

Sagan smiled gently while Korac confessed, "I won't lie. It was her idea to redact it. Once she made her point, I understood. Despite how much pleasure I derive from torturing you, the line has to be drawn somewhere."

I was afraid to meet Tameka's eyes, but to my surprise, her expression never changed. It was, as always, open, pure, and full of regard and love.

Have I mentioned how lucky I am?

"You totally have." Four-year-old you beams. "But you can keep it up."

When everyone seemed more curious than judgmental, I confessed, "Colita helped me through most of it."

Some people winced or recoiled. Eyes went wide. Korac barked out a laugh. "That viper?"

"I knew she was a spy for Nox, but I also knew her entire story. It's a lonely one. Don't get me wrong, she *never* stopped insinuating herself to me, but she never took advantage of me, either."

"Prince Xelan, have you not seen a bath in days?" Colita teased when she arrived for work as my tech. Her eyes took in everything. No doubt every detail would find its way to Nox.

I couldn't be bothered to notice my hair was stringy or my skin was oily. Before I could return with my own barb, Colita collected the excessive length of my hair and pinned it back for me. The next thing I knew, a rag was smeared on my face, smelling of cleansing oils and warmed by the steamer she'd ran it through.

While forcing me out of one white lab robe and into a fresh one, Colita exclaimed, "There. Better?"

Actually. Yes. "Thank you." More revitalized, I resettled Elden's nacre shard around my neck.

Colita's laughter tinkered like a bell. "How many times have I told you? There is no need to thank me. You are my excuse to leave the new Castle. Korac treats me like a—"

"How-is-he?" I blurted the words out fast, which I didn't realize until I was reflecting on it later.

Colita shot me a look with a quirked brow. "The grand General is just that. Grand. He excels at everything and is, simply, too perfect to look at. Or criticize. Or talk to like a normal person. One must contact his lieutenants to schedule an appointment."

The entire time she spoke, I was looking over my calculations for the progenitor. I'd yet to reproduce sustainable imitations of the Vittle crop with the right amount of nourishment to replace our dwindling supply. Yet, talk of Korac properly distracted me as nothing else could.

In response to Colita's recap, I smiled when she said he was excelling and frowned at the thought that Korac's new station was spoiling the core of him. The humility beneath all the regal pretense.

Colita, like an excellent spy, took in my every reaction. She said, "You should visit him, sire."

Yes. I should.

When I smiled, she tried to further encourage it. "I'm sure Nox would welcome you—"

My expression fell into a frown before I could stop it. Nox's name had that effect on me.

A pretty sigh followed, and Colita pressed, "He talks about nothing other than you. How proud he is of your dedication toward saving our species. Your brother misses you. Is it not time to reconsider leaving this haunted place?"

Every pass of wind through the Spire carried my mother's voice. The grieving breath of a specter. I didn't even bother lighting the other rooms. I lived and worked in the labs, surrounded by my frozen friends.

Colita continued reciting a song I'd heard from her many times before. "In Nox's Castle, he created this magnificent lab for you. It sits right off this impossible library, and it's near the baths—Your highness, you *must* see it."

I could do with a change of scenery. I'd built my lab in the Spire from Many Feet's old cave. There weren't any windows. I couldn't remember the last time I saw Li—

"And then the three of you can reunite in bed with me, and all will be right with the multiverse."

When I quoted her in the study, Korac barked out a laugh and choked on a snack Sagan had fed him. Her eyes glittered with good humor and mischief.

Pehton muttered, "Who would ever think I'd have something in common with *that* woman?"

Her brazen admission got Tumu, Bones, and Lamassau into a fit while Caedes gave her a measuring look.

Shameless, Tameka shrugged. "Meh. I could see two out of three."

The look on Korac's face—

My abrupt laughter startled me, and I pulled Tameka in for a hug to thank her for it. For everything.

Andrew put us back on track. "So after this, you went and talked to Korac at his camp. He redacted a lot, but it implied something was wrong with you."

I let Tameka go as I confessed, "My heart broke for my people, reduced to grunts in an army slated to destroy an unknown world. Why couldn't I be further along in my research to elevate their intelligence and reduce their limitations? Why didn't I accept Karter's offer when the Valkyrie had attacked to usurp father and takeover as Cinder's King?"

The room fell quiet again.

Into the silence, I said, "Korac, you found me on the mountain where I often wept for my failings. You called it 'emotional erosion.'"

My General licked his lips before saying, "The next time I saw you, you were fresh and ready to race. It was a night and day difference. Eight thousand years have passed since then. Did you ever learn to manage it?"

I swallowed before saying, "Let's take a break. The next entry will cover the first invasion of Earth."

The twelve-year-old version of you states, "It's a fair question."

And I will answer it. I promise.

ENTRY FIVE

EVERYTHING I WANTED

"Do you still think of it as an 'invasion'?" Little you asks with a tilt of your head. Your pigtails sway with the motion.

It's a good question, but yes. I think so. A nonviolent one, but an intrusion on the human species, nonetheless.

The Shadow took a break to rest, to discuss, to… relate to one another.

Even Tameka backed me into a hidden corner of the ravine. With love in her eyes—such extraordinary love—she convinced me everything was all right between us. After so much overexposure during my Verse, I craved the contact with her. We kept everyone waiting another hour. We weren't the only ones to return with a few buttons undone or sleeves slipped off. Every couple was a little disheveled as they found their places.

Korac glided his hand down Sagan's shoulders, displaying her bare arms, free of their ribbons.

It was oddly comforting. So normal, natural, and healthy. How could everyone having sex in my stronghold come across as so wholesome?

I actually laughed aloud at how ridiculous it sounded in my head.

Tameka quirked a brow at me with a sexy smile. "Are we thinking the same thing?"

It felt good to say, "Yeah. I think so." I kissed her hair and walked us back to the fireplace in my study. When I turned around…

Wow.

One day, we'd return every pillow and blanket back to their respective couches and beds, but it might take a while.

I asked my growing audience, "Is everyone comfortable?" I kept my voice from trembling with anxiety.

They responded with various forms of "Sure, Wingmaster." "Aye, aye cap'n." Or quiet toasts with their drinks and food.

Tameka gave my hand a reassuring squeeze, and I was as ready as I'd ever be.

"Who wants this one?"

Silence stood. "I do."

I gave a small bow with my head. "Yes, foremother."

At my reverence, Silence beamed and glided to one wall covered in journals, asking, "Which will it be?"

"Four hundred and ninety-eight. Page two hundred and eighty-three."

The woman responsible for all of our creation smiled a thousand-watt movie-star beam as she read the first few lines. "If that creature who opened a conduit to Earth was a Thailean Mystic, I would eat my robes."

Kyle laughed. "How did that marinate in hindsight?"

Andrew asked, "Yeah, how could you tell it was Remorse?"

I ran a hand through my hair while I said, "I didn't, but…I knew Mystic sightings were rare, made more ironic given Korac was regularly conversing with one in secret."

The Iona General shrugged.

I confessed, "Still. Nothing is as beautiful as a conduit opening for the first time. The desert waited on the other side. I decided, once more, to forgive Nox. After all, he'd brought me the stars."

"Fascinating. I wonder if the conduit occurs in a place or if he fashions it there? Are all conduits connected by the Seam? If so…" I could go on and on, fidgeting with Elden's nacre shard while ruminating about the physics and metaphysics of blood-borne conduits.

Fortunately, Korac drove me out of it with the lure of a race. How could anything be better than the three of us crossing into a new planet in peace and sport?

Regarding my wingless lover, I said, "Fair race. No flying. Ready?"

Korac said, "Set."

Nox finished it. "Go!"

But it wasn't meant to be. Remorse interrupted us to harass my brother. Meanwhile, Korac and I were the first to reach Earth and the first to…

Well…

In my study, the Iona General suggested, "I think we can skip the sex scene this time."

"Who says you get a say?" Pehton cried from across the room.

Sagan laughed before agreeing with her husband. "Leave it to the imagination, girl."

I could hear the grin in the Lyrik's voice as Pehton said, "Caedes has me covered, anyway."

Wholesome and healthy.

It made it hard to push on, but… "Silence, can you please continue reading?"

With a sad smile, as if she'd already read ahead, Silence continued.

With less of a fight than I'd expected, Nox agreed to let me build my stronghold in peace. For the next phase of my work, I needed complete privacy. It might strain my relationship with Korac, but I couldn't have them peering over my shoulder for their own inspiration.

Life.

I would create it. Soon.

While I wanted a fresh start with my brother, I couldn't trust him enough with something as monumental as this. Baby steps.

Still, when I went to scout a location, it meant leaving Korac for the evening. When I thought about how I felt for him, it was bittersweet. I'd loved no one more, and my heart ached against leaving him, even for a few hours, because I knew the truth.

Many days alone were ahead.

On the bright side, I found the perfect site only an hour's flight away. When I stood on the level ground above a thin sheet of bedrock, it felt…

Perfect. Right.

The stars twinkled in their agreement.

For what I envisioned, it would take time and advances in technology beyond my imagination, but for now, a simple building would do. I found some volunteers to pay after I bought materials from the proper sources. We broke ground in no time.

A few hours later, the foundation was on its way. I worked alongside the men, dirty and entirely too focused. The foreman was remiss to inform me that they'd spent the better part of the night ignoring their duties at the camp to help me.

Even after they left, I kept working, taking pride in the aches even my nacre couldn't address immediately. Lifting one-ton blocks was hard work.

The small version of you giggles. "Those were some big blocks."

Yes. I was properly exhausted by the time I returned to camp for a day in Korac's care. I wasn't expecting to find humans in Nox's tent.

Colita gloated, "I brought them here."

"Quite impressive. Look at you, our lady diplomat." I patted her on the back and instantly regretted it. So much dirt. "Oh… I am so sorry."

She glared at me and scoffed. "There is no way you should expect to confer with the General while looking so filthy."

Point made, but that didn't stop me from greeting our first humans with grimy hands. They seemed to appreciate it.

Elden, they were fuzzy. And varied. Their hair and eye color, muscle and fat composition, intelligence—I spent several hours in Nox's tent recording observations the way we'd often seen Iuo record our histories. I almost managed to sneak a hair sample, but alas…

The sun threatened our horizon.

Nox offered to let the humans stay in our camp, but Colita volunteered to return with them to their homes as an ambassador. It suited her, but the risk to her skin exposure under Sol's radiation resurfaced some ongoing concerns.

To my dismay.

Especially with the considering glance from Nox as he saw Colita and our visitors out of the tent.

New planet. New sky. New problems.

"Korac, you and Nox skipped ahead to the settlement and fortress established, and I think I'll do the same. If you don't mind, foremother, could you please retrieve journal five hundred and three? The next entry is on page sixty."

I knew what I was doing by asking Silence to read. Asleep in Li mountain for millions of years, she'd missed so much of her people's formation. Even though she'd read the other two Verses, I wanted her to feel a part of this paramount time. The discovery, the exploration, and the woes.

Silence's gray eyes sparkled with every reading. Especially this one.

"Come, my prince, keep your eyes closed."
Korac led me up the exterior staircase to the fortress' highest floor. He assured me Nox and his advisers were buried in plans in the tunnels beneath us. We would not see any interruptions tonight.

Still… "Is this necessary, Korac? What is it you want to show me that requires such—"

"Fun? Excitement? Is there a little danger in it for you?" Korac's voice softened and deepened at the last.

It was his bedroom voice, and although it thrilled me to hear it, it also riddled me with anxiety to hear it outside of our sanctuary. "Korac—"

Heavy wood groaned, interrupting my next caution. My captor said, "My prince, open your eyes."

When I did, my mouth fell open.

I knew Korac had worked every night to design the top floor of the fortress. I didn't know at the time it was with Nox's blessing. But seeing the final product…

I almost asked him to decorate my stronghold.

Slotted with shelving, polished and ornate wood covered three walls, while the fourth stood in a testament to historical design. Glass. And the ceiling too. It complemented the impossible telescope positioned in front of it. Above, diamonds twinkled in the midnight velvet reflecting the carpeted floor. The desk and tables matched the wainscoting padded with leather. I was suddenly inclined to test them with Korac.

I had to swallow before I could ask, "Is this… Is this for me?"

Korac rolled his eyes and teased, "No, I designed it for my other lover with midnight blue Atramentous."

He'd earned the laugh from me while I took everything in, unable to speak further.

Less confidently, Korac asked, "Will you work here? Will you stay?"

I wanted to say, 'Yes.' To say I wouldn't part us for my responsibility to our species. I wanted to look into my lover's white eyes and lie to him. For him.

"For a time."

Korac kept his back to me, pretending to peruse a collection of encyclopedias. "Not forever?"

I wouldn't let us dissolve like this. Wrapping my arms around him, I buried my face in his peppermint-scented hair. "Please. Let us not dwell on it. I am here. You are here. Enjoy it now."

The way Korac hung his head... Grieving us—

I stayed for another year. Happily.

"Until Nox asked you to create the Sphere," Sagan recounted correctly. "You wanted to build something like the Martyr Complex to feed the Sphere's mechanism, but only you or Nox bled potent enough nanites to fuel it."

Andrew continued the history up from there. "In his Verse, Nox said he didn't want you exploring your own blood. Obviously, he worried about you discovering the Tritan half of your parentage. But I always wondered..."

I gave him permission to keep pushing. "Yes, Andrew?"

"Surely a scientist such as yourself had already studied your own genetics?"

Korac's expression said he'd never thought of it before and was impressed with the young Progeny man for considering it.

Kyle called out, "Right?! You used your blood to create Many Feet II. So, you must've known."

"Of course. How do you think I knew I wasn't Umbra's son? I'd tested our DNA for a match by the time I was twelve. But with technology as limited as it was, I couldn't perform a proper analysis of the anomalies until much later in my life. You're all correct, but it wasn't just the sphere. It was the Cruor Villam. The unexplained visits from Bin. Then came Thailea. I *believed* Nox had murdered people for the ore."

Silence read the next entry.

NOX TURNED AWAY AND SNARLED, "I NEVER ASKED YOU TO APPRECIATE MY METHODS." He whirled and pointed a finger in my face. "But I expect your esteem for acquiring it. I am your brother—"
"And I am not your excuse for murder—"
"I AM YOUR KING!"

I hate the monster my brother has become.

Now was the time. It hurt to leave without saying goodbye to Colita or Korac, but it was the only way to ensure even they would not follow me.
The Icarean Prerogative.
Save the race.
It was all that mattered now.

Rayne...

The tiny version of you sidles closer and wraps her chubby arms around my neck. More grateful than you can know, I grip you tight, but when my eyes open, I find the preteen version of you in tears. You confess on a sob, "I hate it. I hate it every time I hear it."

I stand, shifting your smaller weight to one arm while you continue to cling to me. Crossing the room, I wait. When pre-teen you stands, I wrap my free arm around you and hold you tight. You bury your face in my side and cry.

I hate it, too.

Tameka brought me back to the moment, standing before an audience of our favorite people. Our family. But at that point in my Verse, I knew only strangers. Never would I have imagined my home filled with so much warmth.

I sought it out.

"Devis?"

My third Progeny sat cross-legged in a corner of the room with his eyes closed throughout my storytelling. I'd wondered a few times if he was using his affinity for memory to live the moments with me. He opened his eyes, bright green contrasting beautifully against his dark complexion. His voice was deeper with meditation as he asked, "Yes, father?"

I smiled at the familial reference, still unsure after all these millennia how to take it. "Would you mind reading the next entry?"

When Devis stood, his locs swayed with him, and the decorative beads tinkered together. He bowed to Silence as he approached the ladder and relieved her for the readings. She picked her way back across the pallets before settling into Kyle's waiting arms—

Their relationship is a hereditary puzzle I will forever try to put from my mind.

I see you smiling about it, little Rayne.

"Hee. They're happy!"

Yes. My foremother and a descendant of my Progeny are happy together.

Ahem. Back to the story.

For Devis, I said, "Volume seven hundred and two. Page five hundred—"

"The beginning. The start. Our song preluded to this Verse."

The people in the room turned to look at T.A.O. who rightly guessed the entry. Or maybe she'd read it during the mystery which was her life.

Andrius tried convincing her to return to the seat beside him, saying, "It is all right, little sister."

I smiled gently at her. I always smile that way for T.A.O. I asked, "Would you like to read with Devis? Would you like to read together, all three of you?"

In an awkward motion, Andrius stood beside The Afflicted One and chafed the shiny nacre filaments down his own deep-complected arm. "Yes. Please."

The First Wave Progeny gathered together at my bookshelf and prepared to read my notes on their creation while I prayed to Elden. Please, let this not offend. Let them understand. Not everything was meant to be seen.

Ore.
Gas.
Soil.
Blood.
Why did the Progeny experiment continue to fail? What component was I missing?

Dozens of efforts, all of them unsustainable—Wasted my resources, time, and mental energy, creating only half-formed things for incineration. Figments of my worst nightmares—

"Why?!" I pounded my desk, while another failure boiled, formless and undone, in my latest progenitor. Gripping the shard of Elden's nacre, I growled, "What am I missing?!"

I'd gotten used to the smell of liquid skin and un-sacced organ fluids. Perhaps that was telling. How long ago had I last seen the night sky? Breathe the desert air? My hair dripped with gross lab work and unwashed perspiration. Blood stained my nail beds blue and red.

I missed my observatory in the fortress.
I missed Colita's care.

But most of all, I missed Korac's peppermint-scented smirk.

With a sigh, I ran a hand through my—

Nope. I couldn't even push my fingers through the cakey strands.

It was time to admit it. "I have failed."

After calculating the passage of time, I'd determined that three months had passed since I abandoned all of which I called home at the fortress. Since I broke Korac's heart and mine.

"Nox…"

While buried in my work, I didn't allow my thoughts to veer onto my brother or linger on our last argument, which drove me here. But although I feared Nox was lost to me, I still knew him well enough. He'd likely spent the last three months trying to think of ways to buy me back or lure me home. The humbling anxiety was good for him.

So much for 'my King.'

Looking about the stronghold, I groaned. How did I let it get this bad? I vowed to both apologize and thank Colita for ever tolerating me as soon as I contacted her for a quick rendezvous. I needed information, but I also needed help. She was the least likely of the Icari to force me to choke down 'return home for the species' sake' rhetoric.

I spent the remaining hours of Sol's harsh radiation tidying my documents, recalibrating my instruments, and disposing of my failed attempts at creating life. When the biological compounds were properly sterilized, I memorialized the ashes in an urn. I'd set it aside for this purpose after the third failure. It seemed too detached to dispose of them clinically. I marked the monument with each attempt.

One hundred and three tallies scarred the bronze basin.

I was tired.

Once the sun set below the dunes, I traveled to the edge of the fortress, wearing a cloak to add some clandestine adventure to the occasion. Three months ago, I'd learned

Colita's routine. She spent early evenings settling disputes in the fortress, but around midnight, she traveled out into the city seeking… inspiration.

Everyone knew of Colita's desire for a harem. I chose to believe she would see the error in such objectification before she began breeding for it. I even provided a few examples and lectures on the inappropriate applications of eugenics—

But I digress.

I found Colita in the city square, accompanied by a two-guard escort.

Easy.

While she browsed inside a shop, her soldiers waited outside, flanking the entrance. I dropped off the shop's roof and onto one of the guard's shoulders. I clapped a chemical-soaked rag over his face, and he fell out instantly. Before the other noticed me and raised the alarm, I rolled behind him and dealt with him quickly. Both guards would wake within a few hours, unharmed.

In my study, Kyle barked out a laugh. "What are you? Batman?"

"Superman!"

That's right, Rayne.

As if Colita had heard the commotion, she stepped out to find me on the stairs with my hood lowered. "Xel—"

In a heartbeat, I crossed the space between us and silenced her with a finger to her lips. "You never saw me."

Colita groaned, but the sparkle in her eyes told me she was happy to see me, too. When I removed my finger, she said, "Carry on. Tell me whatever apologies you wish me to relay to your brother—"

"I need your help."

Sky-blue eyes properly looked me over, and it embarrassed me how Colita's nose crinkled when she sniffed the air.

There was a gentleness in her voice as she said, "Oh, Xelan. The entire time you were away…?"

I lowered my eyes in shame, clinging to Elden's nacre shard for the strength to admit it. "Yes."

Abruptly, Colita took my hand. "Come on." She pulled me into the shop and called out, "Lucas!"

Everyone stopped breathing and stiffly turned to look at the most conspicuous Icarus in my study. All aside from Silence and Smith. They both shared a knowing grin. Andrew in particular raised a very curious brow at his lover.

Lucas was calm and easily met their stares.

I cleared my throat to relieve some of the tension. "Uh. Lucas. Would you like to take over?"

The Icarus in question gave a small bow with his head. His gilded eyes glittered with amusement as he said, "Of course, your imperial majesty, but back then you were only a Prince. Young and devastatingly handsome, if a little naïve. Colita spoke of you often, with nothing but kindness. You came into my shop, precluded by a particular aroma I could only refer to as 'smelted people.'"

Beside me, Tameka winced, and I flinched.

Preteen you asks, "Why did you flinch?"

You know why, Rayne.

"She doesn't judge you."

After talking with you, I've come to see things more your way, but in the moment I felt… so very alone and exposed.

Korac said, "When I first met you, Lucas, you were training future CoN agents in swordplay and helped me design new uniforms for my legions."

Sagan added, "And a few years ago when Rayne was prepping to meet…" she shot me a look before saying,

"Nox at the fortress, you told us you were born during the first invasion."

Lucas crossed his legs and laced his fingers on top of them. "Yes?"

Smith grinned as he said, "I believe they expect you to elaborate."

The golden-eyed Icarus tilted his head. "This isn't my Verse."

Before the room broke into commotion, Andrew said, "Lucas has answered these concerns once before, when we moved his zeppelin to Nikki's Iona. We know he lied about his age initially, and that he's had many roles as a former agent of Imminent across the last few million years. Is it really necessary to interrogate him now because he owned a shop in Nox's settlement?"

Korac conceded with a shrug.

Sagan smiled sincerely at Lucas while saying, "No accusations here. I only want to know the whole story. That's why I enjoy the Verses so much."

Lucas returned the beaming expression. "Absolutely, my dear. If I may continue?"

I nodded, trying to hide my own considerations about Lucas' fluid past.

"Can you help him?" Colita asked, as if I were a charity case.

I certainly shuffled in smelling awful. The shop was full of nice pristine textiles and goods, and there I was, stinking the place up. My shoulders slumped as the self-doubt crested in some great wave threatening to drown me.

Was I really a person if my very existence had no effect on society? On reality? Since I'd failed my people so badly, was I any Prince to them—any leader? Did I deserve Colita's kindness or her friend's charity—

"That is enough, Prince Xelan. This way."

Lucas gestured to a back room, and after I absorbed the shock from his near-mind reading, I followed him into it.

Colita set about heating some water for me in a basin, while the gilded-eyed Icarus used a blade to cut my clothes off of me. They were so matted and caked that they retained the shaped they'd molded around me.

I tried, but I couldn't stop it. A few tears sprung to my eyes.

What was wrong with me? Why did I let myself reach this level of filth and isolation?

For the race. For the people I'd failed, anyway—

"Shh. Your highness, soothe. Soon, you will feel right again." Lucas' good telepathic timing bordered on unnerving and reassuring. Exactly what I needed to hear.

One would think being scrubbed down by a beautiful woman while a gorgeous man tended to your hair would be remembered as the pinnacle of luxury and pampering in a lifetime, but I think I wept through it. My emotional state affected my memory so badly that I lost time entirely. I know I clung to the sliver of Elden's nacre as the cycle played on repeat.

Let yourself go to save the race.

Fail the race.

Reduce yourself to dependency on others while knowing you'd failed them.

I learned later that it took two hours for Lucas to shave off the hair I'd grown since I was a child and for Colita to scrub the grime off of me. Once finished, she assured, "I find your appearance without hair aggressive in an attractive way. Your eyes are more pronounced."

I declined her offer to look in a mirror, but I admitted, "I *do* feel more myself. Thank you. Thank you, both."

Something passed over Colita's face, and I narrowed my eyes at her. "Is there a reward expected for your charity?" At this point, I was honestly willing to give them anything to absolve my dependency and inadequacy.

"I would like to enlist as an officer in your army," Lucas confessed. "But you are free to decline with no indebtedness to me."

I glanced between my new friend and my old one before asking Colita, "And you?"

"I want you to consider returning to the fortress. Your brother and Korac suffer without you. We all do. But I am sure you expected this suggestion from me." Her cherubic curls dipped with the tilt of her head.

It was such a normal and expected request that I grinned at her. "I will consider it. I was alone for long enough." To Lucas, I said, "To repay your kindness, I can grant you a captain's commission. Although, I cannot imagine your motivations as a shopkeeper. Why would you want to enlist?" As soon as I asked it, I knew the answer. "Warrior-caste upgrades?"

Lucas nodded, saying, "And all the reproductive benefits granted to the Icari of this status."

We were a starving race. To prevent overpopulation with our dwindling food resources, we permitted only one child to members of the warrior caste. The servant caste were granted children under very rare and heavily assessed circumstances. With most of them mute, it was hard for them to even plead such a case. But there it was.

I resented the circumstances and easily agreed, saying, "Granted." Running a clean hand over my freshly shaved head, I sighed. What would Korac think of this? With a groan, I turned to Colita as she browsed. I asked, "How is…" I couldn't ask about Korac directly. "Leadership?"

Delight lit up her angelic face as often happened when Colita spoke of Nox. "Your brother is taking excellent care of the Icari and the humans living in this settlement. We are in talks for expansion and establishing additional colonies further west." Here, her voice went quieter. "But your absence troubles him. At every feeding, he asks about you, and he looks crestfallen when I have no word. May I tell him about tonight?"

Lucas looked between us, and even he seemed to know the answer before I said, "Not yet. I need more time to recover without his pressures." I wet my lips before asking, "And what of Korac?"

Colita's face was less pretty as she complained, "Insolent. The moping brat leaves snakes in my bed and denies it when I confront him—"

I laughed. I couldn't help it. "Snakes?!"

Lucas hid a smile. "How juvenile."

"Fine. You two mock me as well. As if I do not look after you both." Colita crossed her arms and huffed, browsing the jewelry at the store's front. All the while muttering her disdain for our ungratefulness.

Korac was fine. Nox was...

Still not my King no matter how much he thought it. I had other, more important matters on my mind. Was I truly finished with the experiment? Did I give up or push on refreshed thanks to Colita's ministrations? I didn't notice, but while I considered my next steps, I'd started fidgeting with the shard around my neck again.

Lucas gestured at the habit, asking, "You toil away in anguish to save our race, yes? Our tortured and burdened Prince?"

I swallowed to prevent a flinch and nodded instead.

He suggested, "Perhaps you should put more faith into your good luck charm."

Colita mused, admiring a bracelet, "Why yes, Prince Xelan. Ask Elden for guidance."

Their remarks forced me to stare at the shard in my hand. The properties of it. The mystery of how Umbra came into possession of it. And all the things I knew of Elden under mother's tutelage.

A Tritan nacre.

The beginning.

"The shard!" I went to grip my hair and found my scalp instead. Too excited to care, I cried, "This is it! This is what I was missing!" In my overwhelming gratitude, I clutched Lucas to me and hugged him. Despite my flurry to rush out of the shop and back to my lab, I kissed Colita's cheek. "Thank you. For everything."

They both chased me out of the store, calling after me, but I would stop for nothing. I'd finally realized the answer.

An hour later, I loaded the components into the progenitor.

Ore.

Gas.

Soil.

Blood.

All of it coalesced into Elden's shard, which I'd set in the progenitor. From it, new material generated into a fresh pearl based on the nacre ore. The gas floating above the nacre allowed the soil and mix of my Icarean and donated human blood to create new cells. From there, bone formed. Tissue. Vessels. Organs. Hair. Skin.

A woman laid in the machine. Her skin was dark and soft, like a purple calla lily. The fuzziness, native to humans, was absent, aside from her lashes, eyebrows, and wavy hair. It formed a halo around her soft face.

Without another thought, I found the only clean sheet in my stronghold and covered her with it. As I waited for her eyes to open, I pondered at their color. It seemed right to clean in the meantime, which took hours. I'd peer in the progenitor here and there to see if the woman had moved at all. Her arms remained at her sides, and her legs didn't even meet the device's end. She was shorter than the average Icarean female—

This was fodder for my mind to cycle while I toiled over her unconscious state. I couldn't hope to consider this a success until her eyes opened, and I performed certain tests once I learned to communicate the ethics of consent to her—

Complicated.

So complicated.

Shelves? Dusted.

Floors? Swept and mopped.

Instruments? Cleaned and calibrated.

Work surface? Cleared and sterilized.

A room...? She'd need somewhere to sleep if she ever awakened. I would need to build another room—more rooms. I could progenerate more like her and save the species—

While I made a bed for her, goosebumps raised on my skin. The back of my neck tingled. With my pulse racing, I turned and faced the progenitor.

The woman was sitting up in it, staring at me.

Blue.

I'd never seen eyes so bright in my life.

There wasn't a trace of fear in her. In fact, her gaze held familiarity. She *knew* me.

I held up both hands and let her see they were empty as I crossed the lab. As gently as possible, I said, "Hello. Is your nacre translating? Can you understand me?"

The woman measured me with her eyes. Something... Something lived behind them. Immediately, I recognized an enormous intellect alive in there. To my immense curiosity, she stretched one leg out one side of the machine and followed with the other. Testing her limbs, she held onto the progenitor as she stood. I almost went to her side, but her wobbly efforts became steady in a matter of seconds. Without a preemptive sense of modesty, she easily tied the sheet around her and settled her hair about her waist.

With her shoulders held straight and her chin held high, my First Progeny crossed the lab to me and smiled.

"Father, I am Celindria, and I will help you save the Icari."

Devis stopped reading and stared at the words on the page.

Andrius peered at me, and there was something in his teal eyes.

T.A.O. gave a voice to it. "Words to douse the sun."

Into the ominous quiet which followed, Korac muttered, "Amen."

There was no chance of anyone wanting to take a break now, but I wanted nothing more. The weight of this scrutiny had left me flattened to the spot, with no chance of fidgeting or scratching without them questioning why. This was the first unexplored dominion of all the Verses. And judging by the naked interest on their faces, everyone in the Shadow wanted to know more about these historic moments with Celindria.

For me, they were personal. Secluded. I'd created an entire cognizant being, and she deserved her privacy.

You're sitting there with your pencil poised over your notebook, eyes down on the page, yet I recognize the storm in them.

Tell me, Rayne. What are you thinking?

You lick your lips as if nervous for what you're about to say before telling me, "Ever since Celindria first visited me in my dreams and showed me flashbacks into her life, I've wondered... What was she like?"

Naturally, you would want to know. She *was* your ancestor.

"It's more than that. So much of our histories intersect over Celindria—They lead to her. But I want to know what kind of person she was. I haven't been able to pin her down."

From the start, Celindria didn't want privacy or seclusion. She wanted mayhem.

"How was I made?" This was Celindria's first question.

I pointed to the machine. "This—I call it the progenitor. With some supplies and my blood, I generated your cells."

Celindria gripped the side of the machine and peered in, searching for something. After a few moments, she set those intelligent eyes back on me and asked a surprising question. "And what else? I am different."

Even before I created her, I'd removed any trace of the former experiments. Yet her insight impressed rather than alarmed me. I nodded along with her deduction, saying, "Yes, you are." I held upon the chain. "It was a gift from my brother, and it belonged to our grandfather. It was a shard of his nacre—"

"Nacre." Celindria formed the word with significance. Then she asked, "Is there more?"

I recoiled, taken aback. "No."

Celindria peered back inside the progenitor. With concrete certainty, she said, "To make more like me, we need more nacres and special blood."

Andrew raised his hand, and I wearily called on him. He asked, "What did you make of her behavior at the time?"

Korac made a sound between agreement and appreciation.

I awkwardly rubbed the back of my neck, trying to recover the head space I was in. "I want to explain it." Moving among the pallets, I reached for their understanding. "A new species! A step toward saving the Icari and Cinder! It was the pinnacle of my intellectual achievements, and it was successful. Celindria was graceful, eloquent, and brilliant. I was so proud of her. Proud to be a part of her making.

"And finally, I had someone to converse with about subjects I'd toiled so long after. Brainstorming and reflection. Revising formulas and estimating new projections for unexpected outcomes."

At some point, Korac winced, and I shot him an apologetic look. "You, more than anyone, knew how lonely I was in this."

"Do you still feel that way?"

From behind me, the uncertainty in Tameka's voice broke my heart. I faced her. "No. Not at all. But these friendships—" I encompassed the room with a gesture before continuing, "They didn't exist yet. I only knew a people reduced to basic intelligence. I was the only person I knew who was like me."

Tumu suggested, "I believe a few of us in this room can appreciate that feeling."

I wanted to hug the old Primary—

Screw it.

I threw my arms around the big alien from behind the couch and muttered against his hearing receptor, "Thank you."

Iuo agreed, "It's difficult being asexual in the porn business."

Miy laughed loud enough to echo in the room.

Twenty-One apologized on her behalf. "It *is* ironic to hear you admit it out loud for the first time."

Beside him, Iuo narrowed his black and blue eyes at the massive Icarus. He asked, "Are you saying you knew all along?"

Bones interjected, "He's saying for three years you've been surrounded by peak Icarean male, and you haven't tried to take a bite out of either of us—"

"Don't forget me!" Lamassau called from across the room.

"—Not to mention our lovely assortment of Lyriks, from broody to bright."

Miy nodded when Bones said broody, proud of her representation. Twenty-One glimpsed the appreciation and tucked her closer against him.

Iuo shifted on the couch beside them, propping on his tail as he said, "But if everyone here knew, then…"

At the front of the room, Tameka finished for him, "There's no point in keeping it secret. Not with us, anyway. We love you. We love each other." The next she said while looking straight at me. "There's nothing that can't be said here, but we won't force anyone into any dramatic confessions. Not unless you want your own Verse." Her cheeky smile at the last was infectious—

"Unfinished."

T.A.O.'s single word arrested me.

Stilted, I turned to face her. The rest of the room glanced back and forth between the pair of us in silence, as I couldn't bring myself to ask her if she meant 'unfinished' or '*unfinished*' without giving away a secret. A secret which didn't belong to me.

Andrius searched my eyes before wetting his lips to say, "Our sister is right. There were signs before our conception, yes?"

I closed my eyes to hide from this.

"You closed your eyes to me, too." Your voice is soft, but still, it urges me to open my eyes. When I do, and I always will for you, you're standing across the room from where I sit with the little version of you, asleep in my chair. You give me a small smile of reassurance. "It's okay to be scared. You're baring your soul to us, but you're doing it voluntarily. That's so brave, Superman."

Thank you, Rayne.

You take your notebook and curl up in the corner of the couch nearest me. "I have a goal," you say, while writing the next line. "By the time you leave this Divine Booth, you'll realize everyone else thinks the same as I do."

Even Tameka... And Korac?

"You are the bravest of us, Xelan. Close your eyes if you need to. We'll still be here when you open them."

Celindria knew things she shouldn't. No matter how many of her mannerisms I rationalized or the breadth and depth of her linguistic knowledge I excused as inherited from my own—She was impossible. But I didn't know then what I know now of Imminent. In hindsight, everything has become clear.

Celindria folded a million lifetimes into every breath, and she expertly hid this fact from me.

"The Coalition. We need their blood," she announced over breakfast the next morning.

I sat across a lab table from her, eating eggs and Vittle supplements which we shared. I slept and ate to take care of myself, as I'd promised Colita and Lucas. But in my sleep, Celindria had ransacked my libraries and labs to sate her unending curiosity. Presuming she'd gathered the knowledge about the Coalition from the Verses, I asked, "How do you propose we acquire these samples?"

Celindria ate with utensils, not with her hands. It wasn't something I'd introduced her to, she just instinctively collected them along with our plates for breakfast. She peered at me as she glimpsed my examination. Her eyes were as impossible as the rest of her, but they lacked…warmth. She took a sip of freshly squeezed juice before answering, "Umbra's vault."

Nonchalant.

Matter of fact.

Never mind that Celindria suggested we claim samples from the most vital repository of our genetic history.

"That answers where, but not how?" I didn't bother to dispute her assertion, because it was true. The vault was the only logical location to acquire those particular samples.

Celindria avoided eye contact and looked off at a painting, which depicted the Great House framed by Earth's conduit on Cinder. Confidently, she nodded at it. "We go there."

No Verse named the exact location of the Coalition vault. Impressed, I smiled at Celindria, and it brought her attention back to me. She smiled back, and it was…

Inviting and kind.

In my study, Devis muttered, "She was capable of it occasionally."

Andrius nodded in agreement.

Sat against the wall, Korac made a bewildered expression as if he'd found it hard to believe.

I believe Celindria's rare smiles were genuine.

Celindria asked, "Are you ready to perform your tests, father?"

The term startled me. By the contribution of my blood alone, was Celindria my daughter? Were the lives we create automatically *our* children? Should Umbra receive so much credit?

In the time it had taken me to process it, I worried I'd discouraged her, but when I met Celindria's eyes again, they sparkled. With firm confidence, she said, "Father."

Yes.

I smiled and gestured at the instruments. "How do you feel about blood work to start?"

Celindria held out her arm, and I inserted the IV catheter.

In my study, a sizable dynamic had shifted. People sat forward on the edge of their seats.

Even you look up from your notebook for what would come next.

Red blood filled the vial and the next. I took about four samples from her and filled them with different serums.

And I plated a small dot of it on a slide for microscopic observation. All the while, Celindria helped with the centrifuge and recorded her own observations. We spent a few hours checking her DNA, muscular-skeletal structure, metabolism, and potential for upgrades.

No wings, but the possibility was there. No inherent thirst or sensitivity to Sol's radiation. Incredibly strong. I suspected Celindria even withheld the magnitude of her strength and the limits of her speed. I almost asked her questions about her reproductive system, but decided it wouldn't present issues for the time being. Frankly, it felt too invasive to ask, even for me.

"Now that we took care of the formalities, are you prepared to leave, Father?" Celindria waited at the door in a clean cloak and held out one for me.

I glanced at the time to see that it was indeed evening, but I needed to eat and find some way to approach Korac about returning—

"I can go myself," Celindria offered, as if this were logical.

I frowned at her. "To the Coalition vault?"

She nodded earnestly.

Where did stealing our ancestor's DNA fall under the Icarean Prerogative? I shook my head. "We must file the appropriate requests and—"

"If we go now, we can take advantage of the garrison change."

My blood went cold. How could Celindria know anything about the military operations? None of my notes nor the Verses contained those assignments since we'd colonized Earth. Despite my initial shock, it seemed unfair to immediately assume a threat in her. She was only a dozen hours old. I asked, "How did you come by this information?"

Like a child, a mischievous grin spread across her lips and sparkled in her eyes. She sounded confident as she said, "While you slept, I left and met a soldier with the intel. Clever, yes? He gloated about his station and answered my questions readily. I think the poor boy fell in love during our brief encounter."

I laughed. I couldn't help it. The sly look on her face and the half-abashed pride was endearing. Still, to avail my concerns, I asked, "Why is this so important to you? And why the urgency?"

"Father, we need to move on from your Progeny project onto the Vittle crop or none of the billions of existing Icari stand a chance at surviving, even on Earth. Now, either we practice some stealth and harmlessly retrieve the samples ourselves, or we go before your brother for permission." Celindria's broad smile shifted into a smirk, and a faraway light brightened her eyes as if in distant thought. She mused, "I must admit. I am intrigued to meet King Nox. In that case, let us depart for the settlement—"

I gently gripped Celindria's shoulder. The thought of her finding interest in Nox pried a nerve in me. The same voice in my head which had said to keep Korac a secret told me to keep my brother and Celindria apart. So, I told her, "We will go to the vault. If we are discovered, I can use what sway I still have as Prince to remove us from scrutiny. What could they possibly do to us, anyway?"

The conduit from Earth to Cinder was guarded, but as Celindria said, the garrison was changing shifts. With her on my back, I slipped through it easily. Once in Cinder, she snickered, and I couldn't help but grin as I asked, "What other trouble is on your mind?"

"All of it."

When Celindria beamed at me, I saw how I must have looked to Nox when I was a boy. Incorrigible and with no clue to the consequences I'd brought not only onto myself, but onto others. It lifted my spirits to know Celindria and I had so much in common, including the passion to save our people.

Within fifteen minutes of passing through the conduit, we approached the Great House. Umbra left it unprotected during his time, but when Nox had moved the capital to his

Castle across the way, he'd restored the urns to the vault in Elden's hall. No longer a ruined shrine, the roof and walls were secure, with no good points of unauthorized entry.

"What of the courtyard, do you think, father?"

I was about to suggest that. Deflecting any concerns regarding my newly formed daughter, I crept up to the eaves of the courtyard and peered down. "Five guards."

Celindria assured, "Give them a few minutes. They will changeover soon." She angled her face so I could see the certainty in her smile.

She smiled so much back then.

I grinned back at Celindria and shook my head, incredulous. "You have only been here a matter of hours and already you have me in mischief."

"Saving the race should not require mischief."

Oh, finally. Someone understood me. I shouldn't need to fight tooth and nail to complete my work without someone interrupting me every five minutes with a new means of destruction grounded in my research—

"There," Celindria whispered and pointed at the guards shifting.

When they cleared the courtyard, I jumped down and went straight to Elden's chamber. Surely the vault would only reside in such an important location—

"My god..." I gasped when I took in the surrounding urns. Hundreds... "I assumed there were only a dozen at most."

Celindria patted my shoulder. "Put me down, father. We will not have time to take samples from all, and I require four specific ones."

I raised a brow at her, but set her petite form down. Celindria's human-shortness amused me, as she stood up to my ribs. From there, she held her chin high with so much regal confidence.

Celindria pointed, "These," and approached the south wall where four urns were decorated when the others were plain. There were emblems engraved on the bronze.

Rope.
Blade.
Tree.
And star.

"I want these," Celindria repeated. "If only we could find their nacres." She set about opening the first one for a sample.

I joined her with a side glance as we worked. "What makes you think anything is left of their nacres? They burned."

Celindria shook her head. So sure. "I believe my grandfather was right about the nacre chamber—"

"Prince Xelan?"

We both spun to find two guards in the doorway. When we made eye contact, they came to attention and saluted. "Sir."

Celindria whispered, "Take care of them. I will finish."

"Greetings, soldiers. I know this looks conspicuous." Tomb raiding wasn't a crime on Cinder, but maybe after this…

The soldiers glanced at one another before the taller one volunteered, "Official royal business is no concern of ours, your highness. We will leave you to it."

I worried about them reporting this to Nox. "I hope you understand this is for the race."

Celindria added, "To dissolve the caste system entirely."

I froze. How did she know my main objective? I'd never referred to it in my journals or discussed it with anyone. The very notion bordered on treason.

The two soldiers glowed with the premise, and a revolution was born in their eyes. The shorter one assured, "Any business to elevate us is no business of our superiors."

I winced.

In my study, Korac winced.
Tameka squeezed my hand.
Sagan looked across the room at Bones, who was an Icarean soldier at the time, and asked, "Was this far-reaching?"

He shook his head. "Celindria's Rebellion didn't reach my ears until Celindria had spent a hundred years on Cinder with Nox."

Devis said, "We forged weapons to arm the humans against the Icari." He didn't look proud of his confession.

Korac asked, "Who ordered you to do it—"

"We are getting ahead of my Verse."

When my General closed his mouth, he also clenched it shut, gnashing on the unasked question. *Did Xelan order Devis to do it?*

Not yet.

Instead, I asked our group, "Here is the time to ask your questions about Celindria."

Hands went up all around the room, and I felt dizzy. Tameka's warm hand smoothed up my back, and I needed the comfort. I kissed the top of her coiled hair to show my appreciation.

This might take a while.

ENTRY SIX

AND EVERYTHING I LOST

After completing my first act of treason behind my brother's back, I spent hours reflecting on my time with Celindria and studying her mannerisms. She was so eager to begin the next phase of the process, but I wanted to keep my promise to Colita and Lucas. So I rested, and we talked.

In my study, hands from all the Shadow waited for me to call on them. Their faces were open with curiosity in most and concern in others. For Celindria, I loathed to expose the secrets she trusts in me.

Curled on the couch, you state a simple fact. "It's for the Shadow's safety."

Not for them. At this moment, they believed Celindria was dead.

You shake your head and assure me, "You won't keep them in the dark for much longer. I know

you. This is your big confession, and you'll finish it right. Until then, Celindria is the manifestation of their worst nightmares—Tell me, how did Chris look?"

Your direct blow made me wince.

Chris cuddled Para at Karter's feet. Both women placed a comforting hand on him, but he didn't feel it. I knew that look. He wasn't in the room anymore. I prayed to Elden he wasn't reliving his time in Celindria's captivity, but I know trauma victims are never so fortunate.

I could do this. I made Celindria, and I could answer for her sins. The first person I called on was the person I wanted to answer the least.

Korac asked, "How soon did she liaison with your biological sperm donor?"

That's what I'd expected him to ask. Clearing my throat, I thought of the best way to answer this. "Straight away. Her scent didn't change, but Celindria possessed massive control of her biological functions. I believe she was already pregnant with Remorse's child when we went to the vault."

Tumu said, "I can confirm Primary Rem was absent from his sanctum during this time, and as Korac noted in his Verse, there were sightings of a Primary in Nox's settlement."

Yito called from the back of the room with Matt, Lucy, Bethany, Puk, and crew. "The Primary was collecting entries into the breeding program. He returned from Earth with twenty-two women."

Lamassau shook his head. "The bastard. I doubt a single one of them consented."

The room went quiet, mourning the millions of anonymous victims to this senseless mess.

"Celindria wouldn't care if they'd consented," Chris muttered, without focusing on the room. He was seeing a horror I couldn't bear to imagine. "She wouldn't care about them at all."

Tameka said, "I want to ask next. How did you figure out she was…I don't even know the right word for what's wrong with her—"

"Cursed," Devis offered.

Andrius spared his brother a pitying look before saying, "Celindria considered it a gift. No sense of guilt to carry, nor the anchor of love to weigh her down. No weakness."

T.a.o. said, "Alone."

Andrew asked, "I'm sorry, but didn't she hurt you shortly after Xelan created you? Why do you three seem eager to defend her?"

The three First Wave Progeny exchanged a look before Devis shook his head with agony in his eyes. In Atramentous, it was hard to gauge T.a.o.'s feelings, but she also didn't volunteer an answer. Leaving Andrius to say, "Celindria spared us her fate."

I offered, "I believe the next entry will answer Tameka's and Andrew's questions. Andrius, would you care to read?" I spared him an encouraging smile while my insides roiled.

In answer, Andrius took the volume from Devis and continued reading.

This morning, I stared at every vial and microscope slide with Celindria's blood in it. One vial was red, three were blue, and the slide was yellow.

Canary yellow.

The same color which had drenched Nox when he returned from Thailea. I'd never forget how he tried to convince me he knew nothing of what had happened while covered in evidence of a massacre.

"That aged well," Korac mused in my study.

Andrius continued the story, unaware of the resentment in me.

"Celindria," I called to her.

She emerged from the bed I'd made for her. "Yes, father?"

I wet my lips, unsure how to approach this. I asked, "May I take another blood sample?"

"Of course. More tests?" Celindria stepped close to me and held out her arm. Her enthusiasm waned when she noticed the change in the samples. "Ahh. An anomaly."

I nodded, relieved Celindria understood without me explaining. I said, "Yes. We should see if this is a recurring phenomenon or…" My voice trailed off as I inserted the catheter and… nothing happened. There was no blood. Trying not to alarm her, I asked calmly, "Celindria, are you feeling all right?"

"I feel nothing."

I frowned. It was such a strange way to answer my question. "Nothing wrong, you mean?"

When Celindria shook her head, that chill returned to my blood.

I removed the IV materials and gripped the lab table, staring at the samples. So close. I'd come so close to creating a fully formed person, but if Celindria could simply stop bleeding—

Something had gone wrong. Giving over to my work, I sat down and began analyzing my notes and her blood work, trying to come up with the cause for the anomaly.

Rudely, I'd forgotten Celindria's presence entirely, so when she spoke, it startled me. "I know what caused it."

I blinked up at her before finally inquiring, "Yes?" How could she know the flaw in her own making? But since she was so intelligent, what was the harm in experimenting?

Celindria pulled up a chair across from me and took my hands. Hers were ice cold, and her voice was remote as she said, "The shard of Elden's nacre was such an intuitive variable to contribute to the experiment. So potent—Of course, it would work. But a nacre as ancient as his was without upgrades for so long… and it was incomplete. I fear the flaws stole my chance of having a soul."

My eyebrows shot up, and I stammered as I asked, "A soul?"

Celindria's smile was without warmth or assurance. There was nothing in her eyes as she confessed, "I cannot feel as you do. Like the Icari describe in their Verses or you in your notes. Sometimes, like now, I feel nothing at all. Therefore, there is no blood. But yesterday, I felt something akin to gratitude and affection for you. The blood came easy then."

I leaned forward and clasped my hands together, considering this. What Celindria called a soul, I considered the mind's conscience and emotion. Without meeting Celindria's eyes, I said, "There is no empirical way to prove emotion, but we can try some qualitative tests. You can keep a journal, and I can interview your regularly—"

"There is no way to prove if I have a soul," Celindria translated. Then she commanded, "Look in my eyes, father."

For the love of Elden, I didn't want to. In Celindria's voice, I could hear the icy objectivity. The deep intelligence which surfaced in her gaze—So ancient and alone. But I did as she told me.

Celindria *was* without a soul.

"I have wronged you," I confessed. To create someone without the capacity for love, conscience, and heartache—What had I done? In my arrogance, I'd created an abomination.

In line with her sobering nature, Celindria said, "Yes, you have." Tears pricked my eyes, but she pressed on, "And I know how to prevent it from happening again. The others—I wish to progenerate them to prove to you that you can create Progeny, whole and complete. Not half-formed things like me."

My voice was thick with the overwhelming emotion as I asked, "How?"

Celindria showed me in my calculations where the experiment required a nacre—whole ones—to succeed. Icarean ones preferably. "My brothers and sister will have souls. They will be your Progeny."

I took her face in my hands and kissed her forehead. "No matter what happens, *you* are my Progeny."

Celindria felt it. I could see a hint of warmth thawing the ice in her eyes. It made me ask, "Is now a good time to draw blood," before I realized how insensitive it sounded. "Uhm…I mean…"

Without a word, Celindria held out her arm, which gave blood as expected. It was red again. She offered me a reassuring smile, and I was grateful she understood how impulsive the scientist in me could become.

Now, all the previous samples were yellow. I pointed to them and asked, "Do you know what causes this?"

Celindria shrugged and offered, "Perhaps the unusual composition of Elden's nacre?"

"Your hypothesis will have to do until we can apply more research. Until then, I need four nacres for the next experiments."

Her smile was so reassuring and kind…and sad…

"Leave it to me, father."

I would do *anything* to rectify Celindria. Somehow, I would give her a soul.

The next day, she returned with four nacres—I didn't bother to ask how she'd came by them because I trusted her—and we created the other four Progeny.

"So is this what Celindria meant when she said you wronged her?" Tameka asked, looking a little tired, but nonetheless supportive.

I swallowed before I could say, "Yes. And I *did* wrong her." I wanted to leave no room for discussion.

"Why, Superman?"

Because it's an irrefutable truth. In my vanity, I created a living being. One who couldn't love or hurt—Not the way we can.

You drop the pencil on your notebook and perch an elbow on the armrest, fist under your chin. All the while, you're gazing at me with so much…

appreciation and kindness. It hurts. "Before you continue, I can already guess Tameka, Korac, and probably Tumu had something to say about you supposedly wronging Celindria."

Do you?

A pretty smile brightens the sympathy in your eyes. "Of course, but if I interrupted every time I thought you a better man than you give yourself credit for, then this Verse would take forever."

With that, I feel more confident in my ability to continue.

Tameka let me have it. "In no way are you responsible for Celindria's *actions*. I might agree with you that in making her there were some depressing flaws, but she still knew right from wrong. Korac, back me up."

Korac quirked a brow at her, but said, "Tameka's right. Celindria's miserable existence is more her doing than yours. Rather than spending all her energies and resources researching treatments or alternatives for her prognosis, she spent it designing an empire—"

"She does research it. Day and night."

They all turned and looked at Chris.

Stricken with the memory, his voice was heavy with nightmares as he continued, "She never stops. Every effort toward Imminent is an effort to feel." He swallowed as he met my eyes. "She will do anything to feel."

Tumu challenged, "But if feeling is a weakness in her eyes—"

"It doesn't stop her from wanting to experience it." Devis looked as far away as Chris.

Andrius said, "Celindria believes there's something in the connection between all the Progeny which might awaken a soul she believes to be sleeping, not gone. Not entirely."

Sagan asked, "What do you believe, Xelan?"

The focus returned to me, and I ran a hand down my face to physically erase my thoughts from being revealed. I wasn't aware Celindria was still trying to find her soul. So long ago, she destroyed any remnants of it.

I said, "We'll get there."

THE NEXT DAY, TWO YOUNG MEN FUMBLED AROUND MY STRONGHOLD WITH THE STABILITY OF NEWBORN FOALS. I dressed them with rugs and ropes. The one with green eyes couldn't take them off Celindria, who cut my sheet into a dress with little regard for her appearance or anything really but our research. She stood over the progenitor, watching the next female sleep. One even smaller than herself.

"Have you given any thoughts to names?" I nudged her with a cup of tea.

Celindria took it with a thankful smile, a sign her *soul* was present. Gently, she mocked, "We are not pets. We choose our own names."

I conceded the point to her and nodded to her two unstable siblings. "Have you learned their names yet?"

With a sip of tea, Celindria shook her head. "They will reveal them in time. Until then, I asked them to read the Verses."

Glancing over, I noticed one held a book upside-down, and the other licked the pages. It made me smile. "Can they read like you?"

"No one is like me."

The way Celindria said it...

I'd finally met someone more alone than myself.

Another thirty minutes passed where I tried to communicate with my sons. Their intellects were less developed than Celindria's, but they learned faster than any non-royal Icarus. Before T.A.O. awakened, Devis read an entire page of a Verse, and Andrius formed his first words, "Elden's grace."

Beautiful.

Ensouled.

Celindria was correct in her hypothesis, and regret threatened to poison me. For as I rejoiced in the Progeny's making, I couldn't imagine the isolation in her. I'd reduced my daughter to a half-life. When T.A.O. emerged from the progenitor with a bright and giving smile, I knew I owed Celindria a debt. These were whole people, and whole, Celindria was not.

I ran out of sheets and rugs quickly. Once Merit's progeneration was underway, same as the rest, I decided to go out and pester Lucas for supplies. Progeny awakened with hearty appetites. In the doorway, I asked Celindria, "Are you sure? This is a recipe for disaster, leaving you alone with your siblings—Leaving *you* alone at all."

Celindria faked a wry smile at my hilarious joke. "We will manage, father. By the time you return, I will have them speaking."

I kissed her forehead and left for the settlement. The Prince's purse was hefty, and I owed a gilded-eyed Icarus a debt. I alighted at Lucas' shop.

"Most people come through the door," he mused with his back to me, where I'd climbed through the window.

In my study, Kyle called out, "Bat. Man," much to Silence's amusement.

Ignoring him, I continued on.

"Apologies, Lucas, but I find myself in need of your wares. Without detection."

Lucas chuckled before taking a pin from his teeth and fixing it into a gown. He offered, "Is your majesty closer to saving our race?"

I wrung my hands, eager to return. Something about leaving Celindria alone with the others gnawed at me. Still, I said, "Yes. Thanks to you."

With a wave, Lucas went about his work, saying, "Take what you need and leave payment under the counter. I must finish this dress for Colita by tomorrow or her exclusive eye will wander to the human merchants."

Without even knowing how things were in the fortress, I assured him, "She already has."

He laughed as I went browsing. Five Progeny and me. Eleven garments should do. I paused at the only white dress in the store and thought of Celindria in the sheet. The absence of color suited her missing soul. It was more expensive than anything else in the shop, but I could afford it. Without bothering Lucas at his trade, I wrapped the clothes myself and left a considerable purse under his counter.

His laughter was rich as I stomped back through his studio and left the way I'd came in, simply for his amusement.

Elden, it made me miss Korac and my brother. Mischief and laughter. I would return home without preamble, I decided. I'd march right up to the fortress with my Progeny and walk in—

Something was wrong.

In my study, I asked, "Andrius?"

My third Progeny lifted his gaze to mine, asking, "Yes, father?"

Devis glanced between us as I refreshed everyone's memories. "You once told Nox what Celindria did to you while I was gone. Some of it, anyway."

T.A.O. shivered beside her brother, who said, "Yes. I did. Would you like me to tell it again?"

"Please," I said before I kissed Tameka. Leaving my lover's side, I crossed the room to squeeze T.A.O. into a side hug.

The ancient Seamswalker buried her face in my arm.

Before Andrius began sharing the details of that night, I whispered to my frailest Progeny, "You don't have to stay if you don't want to."

T.A.O. met my eyes and said, "Unfinished."

Taking the cue from his sister, Andrius told the story. "Before Merit awakened, Celindria asked me to help her fetch eggs. I followed her under the stars—my first stars—and gazed at them while she tended the fowl Xelan kept corralled nearby. Something slipped over my head and a substantial force cinched around my neck. I understood nothing. Not rope, nor breath—My lungs' burning need to breathe, but this is how I learned.

"I fell to my knees, frightened by the pain and uncertainty. The 'why,' and the dire need to know it.

"Repeatedly I thought, 'Stop. Stop it. *Stop*!' Two breaths from death, the rope slackened, and I could breathe. Coughing, begging the air to return, I faced my attacker to find my older sister looking very pleased with a rope in her hands.

"'Why?' I could barely get the word out. I coughed and tried again. 'Why?'

"Celindria said, 'Force me to answer.'

"I was still new, and there was so little I understood. She was the eldest with the most knowledge and speech, so I tried to get to my feet and—

"'No. Not that way. With your will. Compel me to answer you.'

"Celindria's demands frightened me, but what frightened me more is that I knew what she meant. I'd felt it. Tell me. Tell me, 'why.' '*Tell me!*'

"Fluidly, Celindria said, 'I am testing your abilities. You and the others have gifts, and I want you to use them. Unfortunately, I must hurt and scare each of you.' She popped the noose she created for emphasis. 'Will you let me test the rest?'

"The thought of exposing my newly made brother and sisters to this torment sickened me, but I knew so little. Celindria looked after us, and father left her to do so…For confirmation, I looked at the twinkling lights in the sky. One shot by in a blaze of light, and I knew. With a nod, I promised not to interfere.

"Celindria went back inside and tested the rest, and the sounds of them choking haunt me to this day."

I flinched so much through his story. How could I not have seen it?

Devis said, "It was similar with me. She came back into the stronghold and... I went with her into a room." He didn't need to say how Celindria had lured him there. The Shadow knew of Devis' feelings for her. "She choked me until I touched her hand and mined through the memories of her creation. That's how I learned she was different from us. Afterward, she convinced me this was the only way and asked me to stay in the room while she tested little sister."

Eyes in the room fell on T.A.O. She was still in my arms and kept her face hidden. I kissed her hair and whispered against it, "You don't need to speak. I can tell if you want?"

She nodded against me.

Shortly before I returned—and I mean minutes—Celindria had tested T.A.O., but her ability, as we all know, gave her a means of escape. When I came back to the stronghold, I found the door open and Celindria calling for her nameless sister. All while Merit slept in the progenitor.

"Celindria, what happened?"

She met me when I landed and cried with no feeling, "Oh father! Little sister disappeared!"

I blinked at her. "Disappeared?"

Celindria nodded, still searching the grounds to find the missing Progeny. "Yes, father. I was performing a test, and she vanished—I must tell you about their wondrous abilities!"

Abilities.

Missing.

I put my hands on Celindria's shoulders to get a literal grip. "Tell me about the missing Progeny first."

For thirty minutes, we searched, but if I understood Celindria correctly, the other woman truly disappeared. By now, the brothers came to help. She told me the teal-eyed one could control volition and the green-eyed one could manipulate nacre memory banks—All easily quantifiable, but these revelations made me glance at Celindria now and then.

Was she concealing any abilities? And why would she not reveal the nature of this 'test,' which stressed my Progeny into disappearing?

In my study, I reached my arms out to Devis and Andrius. The latter moved into hug me and T.A.O. The former hesitated until I said, "Did you hear me? *My* Progeny. You're my family, Devis. I should never have left you alone with her."

Andrius pulled Devis in, and I hugged my kids.

Across the room, Tameka said, "You should never have to doubt one kid with the safety of the others. Not one with so much obvious intelligence. How could you know Celindria would hurt them?"

"Tameka is right."

I want to believe it.

"I want you to believe it, too."

A quiet moment passed where I let the First Wave Progeny move apart, except T.A.O., who clung to me still. She knew her part of the story wasn't over.

Korac watched us with careful eyes, measuring me—my sincerity, my growth, or my reflection. I don't know which, but it was there. He asked, "How did T.A.O. return?" He glanced at our frail fae before wetting his lips to add, "And how did she come by the name?"

T.A.O. tightened her grip on me, but she found the strength to say, "Weeks. Fires burned my hair. Hands on me. An asylum for lost things adopted me. I heard... the lonely pulse of one I later found. The Seam."

Korac and I maintained eye contact over T.A.O.'s head while she shared her story to the best of her ability. When she sniffled, I kissed her hair again, taking over the telling.

WEEKS WENT BY, AND I CHEWED MY NAILS DOWN TO THE QUICK—BEYOND IT, UNTIL THEY BLED. My anxiety over an entirely lost person never abated, and I worried about Celindria's education of Devis, Merit, and Andrius. In the time since the smallest of them had disappeared, my Progeny named themselves and practiced their abilities.

One night, I went out for supplies when a sight on the horizon stopped me. A storm rolled in on the desert and electricity danced across the sky, illuminating a great dune far off. On this mountain was a silhouette, small and female. Without closer inspection, I knew it was the missing Progeny. I opened my wings, determined to go to her and bring her home, but...

The silhouette flitted to the peak of a closer, smaller dune.

Celindria had told the truth. My fourth Progeny harnessed some form of teleportation. She traveled one dune closer and no further. With a knot twisting in my stomach, I flew to her, fearing her rejection and hoping for her to come home—

Her eyes were Atramentous. This only happens during times of extreme emotion or combat. Nothing about her dainty frame implied aggression or even fear. When she spoke, her voice was soft but firm. "Father?"

"If you would have me?" I wanted to make it clear, I would enforce nothing on her. "Do you wish to return with me—"

"Beware of the flames. The black glow which will consume us all, even the daughter of Elden's making. She will set us ablaze."

Never did I assume what she said was nonsense. There was poetry to her madness, but isn't this what broke my heart? I reached out to her. "I will look after you."

Her Atramentous eyes settled on my hand. With alarming certainty, she assured, "No one will forge a defense high enough to protect me. That is not my story."

Her eyes never shifted back to normal. They stayed in Atramentous as I asked, "Can I be in your story? I should like to be your friend." All the while, I was aware she could vanish at any moment, and I'd never see her again.

Please Elden, anything but that.

"Father, I am The Afflicted One. They call me this wherever I go."

No.

No.

I'd wronged another one. Despite the wave of disappointment threatening to drag me under, I offered, "You could be T.A.O. here, if you like?" After I attempted a small smile, I added, "It is easier to say."

With an avian tilt, she tried the name on for size. "T.A.O." Her smile, when she gave it, took my breath away. "Thank you, father."

When T.A.O. took my hand, I'd felt such relief one other time. After Nox had saved me from plummeting to my death when I was a child. The revivification of the memory, and T.A.O.'s safe-ish return, urged me to visit the fortress. Soon.

T.A.O. warned, "Be calm," before Seamswalking me to the stronghold. That's how I discovered she could form conduits to travel, and I looked forward to exploring this ability with her.

In my study, Kyle asked, "How did you react to Celindria, T.A.O.?"

After she shook her head against me, I answered, "Not at all. She didn't seem to recognize anything. The trauma of Celindria attacking her had sent T.A.O. into a fugue state, and Elden knows the places she Seamswalked to before finding shelter in the Seam."

"Razor's bones," T.A.O. corrected.

Tameka clapped her hands together, drawing the attention of the room. She offered, "Who's up for a break?"

Andrew raised his hand, and Tameka glared at him, but called on him all the same. "Yes?"

"What about Merit?"

I glanced at Andrius and Devis. The former said, "Celindria left her unharmed, as if she already knew Merit possessed no abilities. She was never attacked or ever the target of Celindria's torture."

Devis gave Andrius a look, saying, "Not all of it was torture."

Still defending Celindria. Devis and I have much in common.

I shifted T.A.O. apart from me with a gentle touch and announced to the room, "Tameka's right. Let's take a minute."

The Shadow grabbed food and adjusted their makeshift beds, some choosing to stand and stretch their legs. Others snuggled in for a quick nap. Andrius found me in the ravine, staring at a glass enclosure containing an anatomical sketch of a Mon3 Queen.

"Father?"

I gave him a weary smile. "Yes?"

He chafed his arm before coming out with it. "I spent millennia in Celindria's captivity, and one mistake keeps recurring in your Verse."

My smile shifted into a confused frown. "Oh?"

"It wasn't Celindria's aim to spare my brother and sisters her curse. She ensured us that we knew emotions to imbue us with controllable and manipulatable weakness. A guarantee we were too compassionate to endure another of us being tortured."

I'd feared as much. Hanging my head seemed dramatic, but it was ladened with iron. So heavy. My voice was soft when I asked, "Did Celindria confirm this?"

Andrius nodded. "Yes. Many times while she carved into me without mercy, forcing Devis to watch."

I glanced at him for his reaction as I asked, "You have no love for her, then?"

With a quick search of my eyes, Andrius said, "Like you, I love who she could be, but she continues to disappoint us, does she not?"

The way he said it…

Andrius walked away, leaving me to wonder if he knew my secret.

"I love who she could be."

Rayne, I think I love you the way I wanted to love Celindria. I've never confessed that to anyone, but you are the warmth and joy I needed.

You straighten on the couch and meet my eyes. There's a depth to yours, and it was filled with adoration and respect. Two things I'd never earned.

You say, "I feel the way I do about you because you treated me with as much and never took advantage of that vulnerable teenager girl who admired you so. All those nights outside training me to defend myself and listening to every syllable of gossip. Ray Callahan was my father, and he was a damned good one. But he worked all night and slept all day—weekends, too. Nursing was hard. Raising two teenagers was hard on both of my parents, but I won't deny it. I needed someone like you in my life. Paternal and there for me. We both know the truth: if not for you, I'd be dead."

Little Rayne stirred where she slept in the cradle of my arms. She cuddled my hand tighter around

**her and fell back asleep. Meanwhile, I tried not
to choke on gratitude.**

**"You wouldn't choke if you'd stopped denying it,
but let's get back to the story if that makes you
more comfortable."**

Everyone regathered in the study. Once again, I stood at the front with Tameka at my side, unwavering as a monument to her love for me. Once people settled, I said, "This part is well-documented in the other two Verses, so we'll move through it quickly."

I TRAINED THE PROGENY FOR THREE MONTHS IN LANGUAGE, HISTORY, AND SELF-DEFENSE. We lived peacefully together with no further traumatic incidents that I knew of. Celindria stopped hiding her scent because there was no hiding her growing belly.

I didn't detain the Progeny. I'm not that kind of monster. But Celindria's condition left me confused and curious. Neither are good reasons to invade another person's privacy. Eventually, she confessed it to me.

"Father, I know you know."

We were cleaning the hut where I kept the fowls while the other Progeny cleaned and cooked inside. I spared Celindria a considering glance, letting her decide how much detail she wanted to provide. I said, "Yes, I noticed."

Celindria stopped in the middle of her work to place a hand on her swollen stomach. "I wanted to test a theory."

Interesting. "What theory?"

The way Celindria's eyes reflected *nothing* saddened me. Especially as she said, "Perhaps incubating a fetus could promote the right chemicals to form a bond, reaction, emotion—Anything."

I tried to keep the hope from my voice as I asked, "Did it have an effect? Do you—"

"I feel nothing." Celindria poked her stomach, adding, "Nothing at all. I know I should feel something about the indifference, as well, and sometimes…when I experience the ghost of an emotion…I think it is what you call longing, only very diluted."

I took her Celindria's in my hands and stared into her eyes. "We will find a way. I vow to you. The delivery could always produce results."

Celindria's lips lifted as if by strings, and the forced smile didn't reach her eyes. "Of course. We can only hope."

Days of watching her so unexcited and apathetic with a growing life inside her—I couldn't bear it anymore. Once, three months before, I'd seen her more than intrigued and truly delighted. Celindria had mentioned it three times since with so much curiosity and interest. The very idea of introducing her to Nox went against some loud instinct I chose to ignore. Not to mention, my return to the fortress was long overdue.

"Celindria, Merit, Andrius, Devis, and T.a.o." I'd called them into the kitchen for dinner. Since they'd been 'born' in the stronghold, we'd added seven rooms. The Progeny had transformed my stronghold into a home.

We'd come right back, I told myself.

I kept my eyes on Celindria as I announced, "Tomorrow, we got to the fortress."

A sparkle of delight shone in her eyes. "Truly, father?"

"Yes—"

"Will we meet King Nox?"

Devis glanced at Celindria with barely veiled concern.

I wanted to both smile and grimace at her eagerness. "Yes. And General Korac. Do what you need to prepare. We leave at sunset."

Korac was nodding before I finished the last sentence. "So this is when you lied to me about what happened to your hair? You said it was a 'lab accident.'"

Tameka laughed. "Sorry, but *that's* what you choose to focus on?"

Kyle muttered, "Better than pointing out all the warning signs about introducing Celindria to Nox." Silence nudged him, and he doubled-down. "I'm just saying."

I held up my hands to stave… everything. "I know. I know my part in this—"

"Bullshit." Korac glared at me as he continued. "Celindria was already meeting with Remorse. She would've found her way to Nox, eventually. The only error you committed, dear Prince, was moving off to the stronghold in the first place—"

"Okay." Sagan took his hand and kissed it. "Okay. I know this is the touchiest time for you, but you need to let Xelan speak his peace."

Tameka mirrored the gesture with me, and I smiled down at her.

We're both so lucky.

The display Celindria put on for Nox concerned me. She smiled brighter, and there was something in her movements. I knew it came from her interest in him, which was none of my business in a casual sense. But how do I describe this? My soul screamed against it and rattled the cage of my bones in panic.

But it was so good to see Korac. To be surrounded by my people. I should've known something was wrong when Nox started being more expressive.

In my study, Korac spoke up then. "He was trying to be more expressive *for* you. It had nothing to do with her."

"No, Korac. He was more expressive because he'd fallen in love for the first time."

Sagan suggested, "Couldn't it be both? He was happy to have you home with your Progeny while exploring this budding relationship with Celindria. But Xelan, how often had you seen Nox happy?"

I fell quiet, as did Korac.

Tameka offered, "Please don't mistake this for me siding with Nox in *any* way, but we've all read his Verse. The man was miserable almost his entire life. You did the right thing for your brother when you left Celindria with him, and you did the right thing for her because you let her keep her own agency. There is no other way to look at this."

You point your pencil at me. "Once again, I agree with Tameka."

Rayne, what was Nox like with you?

You fall quiet and contemplative. Sad, even. "Depends on which Nox you're asking about."

No doubt that's a fair statement. The one you first fell in love with? Or the one you still love today?

The small smirk is a little unexpected until you accuse, "You keep trying to pry it out of me, Superman. You're not ready for this talk. But the Nox I found worth knowing, you wouldn't recognize today."

I frown at your use of present-tense, but you're right. I'm not ready.
Let's move on.

When Celindria told me she wanted to stay at the Castle, and when Nox defended her choice to do so, I feared disaster was on its way. Then came the delivery.

I'd never seen Nox so caring as an adult, I think is fair to say. He was kind to me as a child, but as we grew older, I never saw him be gentle with anyone. He tended to Celindria throughout the entire labor. Then the time came to take the newborn to her adoptive family.

In my study, I took a moment to pause before saying, "This is the only time I'll mention Merit or discuss anything about our relationship. As Nox and Korac both stated in their Verses, she was kind and full of so much life. Her energy filled the room with laughter and fun. I appreciate both of you for paying her the respect you did in your Verses."

Korac toasted with a glass of juice.

Celindria was stone cold about the birthing experience. I could handle that. Her scientific mind combined with her quest to restore a soul she'd never possessed had convinced her to attempt the experience of bearing a child. But the way she forced it and everyone out of the delivery room was…

Cold steel. Hard and unfeeling.

Korac and I exchanged a distraught parting glance as I escorted Merit out to deliver the baby to her future parents. I wanted Korac—To live with him and share everything with him. Yet, as I left Nox's castle that day, our paths divided even further apart.

"Xelan, should we name her?" Merit interrupted my thoughts. It was also the first time I'd noticed she was the only Progeny who didn't refer to me as 'father.'

I smiled down at her as I considered her question. "Celindria said she already named her and the parents knew the name."

The redhead in my midst gave me an infectious grin. "But she is not here to stop us from changing it."

We named Rayne's ancestor, "Hope," but just between us.

The walk was mostly me in my head, chasing spirals into my understanding of Celindria, while Merit kept me current with peppy conversation. Until she stopped me to say, "I want to confess a truth to you, but I fear your judgment, given Celindria's clinical approach to pregnancy."

My brows shot up, but still I said, "Feel free. I have no desire to judge you, Merit."

"I agreed to surrogate for a young couple. For similar reasons to my sister, I want to know what it feels like, but I also believe it is best. I serve a different purpose."

Merit's confidence surprised me and enticed me to ask, "What is your purpose?"

Merit grinned at me and poked me in the chest. "To help you, of course. You will always need my help, Xelan, and I will always be there to give it."

Everything dawned on me at once.

Merit's reminders to eat and leave my lab to bathe. Her sweeping up behind my efforts and maintaining my lab. All this time, Merit knew my weakness, and all this time, she was kind enough to help me with it. "Merit, have I ever told you I find you rather extraordinary?"

Her laughter was rich and sweet, like caramel. "No, but say it anytime you wish, love."

"We formed an easy relationship which naturally turned into much more later in the story. I simply wish not to mention it again. Most here know she died saving my life. For the longest time, the nacre in my chest belonged to her. Only when I was resurrected on Gait did I retrieve my birth nacre. And I wish she were here now to see all of this."

Sagan gently chimed in, "That's why we have the Ionas. To remind us of them and honor their sacrifice."

I said nothing. I was angry because Nox was the very reason Merit died. He stole my nacre, and she gave me hers. So how could everyone so easily suggest Nox deserves an Iona named after him—

I spiral with this.

"I understand." You're staring at the notebook again, contemplating.

Do you think I should name the next Iona after him?

You meet my eyes and stare a hole into me before saying, "Like all things Nox-related, I can't give you an answer until we finish your Verse. Until I know everything."

Then let's move onto the last of Nox and I as brothers, Korac and I as lovers, and myself as an Icarus. For once I betrayed my entire race for the beings I'd created, what better name could suit me than "Traitor Prince?"

ENTRY SEVEN

MY PROGENY OR MY PEOPLE

IT WAS MORNING ALREADY, AND PAX WOULD WAKE SOON. After Tameka and I checked on him, we left some fruit on the counter for his breakfast. Once he'd finished eating, he'd brush his little teeth and come play with us in the study.

Until then, we joined the migration of Shadow into the hexagonal space. This break had lasted an hour. Tameka had snoozed on my chest, while I stared at the ceiling and relived events I wished I could forget.

"Every one of them?"

Little Rayne...

You giggle, and that's when I noticed the preteen version of you had fallen asleep. Draping over the armrest, you look uncomfortable. I leave my chair to straighten you out with a pillow and drape a blanket over you. When I kiss your

forehead, the little version of you goes, "Hee. Love my Superman."

I fold myself down onto the floor with you and smile at you under the pillows in your fort.
You're right. I don't wish to forget every memory. Only the ones which hurt.

The Shadow had changed out of their formal wear. All but the bride, groom, and the best man. Pehton enjoyed her silver-coated feathers, and Caedes ran his fingers through them idly. On the pallet beside them, Sagan and Korac cuddled together. The bride was missing all the ribbons on her legs. The way her husband looked at her, the remaining ribbons which kept her decent wouldn't last long.

I was happy for them. Especially as Tameka took my arm and smiled up at me, dressed in short-shorts and a crop top. Enough skin to entice and distract me, as if she knew it would help with what came next.

"Thank you, everyone, for staying with me through this—"

"We got you, Wingmaster!" Bones called, eliciting a few snickers at the use of my catch phrase.

Others cheered and joined in with toasts of orange juice and waffles. I knew it was a long day ahead of us, but my chest expanded with their good spirits.

"Trust them to withstand the worst of it and still love you after."

You're right. I could trust in it.

"Before I move onto my days as a pirate—"
A few chuckles resonated throughout the room.
"—We must first get through some darker nights. Korac, would you read the next entry? Volume one thousand and two. Page twelve."

I caught him midway through whispering something to Sagan. Something stimulating, judging by the blush on her cheeks. Annoyed, Korac pulled himself to his feet as if by strings and glided to the north wall of journals. He muttered, "It'll be unpleasant business, I'm sure." After one glance at the page, he gave me dead eyes. "Truly?"

"Please read."

"'Bin of Yu and his entire colony died of some mysterious plague, but I *know* Nox murdered him. Not to what end or by what means, but I feel the certainty of it boiling in my blood. The Night King assassinated a fellow galactic leader and friend.'" Korac stopped reading to ask, "Xelan, be honest with me. How do you view this after reading Nox's Verse?"

I didn't know how to answer Korac. I still don't.

Rayne, I know you've memorized it. How did Nox introduce you to this moment?

Even though it unnerves me, little you recites, "'If there was one sin, I would keep from you, Rayne. This is it. This is my worst. The ultimate wrong. Not a crime of passion. Not a righteous endeavor. A calculated, cold-blooded, pre-meditated assassination.

"'Of my friend.

"'Elden, forgive me.'"

How am I supposed to feel about that? I understand his motivations—He wanted to pursue a physical relationship with Celindria, and Primary Rem wouldn't manipulate the Weapon to allow it until Nox killed Bin. I understand he was desperate, but is that understanding enough?

How do you feel about it?

You're quiet for a while. When you do answer, both versions of you say in tandem, "I wept when I read it." The preteen version of you never opened her eyes as you both continue, "I felt for everyone involved, and I would erase it if I could."

Yes.

To Korac, I said, "I weep for Legir every time I read this moment in the Verses. For Nox, I..." The words don't come to me.

Korac knew how to pry it from me. "You believed what I said in my Verse. Do you believe Nox felt remorse for this?"

This I could answer. "I believe there are no lies in the Verses as there won't be in mine. Does that suffice?"

Korac stared at me for a long moment before nodding his head. "It will do."

Tameka chafed her arms before asking, "What comes next?"

Bones raised his hand. "Can I take this one?"

I gestured for him to go on. "Please do."

He stood and said, "We lived one hundred years with our King and the General in a sour mood while rumors of unrest stirred. Humans tried to plunder Cinder, dying from the unfriendly atmosphere before reaching so much as the Great House. Security detail kept the garrisons busy. Some tried to scale the fortress walls on Earth. Upon capture, all of them swallowed a sachet and died near-instantly."

"I can contribute here as someone with unique insight from the Razor side of things," Miy spoke up, and with my nod, continued. "Around this time, Razor became interested in Icarean politics. He forced the Lyriks to... interview a few merchants still working with Nox and Korac. The unrest seemed to intrigue him. Meanwhile, those Imminent projection calls he took? Celindria began to appear in them around this time. But Lucas, were you involved yet? I don't recall."

The gilded-eyed Icarus didn't seem surprised the spotlight was on him once more, involving clandestine operations. "I was filtered. You couldn't see me, and I never spoke. Remorse tried a few times to convince me to change my allegiance from following the Mother's orders to the letter, while Razor was determined to tempt me to his vice trades. I followed Silence's descendants and awaited her return, per my orders."

A few people glanced at Silence, who smiled at Lucas with all the love of a dear friend.

Miy took the proverbial mic back. "Whatever. So anyway, Razor funded some of the human revolts. I think he provided them with espionage tech."

I saluted her. "Thank you, Miy, Lucas, and Bones."

Sagan raised her hand, and I called on her. She asked, "What was this time like for you?"

Expecting this question, I nodded. "During the one hundred years when Celindria lived with Nox, I was busy researching ways to survive the sun, building my stronghold, and spending time with the Progeny. I kept tabs on Celindria and Nox." I glanced at Korac before admitting, "And deeply missed the people I left behind in my seclusion. But at first, I knew nothing of the uprising. So when the day came that Devis ran into my home with news of Celindria's public whipping, I raced to the fortress as fast as I could."

THE CRACK OF THE WHIP REACHED ME BEFORE THE SCENT OF CELINDRIA'S BLOOD HIT THE AIR. I shouted, "Stop!" Over the crowd, I soared like a jet until I slammed onto the platform. I had trusted Nox and Korac with her protection, and this was the outcome.

Celindria was a bleeding puddle of split flesh and exposed bone.

I cradled her, muttering, "I should never have left you with these monsters."

In my study, Korac looked away.

"Only *you* can cut him so."

Yes, and I cut him deeply.

Over Celindria's broken body, I glared at Korac, knowing my eyes had shifted into Atramentous. I meant every syllable of my warning to my once lover. "Never come near us again."

On the flight back to the stronghold, Celindria's agonizing screams filled the night while I contemplated so many things. How could Nox *do* this? How could Korac? Why wasn't she healing?

Upon arrival, I tended her wounds and noted damage to her nerves. If her nacre didn't heal her, Celindria might never walk again, and all I could do was ask "why."

I didn't want to cover the next entry. Everyone knew I'd flown to Li Mountain to cope in isolation when Korac found me. I ended the relationship and returned to the stronghold. There I tended Celindria for days before she regained consciousness enough to address my questions.

I didn't like the answers.

Tameka asked, "How *did* she explain all of it to you?"

I stretched my neck and back, feeling tense. "Celindria told me Nox entertained proposals of enslaving humanity for their blood, and already harvested nacres for the Cruor Villam—A monstrosity I still abhor. That he expected Celindria to endure his public philandering and demanded she conceive an heir for him to usurp my inheritance to the throne—"

"You couldn't possibly believe her?" Korac's voiced dripped with venomous incredulity.

I didn't look at him. Instead, I wet my lips and tried to explain. "Understand me. When Celindria said, 'Nox is no better than your father,' I already thought the worst of him after he had you publicly masticate her."

Korac opened his mouth to say more, but Sagan touched his arm gently and asked, "What else was taking place?"

With a grateful nod at her, I said, "Remember, at this point, the Progeny were living their own lives." I gestured at the first Seamswalker. "T.a.o. traveled often, apparently sometimes with Korac. Andrius was married with grandchildren. Devis forged weapons and supplies for the settlement and the rebellion. Merit stayed with me and helped me nurse Celindria back to health. I believe because Celindria didn't view Merit as a threat that she treated her differently from the others, even when I wasn't around. We had a comfortable friendship, the three of us. Not long after the whipping, Merit and I began our romance." It was hard, but I pretended not to notice the faint wince in Korac's composed facade.

This wasn't a happy decade for him, either.

Sagan said, "This was the time of CoN, The Brethren, and Nox's council. But Xelan, you didn't stay neutral, right?"

I sighed, wishing to be elsewhere. "I worked with The Brethren to train humans and coordinate purchases for Devis' materials. Especially the Pretiosum Cruor. Lucas, spying as an Icarean captain, worked with me disguising supply chains as merchant caravans. Then Andrius disappeared. I'd assumed you'd fled at first, but I suspected..."

"You thought so little of Nox that you trusted he would harm the very person who warned him about Celindria in the first place?" Korac sounded incredulous. Sagan touched his shoulder, shaking her head, and he kissed her. "You're right. I'm sorry. Please go on, your imperial majesty."

Andrius interjected, "If I may?"

I tried for an apologetic smile. "Of course."

He continued. "I came home after a day of hard work to find my home empty. Three generations lived in our residence, including two infants. They were all gone. When I stepped back outside, Celindria was waiting.

""Come with me, and they can return home to carry on their lives without you. Defy me, and I will keep them.'

"I couldn't fathom it. 'Sister, why?'

"Celindria shook her head. 'We were never siblings. You have thirty seconds. What will it be?'

"We can all tell by my being here that I went with her and never saw my family again. The Brethren kept excellent records of the Progeny lineage. I've learned since my family prospered and led to you." Andrius gestured to Andrew, who beamed.

Devis cleared his throat before admitting a little uncomfortably, "My children were illegitimate, but successful, as The Brethren told me." Kyle toasted him, and Devis continued, "As we know, Celindria learned of me spying on her and Nox before she found me tampering with the Pretiosum Cruor. I meant to remove her blood from it and hand it over to The Brethren. It wasn't a pretty confrontation.

""You dare defy me?'

"I'd held the device back, to keep it out of her reach, but I knew I'd lose. 'I'm protecting my people.'

"Celindria waved a finger at me. 'Know your place. You amount to nothing in the Cascade.'

"She knew how to wound me. Still, I said, 'Then the universe will pay no heed if I carry on with my work.'

"With a slight lilt of her lips, Celindria's smile transformed from menacing to seductive. She was so cruel to tempt me with what I wanted most. 'We were in love once, were we not, Devis?' She reached out to me, hips swaying with each step in my direction.

"I loved her. I suppose I still do. But I'd seen too much and knew her character was dishonorable. No. I wouldn't let her manipulate me anymore. And she'd take me. Probably kill me, but I'd get one shot in at least. 'I cannot recall. Perhaps you should ask Nox?'

"I think…for a moment I swear I saw her Atramentous, but…I wonder if she stole the memory from me. Never mind that. I woke up on a slab in her labs in New Cinder."

Atramentous.

Even I'd never seen Celindria's eyes transformed. I'd wondered if they even could.

There was no need to torture T.A.O. about how Celindria took her. Between the Verses, we could puzzle together that Celindria took her some time after the calamity on Thailea, where Celindria supposedly died.

"Superman, you're avoiding something." Your admonishment sounds so cute in the little voice.

You're right, Rayne. I can't believe we've already arrived at his part.

The preteen you, still resting in the makeshift bed I tucked you into, asks, "How do you feel about Nox's perspective?"

I'd hoped you wouldn't ask me that. Nox punched into my chest and took my nacre. His Verse poured regret like blood from my chest. It hurt, you know?

Little you nods, quietly.

Of course, you know. I'm sorry, but Merit died to save me.

In my study, I'd fallen quiet thinking this exact stream of thoughts. It's a spiral I can't escape. Yes, Nox regretted trying to kill me. But…

No.
No.

"I can't forgive my brother."

Sagan broke the silence which filled the room. "When Korac told me this part of his Verse—The part where Nox stole your nacre—I wanted to ask you so badly how you felt."

I wiped a hand down my face before I restated, "Even after reading it and understanding it, I can't forgive it. Maybe if I was the only one affected or if he'd handed me my nacre the way he did with you, but Merit..."

Korac surprised me by saying, "I understand." We all looked at him, prompting him to add, "None of Nox's crimes are easy to forgive. Fuck, neither were mine. But... Merit was a bright star, fallen too soon."

In the Divine Booth, I glance over at you on the couch. A heavy tear rolls down your cheek as you stare elsewhere in the study.

Please, Rayne, tell me what you're thinking.

You swallow your heart to say, "I will. When you finish. Try not to worry. I'm not upset with you. Like Korac said, I understand."

Thank you.

Tameka gave me a squeeze before pushing us along. "What next?"

"The Vacating."

Andrew asked, "Were you in on that plan? And how did you not get sucked back into Cinder with all the other Icari?"

Lamassau frowned and pointed at me. "Hey, yeah. How?"

I looked around the room at the puzzled faces before confessing, "I don't know. Maybe Celindria factored in my Tritan blood. I have no idea. She only assured me it wouldn't take me, and I trusted her. As for the plan, yes, I knew.

"One note regarding Celindria's second pregnancy..."

WE WORKED SIDE-BY-SIDE TO ESTABLISH THIS REBELLION FOR THE SAKE OF HUMANITY AND EARTH. So, when Celindria started showing, I took notice and made my own assumptions. She invited no conversation about it, prompting me to leave it alone.

Until the day Celindria returned from a supply run with a flat stomach.

I followed her into my stronghold, and she rushed into it, avoiding me. Yet I couldn't leave it alone. "Did Nox—"

"Father, please. Not right now." Celindria headed for the bath.

I gently took her elbow. "Please. I have to know."

When she whirled on me, there were tears in her usually empty eyes. Fresh ones, and they spilled down her cheeks.

Celindria's duress and the smell of blood left me growling. "I will kill him, myself!"

I spun and stormed out to put an end to Nox's abuse and hatred for someone not even a fraction of his age—

Her icy hand on my arm stopped me. I'd never heard Celindria's voice so sad. "*I* ended the pregnancy."

I took her hand in mine to warm it and brushed a loc from her face. "Please. Tell me."

Celindria swallowed before shaking her head. "I may not feel as you do or as much, but this will kill me if I let it. I must release it. Forget it. Please."

I asked what I couldn't keep to myself anymore. "Was it Nox's child?"

I'll never know if Celindria lowered her head in genuine shame or faked it, but the pain...I felt it in the squeeze of her hand. "It was mine, and now it is not. This is no world to welcome another child of mine. Now please...I wish to wash this away and never think of it again."

With a kiss on Celindria's forehead, I let her go.

"After I heard Celindria had confronted Nox when she terminated the pregnancy, I questioned her sanity and emotional stability. It was chaos, and I sought meaning. Moments before the Vacating, she asked me to eliminate an Icarean soldier. Instead, I left a message with him for Korac."

The room looked at the Iona General, and Korac made a point of looking at the floor. Once she noticed, Sagan took his arm and snuggled against him.

This was the moment Korac couldn't tell in his Verse, because this was when we said goodbye. Not to see each other again for eight thousand years.

I PACED IN THE SAME SPOT FOR THE LAST HALF HOUR. I examined the rut I wore into the sand. Not much longer. I peered up at the stars and imagined them through Nox's Sphere. Shuddering, I couldn't even think of it without grimacing. Everything had went so wrong, so fast. Korac alighted from the sky. He approached from the East. Good. The gust blew back my hair and clothes. Show off.

"You summoned me." Korac's voice dripped with suspicion.

Distract him for ten minutes. Only ten minutes. Enough time to let Celindria close the conduit. Hopefully, this conversation was enough of a distraction. I said, "I never thought you would come."

Korac raked his gaze over me. A compliment—A testament to the remnants of our relationship. He looked back up with mercury in his stare. "I always came for you."

I closed my eyes. Memories washed over me and so much regret. The memories threatened to swallow me. Sand crunched beneath Korac's feet as he closed the distance between us. When I opened my eyes, a breath separated us. The stars above glittered across the constellations, waiting with the patience of immortals for the show to start. Despite the proximity and the loss pouring from my heart, I resisted the temptation Korac offered. Instead I warned, "Please, listen to me. I wish I had more time—"

"Before your unstable *daughter* draws me into Cinder?"

I recoiled, staggering back. "What—How?!" The plan. The plan we'd protected for a decade. How could Korac know? I never told Colita. If Korac knew, then surely Nox must know—

"Do not insult my intelligence. I am General of the Icarean army. Military strategy and affairs of the court are my business. Your treachery is no different." Korac remained as cool as ever. Despite the frost in his overall demeanor, fire sparked in his eyes.

I scoffed. "Treachery?! Nox kills and takes and cannot see he will destroy this planet as much as Li destroyed Cinder. Earth cannot replace Cinder if we turn it into another barren rock!"

"That bitch has poisoned you!" Korac cut me off from responding with a gesture, swallowed, and said, "Time grows short. If you called me here to make amends, I am prepared to accept your surrender and take you home with us. Serve your sentence."

"Nox…" I opened my wings. If his council knew the Progeny's plans, then the Icari had prepared for this.

No.

Could I make it to the fortress in time? "I must warn Celindria." Electricity traveled up my arm where Korac gripped me at the elbow. I peered down at the contact. "Unhand. Me." The three syllables were spoken in ice.

"The ego of you. Can you not see it?! You are a *traitor*. Your title stripped, your research seized—You made yourself an enemy of your people. For *her*!" Korac jerked my elbow until we faced one another.

Short of death, nothing would stop me from warning Celindria. I said, "Let me go before I lose my reason."

"Celindria is the monster. Not your brother. I know it went wrong, and Merit paid the price. I cared—"

I punched Korac in the jaw hard enough to bleed my knuckles.

He spat blue blood onto the sand, but didn't retaliate. The shake of his head was full of disgust and disappointment. Tired and done, I went to fly again. Once more, Korac pulled my arm.

I whirled and spat out, "Merit was capable of more love than you will ever hope to see. You understand nothing of sacrifice."

Korac recoiled with hurt in his eyes. "These are my last minutes on Earth, and I chose to spend them with you. How could you say I know nothing of sacrifice?" Some knowledge dawned in his eyes, and he said, "You never intended to say goodbye. You asked me here to keep me from stopping Celindria." Korac's eyes hardened as he added, "While you try to distract me here, she is alone with my King at *her* summons. Do you not see it? The game she plays?" He let go of my arm.

I looked down at where his hand had been. It burned. I said, "You are wrong. I wanted to see you one last time, but now I must keep Nox from harming her." Although, if Korac was right and Celindria had summoned Nox…

What was her aim?

"You broke your promise." Korac's voice sounded tight, squeezed out. When I met his eyes, he continued, "You said you would teach me to fight and to fuck in the sky. Then you left me with this misery for your misguided children."

I squeezed my eyes shut. The wind picked up around us, and a sharp keening sound grew ever louder in the night. "I cannot—"

"I will miss you," Korac confessed, making me open my eyes. With tears streaming down his face, he said, "I will be alone without you. We have no way of knowing for how long. I weep for you being separated from your people for maybe thousands of years." His hair picked up on the spiraling gusts increasing around us.

The Vacating was coming. I wanted to reach out and touch Korac's face, to take his tears away. I still cared for him, but in the eye of this hurricane I could only say, "I hope in the time it takes, you will learn how to weep. Then we can speak as friends again." I flew into the night, all too aware the next time we'd meet, it would be across the front line of a battlefield.

I didn't want this for us. For any of us. I wanted the Icari to stay on Earth, but not as Nox's personal army.

"The Army of Night." Your words make me peer at you.

Rayne, I never referred to the army by the name the humans called them. How...

You shrug, looking off. "Maybe I read it in your journals."

Maybe.

In my study, I met the sad eyes of my closest friends. When I glimpsed Bones and Twenty-One, I thought to say, "I am so sorry."

Bones shrugged. "We had already evacuated back to Cinder, but we missed the desert and the stars."

Twenty-One admitted, "I had a family on Earth."

I winced. "Did they evacuate with you?"

The enormous Icarus said, "My wife was human and my daughter stayed with her."

Lucas offered, "The Brethren kept close records of all hybrids. We can trace down their lineage, if you'd like?"

Miy peered up at Twenty-One, who shook his head. "Thank you, but there's no point in it now. They're gone. It's one way Nox motivated the soldiers. To avenge those broken connections. Through Dr. Suarez—"

Pablo waved.

"—I learned not all the people on the other side were heartless. Since reading the Verses, I understand it was all ugly business and confusion. Not a good enough crusade to lose my family to, but I could understand the reasons at least."

Tucked between Chris and Para while cooing at Echo, Karter asked, "What about the Valkyrie?"

Andrew added, "Yes. And Lucas and Caedes? The Brethren?"

Devis said, "Celindria could program it using samples of blood from anyone she liked. All The Brethren had signed up for this exclusive privilege. As for the Valkyrie..."

I said, "Once I'd annexed onto my stronghold, I migrated the Valkyrie to Earth in their suspension beds. I assumed the Pretiosum Cruor didn't take them for this reason, but perhaps Celindria had programmed them like The Brethren."

Korac ticked off the next few events on his fingers. "So the Vacating took us, Nox and I discovered Imminent had infiltrated the Castle and he slid into madness, and Colita raided the remnants of your old lab in Umbra's Spire."

Where they delighted in finding the plans for the Martyr Complex.

I kept this to myself because I believed Korac's shame was genuine.

"What about Nox's shame?"

*I want you to always feel free to ask me any question—Ever. But I wish so many of them didn't revolve around him. I believe Nox told the truth in his Verse. Both men do not regret building the monstrosity which I'd designed. They only regret ever putting **you** in it. However, Korac and Nox admitted they would give anything to confine Celindria to it.*

Head nuzzled into the pillow, you stare at me across the room and state, "The distinction bothers you."

The Complex is a nightmarish amalgamation of my desire to save our species and their desire to hurt another being. Why would I revel in either man's need to inflict the agony you they'd subjected you to, Rayne? Do you think anyone—even Celindria—deserves the Complex?

Little you says, "No." Proud, I ruffle your hair until you add, "But I think Celindria deserves to feel what it's like, the same as you think Nox deserved his madness." Pulling you in for a hug, I kiss your pig tails.

I know I'm a monster for it. It's something I need you to know—

"No." You wiggle away to stare up at me. "I understand you. You're not a monster, and you're not wrong. Not entirely. Nox deserved some form of punishment in the end, but doesn't it bother you that you wished it on him when you know better now? That he wasn't lesser until later? And Korac?"

They thought so, too.

Into the sad quiet which settled in my study, Sagan professed, "It was so tragic."

Korac spurred, "Well, your imperial majesty. This is where we part in the Verses. Is there anything you want to say?"

There's only one thing I wanted to say to him. "I missed you." I include a smirk for good measure because it was so very true. Earth was lonely after Celindria banished the Icari.

"Tell them."

I cleared my throat and added, "I missed all of you. You were my people, and I barely got on without you. If not for Lucas' company, I don't think I would've survived."

Lucas gave a little wave, accepting the credit.

"As Korac said, this was where our journeys split until we return for the end of this Verse." Behind me, I retrieve a folded bundle of cloth. Shaking it loose, I threw on my frock and whirled. "Let the space pirating begin."

The room burst into laughter and whistles, but over it all I heard Korac groan, "I am so glad I missed this phase."

Tameka confessed, "I'm glad it's making its way back."

The little version of you beams. "Me, too."

Me, too, Rayne.

ENTRY EIGHT

CHASING ALL THE WRONG I'D MADE

"**For those viewing the hologram, I'll start the next chapter here.** Everything changed with the Vacating of the Icari to Cinder. I know what people thought of me—Maybe even think it in the present-tense. Yes. Celindria is a blind spot for me, but I took Korac's parting words to heart.

"Why would Celindria summon Nox for a confrontation during the Vacating? To gloat? To punish him? And was I wrong for trusting her account about the corporal punishment?" I glanced at Korac. "The look in your eyes... It was the same sincerity I always saw when we were alone together. On your word alone, I knew I would investigate Celindria."

Korac toasted his drink with a dash of irony in the gesture. 'Too little, too late,' it said.

After the tense pause stretched on for a while, Kyle threw his hands up in frustration. "Well, what did you find?"

"Nothing. Celindria had vanished after the Vacating. I went to our designated rendezvous and found a message carved into the sand."

Do not seek me. I must fly on my own to mend this broken heart.

"Decades passed without word. In the absence of a leader to organize their revolution, people gave up on the cause and migrated away. The settlement fell into ruin around the indomitable fortress." I gestured toward Lucas, then at Caedes. "The Brethren refused to stay in Egypt and moved on to form council at a secret location, the capital of what remained of Icarean-human relations. Would either of you like to tell us about this time in your lives?"

With Pehton cradled between his legs, Caedes answered over her shoulder. "I collected the remaining half-breeds and their offspring for the relocation. Some, like myself, were born with nacres. We tracked these lines which had disseminated across the world. Eventually, rumors of the Traitor Prince circulated, stirring trouble in your search for Celindria. When you returned to Earth—"

"You're getting ahead of me," I said with a raised finger and a friendly smile.

Caedes saluted in return and summarized, "My life was political, diplomatic, and more violent than you may think, but certainly not worthy of a Verse."

Pehton kissed his cheek. "You'll tell me sometime."

Caedes' words rumbled from his chest. "Yes, ma'am."

Korac's laughter was abrupt and ended quickly. "Sorry." He did *not* look sorry.

The moment which followed was comfortable, and Lucas killed it. "My Verse is much more duplicitous."

"No shit!" Smith called from the back of my study.

Silence grinned, amused.

My foremother is prone to mischief—
Is that where I got it from?

Little you snickers in your fort. I'm grinning at you, and I know it's the spitting image of Silence's signature beam.

I said, "Lucas, please regale us of a spy's tale."

He hopped his butt up onto the couch between Tumu and Lamassau. Ignoring their considering glances, Lucas began braiding Andrew's hair. He said, "The Mother asked me to look after her descendants." He shot a knowing look at her. "Were you aware of how complicated a request that was, old friend? *Everyone* is your descendant."

Silence lived up to her namesake, smiling at him with affection and patience. A little gratitude.

Lucas continued. "Applying my judgment, I interpreted 'descendants' to mean Xelan and the Progeny. As for Nox… I saw the madness building in him from afar. I knew you would feel sorrow for him, Mother, but there was nothing I could do."

Silence bowed with her head, thoughtful in her steel eyes.

Finishing with Andrew's braids, Lucas stood, saying, "I sought the Traitor Prince and set him on his way to find Celindria while I maintained record on the expanding Progeny line. None of whom had manifested traits as extraordinary as the first or current generations."

Andrew murmured, "Did you feed this information to the Cult of Night?"

True vacuous silence filled the room.

Lucas stared down at his lover, who didn't even look up at him. The rest of the people watched the moment happen, uncomfortable with the implications.

"Yes."

Korac, who'd received the information from CoN, asked, "If your orders were to track Silence's children, why would you give Nox and I intel on their whereabouts?"

I wanted to know that as well, but I believed Lucas was always well-intended. Whatever the cause, it was a good one.

"For the same reason I informed the Icari of Xelan taking his new Progeny to Cinder. My aim was to reunite the quarreling brothers—To reunite the Mother's family. Imminent desired the information as well, but I never imagined Celindria would reveal herself. Even with my access to the Probability Matrix, I couldn't predict what would come of those decisions. Nothing has gone as expected with this particular rope we braid."

Rope.
One made of nacre.
In the two dreams where you came to me, Rayne, you wore braided nacre rope.

"I did, Superman. Now continue with the story."

"Silence, can you confirm?" Tumu asked a reasonable question.

She said, "I am grateful for your trust, and I ask you to grant Lucas the same. He speaks the truth. With each action the Shadow takes, you forge an unpredictable path in the Probability Matrix. One which feeds us with infinite outcomes. Yet still, you choose what cannot be expected." With the last, Silence grinned. "It must have driven Imminent mad."

Lucas bowed to Silence, deep and formal, before saying, "To continue with my story, I sought a friend."

"Me!"

We all spared a glance at Smith, who looked entirely too excited to feature in my Verse.

With a nod toward his companion, Lucas said, "Yes. For those of you not privy to this information, Smith goes back to the early years. After The Brethren migrated, I found this soldier in the mountains who smiled entirely too much—"

"Hey!"

"—Oh, that is not the first time you've heard someone say it. He became my initiate, and he was the only member of Imminent for whom I'd revealed the truth about Silence and the truth about me. Also, my intentions for the Progeny, the Traitor Prince, and the mad Night King of Cinder."

You're smiling.

The preteen version of you shakes your head against the pillow, incredulous. You even let out a little laugh before admitting, "I can't help it. It's such a ridiculously dramatic name for him, but I kinda like it."

I don't tell you, but you often beam when you talk about Nox, and it kills me.

I love you, Callahan.

You direct that beautiful ray of an expression onto me, and it warms me through. You say, "I think I've loved you my entire life, Superman. Ever since I was her age."

The little version of you giggles and beams up at me as well.

Wherever you are, I hope you're safe.

"Keeping telling your Verse, old man."

In my study, I said, "Smith."
He stood at attention. "Your imperial majesty?"
I shook my head at him, but said, anyway, "Read volume one thousand three hundred and ninety-eight. Page four-fifty seven."
Smith saluted and set about the task with grinning enthusiasm.

I couldn't stop pacing across my stronghold, now several stories tall and wider than a Cult of Night compound. No one from The Brethren knew the location. Only...

Well, the Icarus I awaited had proven trustworthy over the millennia since Celindria had disappeared. I trusted him to help me. But three more hours? I was pulling my hair out—Physically. The blood under my fingernails was mine for once.

News.

Actual word had come of Celindria's whereabouts, and a lead of where she would appear next. I could finally ask her why she'd banished my people and promptly disappeared, leaving me alone in this world once more. Was it Celindria's right to leave and live how she wanted? Yes. I would never dream of shackling someone to me, but...

Where were the other Progeny?

What had happened to Devis? One day he wanted to meet with me regarding the Pretiosum Cruor, and the next he was gone. Where in the Twelve Worlds was T.A.O.? Andrius had left with a caravan, but it had never arrived at its destination.

More hair came out.

This was my fault.

After three hours of this spiral, a knock sounded at my door. I crossed the rope bridge spanning the ravine and surveyed the security slot before answering the door for the only person I trusted with the location of my stronghold.

Lucas stepped through, putting me to shame with his expensive robes and slicked-back hair. He took one look at me and sighed. With his hands linked behind his back, he said, "Dear Prince. We have been through this before, have we not?"

"Tell. Me. Please."

In my study, Lucas shared, "Xelan regularly checked in with The Brethren and lived with me, sometimes for centuries, to integrate with the Progeny families, but I could tell he was restless to find Celindria. I knew of one contact within Imminent who'd expressed interest in helping him."

Korac looked between Lucas and me, his eyes narrowed in suspicion. "Is it who I think it is?"

Tameka spared me a curious glance.

In the story, Lucas said, "Celindria was last seen on Gait, and my contact awaits you there."

In my study, Korac shook his head, exasperated. "A few hundred years is all you waited—"

Sagan chafed her husband's arms and whispered in his ear, kissing his cheek. Korac hung his head, and Sagan gave us a nod to continue.

Lucas said, "I promised Xelan to take him only if he gave himself some time to clean up and recover. Within a fortnight, I arranged with Imminent to travel through the conduits of Enki, unimpeded. We arrived on Gait to be greeted by a parade of Lyriks."

Miy said, "I was there, but not me, obviously." She shot a nasty look at Pehton before glancing at me. "Triss seemed especially excited to meet you. Razor had promised you as a pet."

I pretended to clean an eyelash from my eye to hide an incredulous smile at the notion.

Korac asked, "What were you first impressions of Gait? The world you knew I'd come from."

I GAZED INTO THE PURPLE SKY OF ANOTHER WORLD WITHOUT STARS AND TASTED METAL, LINGERING IN THE AIR. The smell of street food, pollution, and waste marred the illusion of pristineness from the freshly packed snowfall. The space-scrapers competed to pierce the stratosphere of a world filled with uncertain mysteries. A ziggurat claimed the center, reminding all the planet's citizens of their debts to society. Convicted or born here, the Vast Collective deemed them all 'less' and deserving of this purgatory.

"Welcome to Gait, your highness."

The red-feathered Lyrik curtsied in her armored minidress, keeping those yellow eyes on mine—

In my study, Echo whistled a soft cry. Korac appeared at her side as if he'd learned to Seamswalk. He and Karter tended to her while Sagan smiled softly from her pallet beside Pehton and Caedes.

Back to my story.

"Thank you for hosting me, but an escort of this magnitude is unnecessary..." I left a lilt at the end of my sentence, asking her name.

The Lyrik smiled, and it was...gorgeous in a hard way. I knew with little interaction that she was lethal and wouldn't hesitate to slit my throat on command. "I am Triss, and the escort is for security reasons. Enki is seeking you, and they offer a pretty price." She let me see her eyes sweeping over me, assessing, before returning them to my face. "Officer Tumu should offer more. Please. Follow me."

Technology across the Twelve Worlds varied greatly. The closer the worlds were tethered to Enki, the more advanced they were as a civilization. Gait was the most advanced world I'd seen. Projected signs in the sky, neon lights, vehicles lumbering above—Not to mention sanitation and water works. The metals...their compositions were so fascinating. I wondered if our parade could spare a minute for me to collect some samples—

We turned a corner and encountered a most inspiring structure. A glass and steel warehouse with a revolving door leading into the twilight. More Lyriks flanked the door as we entered what the sign above called, "Razor's Emporium of Exotic Experiences."

Exotic. Experiences.

As we entered the room lined in antiqued mirrors and floored in parquet, I was dazzled and a little uncertain. Leaning into Lucas, I muttered, "What kind of contact is this—"

"The best kind."

When I sought the owner of the voice, I found myself gazing at the mezzanine. A man stood up there in clothes like I'd never seen before and shiny shoes, leaning in an obviously practiced pose on the banister which bunched his shoulders and emphasized his boxer's build.

But that's not why I was staring at him with my mouth on the verge of dropping open.

This stranger was the first person I'd seen with white hair like Korac's. His eyes were white, and his pupils were split into two crescents in each eye. When he spoke again, I listened for a familiar elegance to his cadence.

"Prince Xelan, I can ease your troubles."

Korac.

I found your family.

In my study, Echo giggled and whistled in gentle excitement. It was the only sound in the room. Korac lifted her from the bed and rocked her in his arms.

After a stretch of quiet reflection, Pehton asked first, "So, you could see through his perception field?"

"Yes."

Tumu went next. "You never told me what he looked like to you. Or that he looked the same as Korac."

Feeling slightly exposed, I pushed my fingers through my hair, saying, "At first, it's because I wasn't aware others couldn't see him as I did. I quickly learned the way of it, and discerned that if it was a secret Razor wanted to keep, then I would keep it for him."

"You knew he was my brother from the onset," Korac stated this as fact, with no accusation or venom, but still managed to sound unhappy about it.

I fidgeted under the scrutiny. "Not your brother, no, but it was quite apparent he was kin to you."

Tameka took my hand in hers, asking, "What happened next?"

"What would you want in return for 'easing my troubles?'"

Lucas coughed into his hand.

Beside me, Triss grinned.

My question hovered in the whiskey lighting amid the reflective tin tiles on the ceiling.

When a full minute had passed, Razor transformed. It was the only word I had for the dramatic shift in his demeanor. The lines at the corners of his eyes, the tilt of his brow, the curve of his lips, and the hollow of his jaw—All of it smiled at me with the deepest sincerity.

"Trust me."

I *felt* the words simply by staring into Razor's face. I knew then I should only do the opposite.

In my study, Matt raised his hand.

"Yes?"

He asked, "Is that how…"

I was already nodding before Matt finished his question. "Yes, Ginger. I see a similarity in you, and I recognized it the day I met you. This might sound a little insane, so bear with me, but it's also how I knew I could trust you."

With that congenial smile on his face, Razor answered my question. "I only ask that you work for me here, at the Emporium, until we resolve both of your little hereditary disputes."

Lucas and Triss looked at me for my answer.

Glancing around the place, which I imagined as full of bodies during the night, I considered my current living situation. Alone, ripping my hair out, and unable to maneuver myself any closer to Celindria. Or preventing the resurgence of Nox on Earth. Perhaps it was about time I let someone adopt me. For a little while.

Lucas gave a brief nod, as if he'd heard my thoughts.

That was good enough for me.

"When do we begin?"

Twenty minutes into another intermission, I found who I was looking for in the kitchen. "Sagan?" I tried to ask softly as not to scare her—

"Yip!" She jumped, dropping an entire plate of canapes, some deviled eggs from Pil, thirteen Reipon cocoa nibs, and one banana. All of which I knew was for her alone. "Shit," she added with a little laugh. "How can I help you, bestie?"

Like Tameka, Sagan has a nature about her. It's a different warmth—Bright and a little hyper. The kind of energy that makes you want to go on adventures.

"Yeah...That's it."

I helped Sagan reclaim her provisions before rubbing the back of my neck, feeling uncertain. "I, uhm...I wanted to check in with you and make sure you're doing okay with the latest stories in my Verse."

Sagan's smile availed all my concerns as she assured, "Don't worry about me, Wingmaster. Get your Verse out. I'll keep Korac on this side of polite."

Relieved, I smiled back. "Thank you. I'm so glad it isn't bothering you—"

"It is. Of course, it is." Sagan was still smiling, but it faltered slightly. There was more pity in it. "I know the version of Razor he let you see, because he showed it to me in the beginning. An ally and a confidant. Someone who could understand the worst in you and wouldn't shame you for it. What a rich friendship..." Before I could respond, she placed a hand on my arm and lost some of the sparkle in her violet eyes. "Then he pushed me into the Seam so I could starve to death, because I refused to die having his baby. All so he could torture Korac further. His poison was—*is*—systemic. You are so lucky you to have only seen the friend in him, and for all he died saving us, I think he deserved at least one person to still feel the way you do about him. But nothing else."

I knew what she was saying. "So no Iona for Razor?"

Sagan shook her head and sighed. "I think not. We're being charitable by telling Echo the good more than the bad about her biological parents."

"Well, since you don't have a problem being honest with me, do you think me childish for denying an Iona for Nox if Razor can't have one?"

Korac chose that exact moment to walk into the kitchen with Pax on his back. His typically composed mask almost hid the ire beneath the play in his eyes. He'd heard our conversation and disguised it well as he announced, "Look, Pax. We found your dad in the kitchen, like I said."

My son wiped the sleep from his eyes and mumbled in a groggy voice, "Thanks, Uncle Korac. Dad, can I have some waffles? Please."

I ruffled his red coils before saying, "Yeah, go find Uncle Caedes and ask him to make them for you the way you like."

Korac let him down, and Pax hugged my side. "Thanks, dad." He took off for the dining/living space where everyone was gathered for brunch, leaving me alone with the two people most likely to advocate for something I didn't want.

Korac glanced from Sagan to me before hopping his ass onto my countertop. "So, what's this about Razor getting an Iona when you won't give one to Nox?"

I sighed and pressed a hand on my brow.

With her arms full of food once more, Sagan said, "You missed some context. Xelan is asking a fair question from his perspective. If Razor doesn't deserve an Iona, why does Nox?"

Korac bit into an apple, and the juice dripped down his chin until he rubbed it away. He chewed and swallowed before admitting, "I know Nox is no hero. His most unheroic actions are what sent me to the Shadow in the first place, but at least, when he wasn't insane, his intentions were good. 'Save the race at all costs.' The Icarean Prerogative."

"Nowhere in Elden's Verse does it say 'at all costs,' and I agree motives should play a part in the decision. Razor's intentions were mercurial at best, but he never killed his brother, then celebrated by…"

I couldn't bring myself to say what happened to you.

Flat and bitter, Korac said, "No. He only sent his brother to men who would, and when I was a child, at that. I know it hurts more for you because it was Rayne, and you cared—care—so deeply for her, but think about it. Razor made a billion credits each night selling the very experience you don't condone."

Sagan, still holding her bundle of food, looked between the two of us.

I stared at Korac for a long minute, letting his words sink in. It was a hard truth to swallow. The only good which had come from the experiences was that I hacked into those accounts and used them to fund slaves we'd freed from Lukemore six months ago. Still, I must be honest with myself. Razor had never intended the money for a righteous purpose.

"You're right." The couple sighed in mutual relief until I continued. "Neither of them deserve an Iona." I wanted so badly to quit the room with their mouths hanging open, but it felt petty.

Korac blinked at me, and Sagan frowned sadly.

I turned to her and said, "I'm sorry some of my Verse is bothering you. If you feel uncomfortable at any point, I'd understand if you want to leave."

Sagan tried for a weak smile, assuring, "I'm here for the complete story, Wingmaster, and I understand. I won't bring up Nox as a candidate again."

A lead weight dropped in my stomach as if I'd kicked a puppy. "Sagan, I never—"

"We're heading back to your study now. See you there." Korac glared at me as he calmly led Sagan out of the kitchen.

Rayne.
You've gone so quiet.

Your twelve-year-old smile is gentle as you assure, "Not for the reason you think. To Korac, Nox is a tragic hero. Maybe even to Sagan and

some others in the Shadow—Hell, the entirety of Iona Pax. But despite that, you are entitled to your feelings on the subject."

You're still saving yours to tell me after, yes?

Little you says, "You know it."

Then let's return to the study.

Pax was full from the waffles Caedes made for several people—

Forgive the long pause. I only realized I'd neglected to eat since before the wedding.

Never mind. I'll eat later.

Tameka stood at my side, and everyone found places among the pallet fort inside my study. I glanced over at Smith, who was peeking at the next few pages in the volume like he sought an answer to a question he'd yet to ask. He mumbled something to Lucas as the Icarus walked in, and I fought the urge to eavesdrop.

Instead, I sought Sagan. When our eyes met, she stopped running her fingers through Korac's hair and smiled at me. Pure and affectionate. We were all right.

"Superman, you were worried that one conversation could ruin nearly a decade of friendship?"

I've lost friendships which spanned millions of years for less, or so I'd thought.

Preteen you sits up on the couch, letting the blanket pool around your waist. Your eyes and all the kindness in them refuse to look away from my face. "Xelan, it was never one conversation, and you're wise enough now to know the difference between another nail in the coffin and one in a complicated structure of friendships and family.

You're not a monster for voicing your reasons to contest Nox's Iona and trust Sagan to know that."

Coming from you...
Rayne, thank you.

***

"Smith, I titled the next entry. What did I call it?"

Smith shot me a quick smirk before reading, "'A Transcript of the Most Unusual Conversation of My Life.'"

Beside me, Tameka gave a half-laugh. "If it was with Razor, I can say the same is true for me, too."

There were a few agreeing sounds throughout the room.

I STOOD ACROSS A KITCHEN COUNTER FROM THE MAN WHO LOOKED SO VERY SIMILAR TO MY FORMER LOVER, YET I FELT THE NEED TO GUARD MY CURIOSITY IN HIS PRESENCE. The voice in my head said Razor would value my interest and exact a price in exchange for sating it. Wanting something from this stranger, who Lucas referred to as the "Pain Curator," was dangerous.

Once Razor finished outlining his proposal, I let all my skepticism into my voice as I asked, "Security? Is that *all* you want from the Traitor Prince of Cinder?"

Something moved in Razor's eyes as he searched mine. After a long moment of silence, he declared, "You are not your brother."

My laughter was bitter and...

Laughter?

How long ago did I last laugh? I straightened from leaning on the counter and shook my head. "Sir, you are indeed observant."

Triss, further down the expansive counter with Lucas, made a sound one might call a giggle, but the same hardness which permeated her smile steeled the rich noise.

Meanwhile, Lucas—Your eyes never left us. There was such an intensity in them which I mistook then as diplomatic nerves, but it went deeper, yes?

In my study, Lucas answered, "Yes, your imperial majesty. I needed you to like and trust Razor, but the man possessed an uncanny ability to put off most people when he was in certain moods."

In the story, Razor smirked at me and rolled back the sleeves on a button-down—foreign clothing to me. A heavy timepiece encircled his pale wrist with tiny gems inside. While at the task, he said, "Ask your questions, dear Prince, and I will answer them honestly to earn your trust."

"How can I trust your brand of honesty?"

The Pain Curator's smirk crooked further. "Because I like you, and now I want you to stay for your intellectual company more than your physical capabilities."

I understood the sentiment. After a thoughtful pause, I opened with the most burning question. "How did you become a prisoner of Enki?"

Vaguely, I sensed the other two in the room react, but I placed my focus on Razor. What felt like an hour passed before he blinked. After which, the Pain Curator spoke in a voice so deep it bubbled goosebumps along my skin and resonated in my chest. "I could insult your intelligence and ask what you mean by that, but this once, I think I will skip the pretense. Instead, I want to know how you came to this conclusion. If I like your answer, I will tell you." At the last, the Pain Curator smiled again.

"Gait is exceptionally advanced in its technology and civilization, making it older than most planets and rather entangled with Enki. A relationship of give and take. Gait houses the criminals too scientifically valuable to execute, and Enki provides the tech to do so. Tell me, Pain Curator, why do you live on a planet inside Enki and are there any others?" Razor raised his brows, impressed, and I pointed skyward. "No stars or moons in the sky. There's also an artificial component in the atmosphere, leftover from before the Tritans terraformed Gait. This world tastes of Dyson's Sphere."

In my study, people gaped or raised their brows or smirked.

Tameka beamed at me. "You knew from the start?"

From the nearest pallet, Pax said, "Dad knows everything."

My son's confidence may have puffed out my chest a bit.

"Hee." Little you takes so much delight in this.

Lucas confirmed, "He impressed Razor so much, the Pain Curator confessed much of the truth."

"I made a bad deal once, and for my penance, I was Gait's first resident."

The first?

Razor was ancient.

I gaped.

Razor smirked, as if gleaning my thoughts, and remarked, "You have no idea, but never mind that. As long as I ingratiate myself to Enki, I can do as I like. As you can see, I established a lucrative business spanning the galaxy. I would like to offer you a place in my organization, but outsiders will only see a fresh addition to my security detail. In return, I will give you any and all information I gather about Celindria from my sources within Enki and the Vast Collective. As a show of good faith, I will provide her next destination: Monarch 3. A planet I understand you are familiar with. Work for me, and you can travel freely through the conduits with a team of your own recruitment."

It was my turn to shoot my brows up. This offer was beyond generous. I glanced over at Lucas, who bowed his head. I took it to mean if anything went wrong, he would be there to help me out. Beside him, Triss smiled like a diamond. Bright and ready to cut glass.

Still cautious, I said, "This is more than I could hope for, but... And forgive my manners... What do you gain from my employment here?" I held up my hand before he could restate his earlier reasoning. "Beside my 'intellectual company?'"

Razor kept smiling while something danced in his eyes. He folded his arms on the counter and leaned forward, conspiratorially. "A little adventure and a little mischief. You may not be aware of this, but the trouble Celindria has caused brought attention from Enki to your rogue Progeny experiment. They want me to use my resources to investigate whether you are a galactic threat. In meeting you, I can see there is not a single threatening bone in your body, but… They want tabs all the same. Easier kept with you in my facilities, and I cannot wait to see what you do next, Traitor Prince."

In my study, I confessed, "In the spirit of this Verse, I wish Razor could give his account."

Korac said nothing while Sagan took his hand in hers. She smiled. He did not.

Noticing the conflicted expressions in the room, I pressed, "Everyone gets so quiet now whenever Razor's mentioned."

With a little encouragement from his wife, the Iona General finally admitted, "I'll never understand how he could do those things to me, to Bethany, and to Sagan, but show you and T.A.O. a completely different side of himself. He gave us an abbreviation of his Verse, but it still wasn't enough to understand his motivations aside from pettiness stacked on top of a massive inferiority complex of which I'm no longer certain was entirely his fault. But it doesn't matter because he died in an act of heroism meant to confound us and scholars until Eternity takes us all."

This elicited a few nods and thoughtful looks.

From the northwest corner, Matt set aside a sandwich, stood, and said, "Razor's clientele kept comparing me to you as Razor's protégé."

Lucy stood and rubbed his back. Bethany watched the two of them from the same corner as their crew, fully integrated into the pride.

I thought a minute before saying, "All those years ago, I knew I could trust you because you were so young and still unformed in your… talents. You needed guidance. I never imagined you would ever face Razor. If I may ask, how was it, looking into that mirror?"

Matt said, "We got along in a way which felt comfortable at times, but while I knew I could learn from him, I wanted to be *better* than him. I think that came from wanting to live up to your expectations, even when you were dead."

I winced. I always winced when someone mentions that Nox had sent me to Eternity for a few years. Still, I preferred it to someone saying 'when I was gone.' To him, I said, "Thanks, Matt. Did you have a question?"

The freckled-face young man glanced around the room before asking, "What did they mean by protégé? I wasn't exactly entertaining his clients through song and dance when they were comparing me to you."

I glanced at Tameka, Korac, and Sagan. I needed to clear my throat to say, "I think Razor was gifted in motivating people and could tailor his trials to each person."

Pehton humphed. "No shit."

"He liked to stretch boundaries. Perhaps until you were so far gone, you found yourself in regret. On day one, I gave him my pain as an experiment in exchange for credits. As for my working responsibilities, I never killed for Razor and I never knew about the basement. I'm not even sure the Numbered were down there at that time—"

Bethany stood up beside Matt and Lucy. Korac clicked his tongue and crossed the room. While the couple watched on, giving Bethany space, Korac offered, "Would you like to go for a walk, Bethany?"

She nodded, and my heart broke. I said, "I'm so sorry."

Korac shot me a look before leading her out. Matt and Lucy followed to flank the doorway for their return. I burned with shame.

Preteen you folds the blanket and straightens the pillow on the couch, not meeting my eyes as you admonish, "Listen to and respect their

experiences. They all understand you knew a different Razor from them."

Like I should understand you knew a different Nox?

You tilt your head before saying, "If that's how you choose to look at it, but it's not a combative arena. Your brother versus Korac's brother. 'Only one man will earn the title of Iona.'"

Your succinct summation of it earned an abrupt laugh. One I maybe didn't deserve.

You're right. I am excluding others' experiences and not appreciating enough that they differ from my own.
To my loved ones in the study, I said, "Let's move onto some adventures where I met so many of our friends and converted enemies to allies, but not before one of them tried to eat me."

ENTRY NINE

AMENDS FOR OTHERS

The wood construction of the Queen's Fare was a marvel of engineering and taste. Nanites carved out the construction to a fine, polished finish, including the bars and tables—All furnishings and structures. I could see my reflection on the floors.

I could hear the smirk in Razor's voice behind me as he said, "Yes, it *is* a wonder. The hive was a husk when I found it. If you ever want a peek at the technology behind it, I would be happy to show you."

A husk in Monarch 3. Surely, this wasn't the same hive—

"The burlesque lounge is through there." With a nail-less finger, Razor pointed to the unlit room off the lobby. "Deliver this envelope to your contact in the VIP balcony. Tell security I sent you. In the meantime, I will be conducting some business in the back." He patted my shoulder in one of his congenial gestures, saying, "It may take some time, so until then, I suggest you enjoy yourself once your errand is finished." After winking at me, he went behind the lobby's bar and through a door meant for employees only.

His bizarre nature left me shaking my head a lot, but often with a smile. Which was better than staying home, alone, pulling out my hair. Right?

I headed for the dark archway—

Behind me, Razor called, "Oh, Xelan?"

With a glance over my shoulder, I caught the mischievous grin on his face.

"Try not to blush."

I laughed, waving him off. Thanks to father's consummation ceremonies, blushing was unlikely, so off I went into the dark. The lounge was decorated in heavy black and purple fabric cascading from the ceiling. The chairs and barstools matched the color scheme in plushy elegance. Darkness congregated around the colors, creating an intimate bedroom atmosphere which smelled of vanilla.

Notably, it was like Razor's scent, minus the coagulated blood. When I asked about it, he'd said the darker scent resulted from a rare bone disorder common in his people. But when I asked about his race, he gave me one of those 'I know something you don't, and I delight in keeping it from you' smiles. It was Razor's favorite smile.

Back to the story.

Women and men of all origins from across the Vast Collective performed on the stages in various ranges of undress. I knew without being familiar with their cultures that each of them represented the peak standard of beauty from their home worlds.

With a glance upward, I noticed the draped material gathered at the base of each balcony until it formed the outline of...

All the females in the Vast Collective must bear the same anatomy to an extent.

I *did* blush. It burned my cheeks as I approached the only set of stairs and the Mon3 drone guarding its base—

Did I... Did I know him? He looked so familiar...

Oh.

It was him!

The drone who had let me give his Queen a nacre. The last time I'd seen him, he'd dropped me on the surface of the magnificent tree where I found Nox and Korac ripping people apart.

Did the Queen survive? Did the nacre and my blood revive her—

"Sir?"

The security drone said it as if he'd tried to reach me several times.

"Pardon me." How do I ask about his Queen in the very same hive my father had ruined and my employer had appropriated? I ran a frustrated hand through my hair and considered my options before I choked out, "Razor sent me to meet someone in the VIP balconies."

Instead of Traitor Prince, they should call me Cowardly Prince.

"Go ahead."

To satisfy one curiosity, I asked, "Do you need some proof of my affiliation?"

The drone chuckled. "You must be green to Razor's company. No one would dare misuse the Pain Curator's name."

Rather than satisfying my curiosity, his answer only fueled it further. I muttered, "Thank you," before climbing the stairs to the balconies. Only one was occupied.

I rapped my knuckles on the archway. "Excuse me?"

"Come in, friend."

Again, I asked as I entered, "What makes you assume I am a friend?" I sat in the chair beside the contact, unable to see him in the dark with his face turned away.

The informant shrugged. "We are all friends here." His accent drew out the 'S' sounds in a hiss. When he turned, his eyes took me by surprise. One half of each iris was was black, and the other half was blue. They were set in shallow sockets, surrounded by red scales. When he smiled, his front teeth were comprised of fangs in varying length, and when he spoke, his tongue was forked at the end. "Hello, your highness. Is that envelope for me?"

In my study, Iuo toasted me with an ice cream cone. "Finally, we've arrived at the integral parts of this Verse."

Some chuckles and snickers sent me back into the story.

After I handed over the envelope, Iuo checked it and smiled. "I never thought a celebrity would run errands for the Pain Curator." He reached out a hand, saying, "I am Prince Iuo of Reipon, and I am beyond delighted to meet you."

I took the hand and reveled in the texture. Fascinated, I stared. Unsure how to take his compliments, I blurted, "May I ask for a sample of your DNA?"

Iuo barked out a laugh. "Yes. Yes, you are living up to your reputation. It would be my honor to contribute as your first Lamian specimen." He plucked a scale from his arm and offered it to me.

Eyes wide, I stored it carefully. "Thank you."

After an amused shake of his head, Iuo got straight to the point. "Regarding the business which brings us here. Your daughter has instigated some trouble, demanding access to local hives. Healthy ones. Those are off limits." Iuo waved a finger for emphasis. "No one can enter a Queen's dominion. When Celindria could not pry them, she threatened the drones before leaving of her own accord, all while promising reprisal. Does that sound like the girl you know?"

This tore at me. Could I say I ever really knew Celindria? But then I thought of the vacancy in her eyes as she'd asked for my help—What it must be like to go through life unable to experience it fully.

I sighed and wiped my hand down my face.

The gesture sparked something in Iuo. He gripped my shoulder and offered, "We can locate her and return her to your care before Enki claims her. Do you know of her next destination?"

If Celindria was demanding the gas…

"Lacceirus Capra."

Iuo kept glancing back at the stage, as if afraid to miss the act, but still managed to say, "We shall venture there next. I am positive Razor can find some lucrative excuse to send you, and I will accompany you."

I couldn't keep from frowning. "Why?" I hated asking when I sought alliances and friendships, but that voice in my head said to doubt everything, everyone.

Iuo's smile was kind, as he said, "I am a 'performative' historian for Enki. They are extremely interested in you, and my presence as an official could tame some of their desire to pursue you and Celindria. It will satisfy Officer Tumu's concern. Consider me a chaperon."

Officer Tumu.

The same name kept coming up.

I said, "Thank you."

With another glance at the stage, Iuo assured, "I will join you once I have gleaned all the inspiration I need from here. About two hours? In the meantime, recruit Seps."

I tilted my head. "Seps?"

Iuo pointed at the stairs. "The Mon3 drone. He was among the individuals your wayward child threatened, so he has a vested interest in your case. No—Wipe those worries away. Seps is a peace-loving individual. Like me, he only resorts to violence when the occasion calls for it."

I frowned, asking, "You saw Celindria. Do you think the occasion will call for it?"

There was a…flicker of something in Iuo's eyes before he said, "Let me just say we may need the additional muscle. Two hours."

Back in my study, I asked Iuo, "Did you actually want to finish the show or were you staging what came next?"

Iuo put on his best innocent face. "I haven't a clue what you're talking about. That burlesque show completely inspired the next series of videos I filmed."

Bones mumbled, "Sure."

I glanced over at Tumu, whose warm expression reminded me of why I valued my friendships so. With a grin, I accused, "You were already chasing me down."

The old Primary returned the expression. "You didn't know it, but your days were numbered."

Lamassau chuffed. "All of our days…"

Korac raised his glass. "I'll drink to that."

The room took a collective sip, even Pax drank from his orange juice.

I reflected on what came next—

Oh.

Hmm.

I turned to Tameka and leaned down to mutter in her ear. "The next part I'd rather tell you in private, but…"

She smiled and said, "We don't have time. It's okay. I'll get through it."

"Smith, please read on."

Seps waited downstairs, and I didn't need to ask if he'd been listening. The determination was set in the line of his jaw.

Instead, I asked, "So will you come with us?"

With a glance left and right, Seps muttered, "I need you to come with me before I can leave with you."

This smelled of trouble.

"Sure."

A half-hour later, I knew we'd exited the tree by the sudden freshness in the air. It smelled wild and uncompromised by technology, just as it did all those millennia ago when we'd first stepped inside. Of course, I needed my nose to tell me this because Seps had blindfolded me and stuffed some wax in my ears, deafening me. If not for the lead tied between us, he would've lost me in flight.

I didn't blame Seps for his caution—

Wait.

A coolness came over me, and the smell changed. It was… more the perfume of fragrant flowers and—

The hood came off and left me facing Seps, who gestured for me to remove the wax from my ears. It was dim in the space. Some light transitioned in color along the walls like the reflection of water. Purple gas hovered at my feet.

We were in a hive.

In the center, a form moved until great wings unfurled, revealing a frail body at its center. I'd recognize those lips anywhere. Having been a Prince all my life, I can count the few times I went to my knees for another person on one hand—Apart from a lover, of course.

In my study, people chuckled, but Pax glanced around, confused.

Tameka shot me an adorably admonishing look, and the story continued.

On my knees, I bowed my head, saying, "Your majesty."

"F8," the Monarch 3 Queen corrected. "Young man, why have you returned once more in the company of our enemy?"

Enemy? "Razor?"

F8 pushed her hair over her shoulder and clicked her tongue. "All men not of this world are our enemy."

"Am I your enemy, your majesty?" My question puzzled F8 into frowning. I gently assured, "No. Not everyone harbors ill-intentions. I seek my daughter. She came here, and—"

"Threatened us. Demanded our clouds," Seps finished.

F8 shot him a look for the outburst, but agreed with a reluctant nod. "He speaks the truth. She is the first to ask for a Queen not for breeding, but for our pheromones. What sin does she wish to commit against our people?"

This was uncomfortable to admit, but I said, "I created her from this..." I waved my hand through the gas. "And other materials. I believe she intends to recreate the process, but I want to stop her. To save her from the...sin I fear she may commit against herself." I swallowed before bringing up the next bit. "An ally mentioned Seps should join us on the journey."

Seps frowned, but F8 conceded the point to me with a bow of her head. "Yes. This is a beneficial alliance. Cinder and the world Enki has named Monarch 3."

I quirked a brow out of curiosity. "What do you call it?"

"Home."

That earned a smile. "Yes. Your home. I would never betray my own intentions. When I revived you, I intended for your people to thrive. Tell me, how many of you possess nacres now?"

F8 glanced over at Seps, who gave an assenting shrug. The Queen said, "All of us. We walk among the worlds of men and do their bidding to prevent further expansion into our home. To learn and subvert their designs. Beware of your new companion with the changing eyes."

It was my turn to bow and concede the point about Razor. "Yes, your majesty. So, what say you? An alliance?"

F8 crossed the hive with the gas billowing around her dainty ankles like thick smoke. The closer she drew, the headier the smell of the flowers became. When she stood not a breath away, I could see her lids were low and her eyes sparked with fire. They raked down and up again, assessing me.

The Queen confessed, "We are a hive. Communal. All arrangements are sealed one way."

I frowned. "How?"

F8 needed to levitate to reach my face with her small hand. She cupped my jaw and flew in to kiss me. Curious, I let her. After which, I grasped her proposal.

"Oh."

In my study, Tameka gaped at me. Shocked, she cried, "You didn't?!"

Sagan grinned at me.

I wet my lips and tried for a good defense. "I'm a scientist, and I was curious."

Tumu barked out an incredulous laugh.

Lamassau admonished me. "That's so weak. You introduced an ex-lover to your current one without mentioning—I mean, you designed Iona Pax with F8 on the team—" He gave a hearty laugh before toasting me. "You, my friend, are messy."

I didn't bother explaining it was a simple one-time business transaction, but the defensiveness was there all the same. Better to save it for a private conversation with Tameka.

Korac jumped in. "How many of our allies did you sleep with, exactly?"

Sagan nudged Korac, but the question still stood.

I wanted to loosen my collar even though I wasn't wearing a shirt under my frock coat. Eventually, I squeezed out, "That is a hard question to answer. Technically, only F8 made it into the Elect, but..." I swallowed, saying the next. "I have taken a partner from each race to experiment with the capability Enki's reproduction program had instilled to see if it was as viable as they'd assumed." My face burned.

Tameka stared at me. I was worried—

"None of that, Superman. It's a simple matter of accepting your varied history. You know how gracious Tameka is about you living so long and acquiring a few exes."

Very well.

Sagan's expression was unexpected. She smiled with something close to admiration in her eyes. "I dig it."

Korac gave a bewildered shake of his head and took a drink like it could wipe away the mental images.

In the back, Puk folded his arms and tsked, near sulking.

Matt asked, loud enough for the room to hear, "What is it, man?"

The Mon3 drone, in his pride, admitted with some disappointment in his voice, "I always thought once you go drone, you never go home."

Much laughter ensued.

Iuo began listing off statistics in which Puk's assumption simply wasn't the case.

In the ruckus this caused, I whispered to Tameka. "Are we all right?"

She gave me wide eyes, a slow blink, and a wary smile. "Yeah. We can talk later. I promise it's not a big deal." With all the kindness in her, she took my hand and gave it a weak squeeze. "Really."

I waved for Smith to keep reading amid the noise.

He looked back at my journal and read, "'With the arrangement consummated, Seps returned with me to the Queen's Fare. We emerged in the lobby with Iuo and proposed the expedition to L. Capra to Razor. He beamed, delighted, and said, "How fortuitous. I have another package for you to deliver, and the recipient happens to reside on L. Capra."'"

The Shadow fell silent.

I made eye contact with each of them before I flicked the lapels up on my frock. "Now the adventure begins."

"Superman, are you trying to exasperate Korac to death?"

Am I that transparent, Little Rayne?

"Little did Razor know, but piracy had already begun. Every source of light, tablet or device, and nano program, I loaded into my homemade tech for analysis and the inevitable replication." I spread my arms, encompassing my study and beyond. "My stronghold required some upgrades if I were to compete on this scale. Analysis and engineering was all I needed." I paused, then held up a finger. "And patience." Another pause. "And to regrow my hair and eyebrows a few times. No big deal."

Little you giggles, and preteen you grins incredulously at me.

I treasure both reactions.

In my study, they laughed and teased. I couldn't tell them I stole samples from my encounter with F8, making me no better than the other men who'd invaded Monarch 3.

"She knows, Xelan. I'm sure of it, and I'm sure her presence in your roundtable proves she's forgiven you for it."

After a sigh, I called, "Lamassau."

The Chef stopped ribbing his significant other and blinked the film over his voids at me. "Your imperial thief?"

Low hanging fruit. Barely anyone laughed.

With a shake of my head, I said, "Volume one thousand, five hundred and sixty-eight. Page ninety-nine. Please."

Lamassau spared a wary glance for Tumu, who narrowed his voids at me. The Tritan known as the Chef crossed the room and didn't need to climb the ladder to retrieve the journal. Everyone stared in anticipation as Lamassau read from the pages.

FALLING.

Falling didn't usually happen when one stepped through a conduit. Iuo, Seps, and I yelped at the sudden drop. The drone unfolded his wings with a buzz, and I followed his lead. Iuo kept falling.

"Iuo!"

Both Seps and I tightened our form to reach him. Maybe it was the panic, or maybe it was the natural response for a Lamia in the sky, but Iuo's legs combined into one red muscle mid-fall. He yelled the entire time—

In my study, Iuo admitted, "I did. Yes."

Seps got to him first and clutched the reptilian humanoid to his side. We flew the rest of the way down into…a crater or a funnel. I couldn't tell until we'd landed, but every instinct in me said that was not a good idea.

Let me elaborate.

When we first visited L. Capra, I expected what my brother described. Meadows with purple, blue, and pink flowers, surrounded by yellow-barked trees with bright red canopies. Fresh scent included.

What I found returned a familiar bitter taste to my mouth, which manifested anytime I thought of Nox and his lies. The sky reminded me of a mudslide, and a toxic stench permeated it. On the surface, gravel scraped along barren mountains and plateaus, eroded by the constant howling wind.

"You paused, Superman."

I did. Even with the others, I did.

Preteen you reaches over the table and squeezes my folded hands. "Tell me."

Nox had lied, and the planet I encountered defied expectation. Korac was sitting there in my study, staring at the floor. I know he feels regret for what happened, but I don't think he realizes it bothered me that he and Nox had lied to me. I was only a kid, a little older than Pax.

"Could you be honest with Pax? Would you tell him the truth that your father ruined the homeworld of millions of people and left them to die in the toxic atmosphere? Or would you bring Pax home a cool new piece of tech and marvel at his wonder at it, keeping your tears and shame to yourself?"

For the next, you lean closer until our eyes meet. "Here, in this booth, you can tell me. I won't judge you."

I know you won't. I can see it in the blue of your eyes. So I'll answer as honestly as possible.
I don't know.

A small smile forms on your lips. "That's a fair answer, Superman. One day, Korac would like to hear it."

I alighted on a plateau overlooking the crater, and Seps followed, setting Iuo down. Something about the formation of the six kilometer-wide funnel directly beneath the conduit to Enki left me apprehensive.

To voice my concerns, I pointed. "Do you see the perfect slope in the crater's bowl?"

Iuo shook his head. "Alas, I am a man of letters. Geometry and trigonometry frighten me so."

Seps caught on though. "It is not of nature."

Agreeing with his observation, I said, "Artificial. The result of a massive feat of engineering and patience. Truly, I find it beautiful, but also, a mite threatening."

Iuo asked, "Why so?"

Again, Seps answered with my exact concern. "The Tritans cannot fly, like you Lamias and other species. Anyone without wings would step through the conduit and plummet to their demise."

I admitted, "It makes for an elaborate death trap, but all the same..."

"Unfriendly," Iuo concluded.

A stranger called from behind, "You have no idea, trespasser."

The three of us whirled, but too late. We found ourselves surrounded by aforementioned unfriendlies. In togas. With bent-backward joints.

"Just as I said. King Nox has returned." It was the first stranger's voice again. He projected the depth of it so that his words carried down the cliffs into the gorge below. "We have much anticipated your return, Icarean filth."

The three of us glanced at each other before I licked my lips and tried for reason. "We look alike, but I am not—"

"Silence!"

In my study, she waved, and Kyle kissed her grinning cheek.

The original stranger swept his toga up into the reversed bend of his elbow and glided toward me with an air of aristocracy. "I told them you were too arrogant not to return for more of our precious resources. Now here you are to gloat in the face of our devolved people. Look around, boy."

I stared into his angry eyes before doing as he said. All the men and women looked civilized, educated, and incensed. When I met his gaze again, the Caprent smirked while saying, "Yes, child. We evolved and thrived despite your attempts to destroy us. Now you will stand trial for your crimes."

At a loss, I asked, "What crimes has Nox committed?"

The Caprent waved a finger in my face. "Do not pretend."

On the other side of Seps from me, Iuo cleared his throat and spoke up. "I believe they are referring to Umbra's atmospheric disturbance. The maneuver which ruined the planet's surface, making it uninhabitable."

I blinked at him. "What? Nox—"

"You introduced yourself right as you poisoned our skies, murderer," the Caprent said with conviction. To his people, he ordered, "Take them. The trial begins today. See that Yu and Lukemore are informed. I am certain they wish to witness justice at our teeth."

Teeth.

This race didn't possess wings. Seps and I could fly away and leave Iuo there, but I wanted to see this through. I wanted to know if Korac and Nox had lied to me, and if they did, I would see it made right.

Lamassau stopped reading to ask, "What did you make of their accusations at the time?"

I glanced at Korac before admitting, "I was devastated. How could my brother ruin another people? But the initial disbelief only lasted a minute before I thought, 'Of course, he did. Anything and anyone who got in his way was damned.'"

Korac clicked his tongue in disdain before asking, "So you're saying if anyone accused us of anything during this time in your life, you'd simply believe them?"

Tameka touched a hand to my back as if she knew I was fighting not to wince.

"Yes."

Sagan gently reminded her husband, "Nox eventually killed half the people on my homeworld. Cut Wingmaster some slack."

Her sound reason reached Korac, who conceded the point with a nod.

Tumu waved for Lamassau to go on. "You won't believe what happens next."

Iuo grinned.

Lamassau did as his lover told him to do.

We've all seen the underground cities of L. Capra by now, so I'll keep the details to a minimum. Their race is a testament of perseverance and architectural genius, evidenced by the elaborate columned cities dissolved from rock by their personal acid glands.

It was in such a city I stood trial for Nox's crime. It surprised me to find the courthouse was an arena with a drain in the center.

Not reassuring.

On my knees with my hands cuffed behind my back, I asked, "So when you say 'justice at our teeth,' does that imply...?"

My accuser, standing in the center of the arena with me, grinned perfectly white teeth at me. "This will be an execution via ingestion. I look forward to exacting retribution from your gray hide, Nox."

As non-offenders, Iuo and Seps would stand trial separately as accomplices after my punishment was served.

Literally.

"You're so cheesy, superman."

I wink at you before we return to the story.

The stands were filled with people from all across the Vast Collective. Nox and Korac had racked up some enemies, all too happy to see him eaten. One I recognized.

Legir was an older replica of his son, Bin, the wonderful Yun healer I was sure Nox had assassinated. Legir's presence here confirmed it for me. He sat in a special box in the stands beside the main podium. There, a lanky Caprent stood proud in his azure toga where all the others wore white.

This man opened the proceedings. "All here today to witness the trial and execution of King Nox of Cinder, remember the day you—" He pointed a long-nailed finger at me from his backward arm. "Destroyed our homes. Murdered our women and children. And left our planet to choke on your avarice. Yet, you can see, we defied your condemnation. Now we bring forth evidence to sentence you to death by ingestion."

I opened my mouth to say I wasn't Nox—

My executioner slapped the back of my head. "Down, filth."

They bound my arms in chains but not nacre. I could break it. Fly away. Yet...Some part of me wanted to hear.

And I did.

On my knees for hours, listening to firsthand accounts of how Korac and Nox rushed to distract the people of this world as Umbra launched an apocalyptic weapon into the sky.

Children dissolved in acid rain.

I was weeping by hour one. After three hours, I was ready to let my executioner eat me. These people deserved justice, and they'd never receive it from Nox. Returning here was not in his plans. That I knew for certain.

Once the witnesses finished, the arbiter declared, "King Nox of Cinder, we find you, your general, and your deceased father responsible for these atrocities—Lacking in compassion or mercy. The only measure left to us which could match your brutality is a death penalty we designed especially for you. An acid bath and consumption at the hand of the most wronged, Kombuchi."

Kombuchi, the Caprent primed to eat me, snatched my hair and pulled back on it to expose my throat. He muttered in my ear. "You have been quiet. Respectful. But now you will listen to my story, vile demon.

"We were a simple people without nacres before you ruined our world. I was fortunate to live among five generations of my family. Five. Including my children and their children.

"Your genocide took them and left me sterile. I am the last of my line.

"If not for the Primary, who came to us with nacres, we would cease to exist. Instead, we evolved and look at us now..."

As Kombuchi kept repeating, his people were marvels of scientific evolution and—

Primary.

Nacres.

Something was wrong, and my mind was trying to work it through. It couldn't care less that Kombuchi had opened his double-hinged jaws like a snake and bubbled up a boil of acid at the back of his throat, aiming for me.

Why would a Primary leave sanctuary to aid a solitary planet? Why not send an Officer or an Eminent? And why L. Capra but not Cinder when Li exploded—

"Xelan!" Iuo cried.

Seps shouted, "Stop!"

A commotion erupted near him in the box beside Legir. The Yun leader had moved, but where did he go—Oh. Legir had climbed the podium to talk to the arbiter.

Meanwhile, Kombuchi gripped me in his backward-bent arms, prepared to soak me in his acid.

In my study, Iuo said, "I thought you meant to let him kill you."

Puk added, "I heard through the grapevine you closed your eyes and everything."

I shook my head and waited for Lamassau to start again.

There was too much noise. I couldn't hear...

I closed my eyes and listened.

The voice.

The deep voice coming from the podium. It wasn't the arbiter, and Legir spoke using telepathy. Iuo and Seps kept shouting, so who was talking so calmly and rationally?

"That is Prince Xelan, and he is my quarry."

The arbiter squeezed out with a nervous tremor in his voice, "Of course, Officer Tumu."

My eyes snapped open, and I broke my bonds—Flying away half a second before Kombuchi dumped a vat's worth of acid on me. Once finished, he glared up at me with hatred in his eyes until...

"Stop! Kombuchi. We made a terrible mistake." The arbiter sounded properly scolded and shamed.

The Caprent who still looked like he wanted to eat me shouted up at me, "Who are you, Icarus, so like Nox?"

Not meaning any threat or malice, I hovered above him. I understood him, and let that into my voice. "I am his brother, and we both want to exact justice from the King of Cinder. For my daughter and the planet of Earth."

Kombuchi narrowed his eyes at me, but seemed to take my word for it. "Let us meet this Officer. I promise not to bite."

Without hesitation, I flew back to the stand and met the Caprent's eyes.

He eventually stopped glaring at me with suspicion before muttering, "I knew you looked too pretty to be your brother."

I laughed. Elden, it was such a surprise to laugh right then, but the graciousness between us left me in a better mood. "You have good eyes."

Kombuchi laughed and patted me on the back.

Like that, we became friends.

Preteen you is grinning at me across the coffee table. You even shake your head incredulously before saying, "It's like me and the tiger. We can make friends with anything."

I shrug, the picture of humility.

Charisma is a rare gift. Another one you clearly got from me.

Your laughter is pure serotonin.

In my study, Tumu raised both of his drinks, one nectar and one lobster juice. Now I know why Tritans rarely eat in front of others. The old Primary said, "It's my turn to shine. Fellas, try to remember I'm taken."

Lamassau tsked and rolled his eyes, muttering, "The next five pages in this volume are all you flirting with our imperial majesty."

Sagan spat out her drink, laughing.

Korac cleaned her up, shaking his head but secretly smirking the entire time.

Tumu pointed a glass at Tameka. "Forgive me, peaches. I was wilder in those days."

"Oh, I've seen you in action. Yesterday, in fact." Tameka put him to shame before raking her gaze down me, shirtless in my pirate frock. "But I can't say that I blame you."

There was so much heat to the look Tameka gave me. I had to clear my throat before suggesting, "How about a break?"

ENTRY TEN

MY ULTIMATE WEAKNESS

CAEDES AND PEHTON BABYSAT PAX WHILE I DRAGGED TAMEKA INTO A ROOM I'D FORGOTTEN EXISTED AND SOUGHT REFUGE IN HER WARMTH. I knew what awaited me when we returned, and I loathed it. So much so that I kept us locked in there for over an hour.

With Tameka was better. She was my shelter.

Eventually, my shelter dragged me back to the study, where I noticed Sagan wore Korac's button-down over her transparent dress. Some honeymoon. I should apologize to her for stealing their reception.

As if sensing my thoughts, Sagan caught my eye from the loveseat, and her smile radiated love, comfort, and happiness.

I tried my best to return in kind.

I could do this.

"Let's wrap up L. Capra before moving on. Does anyone have any questions?"

All hands went up. Except Bethany. She'd returned to my study, hugging her knees and staring straight at me with only an occasional blink. Her expression was eerily similar to T.A.O.'s, but I knew my fae Progeny chased the cosmos. What did Bethany chase?

I called on Karter first.

Glowing in her grandmotherly duties, she asked, "How does Celindria tie into L. Capra?"

This was expected. "Kombuchi asked about my daughter and what Nox did to her. I told him an abbreviation of events and let her name slip. I'll never forget his face."

Kombuchi's mouth hung open, and his eyes went wide. "*The* Celindria? My friend, you keep interesting company."

Baffled, I pressed, "Why? How do you know her?"

Bewildered, Kombuchi said, "All Caprents know her. Celindria cured us of a reproductive malady caused by a radioactive mineral the Primary asked us to mine in exchange for our nacres."

"What was your opinion of her?"

Kombuchi gave a little shrug, as if making an allowance for something. "A scientist through and through. Clinical, but Celindria's work saved us, so we revere her as kind. We created an annual festival in her honor. She recently joined us for it. Is that why you came here?"

Something wasn't adding up.

Primary.

Celindria.

Gas. Mineral.

I'd gone too long without answering his question and finally offered, "I seek resolution."

Kombuchi bowed with his head, saying, "A worthy endeavor. I wish you luck on your journey. Thailea is no easy place to traverse. Beware of Inanis."

"No shit," Korac muttered.

Pehton agreed, "I'm glad that won't ever happen again."

For the first time since they'd arrived in my study, Torch and Aria contributed, providing a simultaneous whistle.

I nodded. "I understand. There are so many mysteries still unsolved. For instance, recall the conduit into L. Capra was a plummeting trap? Tumu, do you want to share how you and Rem accessed it since Tritans can't fly?"

Tumu shrugged before answering, "We had Icari or drones fly us down. It was too deep for us to enter at thirty-five feet, and before Sagan split Gait in two, conduits couldn't stretch larger than sixty-five feet."

I confessed, "To this day, I'm uncertain how Celindria traveled there."

"None of us First Wave Progeny have wings," Devis confirmed.

Andrius muttered, "Yet."

Chris said, "I know how." All eyes fell on him. "She could manipulate shadows for travel. I can't tell you how many nights I was in the room guarding Pax when she'd manifest from darkness."

Jack turned to his girlfriend with a hand on her shoulder. "Ross, remember how she appeared in the room right as you opened the only way in?"

Ross shuddered while confessing, "I still dream about it."

Bones chuffed. "Nightmare fuel."

I let them discuss it before changing the subject. "Who's next?" I called on Kyle for some Elden-forsaken reason.

"What was Legir saying to the arbiter?"

All right. That was a good question. I'd give him that much. "This was how I first became an ally with Legir. He was letting the arbiter know I could break my bonds at anytime and fly away. It didn't sit right with him. He also mentioned I wasn't the same proportions as Nox. After which, I talked to him in depth about his sons. Apparently, Celindria had recently visited Yu and asked Legir for specimens. He'd denied her, of course. At least in this one instance, there was no complaint about her demeanor. I think she was having a good day when she met with our friends on Yu."

Lamassau raised his hand, and I regretted calling on him as he asked, "Did you also sleep with Legir?"

Fortunately, Tameka laughed this time.

I shook my head, refusing to answer. Let them speculate. Instead, I snapped my fingers and asked, "Did I mention X and R were there?"

The Shadow blinked or shook their heads.

With a gesture toward Tumu, Yito, and Lamassau, I asked, "Did you know Umbra stole an entire generation of Lukemore females for Remorse's breeding program? It nearly left them unable to reproduce."

They looked clueless. Tumu said, "Remorse committed so many misdeeds, it was hard to keep track. I think I was investigating Gait's children when this could've occurred."

Korac admitted, "I knew nothing of this."

I elaborated, "No. You and Nox were too young when this happened. That aside, I met X and R at this trial. The Caprents invited them to witness Nox's execution."

The next person I called on was Tameka. She gave me kind, apprehensive eyes as she asked, "What was your position on Celindria at this point in time?"

I took her hand and kissed it. Such a good question, which I slightly skirted. "Although she'd done some good, the galactic leaders were understandably concerned. Tumu, what happened next?"

The old Primary leaned forward, placed his elbows on his knees, and steepled his fingers to his chin. "I was there to detain Xelan for Celindria's meddling and take him back to Enki for interrogation. Her trajectory was drawing a decent amount of attention, but now, I believe it was a ploy to distract me from Razor's Inanis trail."

Lamassau muttered, "It wouldn't be so distracting if you'd quit looking at Xelan's royal ass."

Korac chuckled, hidden behind his hand.

I ignored them and pushed, "What did you tell me, Tumu?"

With his voids on me the entire time, Tumu said, "Across the Vast Collective I have followed you and judging by eyewitness accounts, I thought you would be taller. But no worries, Traitor Prince. I prefer my men short."

Lamassau scoffed.

Sagan and Tameka shared the same grin.

With a toast of his cheesecake plate, Bones repeated, "Messy!"

Pehton asked on the end of a snicker, "But what were your first impressions of Tumu?"

This was no ordinary Tritan. Officer Tumu was a Primary. It wasn't his compression orb which gave him away, although I recalled as much from the Tritan Umbra had referred to as "Primary." It was in Tumu's posture. He was ancient and out of his element. Here was a man whose beliefs once carried the weight of a civilization now reduced to arresting galactic fugitives.

Tumu slouched with a heavy burden on his shoulders. We'd get along just fine.

I grinned at him. "Take me to your leader, *Officer* Tumu."

Iuo balked.

Seps glanced between us, calculating the effect for his people.

Tumu winked.

It was the second time I'd been handcuffed in as many hours, but this time, the cuffs were made of nacre glass.

When Tumu linked my wrists through them, he assured, "I promise to remain professional while you are in such a compromising position. Contradictory to your explicit opinion on Tritan affairs, you can trust me to be honorable. Until the cuffs are off." He turned to Iuo. "I require you and your Monarch 3 friend to witness the arraignment."

"Am I to be indicted? And here I thought we would become good friends." I let all the humor sparkle in my eyes. "Come now, the last thing you want from me is *submission*."

In my study, Lamassau toasted himself. "You heard him right, folks. I'm the top."

Abashed, Tumu hid behind a long drink of lobster juice.

In the story, Tumu was less chastened as he said, "Friend, we both know you would never give me what I want. Lucky for you, I like the chase. Now come on."

An entourage of drones escorted us to Enki, where Lance and a more wizened Tritan named Wiw awaited us.

"You paused again, superman."

While I told the story, Tameka was staring at me with the most bright, mischievous grin on her face. One I'd seen many times on our son's face.

I know I've mentioned it before, but I am so lucky.

"Ask."

Tameka vibrated with excitement as she asked, "Is this it?" She peered over at Tumu. "The story you told me about on Iron Hope?"

Pax cheered, while Tumu said, "Nothing gets past you, Peaches."

For the formal citation of reacquiring materials to outfit an army of Progeny in partnership with my First Progeny, the Tribunal snatched Lucas out of The Brethren and Triss from Gait as witnesses. Iuo recorded the history while Seps represented my testimony.

The proceedings were boring. Lucas and Triss both explained I was trying to stop Celindria. Seps and Iuo confirmed it. Tumu looked convinced, but Eminents Lance and Wiw needed to consult a higher authority.

We now know this was Imminent stalling to let Celindria reach her next destination—I was catching up faster than she'd expected.

Either way, Tumu escorted me to Primary Rem's sanctum, where I'd await ultimate judgment. On the way there, Tumu and I were alone, so I asked, "Where is *your* sanctum?"

Tumu's voids widened slightly in surprise. He muttered something about having a thing for geniuses—

In my study, Lam toasted himself once more.

—I took it as a compliment and preened the rest of our silent journey through the maze of conduits.

Why did I preen? Why was I beaming with so much elated enthusiasm when I was facing a potential lifelong confinement on Gait?

My cuffs were undone. I discovered this fact midway through my arraignment, and I worked hard to keep them looking secure.

To this day, I still don't know how it happened. I don't believe in divine intervention, but I think Elden was watching over me. I was grateful as Tumu set me in front of a sixty-five foot Tritan surrounded by a cascade of black fire. The sanctums remain some of the most beautiful structures in my recollection. This one was no exception.

Primary Rem waved Tumu off. "Your presence is not required for this interview, *Officer* Tumu. I will summon you to fetch the Traitor Prince once our business is finished here."

I winced and let Tumu see it. Let him see I was a friend as he left the space. All the while, my eyes kept flicking back to the fire. I desperately wanted a sample of it.

"Touching it would change your world, son. Perhaps not for the better."

Son.

In my study, Korac humphed at the word. As he'd mentioned earlier, scholars still puzzle over Razor's exact motivations for turning on Remorse. This term of affection meant more between the Pain Curator and the villainous Primary. Or did it ever matter as much to Remorse as it did to the Aegis he'd required for so much?

Back to the story.

I stepped over to where the fire falls pooled around Primary Rem's feet, surrounded by columns. It was tricky to maintain my ruse while itching to examine the phenomenon. I asked, "Where does it come from?"

"A conduit of its own making." Primary Rem shifted to keep his eyes on me from such a great height. He asked, "What can you glean from it?" There was something… It wasn't assessing—

What was in his voice? Adoration?

Ignoring it, I answered, "If this—"

"Cascading Light."

"—Is naturally occurring, then the conduits are spatial folds or rifts determined by the flames' path."

I could hear the smile in his voice without looking all the way up to see his lipless face. Primary Rem glowed with pride as he said, "Yes. Most cannot see it. Conduits are the natural result of the Probability Matrix. Paths for instances seeking the optimum thread. We want you to study it, as well as continue your research here on Enki. Rather than serve your sentence on Gait." He compressed to seven-feet tall and faced me. "Imagine it. All the resources of Enki at your disposal. The races—the worlds—you could save. The Icari and Cinder from your own brother."

Preteen you scoots to the edge of your seat, enraptured as you ask, "Were you tempted?"

I can't explain it. Something about the Probability Matrix repulses me. With every mention of it, I want to get as far away as possible. It's unnatural. Everything else… Well, of course I was tempted. But I knew the truth of what they wanted from me.

Little you asks with a cute tilt of your head, "What?"

For the same reason any government kidnaps an innovative scientist. Weapon design.

Still pretending to be confined, I feigned contemplation before saying, "I only want to find my daughter and save my race. In peace and solitude."

Too much knowledge flickered in Primary Rem's voids, along with an emotion close to disappointment. He said, "Very well. Convert Celindria into an ally, or bring her to face the Tribunal. If not, you'll face it in her place. She makes for Thailea."

I nodded with gratitude and relief until…

"After you spend some time reflecting on my offer," the Primary added. "I will leave you in my sanctum here, with the gateway to the Probability Matrix at hand. Consider wisely, son. We could use someone of your intellect and imagination."

In my study, Lamassau scoffed. "He left you alone?"

Sagan, a little in her cups and draped across her husband's legs, snickered. "Big mistake."

I grinned at her and continued, "As we all know by now, one entrance to the Pantheon was in Remorse's sanctum. In a manic frenzy, I explored as much of the continent as I could afford to do with the short time left to me. I drank deep from the well of history and science—Learning everything I know of the Tritans."

Tameka asked, barely containing the giggles, "But why were you naked?"

"Oh, yes. That."

Korac barked out a laugh. It was a rich sound which warmed me to the bone.

With permission from Tumu, I said, "I was pale enough to blend into the white scenery of the Pantheon. The Overseers couldn't detect me without my clothes. It was the last time I'd seen this coat until Tumu returned it to me."

"We could see you the entire time." Tumu burst my bubble and left me gaping incredulously as he continued. "Primary Rem must have programmed them not to attack you—Seriously? 'Pale enough to blend in?!' How does that even explain your hair?!"

"I…" I closed my mouth.

Lamassau pointed and laughed hard enough to hurt his ribs.

Korac frowned. "But if Tumu found your coat, where did you get that atrocity from in the first place?"

Iuo snorted into his drink, muttering, "It was a prop."

Everyone looked at him until Bones cried out, "Wait a damn minute!"

Twenty-One asked, "Do you have a film, imperial majesty?"

Tameka's eyes grew wide and sparkled, both with humor and curiosity.

"Well do you, Superman?"

A wink is my only answer.

<hr>

I think Remorse wanted me to find the Pantheon. I'll never understand Imminent, not fully. Lucas assured me it's impossible to unravel it all without touching Cascading Light.

Little you snores inside your pillow fort while Preteen you sits across from me with attitude written all over your posture. No one messes with this twelve-year-old girl. It's enough to make me smile.

"Try not to worry about Imminent. They're gone and what remains will bite the same dust."

You win. How could I not smile at that? I'll need it, too. Do you have a question for me before I move on, Rayne?

You ask the most precocious question. "What did you steal from L. Capra, Cap'n?"

Your question makes me grin.

They inspired me to bury the stronghold using the same technology Razor had used to carve out the Queen's Fare. And a few artifacts on display. Which you can come and see when you're ready.

"I hope to, Superman. Carry on."

With all the anxiety, I'd needed a shower to help me with the tension.

Alone.

It sounded awful, but my head space wouldn't make for the best company. Tameka was beautifully understanding. With my pirate days behind me, I slipped my frock into the closet and hopped into a clean pair of pajamas, certain the rest of the Shadow was doing the same. A glimpse of myself in the mirror left me staring.

No lines. No gray hairs. Nothing to denote the lives I'd lived. The damage I'd taken. Caused. Repaired.

I'd never felt so old.

Our bedroom was in a wing of the stronghold with Pax's and some other amenities for the imperial suites. With a sigh, I left the bedroom for a sitting room, where I found a visitor.

"Tameka let me in," Korac explained. He was spread across the chaise, reading one of my first editions. As I entered, he licked his fingers and turned a page. "You got a minute, your imperial majesty?"

I wanted to groan, but that would admit defeat. Instead, I folded my arms and leaned in the doorjamb. Yes, I made certain my unbuttoned pajama top gaped. "What do you want, General?"

Korac glanced up, licked his fingers, and turned another page with a patronizing bob of his head. "So, out in the study it's 'my general,' but here in private…"

"Here, in my private quarters, I expect you to answer your Co-Emperor's demands."

That.

Smirk.

"Careful." Korac folded the corner of a page, marking it, before closing the book and leveling his glittering eyes at me. "You're starting to sound like Nox."

That stung.

With a sigh, Korac stood and crossed the space, saying, "It's a low blow, I know, but you two are more similar than you think. Still…" He majestically folded to his knees, put his fist to his chest, and gazed up at me with white eyes I'd seen in this position before. Smirking, he asked, "Can you forgive me?"

I swept by him, not willing to fall into this trap. Recovering the book, I'd found the crease in the folded page was permanent. Tired, I repeated, "What do you want, Korac?"

When he chuckled behind me, I nearly threw the book at his head. Again, that would mean I'd conceded the game to him, and I refused to lose. So imagine my irritation, when I turned and found him leaning in the doorway with his arms folded as if schooling me on how to do it properly. I could never pull off the 'bad boy' image.

Korac said, "Sagan has kept me from saying anything in the study, so I'll tell you here in private. You mishandled the situation with Celindria from the start, and I know you. I know you are fully aware of your shortcomings." He gave a little shrug, admitting, "I want to understand better. Celindria told you she'd felt nothing, so you pitied her and shouldered that responsibility. But then you didn't contain her, knowing she was missing a conscience—"

"And the other Progeny paid for it—"

"All of Cinder paid for it. Some of humanity, too." Korac was never this animated outside of the bedroom. Even with his arms crossed, frustration signaled in the movement of his hands and the tightness of his brows. "I'm not even including the fallout. Nox and I took full responsibility for our cruel invasion strategies. But Xelan…"

Now Korac had my attention. He *never* used my name like that. My General asked, "Did you ever wonder why Celindria kept insisting she wanted emotions when she readily referred to them as a weakness—"

"To feel!"

I'd lost.

The frustration and exhaustion overtook me, and some part of me was protective of what I'd borne in Celindria. "Her biology allowed for a window into a world of warmth and pain, but forgot to provide a door into it. She knew what emotions were like enough to crave more of the sensations and fulfillment. Dopamine, serotonin—All the endorphins. The relief after a good laugh or the cleansing purity of a good cry—Celindria wants it all."

A hush fell between us.

No.

What had I said?

The almost invisible narrowing of Korac's eyes told me I'd slipped. He disguised it by looking me over and asking, "When was the last time you'd slept?"

I couldn't answer his question. I can't—I don't...

"Shh...I know, superman." You lean forward and boop your forehead to mine. "You don't have to say. I know you haven't slept since before Ishkur."

How did you... But of course, you'd know. You're in here with me.

"I'm always with you." I kiss your forehead, and you smile at me as you relax back on the couch. You ask, "What happened with Korac?"

I brushed by my General to return to my study. Behind me, he called, "You never learned to manage it. Not completely." It wasn't a question, and therefore, did not require my answer. Let him have his assumptions. I had better things to do.

The Shadow had converted my study into a pajama party since the last story had taken us into the evening. It settled my nerves to see everyone I loved so comfortable, and it reinvigorated me for this underhanded entry. Without preamble, I went straight into the story.

Tumu released me into Triss' custody. She escorted me, Lucas, Iuo, and Seps back to Mon3. Razor was magnanimous enough to let me sleep in his Queen's Fare apartments below ground. The place housed several rooms. One I glimpsed was painted the same violet as a pair of eyes I hadn't seen in a thousand years. The bed inside was a single, and the room was decorated in trinkets from across the Vast Collective.

T.a.o.

How could my Progeny ever be far from my mind? Wouldn't it make for a lovely story if my afflicted child had spent the last millennia here, with Razor in safety as opposed to the fate she'd likely met?

Stretching the kinks of sleep from my neck, I endeavored to ask Razor about whose room it was. Later. Triss returned to the Lyriks in the Emporium back on Gait. While I'd been considering my Progeny, I wondered if Triss and Razor had ever raised children of their own, as old as they both were.

When the Pain Curator found me trying to sort out some kind of practical clothing from a room he'd dedicated to clothes—A combat suit, shirt, normal pants, anything—I asked, "Are you a father, Razor?"

I think I made him snort as he shooed me away from the door. He said, "No. I am not interested in extending my lineage." He handed me a suit meant for a technician.

Without thinking, I changed in front of Razor, asking, "Does Triss not want children—"

I stopped.

Razor was peering at me with his bizarre eyes, assessing.

"Forgive me. Was I being too inquisitive?" I finished dressing and found some way to pull my hair back. I was ready for the next leg of my journey to stop Celindria.

"Xelan, how long have you been under my employment?" Razor asked, taking a seat on the bed.

I sat down on the edge with him, quirking a brow at

his line of questioning. "A decade, now. Most of it in the Emporium. Why?"

The Pain Curator… blushed. His cheeks went yellow. Thailean yellow. He said, "Your personal questions prompt me to ask, why do you rarely take partners? Keep in mind I have noticed your methodical fetish for different races, but that is not the same as a relationship."

Razor's coloring distracted me from his questions. I was burning with curiosity. What *was* Razor? Some form of Mystic? Or something older? Could he truly be Korac's brother—

The Pain Curator brushed my hair from my face, bringing me back around. He said, "There is so much tension in you. Too much pressure boiling under that altruistic surface. You may not think you deserve release, but I am happy to change your mind."

I only realized I'd leaned toward Razor because his lips crooked into a smirk.

Searching my eyes, he said, "Young Prince, when you return from your next errand on Reipon, we can invite Triss and cross off two more races on your list. But I'm afraid if I kiss you right now, we would neglect my siren, and I could never live with myself if I lost her."

Korac said from the doorway, "I'm so glad I have arrived in time for this."

"Were you trying to make Korac aware of how similar he is to Razor?" you ask with a little crinkle in your forehead, trying to understand.

I can only shrug.
Sometimes adults are just petty. I wanted Korac to feel how uncomfortable he'd made me.

In truth, the entire room looked uncomfortable. Except T.A.O. She was smiling.
And Echo whistled happily in her bassinet.

Tameka scratched my back. I wasn't expecting the comfort and poured my appreciation into my eyes as I leaned down and kissed her cheek—

"It's okay. You can still hold my hand," Pax muttered to Bethany.

Korac, Matt, Lucy, Ross, and Kyle peered at them, checking. The quiet girl was seeking comfort from my son. With a nod, she took Pax's hand once more.

Damn me for letting my spiteful vendetta hurt someone unintended.

You level your eyes at me. "Hurting others because your spite is mightier than you expected? That sounds like Nox."

I say nothing because we both know you're right.

Sagan was supportive, as always. "I understand you, Wingmaster. How about you get us to Thailea? It's the only planet I haven't visited, and I'm dying to hear about the rainbow rings."

Thailea.
The source of so much...
The source of everything.

FORTUNATELY, RAZOR REQUIRED ANOTHER CONVENIENT ERRAND ON THAILEA. He came to me the morning after... our one and only night together. He said, "Cascading Light. Have you seen it before?"

The Pain Curator had caught me after a shower—A habit of his, I'd noticed. I was trying my best to keep up with self care like Colita, Lucas, and Merit taught me. While I wrung my hair out in a towel, I answered, "Yes. In Primary Rem's sanctum." I couldn't hide my shudder.

The Pain Curator absorbed it like oxygen into blood as he said, "While you and your crew are out there, I want you to gather Cascading Light for me using these devices." He pointed to several glass boxes—almost like tiny caskets—beside the bed. "Do you think you can manage?"

I left him in the bathroom to study a box, prepared to disassemble it to satiate my curiosity. How did this contain a fire which didn't burn? How could I capture a flame without touching it? Could I steal one for myself—

"Xelan."

Razor said my name as if he'd been calling me for a while.

I glanced at Triss, still asleep on the bed, tangled in the sheets, and shushed Razor with a finger to my lips. With a wary smile, I whispered, "Forgive me. Of course we can manage. How will we find it?"

A deep chuckle resonated in Razor's chest. "On Thailea, finding Cascading Light will not pose a problem."

I stopped telling the story because T.A.O. crossed the room to stand in front of me. Her Atramentous eyes searched mine frantically. Despite my initial uncertainty, I stayed still and let her evaluate whatever she needed in me.

"Father, secrets will unmake you."

I was frozen, unwilling to breathe or flinch for fear it would lend support to her words. This Verse would expose me for the monster I am, but in *my* time.

Carefully, I cupped T.A.O.'s cheek. With everything in me, I tried to tell her without words, *'Please. Not yet.'*

In my periphery, Tameka looked between us with open curiosity, not accusation or suspicion. My relief almost rushed out with a sigh. Especially as T.A.O. appeared to receive the message. Instead of giving away my secret, she took my hand.

I followed the tiniest Progeny to the middle of the pallet pile and sat where she'd insisted. The Shadow surrounded me in a dizzying circle of familiar faces, filled with love, respect, and warmth.

And I'd lied to all of them.

You reach across the coffee table and take my hand. "You'll tell them when it's time. Try not to worry about Celindria."

I feel the need to justify myself to you. To tell you that I've kept careful tabs on Celindria all this time. The reports leave me optimistic about increased emotional activity. I noticed leaks in our supplies for Iona projects from the onset. For every shipment of materials stolen, an orphanage appeared on Pil. Or a new research hospital on Reipon. All of them are kitted out with advanced technology and comfort. Witnesses reported an ethereal beauty in gold and white on the scene. I think Devis' memory did some good for her. But there are other rumors...

"Celindria is recruiting." You say it with so much conviction as if you know—Not suspected as I did, but like you'd seen it in person.

I lift your hand to stare at the lines of your palm, seeking the right path in them.

I've failed. Again. This time I've failed the Shadow.

"Put that from your mind. Tell me about Thailea. Before I killed Nox, Kyle downloaded Celindria's memories and showed them to me. They were static-y. We understand now that's because of Cascading Light, but I glimpsed something about her from Thailea. What happened there? And don't forget Sagan's description request."

I would never let Sagan down.

Enki's conduit into Thailea put us in a snowstorm, six meters from the base of a

MILE-WIDE CONICAL MOUNTAIN COATED COMPLETELY IN WHITE. The pristine frost glittered in the starlight, reflecting the sheen in a ghostly halo. It was beautiful, but not as impressive as the tornado encasing it. Fire swirled in a black funnel on a wind of its own making, smelling of—I could only describe it as the strike of steel against steel. Harnessed potential. Beyond it, in the sky, the planetary rings challenged the diamonds for the most remarkable view with a diagonal arc across all that velvet mystery. A rainbow reaching out to meet the cosmos which answered in branches of lightning behind the flames.

All across the horizon, the snowy scenery repeated.

We stared.

I don't know for how long until...

"Dear Elden," Seps breathed.

"Indeed," Lucas contributed, as he straightened his elegant clothes.

Iuo shifted into his tailed form upon entry, and his gear conformed to the transformation. After absorbing some of the initial shock, he said, "I seem unable to walk on this planet."

I tried not to study and analyze my friend despite my curiosity. Instead, I asked, "Has this happened anywhere else?"

Seps and Lucas checked the parameter as Iuo said, "Never." Then he beamed at the discovery. "This will make for an interesting entry to my records—"

"Look!" Seps pointed a meter to our right. "Another."

We followed his gaze to find another split into the Seam—Another conduit. Through it, we saw a world with green skies—

"And there!" Lucas nodded beyond it. "Another one, and it leads to Earth."

Before our eyes, the conduit to Lukemore closed, and a few meters away, another to Cinder opened in its place. All around us, conduits formed and dissolved in a breathtaking carousel.

Iuo startled me out of my reverie as he declared, "They form naturally here on Thailea. The phenomenon occurs at random."

I didn't speak up, but I knew that wasn't entirely accurate. As we'd watched, I'd discerned a pattern. It was only visible to someone who'd seen the shape of the galaxy, and I could see the conduits were formed based on the planet's distance from Thailea in descending order. Furthest to closest.

Wait.

"Do they form like this anywhere else?" I turned and searched Iuo's black and blue eyes.

The muscular bulk of his tail let Iuo pivot and turn away from me after his eyes gave away more than he'd intended.

Seps answered from behind us, "Some say they once formed everywhere until the Ancients harnessed them for travel."

Lucas finished, "Then there was Enki, and the natural order became a construct of control."

Para stopped reading volume one thousand, nine hundred and two to glance over at Lucas, along with everyone else in the room. What they found surprised them. The golden-eyed Icarus was looking at Tumu, and Andrew was doing the same. They were waiting.

Tumu let Lamassau's hand go so he could gesture at Korac as he said, "The Exalted would know this story better, but I see our resident bad boy Atheneum is wasted."

Korac chuckled against Sagan's neck, purring secrets to her while ignoring the proceedings.

I winced.

Preteen you goes right for the same question I was asking myself, "Do you think you drove Korac to drink?"

It's his honeymoon, and he's a grown man. But yes. I'm worried I'd given him sorrows worth drowning.

The smile you give reminds me of an ocean sunset. "You two will move past it. I know you. I'll bet you two strawberry milkshakes that you make up before the end of your Verse."

I tap my temple.

That's a hell of a bet when I already know how it ends, but I'll take it.

Despite Korac's attempts to distract her, Sagan asked, "So Cascading Light creates the conduits to influence the paths in the Probability Matrix?" She was practically bouncing with excitement from the epiphany. "We know from what the Exalted has told us that Cascading Light first occurred when they entered our reality. When the Aegis first set foot on what became Thailea. Does that mean..."

I beamed at Sagan, so proud she'd made the connection. Still, I held up a finger to stave her train of thought. "We're getting there." No matter how much her realization impressed me, my smile faded with the recollection of it all as Para continued.

A few feet from the conduit, a cave heralded us. I pointed at it and stated the obvious. "I suppose we should go inside."

Seps glared at the rock opening in the snowy landscape. "This is nothing like my home."

"Cheer up, friend. It will feel like a tree once we have reached the cavern," Lucas promised.

Iuo nodded in agreement. "Razor said we should find what we need in the 'Oblivion Cathedral.' Like everything else from our cryptic benefactor, he promised we would know it on sight."

Funny, but as all three of them assured each other the cave was the right way to go, neither one of them took a step toward it. There was something about Thailea. I could only describe the sensation as feeling 'found,' the opposite of feeling lost.

I went first, and the three men followed. Each of us carried a box into the cave. It was pitch black until Iuo raised a glowing baton with a nod of his head.

How did the baton work? Was it phosphorescent? Organic or artificial—

"May I have one of those, Iuo?" I couldn't resist. He handed one over, which I pocketed, not intending to activate it until I'd returned to a lab. "Thank you."

I glimpsed a look on Lucas' face. He definitely knew what I was thinking. It made me smile as we—

Fell.

Into a sudden and unexpected ravine.

Next time, I'd let the Lamia with the light wand lead the group.

My sudden yelp wasn't dignified, but I compensated for it with the quick release of my wings. "Careful!" I called, as if the others clearly wouldn't learn from my mistake.

Seps and Lucas gazed at me in the center of an abyss. The drone scolded me, "Tread carefully. My Queen would castigate me if I let you die."

Lucas held his hand out for me. "Yes. The Progeny need you back on Earth once all this Celindria business is concluded, dear Prince."

The endearment made me wince as we clasped wrists. Only Korac had ever called me that.

Lucas caught it and said, "Forgive me, your highness." He pulled me back to the ledge, and we shared a friendly pat on the shoulder.

"If Celindria is here, we must have alerted her to our presence by now," Iuo warned.

It was a good point.

I exhaled and nodded toward the path leading deeper into the mountain. "We keep moving."

The ledge hugged the hewned ice rock which formed the cave. It was smooth, not broken or loose. Instead, it looked almost hammered into this condition—

"Shit," Iuo cried.

—And it was slippery.

I helped him straighten after his tail nearly slid off into the nothing again. "I got you."

Lucas glanced back at Seps, who was counting on his fingers.

"What is it?" I asked.

Seps said, "Four times now you have said those exact words."

Iuo claimed, "And I still find it reassuring."

Lucas smiled at me. "Perhaps the Traitor Prince has a catch phrase."

But Seps stopped smiling. Stopped looking at us. He was gaping beyond us into where the next turn led. The Mon3 drone gasped, "In all of Eternity's creation, I have never seen such a sight."

We all turned and...

The Oblivion Cathedral.

"Superman?"

Yes?

Preteen you tilts your head to the side with concern in your eyes as you say, "You've paused. Can you describe to me what you saw?"

No.

You let out a little incredulous laugh. "No?"

No. I don't remember it. No one does. Except maybe...

In my study, I asked, "Lucas, can you recall it? Do you have some advantage as someone who has touched Cascading Light?"

The entire room focused their attention on my enigmatic friend yet again.

Sagan entreated, "Pretty please say 'yes.'"

With a chuckle, Lucas met all of our gazes before shaking his head. He said, "No nacre can retain it, and I'm afraid anyone without a nacre would simply perish at the sight of it."

Iuo waved for everyone to look his way and said, "But I remember the eye of a tornado went through it—A tight spout of Cascading Light. I remembered who was staring into it as we arrived."

"CELINDRIA!" I called out to where she stood on a higher ledge, of which I couldn't recall the color or material. Not ice nor stone, but only oblivion occupies my memory of it. Her white gown billowed around her as she gazed into the flames. Again, I shouted, "Celindria, what are you doing?!"

"Xelan, the vacuum is stealing your voice," Lucas explained before taking my container. "Go to her. We will collect the flames for Razor."

I glanced at Iuo and Seps, and both nodded for me to go. Without thinking, I pounded a fist to my chest where it felt warm from their kindness. "Thank you and be careful." Steadying my hands, I went to her, alighting behind her.

With her back to me, Celindria said, "I could hear your heartbeat when you arrived on the planet, father. For giving me life, I will grant you one warning. Do not follow where I go. It will break your heart."

I was ready to beg. "Please stay. I have seen your work on L. Capra. We can do more good in this world and undo the ugly done by the Tritans and Nox."

Celindria turned and faced me. Tears poured from her eyes. Crimson, cobalt, and citrine. Rivers of blood rained down her face. She confessed, "I can feel what you feel. This close to the source. Here, where the Ancients first came into our world and pierced this mountain we will never remember, I can feel."

Celindria was right.

It did break my heart.

I choked on the tears as I cried, "Celindria, please. I know you want to feel, but Cascading Light could only fracture you more. By giving you a glimpse into Probabilities where you experienced emotions, yet never able to do it yourself—It will shatter you." I reached my hand out to her. "Please."

Through the blood on her face, Celindria smirked. "You always say this, father. Never once have you understood." She took a step back with violence in her unhinged smile.

I lowered my hand. With tears blurring my vision, I asked, "Where did I go wrong with you?"

With the spout of Cascading Light behind her, Celindria backed another step until a breath kept her from falling off the ledge. "You cannot see the worlds as they could be. Everything I do cascades into reality. We must break events and people to find where we are meant to be."

After a hard swallow, accepting the finality of this moment, I offered one last warning, "If you do this…you will never recover your humanity. Your sanity."

"I will be Imminent."

Celindria fell back into the flames.

Devis asked first, "What happened?"

Para stared at the page without reading it.

Bones climbed up from his pallet and crossed the room to read over her shoulder. "Is everything okay—Oh."

I couldn't imagine speaking just then. I struggled to form the words to ask, "Andrew, Pehton, Sagan, Bones, and Pax?"

They all straightened and gave me their attention.

Korac sobered up, if he was ever truly drunk, and stared right into me. He knew I was upset.

"Do you remember when Remorse was killing Celindria? How she cried for help?" When they nodded, I continued, "I'd felt it before. The pulse of every reality surrounding me at once, and her screams rippling across the Probability Matrix—It's her asking for help. And I—"

Collapsed to my knees in front of everyone.

Have you ever heard thirty-seven people getting up all at once and rushing to you?

You shake your head.

It sounds a bit like an attack.

With your voice softened, you assure, "You know it wasn't. They were checking on you."

I know that now, but in the moment, I panicked.

As hands came from everywhere to touch me, I opened my wings for protection. They formed a cocoon around me until only one hand remained.

I hadn't slept in so long—I'd never gone this long before. My bones felt cold and heavy, and the remaining hand radiated warmth and love.

When I peeled my wings back, I expected to find Tameka or Tumu even.

Korac stood over me in black silk pajamas Tameka had loaned him from my closet. He gripped my shoulder and knelt, gazing into my eyes which must've been in Atramentous. I felt like a wild animal—tired and bruised. Starved for shelter, food, and affection.

My General chuffed. "I know. I'm not who you were expecting. Well, too bad. I'm the only one here who can see past your bullshit, your imperial majesty." While I was still stunned, he threw one of my arms around his shoulders and lifted us both to standing. "Come on. Close this chapter, and we'll get you to bed. Where you *will* sleep."

My throat was dry, and I had to lick my lips to say, "Iuo and Lucas, can you cover the storm and the boxes, please?"

Iuo saluted with a fist to his chest. "Yes, sir."

Lucas gave a nod before taking to the front of the room with the Lamian Prince. "We'd just finish gathering the flames for Razor when the cataclysm erupted into a hurricane of snow, which still dominates the planet to this day—Yes, Sagan?"

"Did I guess right? The conduits occur wildly on Thailea because it's the source?"

Iuo sounded pleased to say, "You were completely accurate. Now, Thailea is nearly impossible to traverse. One unique aspect of the storm is the eye. Within, it holds a solitary day of spring for wherever it lingers."

Lucas continued on with the story. "We returned to the Emporium with only three boxes."

Andrew asked, "What happened to the fourth?"

Lucas and Iuo both turned and looked behind them at the single black flame in my fireplace while Lucas explained, "I told Razor it was destroyed in the storm, but who knows if he believed me?"

All the while, Korac carried me out of the study and into the synchronous steps of the ravine. Tameka followed us with Pax in hand.

It's odd. I didn't feel any shame in this.

You blink at me before asking, "Mister, why should you feel ashamed?"

I shrug.
I don't know. Maybe because I needed my ex-lover to carry me to bed after depriving myself of sleep for months?

Your laughter helps heal some of the ache of reopening the wounds from Thailea. The mischievous smirk which followed nearly had me laughing. "Did he give you a kiss goodnight?"

Now you sound like Sagan. You already know the answer, anyway.

Korac threw me onto the bed, big enough to make Razor proud, and my General sat on the edge with his back to me. Tameka and Pax, who'd been lingering in the doorway, discretely disappeared. I had to admit, the cool sheets, smelling of a fresh wash, soothed my overall agitation. Enough so that I broke the silence first.

"Thank you, Korac."

He let out an incredulous laugh before saying, "Your voice sounds like shit. How many weeks has it been?"

I didn't answer. Twenty-eight simply sounded too high.

After a sigh, Korac ran a hand through his hair. "You have a son and mate, now, your majesty. You need to take better care of yourself for their sake. And if you can't, should you really be running this empire?"

While Korac's admonishment was true and gentle, I couldn't answer his stinging questions. There wasn't an answer to give. I tried—Elden knows I try to be a good man. This Verse was a test of it. Bare my conscience and all its dirty secrets to everyone—

Am I fit?

I sat up in bed—

"Lay your ass back down before I knock you unconscious for your own good." Korac stood and leaned on the end post, facing me. He'd invented the 'bad boy' stance. "Do you know why I continue to help you after the stunt you pulled?"

With a swallow, I shook my head.

Korac averted his gaze while saying, "I couldn't help but think Razor would love us arguing over which brother should have an Iona named after him. He'd be tickled pink I'd let your impressions of him get so far under my skin that it cuts like fiberglass." A small smirk quirked his lips. "Don't you think?"

I let the idea live in my head for a minute and smiled. "Oh, yes. Delight is the only word to use. He'd consider himself the host to our game-show. I'll let you have that much."

Korac said, "Before I let you go to sleep, I wanted to say that Nox wouldn't want us fighting at all. And I think I like how that sits with me better."

It was a simple truth for which I couldn't argue. With a nod, I conceded.

Korac gave me a mock-salute. "Sweet dreams, your majesty." Then he left the room.

When Tameka didn't come into the room, I chose not to sleep. How could I? I was left alone with Thailea.

I never told the Shadow how I was before they met me. Even now, I dread them learning the truth. Could you accept how weak I was, Rayne? Could you still think of me as your 'Superman' once you realize I was never a hero?

You leave the couch to sit on the coffee table inches away from me, and I can't meet your eyes. With so much conviction, you say, "I can only know the half-Icarus who saved me so many times. Who trained me to be strong and to save the Worlds. Who loved us all so much that you gave your life for us. Xelan, no matter what's in your past that has you so afraid, I will love you just the same."

Then into Enki we go.

ENTRY ELEVEN

MY BROTHER, THE VILLAIN; MYSELF, THE MONSTER

"**Let's ante up the other Verses before we proceed.**"

It was the next morning, and everyone had gotten a good night's rest.

Everyone but me. I couldn't see the point in sleep with this secret haunting me. Every time I closed my eyes, I saw Celindria in her lab with her bones protruding from bloodless wounds. Her eyes…

The emptiness preyed on my sanity.

An hour after Korac had left me, Tameka came in smelling of a fresh shower, and I couldn't let her fall asleep like that. I wanted her to dream smelling of me—of us. Even after we woke and prepared for the day, I'd asked her to wear one of my t-shirts. The smile she gave me in response was precious to me.

There we stood at the front of my study. Me in black slacks and a white button-down. Tameka in jeans and one of my black tees, with the excess tied at the small of her back.

The Shadow filed in, returning to their pallets and couches. I tried for some eye contact and a warm smile with everyone as they took their places.

Reassurance is my middle name.

Little you teases me from inside your pillow fort. "You don't have a middle name, silly."

"Oh, I don't?"
I hop on the floor and reach into the fort after you.

You squeal and giggle, burying yourself deeper in the cushions from my reach. "No! You don't have a last name either!"

I clutch my hair.
"My heart! You've wounded me."
The faint I feign is dramatic and sweeping. I deserve an award.

The little version of you emerges from the cave, whispering, "Superman?" On hands and knees, you inch closer. "Superman?"

Closer.

Closer.

I can hear the air displace where you've reached out a chubby hand to check me.
Rawr! I got you now!

I jump up and snatch you before you can run away. These squeals belong to my victory as you submit to a tickle fit. Giggles galore.

Preteen you sleeps on the couch through the commotion, resting as if you're burning through some oil which animates the both of you.

I needed this.
Back to the story where I was equating the Verses.

"At this time, Korac—"

He nodded at me from the blanket where he was spread out with Echo and Sagan. The infant was fascinated by her feet and beaming at her dad.

I was—*am*—happy for them.

"He's just delivered the news to Nox that Celindria died on Thailea and I would face the Tribunal. For *their* Verses, events sped up significantly as they moved toward Invasion Day. However, my life was much more involved during this time."

Pehton asked, "Who gets to read?"

I glanced across the room at Tumu, and the Tritan's voids met my eyes as if he'd expected the answer.

"I do," he said.

Tameka grinned at him and teased, "You're in trouble now."

"I'm never in trouble with your husband, Peaches. Well, except maybe this one time on a plane…Some of you were there for that one." He winked at Tameka before returning the jibe. "And some of you were asleep."

She pouted.

Kyle groaned. "Here we go again. We'll never hear the end of you missing that plane crash."

Andrew joined in, saying, "It's not like we haven't survived so much since then, but nope. The one plane crash—"

"Hell, I'd be happy to crash a plane for you, Tameka."

Bone's offer was so genuine that Sagan snorted into her tea.

The ribbing continued, but my eyes were on Tumu. As not to disturb the good time, I muttered so only he could hear. "Volume two thousand and twelve."

When Tumu found the page, he turned and faced the room. His deep voice boomed with the words. "'The voice in my head said not to trust the Primaries. My subconscious wasn't weary of the Eminents, even as I faced their Tribunal, but the Primaries' absences resonated badly with me.'"

The Shadow settled into their places as the reading continued. Discussions of staging a plane crash would have to wait for another time.

"Give your testimonial, Xelan, Prince of Cinder."

I liked Eminent Wiw. He emanated kindness in waves of understanding and something akin to justice. Eminent Lance stood at the podium beside him. Justice was on his mind, too, but best served cold. That Tritan was all about business.

There was a third podium. It stood empty. I very much wanted to know why.

Iuo caught my eye beside the podium. As if he'd heard my thoughts, he shook his head.

Now wasn't a good time to ask.

Lucas and Seps took up seats behind me as witnesses.

At my side, Tumu dwarfed me with his compressed height of thirteen feet. It was worse after he gestured for me to kneel with my wrists and ankles encased in nacre chains.

I went to my knees and stared up at the blue men, judging me. With the utmost sincerity, I said, "I have no testimony to give. I tried to save my race, and I failed. When I tried to save my daughter, I failed. While I appreciate the good people I met along the way, I can see no other end for me than execution because I wish not to live to see Nox ravage the Earth in his vengeance. More than that, I fear whatever it is that Enki wants with me."

Tumu shifted beside me, but I couldn't see the look on his face given our height difference while I was staring at the floor.

Behind us, I think Lucas gasped, and Seps cursed.

One other person took up space in the white stone amphitheater.

The Executive Warden of Gait.

Pehton approached the podiums. She glanced back at me with something in her garnet eyes. It wasn't pity, but an emotion in the neighborhood. With her shoulders straight and her chin high, Pehton addressed the Eminents. "There is no place for a good man on Gait, and Prince Xelan has done no real wrong."

Lance narrowed his eyes at her, but Wiw gestured, saying, "Go on, my dear."

"Before Inanis, you helped me free the children of Gait." Pehton paused and glanced back at Tumu. "Then, you were an Eminent. What did you tell me about a Prince named Xelan?"

Tumu stopped reading and met my eyes.

The room went quiet.

Into the stillness, Pehton quoted, "'No one could love their people as Prince Xelan loves the Icari.'"

Twenty-One, Bones, Karter, Para, Caedes, and Korac put a fist to their chest.

The sight moved me, and I wavered. Tameka caught me and shifted so she discretely took some of my weight. A rest. That's all I needed.

With a glance at our connection, Tumu shared, "I know now you care for any people you consider your responsibility in the same measure, and we are grateful to know you."

I couldn't hold it in. Tameka helped me cross the room, and I threw my arms around my seven-foot compressed friend.

With a grin on her pretty face, Pehton said, "I'll continue the story while you two hug it out."

"I believe this to be true, your Eminence," Pehton entreated. "Please consider another form of punishment for the wayward Prince, because he tells the truth. Nox hungers for vengeance, and I fear he will not stop with Earth. We need Xelan to combat his brother."

"Perhaps he should serve the Primaries or face exile on Earth." All the Tribunal attendees looked at Lucas, who shrugged gracefully as he continued. "I am a witness. This is true, but I serve what is best for Earth and Cinder. The Progeny could use supervision from their maker. Do you not agree?"

Wiw and Lance muttered between themselves while I exchanged a look with Tumu.

Serve Enki by spying on my Progeny in preparation for Nox's return. Or serve the whims of the Primaries.

Pehton used this quiet moment to approach my stand and held out a tiny hand. With the cuffs, our handshake proved awkward, but still I marveled out how my hand swallowed hers. She was even teenier than T.a.o.

"Hello. I meant to introduce myself while you were on Gait, but this is about as comfortable for me as the Emporium. My name is Pehton."

I offered, "Xelan. Or Traitor Prince, if you prefer. Everyone else seems to."

Tumu mumbled, "It gives you an air of danger and mystery. Accept it."

Seps leaned over the rail to poke Tumu's ribs.

The ticklish Officer spun around, whispering, "What?!"

"You took us from the Queen's Fare. What will Razor think?" Seps asked a reasonable question for an agent in his position. Drawing attention to Seps like that risked his work for F8.

Tumu mulled it over. He'd opened his mouth to say something when Lucas cut in, saying, "I will provide a fitting excuse for our benefactor."

Iuo flagged us, and we all glanced at him. He made a cutting gesture at his throat and pointed at the tablet he was recording on. He mouthed, "Stop. Talking. About. Razor—"

"We are ready with our decision, Prince of Cinder." The gentleness in Wiw's voice told me they didn't plan to execute me.

If I were them, I would've executed me.

Lance announced, "Service to the Primaries on Enki for one hundred years. After which time, you will serve the rest of your sentence in exile on Earth. No contact with anyone." He met Iuo's, Seps', Lucas', and Tumu's eyes. "We mean absolutely no one."

Alone.

I swallowed. I'd rather be dead. People to care for kept me able. Without them, I fell apart. I'd done my best when I was working with Colita and in a relationship with Korac. I was at my worst when I isolated myself to create the Progeny. This was—I—

I was hanging my head until my hair covered my face when a warm hand on my shoulder brought me back.

Tumu.

His voice came from inside my head, saying, "Keep this a secret. I will be there when you need me."

I wanted so badly to glance at his face, but stopped myself. Instead, I met Pehton's eyes. Strange. The same message was on her face. From the presence of Seps and Lucas at my back, I felt the same impression. And Iuo mouthed, "We. Will. Meet. Again."

Warmth radiated the study from all the smiling people. Pehton was at the wall of journals with me, Tumu, and Tameka. The Lyriki Warden hugged the latest entry to her chest. I leaned back against the volumes to steady myself, disguising the crutch with a cool 'bad boy' pose. Tumu read over Pehton's shoulder and a tear glistened in his black voids.

"I miss when we were young together," he confessed.

"Hey!" Lamassau called from across the room. Emphatically, he said, "Growing old together is nice, too, Tumi."

Sagan changed the subject, asking, "They took you from the Queen's Fare, but what happened directly after Thailea?"

I fired a finger gun at her. "You're so sharp, Planet Breaker. Iuo, would you like to answer?"

The Lamian Prince waved. "Yes. Yes. Once we escaped Thailea, carrying Xelan between us, we fled back to the

Queen's Fare. Razor harbored our fugitive asses for a few weeks before Officer Tumu came knocking. I think it was more business than pleasure, but didn't you and Razor disappear during this time, Xelan?"

"I worked with him to create new accounts for the Emporium. Five of them were for me. I used them to develop the nanotech which carved out this stronghold and purchased properties for my safe-houses. Eventually, those accounts funded the installation of the Ionas."

Any mention of Razor helping the Progeny always left the Shadow squirming.

To break the tension and because I desperately needed one, I offered, "Let's take a break."

"While Rome was falling on Earth, I was earning my reputation as the most deadly warrior in the galaxy," I said while Pax force-fed an orange segment into my mouth. The sweet citrus reinvigorated me, and I smiled my appreciation at my son and his beaming freckles.

Caedes humphed, and Pehton laughed.

Lamassau snorted into his juice. "Truly lethal."

Bones defended my honor. "Deadly doesn't always mean combative. There are other means of delivering mortality onto a populace."

Yes.

There were.

How many nacres had I converted, and how many had failed?

I checked my lab notes, running a hand through my stringy hair. My hygiene wasn't as bad as that one time with Colita and Lucas, but bad enough that I could imagine my close friends' admonishments.

"Prince Xelan, see to your skin. Wash thoroughly to keep the chemicals from corroding it, but also for the smell."

My hallucination of Colita wrinkled her nose prettily and affection glowed in her eyes.

Lucas looked me over and, without words, let me know how much help I needed. "To the baths with you. At least this time you can keep your hair."

I wasn't taking care of myself as I had promised. And how could I, while I modified nacres into weapons on Enki's behest?

Primary Rem had tried to justify it to me. "Imagine all the lives you could save by eliminating Nox's horde the moment they step foot onto Earth."

"Eliminate?! Those are my people!" I had cried until my voice broke. I railed until my nails bit into my fists. "I want a peaceful resolution between Earth and Cinder."

The Primary's voids weren't without understanding as he easily worked through my reasoning. "Son, you want peace for Cinder, but you know well enough it means war for Earth. These nacres and the soldiers they would inhabit could deter your brother from ever attacking."

Sound reasoning.

I bit my lip, staring at a nacre in my palm which I'd adjusted it with increased speed and agility. To the universe, I argued, "There must be a better way."

Yet here I was, doing as they told me. Well, not quite.

Easily, I could create nacres with improvements to all things, but I dallied by perfecting one combat attribute at a time. Only eighty more years, and I could be free, leaving Enki without their perfect weapons.

The lab was exceptional. Every surface was sleek, white stone. The devices projected screens onto the walls with my notes and data. The instruments came from Pil, supplied by an inventor there named 2Lip. I was dying to meet him and share information, but the Tritans kept me there alone.

I stole so much stuff.

After I'd finished with a nacre, a younger Tritan would collect it for testing.

"I swear I never knew." I didn't say this to the Shadow in the room. Over their heads, I looked Aria and Torch in their sapphire eyes. Again, I repeated, "I never knew."

Pehton let out a soft noise, and Caedes pulled her against his side.

The room altogether looked uncomfortable and sad.

Tumu muttered, "I wish I'd known. I would have—"

"The manipulators didn't want you to know," Torch said, his voice ringing through the room. "We were kept hidden to soothe your conscience."

"But I could hear your voice," Aria assured. "You were near."

I crossed the room to where they flanked the door, insisting on guarding me despite the sins I'd committed against them. I needed to know more. To understand and perhaps to earn their forgiveness. I asked, "Can you please tell us about your experience?"

Torch and Aria shared a look before Torch said, "We were beneath your floor. Through it, we heard you speak. Kept in tanks not unlike how the Martyr Complex is described, only ours was solid and not glass—"

"There." Aria pointed at my face, saying, "I can see it. You recognize them."

All the blood had drained from my body. I went light and heavy at once.

The tanks.

Primary Rem came to visit me one day and opened with, "You are making excellent progress, son."

I said, "However you simulate the nacres, they are proving adequate." I couldn't keep the agitation from my voice. My mind drifted with the exhaustion, and I missed my friends.

"Would you like a visitor?" the Primary asked as if he'd heard my heart grieving.

His sudden offer left me suspicious. I asked, "Is this visitation in exchange for something more out of me?"

Primary Rem chuckled, and his voids glittered with pride. He said, "You are quick-witted. Despite how hard you have made every conversation since your sentencing here, I prefer your company over the others." He gestured to the hallway. "Out there are failed experiments. Help your assistant dispose of them, and I will permit one visitor of my choosing."
Hardly incentive.
Still.
"Where do we dispose of them?"
I wasn't expecting a trip to the Pantheon after my last rampage through the pale stacks. This conduit was in the middle of an empty field at the great archive's center. Every muscle in my body twitched with the urge to snoop through the stacks, but I kept to the task with fatigue weighing me down.
The tanks weren't heavy for my strength, but their weight still surprised me. "What's in here?" I asked.
"Subjects," the unnamed Tritan answered before chucking one through the lone conduit.
I went to open one—
"No!" The Tritan reached out to stop me. As I blinked at him, he offered an explanation. "They are hazardous. Primary Rem would kill me if I let you risk exposure."
The metal under my hand was solid. More real than this half-living existence. The dream state Enki kept me in beckoned me to return to the haze—
Genuine fear sparked in the other man's eyes, and I couldn't have it on my conscience.
I threw the tank into the conduit without looking inside.

"I'm ashamed of ignoring my instincts."
Aria shook her head. "You still don't understand."
"We love you," Torch finished.
Bewildered, I blinked.
They continued with Aria saying, "We heard your kindness above. All those conversations you had."

Oh.

"We learned of Lucas and Iuo. Tumu. Pehton. Seps— Everyone you loved from the words to yourself. We listened and became your friend," Torch explained.

Their observations left me raw.

Tameka looked a question at me, Tumu frowned, but Korac—

"We all talk to ourselves when we're busy at work. Our imperial majesty simply covered both sides of the conversation. It's not worth analyzing."

I owed Korac an apology. His explanation was pure charity, and I hadn't deserved such kindness in the last few days.

"Thank you." I bowed to my General, to Aria, and to Torch.

Tameka cleared her throat, and everyone's attention went to her. Her folded arms showed off the slightness of her shoulders in my shirt and bunched the material to expose a line of her tawny skin at her midriff. The smirk on her face was meant just for me as she asked, "So do I need three guesses to figure out who Remorse let you have in the lab, or should we all know by now?"

Well, Rayne. Who do you think it was?

Little you shakes your head and grins at me. "I don't even need to guess."

RAZOR ARRIVED WITHIN THE SAME DAY.

Now, I realize he was likely already there to see Remorse.

"He's a big fat liar," little you cries with a giggle. You hide your face when I frown.

You're right, Rayne. I know that now.

Razor came into my lab escorted by a Tritan, who soon vanished, leaving us alone the moment the Pain Curator drew me into a hug.

Physical interaction and the smell of vanilla—I confessed, "I have missed you."

"You smell awful," Razor said with a chuckle. A warm sound which I cherished. He looked me over as he asked, "Do they ever let you take a break?"

I shook my head against his shoulder, saying, "There is no rest for the wicked."

Razor gripped my arms and separated us so he could look into my eyes while saying, "You are the least wicked person I have ever met. These are theoretical weapons. I doubt they will ever see a battlefield. No, you will fight your brother another way." He gave my shoulder a good pat. "Now. I have a task for you, and I think you will enjoy it."

Two hours later, I had a map of the Pantheon and the promise of an adventure. A welcome distraction from the soul-destroying activity of weapon-smithing. Also, somehow Razor had negotiated a bath for me.

When I returned to my lab, finding Iuo, Seps, Kombuchi, X, and Lucas there startled me. Including the addition of a new face.

A dark-haired Dwarf in his mechsuit held out his closed, armored fist, saying, "I am 2Lip, and I want you to pilot my newest experiment."

I bopped my fist on top of his and grinned at the legendary inventor. "Why me?

2Lip disapprovingly glared at the rest of our team through heavy brows. "Because the others fear a fiery demise."

"It would be my pleasure."

Each Primary sanctum housed a conduit into the Pantheon, and one sanctum was left unguarded.

"I'd always suspected Tumu was a Primary," I admitted while standing in his abandoned apartments.

Iuo eyed the massive machine hidden in the central space. It was covered and, therefore, all the more enticing. The Lamian Prince said, "Tumu was famously against most of Enki's designs, and I believe he would approve of our activity today."

Curious, I asked, "Where is Tumu, and does he still live here?"

X was wiggling into his suit as he said, "He went on an annual retreat to Yu with his lover, the Chef."

The Chef?

I frowned. Tumu flirted with me constantly, and I never knew he was taken. Feeling guilty, I asked, "Has anyone ever met this person?"

The seven-man crew exchanged glances before shaking their heads in unison.

Lamassau glared a hole through Tumu's head, while the drunken Primary beamed goofily at me.

Iuo reiterated, "All that matters is Tumu would approve."

Seps' faceted eyes flashed with excitement, and his voice buzzed with it from his needle nose. "F8 approves."

"I wish R were here," X admitted.

Kombuchi stared into the Pantheon through the conduit, saying, "Today, we will make history."

At 2Lip's nod, Lucas whipped the cover off the machine. Aircrafts weren't common in the Vast Collective, presumably suppressed by Enki's propaganda machine, according to Iuo. This specimen of genius we'd carried through Enki weighed very little. Pil titanium was the lightest alloy in the Twelve Worlds, and the shiniest. It reflected our adoring faces like a glossy mirror.

"Beautiful," I gasped, fogging the exterior.

2Lip said, "I wish I knew what to call it."
Lucas nudged me until I blurted, "May I?"
The Dwarf nodded, while Iuo chuckled with anticipation.
They all felt it. This was momentous.
"Mercury Turbo."

"Oh, I give up," Korac muttered before blurting, "Ow."
Sagan finished swatting him and gave me a nod to
continue.

X hid a snicker behind a cough.
Kombuchi slapped my back, saying, "Well-named. Do
you think you can pilot this gorgeous machine?"
"Oh, yes. Do you think you can hang on?" I beamed at
him, so happy to see my friends and share in this occasion
with them.
Iuo assured, "You get us there and leave the rest to us."
The cockpit fit me and no one else.

Lucy said, "Yito took me on one of those once. It was an
itty bitty plane, and I was squished into the floorboard."
Yito gave a little wave while Matt grinned at his girl.
I shook my head and gestured for Tumu to continue
reading.

The rest of the crew gripped the seamless aircraft with
magnetic suits, with strips of Pil platinum woven into the
boots and gloves. All of which were prototypes. 2Lip's
entire mechsuit was made of the alloy and meshed to
Mercury Turbo's underside. I flew us through the conduit
in Tumu's sanctum and into the Pantheon.
There, I let loose.
Propulsion carried us across the white archives, and I
followed Razor's map to the destination. Only in flight did
I question how the Pain Curator knew the whereabouts
of the tomes he desired, but never mind.

I was flying through Enki with my friends strapped to a plane.

"I'll bet you were grinning," Tameka said with love in her voice.

Pax raced one of his toy cars in the air like a plane. "This was daddy."

I shared, "In hindsight, I can see it was an exercise devised by Remorse and Razor to boost my morale. To let off some steam."

Iuo toasted his wine glass. "Which we did."

"All of it," Lucas added.

Tumu said, "May I please keep reading so I can see what your non-naked ass stole from the grounds this time, you precocious pirate?"

Korac barked out a laugh. "P.P."

I waved for Tumu to continue, but I won't deny it. That got a smile out of me.

The Overseers were a problem.

One approached from the North, flying low.

On an earpiece, Iuo said, "We need to get topside. Now."

Muffled metal thumps sounded all around me as they crawled into position. Seps waved to me through the nacre glass between us, and I grinned at him. Flying higher than the Overseer, it raced under us, and we watched it go by with bated breath.

2Lip assured me the reflective surface would confuse the security bots similar to how my stripping naked had confused them in the past. But even though he sounded confident at the time, I could still see his fingers were crossed inside his mechsuit.

It made me chuckle.

I knew even if the Overseer spied us, I could easily maneuver my friends to safety. This was an adventure I desperately needed, and I relished every second.

Indeed, we were safe as the machine continued zipping away from us, and we continued northward. The further we went, the lighter the stacks became. And dusty. Until we came across a grove of decayed shelves and their crumbling volumes.

This was it.

I lowered the hovering ship, and they closed access to the platinum on their suits, disengaging from the magnetic hull. Even though the platinum strips were finely woven, it was still the most dense metal in the galaxy. They moved slowly in their pursuit.

Lucas asked, "What was the number again…" He paused and clicked his tongue in frustration. "—Must I call you Prince on a heist?"

I thought about a codename for only a second before I knew. I blurted out—

"Wingmaster!" the Shadow all called out in unison. Even Pax.

Kombuchi snorted. "Are you serious?"

"I have heard worse," Seps assured.

"Where have you actually heard worse?" X asked with a whispering chuckle.

I grinned. Truly. My heart felt light, and my nacre was warm in my chest. I recited the numbers over my earpiece and kept beaming. Nothing could ruin this good mood—

A rumbling sounded. Near… too near. I warned, "Overseer! Find cover!"

They hid inside the stacks, except for 2Lip. He couldn't fit with his mechsuit, so he scurried under Mercury Turbo. I held her steady while the Overseer trundled above.

That was close.

My heart pounded a little with the excitement. After checking the visuals, I said, "All clear."

"I owe Razor a favor or I would not risk a tenure on Gait for this," Iuo confessed.

They returned to work, pilfering through delicate archives the size of their bodies. It was Seps who called, "Found one."

Lucas asked, "Pray tell. What mysteries do these valuable records hold?"

2Lip muttered, "It's best not to anger Razor with your curiosity."

"It's best not to anger Razor with anything," X whispered.

I was dying to know myself.

Kombuchi confessed, "I am not fond of him."

Iuo sided with 2Lip. "They call him the Pain Curator for a reason. Take a few extra with us for our troubles—"

Rumbling sounded nearby.

Before I could warn them over the earpieces, Seps pointed to an Overseer only a meter from us. "Take shelter! They found us!"

Not on my watch.

As they went for the stacks with poor 2Lip out in the cold, I whipped Mercury Turbo into the Overseer's sights and activated frost matte mode. Cooling jets breathed on the reflective surface to hide the polish.

Now the Overseer was my problem. I said, "Get the tomes while I see to our nosy friend! Be ready for my signal."

The Overseer opened its cubical front and revealed a red horizontal light inside. It grew brighter as I stared into it.

Right.

I whipped out of the way as the Overseer fired a red blast across my matte bow. The shockwave from the blast jolted Mercury Turbo into the nearest stack.

And the next.

And the next.

"Dominoes!"

That's right, Rayne.

"Fuck!" Seps shouted into the earpiece.

X whisper-shouted, "For the love of Elden, I am stuck under the stack!"

2Lip ordered, "Wingmaster, engage the weapon's system. The amorphous blob on the right. Stick your hand in it."

With a squelch, I did as I was told—

Mercury Turbo's polished titanium exterior transitioned into a matte black killing machine. Barrels raised from the nose, releasing a steady stream of laser light. I felt a trigger inside the blob.

I was ever so tempted.

Four-year-old you smirks and fires a tiny finger gun at me.

Opening fire in an ethereal library lightened the load I was carrying. My entire world became searing destruction aimed at the offensive Overseer in the sky. The beams of bright light took out the top shelves on the decrepit stacks sheltering my friends. Smoke ruined the purified air, and I knew it wasn't safe here.

"Turbo and I will fly higher. Free X and be ready when I fly back through."

Antagonized by my counter-attack, the Overseer narrowed its infrared targeting beams on the matte black surface of the aircraft. Perhaps more excited than I should be, I laughed as it pursued.

Low through the stacks.

Cut right at the next junction—

It followed.

Straight up.

I heard it trundle clumsily as I went for a dizzying loop.

Over the earpieces, Iuo asked, "Is the mad scientist cackle really necessary?"

In my study, Tameka said, "I'm pretty fond of it."

Pax gave her a high five.

"Wingmaster, we await your return. Have you lost your new friend?" There was more than a hint of amusement in Lucas' voice.

The Overseer kept tight, but refused to fire at me among the stacks.

I gripped the helm, saying, "Coming in low. In five."
Four.

"Three."

Two.
I deactivated the weapons system, replacing the matte black with polish titanium once again before banking on the main aisle where my team waited. All the while, I counted down my one hundred and twenty-six second advantage. They stood at the base of the stacks, lower than I should hover, given the debris falling from the earlier decimation. Pil platinum shone from the threads of their suits.

With one last maneuver up my sleeve, I flipped Mercury Turbo upside-down and picked up my team on the spiraling arc while calling—

"I got you!" The entire study shouted in unison.

Then I zipped off the major thoroughfare and headed straight for the conduit into Tumu's sanctum without a backward glance. The poor aircraft was smoking from how hard I'd pushed it. Which may or may not have contributed to the Overseer firing at us once more.

Kombuchi's magnetized boots thunked as he walked across Mercury Turbo to my cockpit. He gave me a thumbs-up as he instructed, "Get me over it."

X whispered-shouted, "Are you insane?"

2Lip offered, "Use the boosters."

I tapped the boosters and spun in an arc, facing the Overseer. Propulsion on full, we rocketed straight at it. All the while, the target beam lasered in on my forehead.

Iuo's voice was tight as he warned, "Get ready, Kombuchi!"

"This will be glorious," Lucas promised.

Six meters from it, and I activated the lateral boosters, sending us up and over it. A glorious belch of bright green acid poured from the underside of Mercury Turbo.

The Overseer and everything below it melted with a searing stench.

"We cheered so loud. Even as we crashed and skated into Tumu's sanctum with the spectacular aircraft ablaze." I grinned at Iuo and Lucas.

"Twas a good day," Iuo admitted with a reminiscent sigh.

Lucas chuffed. "Speak for yourselves. I lost my eyebrows. I had to shade them on for the next two months to keep above suspicion."

Tameka peered at me with admiration in her eyes, asking, "Did you get into trouble?"

Korac said, "Yeah? Nox and I learned of your naked adventure in the Pantheon, but why had no one heard of this?"

I said one word. "Tumu."

The old Primary sat forward, elbows on his knees to explain, "I hid their little escapade in the stacks and warned our imperial majesty to stay out of trouble the next day or risk being my roommate for the rest of his tenure in Enki."

With a laugh while running a hand through my hair, I finished, "So, naturally, I moved in right away."

Lamassau did a double-take. "Come again?"

No one wanted in the middle of that.

Little you beams at me, saying, "Can you blame them?"

I changed the subject.

"Foremother?" I called to peel Silence's attention from the Tritan lover drama. "I could've used a nanite shield like yours during the action."

The grin on her face lost some of its wattage as she offered a non-committal nod.

Silence is concealing the truth about the shield she created when she, Lucas, Smith, and Tameka were escaping the destruction of Enki. I want her to feel safe and to know she can trust us with anything. Including exactly how the shield was formed.

"We can trust her. I have faith in Silence."

Your kindness knows no bounds.

From where twelve-year-old you sleeps on the couch, you say, "I get it from you."

Let's hope you still feel that way after the next entry.

ENTRY TWELVE

AMENDS FOR MYSELF

DURING OUR NEXT BREAK, **A**NDREW FOUND ME STARING AT A SHARD OF **M**ERCURY **T**URBO'S EXTERIOR SHELL **I** KEPT FOR MY MUSEUM. In its invisible display case, it transitioned between matte black and polished titanium silver in a perpetual wave of motion. I'd been using the moment to reflect on how to approach the next entry when I heard him call my name.

"How can I help you, Conscience?"

Rayne, since you've left, Andrew's been running the Probability Matrix observations with Silence, Lucas, and Smith. Occasionally, Aria and Torch help. I'd hoped T.A.O. would stay and work on the team, but, like you, she has her own way of doing things.

"I won't be gone forever. I promise," little you assures.

Andrew joined me on the glowing landing at the top tiers of the ravine. His expression said something was... interesting. "Sorry to bother you. I'm sure you could do with some privacy, but I've gotten word on a trend I'm currently monitoring." From his palm device, a graph illuminated in a projection. He said, "See, here are the number of Probabilities which erupted after Rayne… destroyed Enki."

Before you left us, the Probabilities ended with you. Once you'd completed your mission, billions shattered into existence. This graphic depicted those fresh instances.

"Go on," I encouraged with a nod.

Andrew wet his lips in a nervous gesture before swiping to the next graph.

Ah.

I frowned. "I see."

With another gesture, Andrew increased the size, saying, "The Matrix is shrinking. Little by little, Probabilities are dying out."

Biting my thumbnail, I considered the causes. "What percentages are we looking at?" Something about this rang in my ears. Something I knew, but couldn't quite place.

Andrew closed the projection and lowered his hand. "Only five percent, but five percent of billions is millions. Hundreds of millions of Probabilities."

I looked up from my thoughts and glimpsed the concern in his eyes. How could I allow apprehension in my Progeny? With a gentle pat on Andrew's shoulder, I assured, "You're on my time, right now. Don't worry about it until we return to our roles. Then, I want to discuss it with Silence and the others. They're older. Perhaps they've seen this before."

A little more confident, Andrew nodded. "Yeah. Okay. Thanks, Wingmaster."

"No. Thank you for taking your job so seriously." Another pat. "We'll figure this out. Let's get back to the study. We're getting closer to when I first met all of you."

While we headed back, Andrew rolled his eyes, asking, "Do we really have to rehash all that?"

I chuckled. "What's the matter, Conscience? Afraid I'll remind everyone what a spaz you were?"

"Don't worry. I remind him every fucking day," Kyle said from the bottom of the synchronized steps.

I laughed while Andrew grappled Kyle into a headlock. My Progeny.

"I miss them so much," both versions of you confess.

They're waiting for you here, Rayne. Just come home.

Little you waves a finger, while preteen you answers in your sleep, "Not yet, Superman. But as soon as I'm done, I'll be there to claim my two strawberry milkshakes."

Is one for Nox?

Your silent, precocious smirk on both your faces is a mixture of adorable and nerve-racking.

You enjoy torturing me.

At the front of my study, Tameka ate from a vegetable tray meant for our little family to share. I enjoyed the cherry tomatoes. Pax favored the celery sticks.

To my waiting audience of snacking Shadow, I said, "The zero millennium turned during my tenure at Enki, and I perfected the Weapon unit a thousand times over. But they didn't know that."

Tumu chuckled where he snuggled close against Lamassau, having learned a valuable lesson about not appreciating his lover more.

Completely on a sidebar, I asked Aria and Torch, "What was it like for you at this time?"

Their wordless exchange spoke to their twin connection beneath the flames of Cascading Light. Aria said, "By now, you'd disposed of us."

"And we'd built an empire of lost ones beneath Torrentus," Torch finished.

Pehton squeezed her eyes shut and let out a sound I could only assume was involuntary. Before Caedes could hold her or her children could say anything, Korac was there.

Immediately.

My General pressed his mouth to my Executive Warden's ear and whispered so only she could hear.

Pehton turned those teary garnet eyes onto my lover and asked, "Tameka, what was it Aya had said about introducing you to Aria and Torch?"

Tameka looked from me to the two Gargantuan Lyriks in question. They nodded their approval for Tameka to answer.

"'We'll need permission from our gods to speak to you.'"

Korac repeated, "'Our gods,' Pehton." Without taking his eyes off hers, he called to the twins. "Tell us. Tell us about your life."

Pehton's eyes were transfixed on Korac, but she still took Caedes' offered hand and listened to her children.

Torch seemed to understand. "We were happy and healthy. A little deprived of sunlight, but we have more than made up for it since reaching Ishkur."

Aria said, "We wanted for nothing. We *want* for nothing. Our family came from Gait, and we will always remain."

A hush fell over the Shadow.

Yes.

Locked in this moment, Korac gripped Pehton's biceps, and she clutched the lapels of his shirt. Her children's words sank in, and Pehton lowered her head onto Korac's chest. He heaved her up and led her to the door where Torch and Aria stood guard. With a nod at both of them, they followed him out of the room with Pehton.

Caedes stood and saluted me. "Please continue. We'll be back in a minute." He took his time leaving, affording Pehton and her kids some privacy.

Korac returned and took his place once more with Echo and Sagan. He said, "Go ahead, your imperial majesty." A warm smirk appeared, as if he couldn't hold it back any longer.

Good for Pehton, Aria, and Torch.

"During the one hundred years I spent on Enki, Korac was earning money for Nox's campaign in the fighting matches at the Queen's Fare. T.A.O., you were with him. Do you want to share anything?"

T.A.O. glanced between her brother and met Korac's eyes across the study before returning to me. "All the Worlds opened to me and let me walk among their people. But purposeless. The Seam offered me a room, and Korac was there. I was safe…until I wasn't."

Andrius knew how to talk to her better than anyone. He gently touched her shoulder and asked, "Why didn't you visit our father during this time?"

A shadow fell over the Atramentous star in T.A.O.'s eyes, and I hated it. I knew the answer before she confessed to me, "The miasma never left you."

Devis said, "But you touched Cascading Light. You knew Celindria would find you eventually."

T.A.O.'s gaze made the rounds again, lingering on Korac. When she met my eyes, the ice in her made me wince. She said, "My daughter…"

Of course. The child Abresson had forced on her was the beginning of her line, which one day led to Sagan.

Tilting her head so all those waves cascaded to the side, T.A.O. said, "Korac kept the dawn safe until I succumbed to the night."

I'd never heard Korac as gentle with anyone as he was with T.A.O. I'd noticed it all those millennia ago in Nox's castle, and I noticed it now. He asked, "Tell us about Razor. He was my brother, and I want to know how he treated you."

"The Seam asked nothing of me but words and smiles. Laughter filled the halls every day." T.A.O. touched a hand to her chest and shored herself up for the next confession. "I made him cry when he couldn't protect me. He hated goodbyes." A single tear fell from her lashes.

Andrius pulled her against his side and chafed her tiny arm. He whispered, "I know he cared for you. He protected you from Celindria until you knew it was time."

T.A.O. nodded, confirming his interpretations.

I crossed the room and knelt to kiss her hair, muttering, "I know. I miss him too."

Sagan stood Echo up and walked her by moving her baby feet, while Korac watched, deep in thought.

It was time to change the subject.

"Jack, can you please read the next entry? Volume two thousand, four hundred and ten. Page seventy-two."

You smile with so much warmth as you say, "I'm proud of my delinquent little brother."

We all are.

Ross kissed his cheek, and the young man stood with a blush, giving a goofy wave under the spotlight. Jack found the volume and read with a clean and steady cadence. The room drifted into the story within seconds.

THE STARS CRIED TO ME.
They said, "Father, forgive me. I am lost without you."

I choked the words out. "Can you feel?"

"Only sorrow, bitterness, and rage." Constellated across the sky, Celindria's eyes blinked back tears. Her voice came on the wind across the Earth's desert. "I would rather not feel at all."

I cried, "Come home! Please!"

The stars blinked again, and her fading image promised, "When my work is done."

"Celindria!"

I startled awake in my lab on Enki. Something smelled… foul.

A Tritan leaned with his hands behind him against the far wall. He was darker than any Tritan I'd seen, almost indigo in complexion. I didn't like his voids. Beady buttons of everything wrong in his heart.

This was Abresson.

When he waved at me with his fingers, the sleeve of his robes slipped to reveal fresh scars. Malice permanently painted on his skin. With entirely too much authority, Abresson said, "If it were up to me, I would give you another one hundred years." His voice grated. He trailed a grubby finger along my stainless steel surfaces as he sidled my way. Frost lingered in his wake. "Your work is so impressive. The others cannot stop talking about it, but I suspect you of subterfuge."

In.

Out.

I breathed to calm myself, while I laid eyes on perhaps the dirtiest soul in the Vast Collective.

Abresson seemed disappointed he didn't get a rise out of me. Cavalier, he shrugged it off before saying, "I wonder if you would practice more caution if you knew the resources you waste with each failed test."

"What resources are those?" I asked, not really caring about the answer, but there was a flicker of humor in his eyes which told me I wouldn't like it.

Abresson looked through one of my instruments, unthreatened by me, and offered out of hand, "Only those children stolen from Gait with Inanis."

As the blood drained from my body, a ringing filled my ears and threatened to pop my eyeballs. I couldn't breathe or think.

The test 'simulations.'

The tanks.

Not clones or knock-off Progeny failures—

"Eight million, three hundred thousand children no one would miss. It was Celindria's idea to use them, back when she was still alive and building weapons for us. A genius, that woman. Too bad about the ice in her veins or I would not mind—"

"Get.

"Out."

Abresson's face shifted. His voids widened slightly, and his lipless mouth quivered.

I knew I'd shifted into Atramentous. When I opened my wings, Abresson hopped back a full meter. I repeated, "Get. Out."

The indigo Tritan kept his eyes on me, moving backwards and feeling for the archway. All the while, Abresson assured, "To go against me is to go against Primary Rem himself. You will face Imminent if you incite violence against me, boy."

Imminent.

The voice laughed in my head.

Nox.

The Tritans.

Surrounded by corruption and vile intentions.

With every step I took, Abresson pooled more and more into a frightened liquid as he shrank for the door. In three pitches, I said, "Tell your master to send me to Earth. Fetch Razor and Tumu for my escort. Send all your Primaries and Eminents to witness. Watch this Prince leave and fear his return."

The Shadow stared at Jack and me, transfixed in the moment.

Until Tameka asked, "What did you do?"

I grinned at her so she'd repay in kind before I said, "What any disgruntled mad scientist does. I destroyed all of my research except for what I had commandeered for myself. The same goes for the Pantheon. Tumu..." I gestured at him on the couch, and he bobbed his head, still drunk. "He helped me smuggle it out."

Sagan asked, "Why did you call for Razor?"

Iuo answered, "For us. He had a way of gathering us for Xelan that I'm not sure even Remorse knew about. If I may?" He waited for my nod, then continued. "I think Razor liked our Traitor Prince stirring up trouble."

Lucas concurred, "The more trouble, the more Probabilities."

Pehton said, "So he brought us together for one last roundtable before our fearless leader faced a sentence of pure isolation."

I looked away from their knowing glances.

Preteen you has rolled over onto your stomach so you can stare at me with your chin set on arms, laying across the width of your pillow. You ask, "Did you look away because they know about your mental illness and how badly solitude affects it?"

I nod.
Yes.

Little you is curling up on top of the remnants of your fallen pillow fort. You say, "We love you."

My lips are suddenly dry, and I lick them before I choke on tears.

I never doubt that about you, Rayne, and I don't doubt it about them. But sometimes, it's hard to bare your vulnerabilities and expect a good outcome.

"What was the outcome, Superman?"

Iuo laughed. "And then F8 asked him to lead an empire. Right there in front of all of us."

Lucas was beaming as he recalled, "Do you remember how he answered?"

"How could I forget?" Pehton was holding her sides.

Tumu, merry in his cups, held his hands up like a conductor. "Everyone. All at once. Three, two, one..."

"I got you!" The Shadow called in a chorus of chuckles, smiles, and love.

Kyle said, "I don't understand. How were you having this meeting in private?"

Andrew echoed, "Yeah. How did Remorse not learn about this?"

Silence answered, "They were in the Opal Mezzanine. Weren't you, Lucas?"

He grinned at his ancient friend and bowed with his head to confirm her assumption.

Sagan begged with a gesture of both hands. "Gimme the descriptive, baby. What's this Opal Mezzanine like?"

While they indulged Sagan with the description of yet another beautiful Aegis construct, I nestled Tameka into my side. I asked, "Are you overwhelmed yet?"

"No. This has been a heart-warming past few days. But..." She climbed to her tiptoes to whisper in my ear. "I'm worried about you. How are you doing?"

I let Tameka set back down on her feet and lied to her with a reassuring grin—

Pax wiggled into our couple's snuggle, turning it into a family affair. I ruffled his red coils. He's at that age where it's not 'cool' anymore, and he glared a reflection of my own eyes up at me.

"Daddy." Pax sounded exasperated and disappointed in my clearly uncool dad behavior.

It made both Tameka and I laugh.

Preteen you says, "I'm with Pax."

I laugh because I know it couldn't be further from the truth.

Jack sobered my good mood by reading, "'After the ally summit, Razor told me Nox became obsessed with an image of one of Celindria's descendants. The same girl who would one day destroy Enki.'"

The room stopped celebrating how well things turned out and refocused on the matter at hand.

Wearily, I admitted, "My Verse wasn't over yet because I agreed to build an empire with my allies. Those allies would only give aid to Enki after I first defeated my brother. The Twelve Worlds saw the Night King's growing army as a threat to the entire galaxy. Still, I strategized with the end goal in mind.

"For crimes against the children of Gait, drowning Enki took priority.

"Around 400CE, Razor agreed with me. Whether to further Imminent's agenda or for the sake of our friendship, he helped me prepare for the isolation with enough funds to install the Ionas and enough technology to research myself into several strongholds of labs.

"But Razor also took a shipment of Cascading Light to Nox."

Sagan reinforced, "To help with his mental health."

Korac caressed her face in gratitude.

Tameka confessed, "I appreciate Nox's raw honesty in his Verse. He saw that image of Rayne destroying Enki and became instantly fixated."

Jack wondered aloud, "But what did Rayne redact during that part?"

I raise a brow at you.
What, indeed? Care to sate my curiosity?

You plant your elbows in the pillow and rest your chin in your raised hands, staring, until you make up your mind and quote, "'I've never loved anything more.'"

I wince.
I suppose I asked for that, didn't I?

You shake your head. "I'm not finished. Nox said he could see 'unmistakable determination' in my eyes and that he wanted to test it. I suppose he learned the hard way. My skull is thicker than his."

Is.

In my study, I said, "I think it's best left for Rayne to know, Jack."

The King Elect of Earth gave me an understanding smile before returning to his pallet.

I waved at Ross. "Would you like to read?"

She hopped up in a sweatshirt and short-shorts. The entire study noticed Jack's eyes never left her long, exposed legs as she picked her way over the cushions and blankets to my wall of journals. Kyle shook his head in disgust, and Silence gave him a playful nudge.

"Which one, Wingmaster?" Ross asked, tentatively tracing the leather spines.

I addressed the room. "At this point in the other Verses, both Nox and Korac jumped from 400CE to 2002CE. I want to be a little more transparent with how I spent my time in exile, because it applies to this next chapter. We'll start it after the entry and some private sessions. Full transparency is hard to offer, especially since the audience extends beyond my study. But I want people out there to know we were not always level-headed. Nor were we always strong and steadfast. We clawed our way out of the ashes and grasped for this diamond we have now.

"Ross, please read volume two thousand, six hundred and sixty-two. Page fifty-eight."

{819CE | Day 152,935 in Exile}

I am a monster.

All those nacres I intentionally failed to delay the Primary's plans.

All those tanks I threw into the solitary conduit in the Pantheon.

The people who my brother hurt on Monarch 3, L. Capra, Lukemore—

Where are my children?

No matter how many times and ways I ask anyone, they cannot tell me what happened to four of my original Progeny.

And oh, Elden, let me forget about Celindria.

I quit sleeping one hundred fifty-two thousand, five hundred and seventy days ago. Inventing stimulant after stimulant to keep from dreaming of my lost daughter.

My abomination.

I am a monster.

I laugh into my empty lab, with books, tablets, instruments and rotten food strewn everywhere. The smell of it..

The smell of me…

It's all my fault.

I brought this on the Earth by not reinvigorating the Vittle crop. By creating the Progeny who Nox coveted so badly. The Vast Collective coveted so badly.

The invasion would come, and no one would be prepared because I stormigated an entire planet and invited exile unto myself.

Where I think every day about ripping out my nacre and ending it.

When I sink to my knees and curl onto the floor, my hair is so long it surrounds me in an inky pool.

Enki.

I laugh again.

The indomitable Dyson's Sphere destroyed by a crying little girl—

I could see.
I could see it in the flames.
Brought this on her. That's what I did. I brought this on her, too.
Rocking, I cry. Aloud I repeat, "I did this. I did this."
It soothes me—The sound of a voice.
It no longer mattered if the voice was my own.
The Icari.
My Progeny.
Humanity.
The Vast Collective.
And now this girl…
I let them all down.
I did this.
I did this—

Ross stopped reading. The study was dead silent. No one smiled or laughed or pecked their partner a kiss.
Everyone stared at me.
I tried to smile. To reassure them. But a tear rolled down my cheek.
Pax left his toys—the only movement in the room—and clung to my side. I peered down at the boy with eyes so like my own and lost it.

You've escaped your blankets to sit on the end of the coffee table across from where I'm sitting in the armchair. With a little work, you maneuver your face in my line of sight to say, "This is good. Being honest about this is so brave, and they will understand."

I still can't hold my head up enough to face you. To say I am better or capable on my own. I wish I could.
I couldn't face them either.

Tameka pulled me into her shoulder, and I cried in her arms. She whispered, "Was it like this every day?"

I nodded and choked—swallowed to say, "Not exactly. Some days, my thoughts raced less, and I could be productive in my research. The same old stuff: Vittle crop and nacre defenses. But never enough to take care of myself. I need people—"

The words left me as I glanced around and noticed the study was entirely empty.

"I need them," I repeated.

Pax said, "They went to eat. Uncle Andrew is making barbecue. Can we have barbecue, dad?"

Tameka asked, "Why don't you find some seats for us, sweetie? We'll be right there."

Our son glanced at me for permission, and at my nod, took off for the kitchen.

The woman I loved most in the world watched that kid go and said what was on my mind. "I'm so grateful we've made it here." Tameka turned her stained glass eyes on me, and, in the reflection, I saw someone she deemed worthy. She said, "Now. Tell me everything. Get it all off your chest. The others will see to Pax, even if it takes all night. Xelan, give me everything. I will still be here when you're through."

Tameka told the truth. For hours alone together, we worked through a part of me I'd kept to myself. She was still there when we came through the other side.

"Of course Tameka was, because you're no monster, Xelan. Everyone is entitled to weakness. It's how your strengths emerge even brighter, and an Icarus with as much strength as you would surely carry an equal weight of burden *and* loss." You wet your lips before asking, "But can you do me a favor?"

Humbled, I nod.

You take my hand and squeeze it. "Please stop using the word 'monster.' The more you use it, the more power you give it. And if you're a monster, that would make me one, too, because you made me. Now, do you think of me as a monster?"

Never.

You give me a knowing look, saying, "Exactly."

If I did anything to deserve all of you, I am so very lucky.
Thank you.
I hope you stay. When I tell the truth—
I'm so afraid to be left on my own.

"I got you."

ENTRY THIRTEEN

ALONE WITH ME

TAMEKA IS THE MOST GENEROUS PERSON I KNOW, AND I STILL LIED TO HER. When I tell my secret, I want everyone to know the truth. So, while she and Pax slept in our study-fort overnight, I had remained wide awake. I faked with my eyes closed to avail her suspicions.

My love, I am sorry.

> You're still sitting across from me, inches away. Your hand is so much smaller than mine and warm. The fingernails are painted black with sharpie in your preteen rebellion. While I stare at your fingers, you squeeze, saying, "Tell Tameka the truth that you can't sleep and something keeps you up at night. She'll understand."

Yes. You're right, of course.

The Shadow returned to my study well-rested and wearing fresh clothes. Even Sagan had abandoned her wedding dress in the absence of the Icarean ceremonial ribbons. Everyone had dressed down, comfortable and prepared for the day.

You wince slightly as you ask, "Was it awkward? You know after..."

I don't know. Yes? Maybe. Perhaps it was only me. You have convinced me I see doubt and questioning glances when it's simply concern and love. But at the time...
I was afraid to let them go. To tell them the truth and drive them away. So, I stalled.

Wearing the same clothes as yesterday was usually one of the first signs I was slipping. Well, that and sleep deprivation. In the same black slacks and white button down—wrinkled—I smiled and clapped with a quick chafe of my hands before asking the wonderful people in the room, "Who wants a private session with me?"
Hands went up.
Work had been non-stop since you'd destroyed Enki, so it wasn't common to be alone in a room with me anymore. Signature Wingmaster pep-talks were in high demand and in short supply. So...
Everyone wanted a chat.
Even Kyle.
"Sagan, do you mind...?"
Korac's mate stood and said, "You heard the Icarus, people. Out in the ravine and form a line. You'll all get a turn. Come on!"

I started with Karter, who of course wanted Para in there with her. Chris, too. We exchanged hugs, and I sat on the coffee table with them on the couch. "Before you ask questions, I've always wanted to ask you something, brave Valkyrie."

Karter and Para grinned at each other and both nodded.

"Can you tell me about your battle on the rainbow rings of Thailea?"

Chris smiled, and for once, it was an easy one. With his chin on his fist, he stared at them both dreamily, saying, "I love this story."

He got a smile out of me, especially as the ladies started their tale.

Para went first. "We'd pursued ourselves—our Inanis selves—through the stratosphere. High, so very high. Our ears popped, and our skin flushed. We thought we might burn but our nacres stayed true."

Karter went next. "Then there was nothing. No sound. No air. Just gas clouds and the ice… The multicolored ice crystals. I met myself in red."

"I was blue," Para added.

They both went quiet a minute before Karter said, "Thailea is beautiful from space. So bright and cold. Cascading Light showered in from the black. It was hard to take in…"

I asked, "Because it was so mind-blowing?"

Para snickered. "No. Because all the other versions of me had a mean right hook, and Karter's legs aren't just for show. Ourselves beat the shit out of us until I went unconscious, and well…"

"The rest you learned in my son's Verse," Karter finished.

Chris, still dreamily, requested, "Go back to the part where there were dozens of you—Ow." His small smile while chafing his arm was a testament to the progress he'd made. As if he'd heard my thoughts, Chris glanced at me, asking, "Can I get a moment with you, imperial majesty?"

I nodded and looked at Karter. "Was there anything you wanted with me—"

The Valkyrie were already shaking their heads. Para assured, "We wanted to see you for a bit and let Chris talk to you."

Karter grinned, and it was perfect. "We know how to find you."

Both ladies left me with a man I had trouble looking in the eyes. "Yes, Chris?"

The veteran stood and saluted me, saying, "I never got the chance to thank you properly. That day you sent me to watch over Jack changed my life—*saved* my life. I will be forever grateful to you—"

The look on my face stopped him.

I couldn't... It was too much, Rayne. Celindria had tortured him—unforgivable torment. And I'd let her go.

You reach higher and squeeze my shoulder, saying, "You can tell him without giving it away. Tell him why you're crying."

"Chris, please. You protected Jack, so you owe me nothing. *I* owe *you*—I am so sorry." With my head hanging, I tried desperately to keep myself from falling apart again.

I couldn't see Chris, but he sounded so distressed. "Sir, how do you... Please don't blame yourself. You can't control what happens to everyone every second."

You force me to meet your eyes. "Listen to him. He's telling the truth."

Before I could say anything else, Chris said, "I only wished she'd survived."

Of course.

So we could repay Celindria in kind—

Chris confessed, "I don't think *I* could hold my sanity together if I couldn't feel anything."

That brought me around. "What did you say?"

Chris was mid-reach to console me when he settled back and said, "I've seen some awful things, and a lot of it, before I'd joined the Shadow. People all have their excuses for the decisions they make, but *they* can all feel. They all have a conscience they rationalize away to validate their misdeeds. Celindria doesn't have that luxury. I wished she'd survived so we could cure her and force her to feel it. All of it. Then maybe, one day, she could make up for it."

Yes.

Yes. That's exactly it.

I gripped this human by the front of his shirt and pulled him in for a hug, squeezing tight to the only person who'd voiced exactly my reasoning. On the verge of tears, I kept repeating, "Thank you."

You look thoughtful, Rayne.

A little smile appears on your lips before you say, "I like his idea."

I walked Chris out, and Sagan let in the next pair. I must say it surprised me to see Miy and Twenty-One. We didn't really know each other, but they brought an interesting flavor to the group.

"We want to fly into space, together." Miy didn't waste time with pleasantries.

Twenty-One, with all his size, beamed down at her, amused and proud. They were quite the pair.

I grinned. "Done." That was surely the easiest conversation I'd have today. I said, "We'll vet you for the program. Health clearances and such, but of course. I'd love for the Shadow to get out there and explore."

Twenty-One put a fist to his chest, bowed, and said, "Thank you, your imperial majesty."

They turned and let themselves out, all the while Miy mumbled, "I'm so glad to get out of this Dyson's Sphere with all these people..."

It genuinely made me chuckle.

Sagan sent Bones, Iuo, and Smith next. I'd always liked Smith, so I was happy when the Shadow had let him return to the fold. Still, there was something slightly condescending about his constantly grinning face, given the betrayals and all.

"Gentlemen."

They bowed.

Honestly, their formalities had intimidated me until Iuo said, "I'm so glad I met you."

Bones nodded. "Same."

Smith simply grinned.

I hugged the Lamian King Elect, saying, "Me, too, old friend. But tell me what's on your mind."

With the hug over, Iuo glanced sheepishly at his comrades before confessing, "The first film will release in a month."

Ah.

Rayne, I don't know if I've mentioned it, but Iuo has rights over your franchise.

Your laughter is pure joy. "What?! I have movies? Wait, are they all porn?"

Now, I'm laughing.
No, they're legitimate works of fiction under the guise of biopics. Someone is also releasing a series of novels about you; although I can't imagine why. There are already textbooks on you as a subject—Are you all right?

You're blinking big blinks and a little rapidly. "Uh huh," comes out of your mouth.

I couldn't help it. I had to press.
Some fictions depict you in love with Nox. How do you feel about that?

Still blinking, you shrug. "Whatever makes people happy, I guess."

Let's move on.

Bones said, "I appreciate this vacation, boss. It's a nice break from the constant travel."

"Oh, is it daunting?" I asked, completely clueless.

The Icarean warrior shook his head while saying, "Not at all, sir. I simply appreciate my time around the Shadow."

Smith chuckled and mumbled, "Sure 'the Shadow' and not a tiny shorts-wearing Valkyrie."

Iuo nudged him in the ribs.

They got another laugh out of me before I clapped my hands together, asking, "Are there questions or requests?"

Bones shook his head. "Nah, your imperial majesty. Just keep doing what you're doing." He gave me a heavy pat on the shoulder.

I smiled at him and looked at Iuo and Smith for any further duties.

Iuo took the hint and waved for Bones to exit. "Let's leave the former member of Imminent for a lone pep talk with the Co-Emperor."

Smith stared up at me with his brown eyes, smiling so his irises twinkled. He said, "It's been a long road, boss. I never lied to you. Not really."

I nod, agreeing. "You were careful, as only someone as old as you can be. I understand you, Smith. Is it really over?"

Smith grinned at me, unblinking, for a long time before saying, "I think you know the answer."

I couldn't keep my eyes from flinching.

With a cordial nod, acknowledging it, Smith grinned as he let himself out.

My heart was still racing, but I wanted this to be the last day. I *needed* to tell them the truth. I called, "Next, please, Sagan."

Puk and Yito were a breath of fresh air.

"Movie nights?" I asked, trying to keep the bemusement from my voice. "You're speaking to the Co-Emperor of the Concerted Empire of Iona Pax, and you're requesting a monthly movie night?"

Yito nudged Puk. "I told you this was silly."

Puk shook his head, adamant. "No. We need to keep this crew together. A movie night is a perfect excuse for all the traveling peeps to roll in and spend some time with the home bodies. And honestly, after spending two months on a rock while Matt tried to guess *Armageddon*, I learned the Shadow are sorely lacking in pop culture education. I'm not requesting this. I'm demanding it." He pointed at the floor to emphasize his point.

My brows shot up. "Well, I can tell you're serious, gentlemen. Aren't you about to leave with Matt and Lucy on an adventure off-Sphere?"

Yito came clean. "I've gone several millions of years without a partner, and while I enjoy Ginger and Morning Star's company, sometimes they remind me of how deprived I am."

Puk nodded vigorously. "It's true."

I was getting the full picture. "So you would like an excuse to come home and have opportunities to socialize. You know you don't have to go with them, right?"

"I love every second of it, but one night a month for some company would do me some good. If you get my meaning, sir." Puk tacked on the 'sir' as if he'd just realized who he was talking to. The Mon3 drone even stood a little straighter, near attention.

I bit my thumbnail, feigning contemplation. Added some pensive nods… "Yes. I think we can do that. I believe Matt and Lucy would like the challenge of balancing their work with a regular social life as well. And it'll be good for Bethany to maintain contact with her brother and sister.

"Yes. Movie nights. Once a month. I'll make it official."

The two high-fived each other hard enough to ring through my study before they both seemed to remember in whose audience they were lingering.

"Oh, sorry. Thank you, sir."

They both nearly tripped over themselves on their way out.

The younger Seamswalker let Matt, Lucy, and Bethany into my study.

I didn't waste time. I knelt at Bethany's feet and looked into her honey-brown eyes to say, "I am so sorry for making you uncomfortable."

She surprised me by laughing in my face. It was a bright, happy giggle of a healthy teenage girl. I looked at Matt and Lucy for some assurance. They exchanged a look and smiled at me.

Matt said, "It's okay, Wingmaster. Bethany simply finds the entire situation funny, is all."

Funny.

Lucy tried to elaborate. "I think Bethany likes you just fine. Some parts of your Verse reminded her of a famine in her life, but now she's well-fed. We see to that."

Bethany tucked strands of her curly brown hair behind her ears and put her face inches from mine. Her voice was soft and under-used, as she said, "I ate Razor. Triss missed you. She brought you up all the time, and it hurt Razor's heart because he couldn't bring you back for her."

My heart stopped.

Ate.

Downloaded.

I muttered, "You weren't upset that my Verse was reminding you of Razor. You were living his memories. Memories of me..."

Bethany nodded and whispered, "He was happy you and he were so generous with Triss and that you could both use some more—"

"Later, Bethany. You can tell me about that stuff later," Lucy kindly and sweetly said into Bethany's ear. Like two girlfriends planning a chat over brunch.

I cleared my throat, wondering how I felt about Bethany seeing those exact memories before asking, "Would you consent to giving us Razor's memories? We could really use them to operate Ishkur."

And to sort out once and for all what kind of man the Pain Curator was.

The teenage girl cocked her head to the side. "Can I still keep them? They taste like vanilla and blood."

Both Matt and Lucy beamed at her like two proud older siblings.

I needed to swallow before I could answer. "Of course."

A tingle crawled up my spine at the sweet smile which spread across Bethany's lips. She nodded.

Matt held his hand out to her and Bethany took it as he said, "Come on, now. I think you used up all our time."

"Wait, is there anything you wanted, Matt? Lucy?" I could spare a few more minutes for original Shadow.

The redhead's freckled face sported a handsome smile, which I'm sure he was faking. "Naw, Wingmaster. We're just glad we followed you to the Callahan's Bookstore on Invasion Day."

Lucy was still beaming as she said, "We couldn't be happier. Thank you."

Hand-in-hand, that beautiful, bizarre trio let themselves out.

Sagan announced Pablo and Lynn next. I hugged them both and didn't hesitate to say, "I am so proud of you."

Lynn stepped back, hands on her pregnant stomach, and beamed. "Yeah. That's all I needed to hear."

Pablo smiled and agreed. "We don't really need anything. We only wanted a little time with you. And..."

"We wanted to invite you to the naming ceremony," Lynn finished.

Judging by her size, it was a week away at the most. For those smiles, I could spare the time. "We'll be there. I'm sure Aria, Torch, and all of our security teams will fuss, but this is essential. Have I mentioned again how happy I am for both of you?"

Happy they survived the last few years, and here I was keeping a most dangerous secret.

You shake your head, reminding me, "You'll tell them. I know they'll come to understand once the concern passes. The Shadow are constructive in their criticism. We've learned lessons from each other's mistakes, and that's how we've survived Imminent."

I hope so, Rayne.

We discussed the ceremony, Lynn's research on the defense weapons throughout Ishkur, and Pablo's latest efforts for public health education throughout Iona Pax.

It was easy going until Lynn asked, "Have you discovered who stole the shipments of Pil platinum?"

I looked into their honest and open eyes, swallowed, and said, "I plan to address the matter with everyone here soon." I know my smile wasn't nearly reassuring enough, but Lynn, Elden bless her, gave me another hug before the pair left my study.

I called out to Sagan, "Please send in the next."

"Pehton, Caedes, Aria, and Torch."

The tiny Lyrik flew into my arms without prelude and squeezed with surprising might. I returned in kind, saying,

"Hey there, Executive Warden. Did you come to ask me something?"

Against my hair, Pehton said, "Oh Elden, it's true."

I laughed incredulously while asking, "What's true?"

"You *do* give the best hugs."

All five of us laughed.

Afterward, I separated us and met her garnet eyes. "Talk to me."

Pehton gave Caedes, Aria, and Torch a nervous glance before wetting her lips to say, "In a roundabout way, my meeting you led me to my children, and I wanted to tell you how grateful I am that you would go to any lengths to keep a promise. Apparently including resurrection."

I couldn't resist ruffling her feathers and saying, "Dork. I'm glad the Shadow were there for you."

Caedes nodded silently behind her with respect in his dark green eyes.

Aria and Torch stepped forward and gently touched their mother's shoulders. "The others await their turn with the Co-Emperor."

I gave Pehton another squeeze and offered her children an appreciative smile.

Before they left, I called, "Caedes."

The gruff Icarus turned with a raised brow. "Yes, your imperial majesty?"

"Can you hang back a second?"

Caedes kissed Pehton before Aria and Torch left with her. Then he faced me alone.

I leaned against the arm of a couch and considered him for a moment. When I spoke, I conveyed my sincerity. "You've come a long way from exploiting The Brethren resources to move black market merchandise. Now you're a head of security for Iona Pax. I think I'll always feel indebted to you for looking after Tameka and Pax while I was dead."

Caedes' wince was faint and unexpected. He confessed, "She's worthy of loyalty and support, and Pax is a joy. Always has been."

"Are you happy?" I'm not sure why I asked such an intrusive question, but I think if he'd said 'no,' I would try to fix it.

The half-smile suited the bald Icarus as he said, "Yes. Truly. And possibly for the first time in my life. With the Verses all intact now, it's almost as if Elden meant for this to happen—For me to be stationed at Iona-28." Caedes chuckled, giving an incredulous shake of his head. "But as you know, it was Lucas' idea. However it all came together, I'm grateful." The light died in his eyes, and his smile dissolved as he added, "I will live up to my role and keep everyone safe."

"Iona Pax thanks you."

After speaking the most words I'd heard from him at once, it was as if Caedes had used his allotment for the year. To dismiss himself, he saluted with a fist to his chest, nodded, and left. The entire time, I beamed at Caedes, happy he came over to the Shadow all those years ago. For the love of redheads.

"C'mon, Sagan, doesn't someone else need to go next?"
That was Jack's voice.

After he said that, I glanced around the corner to catch Sagan physically dragging him in. Grunting, she said, "You. Are. Too. Strong." She gave up. "Ross, help me out."

Kyle's middle sibling took the bend of her boyfriend's elbow. "Come on, Callahan. Wingmaster will be happy to have a minute with us."

"I am, yes." I waved from the door where I could see this comedy show. "Uh, Sagan?"

"Hm?"

"You can let Jack go now."

Sagan looked at where she was straining with her entire body to pull, while Jack remained utterly unaffected. She giggled. "Right. I'll get the next pair rounded up."

I grinned at her. "Thanks." It stayed on my face as I turned to the young couple, saying, "Please come in. Of course, I'm happy to see you both."

Rayne, if you grin any wider, your face will hurt. Trust me. I know.

Your giggle is precious as you admit, "I still can't believe my little brother grew up to be—Well, that's not true. I *can* believe it. I'm happy for him, is all."

This private session isn't totally necessary. I see Jack at least three times a week when the King Elects give reports on Earth's migration, and Jack provides the voted specs for New Earth's design in Ishkur.

Still smiling with so much pride in your eyes, you say, "I'm glad he sees you so much. You really were a wonderful influence on him. Chris, too, obviously. But seeing Jack for work stuff isn't the same as a one-on-one with *the* Wingmaster."

True enough.

Ross went first. "I'll give you two some privacy, but I wanted to ask about Bethany. Can I be there for her Razor-memory transfer? I'm worried the resurgence might trigger her PTSD." Her hopeful eyes held something else inside.

I tried to keep from frowning at the doubt there, but I couldn't keep the concern from my voice. "What else is there, Ross?"

Exposed, Ross cleared her throat and glanced from Jack to me before saying, "Uhm. Well." Her eyes became glassy and her voice thickened. Jack took her hand for support as Ross said, "Bethany is pulling further away from Kyle and I, and I worry this transfer will make it worse. I worry about what's in her head. And—" She choked and shook her head, unable to continue.

I pulled Ross in for a hug.

It's funny how the gesture doesn't solve any problems, but it makes them bearable.

"Especially *your* hugs."

Ross seemed to agree. By the time she pulled away, her eyes were dry and her chin was stiffer. Especially after I assured, "Of course you will be there. Kyle, too." The next point I wanted to make might sting, so I captured her eye contact. Let her see the sincerity in me. "You may need to accept Bethany's estrangement."

Ross winced.

Jack chafed her arms, but he gave me a look which said he'd been thinking the same thing.

I pushed through Ross' initial aversion. "Bethany is making her way in another circle. Still wonderful people, but more similar to her mindset without the pressure of returning to 'normal.' Matt, Lucy, and the others don't place expectations on your sister. Whether you and Kyle intend it, that's exactly what you're doing."

"I know." The defeat in Ross' voice hurt, but there was hope in it. That mattered. She said, "That's why we're letting her go with them to Pil. I'll worry the entire time she's gone, but I trust them to keep her safe."

I almost winced because the next part wouldn't be easy to say either. "Ross, I think your sister keeps herself safe. If anything, Matt and Lucy will keep others safe from her." Something shifted in Ross' eyes, and I knew I was getting through to her suspicions. I said, "They'll teach her the right and wrong of it. I trust them, and I think that's what Bethany needs right now."

"Having Razor's history in her head couldn't be helping," Jack muttered.

While I couldn't disagree, my first reaction was always to defend Razor out of hand. I should work on that.

Ross visibly steadied herself and straightened her shoulders. Fitting her place in the Shadow, her words were clear and genuine. "Thank you. I'll leave you two alone now."

I gave Ross one more hug before she could go. The strength of her squeeze told me she needed it.

Jack waited for the door to close behind her before he blurted, "I think Rayne's really alive."

I blinked at him. "Absolutely. I've been telling everyone—"

He interrupted me, shaking his head, with his hands on his hips trying to figure out a way to word what he wanted to say. After a few heartbeats, Jack said, "I think she's in my dreams. Like not her. But... her presence. It's warm and smells like the beach we went to on Labor Day forever ago. I can't mistake it though: ice cream and surf. The cotton candy and sand. It's all there. Sometimes I'm even on the beach—"

"Are you saying you didn't believe she was alive this entire time?" Was everyone keeping up a pretense for my benefit?

Jack scruffed a hand through his short hair, finding the words. When he finally met my eyes, I knew.

Everyone thinks you're dead but me.

You look away, tucking a strand of hair behind your hair, muttering, "That was kind of the idea..."

Are you visiting your brother?

Still not meeting my eyes, you swallow and simply nod.

It's okay, Rayne. I told him what everyone should already know.

"Nothing could kill Rayne Echo Callahan. Not for long."

Jack gripped the collar on his t-shirt and pulled like it was choking him, shaking his head repeatedly. "No. She would come home, wouldn't she? Where is she, Xelan? Why would she stay away from us—"

Another hug. Another person who needed it.

If I hadn't grappled your brother into the hug now, he'd head down a dark road. One which led to self-blame and lessening his opinion of you.

My voice was tight with emotion as I tried to assure him, "I know, Jack. I know. But trust me, she's working on it. Rayne will come home the second she can."

Against my shoulder, the King Elect asked, "What's so important that it would keep her away from us?"

You meet my eyes, and the answer is there.

"It's my fault."

Jack pulled away and stared into my eyes, close enough to see the secret inside.

I swallowed and repeated. "It's my fault. There's still work to do, and your sister is doing it. I know it."

He searched my face with a twinge of anger emerging in his brows as he asked, "Are you in contact with her?"

"No. Nothing like that. Can you wait for me to explain to everyone? Please? She's not in danger, I promise."

Again, suspicion and conflict warred in Jack's eyes. There was more than a hint in his voice when he asked, "You're certain? She's alive, and she'll come home soon?"

I nodded. "Dead certain, little Jack Callahan."

All the tension rushed out of his body with a sigh. The relief changed his entire demeanor. He breathed in deep and exhaled long as if exorcising stress from his blood. Eventually, he confessed, "I thought... Damn, Xelan, I thought I was losing my mind with grief and survivor's guilt, but…It *felt* like her. You know?" The last squeezed out of him as tears spilled from his eyes. "Rayne's alive. Really alive."

"Your sister is a juggernaut. Nothing can stop her."

"You did *not* say that." Again, that incredulous laughter is almost as priceless as your four-year-old giggles.

I did, and I meant every word.

You fall back on the coffee table and cover your face, mortified. "You're so cheesy, Wingmaster!"

Well, it seemed to do Jack some good.

After another more celebratory hug, I saw him out of my study with one final caveat. "Don't tell anyone, yet. Rayne's not coming home for a reason, and I think it's keeping us safe."

Jack admitted, "I don't know how long I can keep this secret, but I'll try to think of what she wants."

Tumu and Lamassau were waiting at the door. A non-brow was raised on Tumu's face, and Lam simply blurted, "What 'who wants?'"

Jack shook his head, lighter and laughing easier than before.

Without answering the rude Tritan, I said, "Come on in, fellas."

The only green Tritan—the Chef—perched his butt on the arm of a couch and folded his arms, watchful. "I'm only here to keep Tumu behaving, since he can't seem to control himself around you. After all, you two are the 'Eternal Bind.'" He rolled his voids.

Tumu beamed at me.

Here was an important face. A heartbeat I'd recognize anywhere. Tumu emitted a special warmth of someone who understands.

"Understands what?"

Everything. About you. About how the worlds work. He gets it because he's old enough to have lived it, but unlike his fellow Primaries, Tumu learned from it all.

Sometimes, I think he would make a better Co-Emperor for Tameka than I. He was certainly more sound of mind. The only reason I never suggested it was because he's a Tritan. And after you destroyed Enki, the Tritans aren't popular. The Shadow's immediate alliance with the old race was the only thing to save them from genocide, I think—

Or perhaps I've become jaded.

Either way, Tumu is one of my favorite people in the entire galaxy.

"Tumu, you're one of my favorite people in the entire galaxy."

He pulled me in for a hug—yes, another hug—and with this one, I knew what it was like to be Tameka. My head barely came to Tumu's chest, compressed down to seven feet tall. Over his shoulder, I could see Lamassau watching us. He'd exaggerated his jealousy. The only emotion on Lam's face was kindness. He was happy for Tumu to have a friend like me.

I wonder if his opinion has changed since I told them the secret. I should really leave the Divine booth and check on them...

You sit back up on the coffee table and catch my eye with a little wave. "Not yet. Finish telling me your Verse. You're almost done, anyway."

You're right.

Against Tumu's shoulder, I murmured, "I'm so glad you answered my call from Iona-29. I don't know where we'd be without you."

"You're lucky your warrant for meddling with shit while in exile came with a hefty bounty." Tumu was full of shit.

I'd never believed he would actually arrest me, but…there were some offenses along the way. With a step back, I stared into his voids, wondering. "I have to ask, did you know Lance was using one of my Weapon nacres on Rayne?"

No features to speak of, even so, lines tightened around Tumu's voids as he said, "I'm not sure Lance did. I know he said he went through your old lab for one, but Lance may have used a nacre created by Celindria, supposedly to control Rayne's volition when the time came. I never imagined they'd imbue her with the means of our destruction. Not until you said as much the very same day."

Rayne, do you remember when you went with the other Progeny to see Primary Rem, and I stayed behind to speak to Tumu on the platform in the ocean?

You run a hand through your hair, tension in your shoulders. "How could I forget? That was the day you died."

I wince, but nod.
Yes. Well, Tumu told me a little about your nacre. Celindria's blood activated it because she had some of my half-Gargantuan blood. Of course, I didn't know it at the time…

You're nodding now, saying, "Yup. Yes. Between all the Verses, I think we've put that together. But I'd always wondered about the Primary they killed for it."

I smirk.

Des, Tumu's twin. He deserves his own Verse, and one day, I'll tell you. Me and Tumu will. Together. When you come home…
For now, the idea that you're carrying a nacre made by Celindria inside you… Well, it leaves me sick.

"I'll be fine, Wingmaster. You get back to the story. These private sessions are beautiful, but they are carrying on."

I said, "We'll need to meet with Lance, Silence—Anyone who might know how Celindria's nacres operated. We can't leave Rayne out there with an unknown threat—"

There.
Lamassau and Tumu shared a wince.
Both of them assume you're dead and hide how my inability to handle it affects them.

You crook a finger at me. "C'mere." I move closer until you boop our foreheads together where you can say, "That's the sleep deprivation talking. They love you and worry about how you're grieving for me. Everyone here has good reason to think I'm dead. I exploded, remember?"

I nod, nudging our heads.

"But look how they try for you… It's remarkable, really. When it's all said and done—when I come home—then you can throw an 'I told so' party of epic proportions. Until then, cut our people some slack."

I chuckled at Tumu, which made him frown, considering the subject. With a slap on his arm, I said, "Stop worrying. There's still a bit of Verse left, old friend."

Lamassau mumbled, "That's right. '*Friend*.'"
It left us laughing all the way to the door.

My children came in next.
Devis, Andrius, and T.A.O.
Merit's absence left an ache in my chest, but I maintained a grin for the gentler three. For all of Celindria's faults, she'd created some pretty amazing people.
"Hello, my Progeny."
Andrius saluted with a fist to his chest, Devis nodded, and T.A.O. traced her fingers across the spines of my journals. I couldn't blame her, as I'd often caught myself doing it.
I noticed how they filled the space with an awkward, uncertain energy. They were unsure of their place in this world. While I assigned everyone else work which would suit them, I'd left the First Wave Progeny free to do as they wish. It seemed only right, given how long Celindria had kept them in captivity. T.A.O. was the only one who took full advantage of it, and I often missed her.
After another stretch of silence, Devis finally clicked his tongue with impatience and blurted, "We want jobs."
Andrius looked at him sharply and nudged him with an incredulous expression.
T.A.O. blinked.
I let them see all the acceptance I could muster in my smile. "Whatever I can do, I will do. Name it, but remember, nepotism only goes so far."
At my joke, T.A.O. let out a single laugh. That one second of joy from her was enough to swell my chest with pride.
At Devis' insistence, Andrius stepped forward, saying, "I would like to help Caedes with security. I could help with *suggestion*, as you call it. Although, my combat skills could use refreshing. It has been too long since you've trained me in self-defense."

I clasped his shoulder and gave a nod. "Done."

The relief in his teal eyes made me smile brighter.

"I want to teach the Progeny meditation," Devis volunteered. "They could use it to better hone their skills, as I feel they are missing a center. This affects their performance by mere seconds, but seconds are hours when it counts."

"Done. We'll work with them all to schedule it. Are you fine with home-visits?"

Devis nodded. "Absolutely."

Purpose and function brought a new depth to their eyes and anchored their usual uncertainty.

Confidence.

This was good for their self-esteem.

Now it was the most fae of my Progeny's turn. The Afflicted One pulled a volume from the shelf, and the color drained from my skin.

How?

It was my most recent journal. I'd hidden it randomly among older entries.

T.A.O. stared at me as she said, "The hunt. I will join you, Father."

Andrius looked less confused than Devis, which increased my anxiety. Did he know as well? Andrew's ancestor tapped his brother's shoulder, saying, "Let's leave them. Sister needs some time alone with father."

Devis was unaware and still beaming from his newfound occupation. On the way out, he stopped to say, "I wished Celindria were alive to see how much the Shadow have accomplished and how we united the Twelve Worlds. Perhaps it would be enough to change her mind."

So close.

It was so close to my own feelings that I needed to swallow before I could even nod at him.

Both sons left me with my afflicted daughter. Unlike the memory and suggestion Progenies, Seamswalkers have an air of confidence about them. Unbending faith in their ability to remove themselves from any situation.

T.A.O. was not threatened alone with me. She repeated, "I wish to join the hunt."

I nodded. "Yes. You would be an asset, but T.A.O., no one else knows she's alive. I don't even know how you know."

"Her eyes appear in black flames in the skies of all the Worlds, beckoning me to return to her. I will not." T.A.O. tightened both fists, emphasizing the striation of her muscles and straining the veins under her skin. "*I* will not."

Gently, I placed my hands on her shoulders, brushed back the curtain of her wavy black hair, and assured, "I'll never let her take you again, but that means I don't want you chasing after her on your own."

T.A.O. nodded.

"Would you like your own apartments back here in the Stronghold?"

She blinked at me. "My home is in the Seam."

An image of a little nest with a bundle of blankets and a short supply of food stored in Monarch Hall's violet architecture brought a small smile to my lips. I said, "I think Razor would like that."

When T.A.O. found an occasion to smile, it was more radiant than the sun. She Seamswalked back to the ravine, beaming.

"Kyle and Silence are up next," Sagan announced before letting them in.

I already knew I'd need a moment alone with my foremother. There were… too many questions.

Silence entered wearing a slitted pencil skirt and a bikini top with a blazer over it. I'd heard about her unusual dress habits from the younger Shadow, but seeing it in person explained my fashion sense. Kyle followed her with a certain air he had around me ever since the two had taken up their relationship again.

Ugh. How else could I call it but 'I'm doing your grandma' face?

You die laughing.

In fact, I wonder if that was the entire reason Kyle asked for a private session. With one arm possessively around my foremother's waist, Kyle grinned, and I was inclined to believe my assumption.

"Hello, you two. I'm glad you've joined me for this brief meeting because I wanted the chance to tell you how fantastic a job you're doing in your roles. Thanks to you, Iona Pax is safer with every given day."

Silence possessed this way of speaking without words. Her eyes and mouth were so expressive. The movie star beam she gave me lit up those steel irises with joy and gratitude. Silence needn't say anything. This second chance here was more than she'd ever thought she'd get.

Kyle was less gracious as he said, "Well, yeah. We kind of have to or everything falls apart without us." His grin was shit-eating, and he knew it.

I clapped my hands together with a little chafe, asking, "So, do you have questions for me? Requests?"

"Naw. I'm glad Rayne made you train me all those years ago, and I'm damned happy I ignored your B.S. about not telling my sisters. But yeah, overall, this roller coaster turned out all right. Thanks, Wingmaster." Kyle presented his fist.

I bumped it with my own. Very imperial. With a glance at Silence, I made to dismiss my most errant Progeny. "Kyle, do you mind giving me a moment alone with my foremother?"

He glanced at her, then back at me with a shrug. "Sure. I guess." He paused at the door to ask, "Hey, when are we doing Bethany's memory transfer? ASAP, I imagine?"

I licked my lips, barely able to think of anything beyond telling them my secret, but still, Razor's memory was a priority. "If you don't mind, yes. Tomorrow, I should think."

"Roger that, Wingmaster. Don't keep Silence too long, we have..." He licked his lips to say, "Extracurricular activities scheduled while you've finish with everyone."

Preventing my eyes from rolling proved impossible, and my voice was flat. "Get out of my study."

We could hear Kyle's laughter until Sagan closed the door for us.

Silence was shaking her head, laughing. No shame in her. And how could there be? She was truly ancient. Gentle, too. Silence brushed my hair over my shoulder and straightened my clothes, making me presentable.

The softness in her made me smile, but it also hurt my heart. I wondered if my mother would've been a softer woman if Silence had been there to raise her.

It must've shown in my eyes, because Silence's smile faltered. She confessed, "I wished I was there for Savis. For you and for Nox."

"For Cinder?" I asked.

Silence nodded, and it was truly solemn. "Yes. I loved Elden. I still do. So much regret lives in me for how you've suffered. For how *all* of you have suffered."

I couldn't look at her. This conversation was long overdue, and now, with all three Verses done, Silence knew every truth. Still...

"I don't want you to shoulder any blame for how events unfolded. My mother... Yes, her life was hard, but that doesn't excuse all of her decisions. Nox, too."

A shadow flickered in Silence's eyes. A knowledge she was keeping from me. Her blood must run with the unknown. She said, "Ask me."

I licked my lips and did as I was told. "Did you create the shield?"

"No."

I knew it.

You take both my hands and give them a shake. "Be careful with Silence. She's gentle, like you said."

With a sigh, I press a hand to my head, thinking. How to proceed? What do I do with this information? I suppose the first thing I should ask is, "Do you know where it came from?"

"Yes."

Silence's one-word answers were pulling doubt from my faith in her.

I dropped my hand and met her eyes. I knew the answer before I asked, "Can you tell me where?"

"No."

Frustrated, I sat down and steepled my fingers to my lips.

Circumventing my anxiety, Silence added, "Not yet."

There were only so many options. When they'd escaped through the conduit from Enki into Ishkur, Tameka was unconscious. It was only Silence, Smith, and Lucas.

Lucas.

I'd ask him next.

The couch dipped when Silence sat beside me. She reached over and placed a warm hand on my back. Gently, like so much about her, she said, "It will all make sense soon. The Probability Matrix is a difficult labyrinth to navigate. Please trust me. You are safe and loved. Keep protecting Iona Pax, and the path will make itself known to you. Do not repeat my mistakes by acting against it."

I offered Silence a weak smile, saying, "Yes, foremother. I will honor your wishes and keep my faith in you a little while longer."

As expected, recognition warmed the steel in Silence's eyes. To which she bowed with her head before getting up to leave.

When she reached the door, I asked, "Silence?" She paused to look at me. "Will you provide an account of Elden's physical appearance to Iuo? There isn't one on record."

There.

That same shadow flickered in Silence's eyes. She smiled, nodded, and left.

Twelve-year-old you tilts your head to the side and blinks. "No one knows what Elden looks like?"

No. And I suspect my foremother will lie about that, too.

"Xelan, I think I've seen him."

Tell me, Rayne. What did you see?

You swallow before getting the words out. "When I was dying—"

I wince.

"—yeah, there's no pretty way to say that. But... I saw this figure with charcoal skin and gold tattoos. His hair was as long as mine, except it wasn't just black. Every strand was half black and half white. He was tall and built like Nox. Imposing really, but I still sensed so much kindness in him. Like Silence, he seemed gentle."

This is momentous. Any details about his face and eyes? We know his eyes were like yours, but... I've never heard of a firsthand account.

You shake your head and admit, "I couldn't get him to turn around before I was resuscitated."

Resuscitated—By who?!

"Well, Razor was around—"

I can't keep the bewilderment off my face.
Razor took on physical form to perform CPR on you?

With a little wince, you wave your hands. "No. That's not—It's complicated. And not important. I died within an hour, anyway, but I know it must've been Elden."

I have to be honest, at least fifty more questions come to mind. Like was this a visitation or a hallucination?

"Visitation. I know. He came to see me." You nod with certainty.

Is he still alive somehow?

Brushing more hair behind your ear—a nervous gesture—you confess, "It's not the first time I've talked to him. It's just the first time I've seen him. I think he's still alive inside his nacre."

My god. We should resurrect him—

"No!"

I blink at you, waiting for a reason.

You frown as you try to explain, "Sorry, but... I think he wants to stay sleeping for now. Please don't go to him."

I have absolute faith if anyone could develop a relationship with a deity, it would be you, Rayne. I'll wait until you say otherwise.

"Thank you."

"Lucas and Andrew."

A pair couldn't look less alike. Andrew was wearing a polo and shorts while Lucas sported a three-piece. Although, the two were closer in height than any other couple. An advantage I remembered for snuggling and other…positions.

Never mind that.

You shake your head, laughing with a light blush.

"Hello, Conscience. I suppose you already know I'll need Lucas alone before this is over."

Andrew, laid back as ever, nodded. "Yeah. Whatever. Uhm…I think I've already said everything I needed to say to you. You and I see each other enough that a pep talk isn't really necessary. Just know the Probabilities have been steadily shrinking since their formation, and especially in the last few days."

We clasped hands and ended in a fist bump. "Thanks for keeping on top of it, but try to relax. This Verse isn't over yet."

"Fucking tell me about it. How many more do you have after this?" He patted his pockets until he found a piece of hard candy to suck on.

After a moment of considering his question, I said, "I guess only Korac and Sagan after you two. We'll return to the story proper after that."

"Great." Andrew glanced between me and Lucas before letting out a sigh. "Okay. Well, you two have fun." He kissed Lucas' cheek on the way out. "Don't get into any trouble."

Lucas' eyes glittered as he said, "I try not to, but no one believes me."

When the door closed, I said, "I believe you."

The smile Lucas gave me in return said he didn't really care either way. Here was a friend and an ancient adversary with far more behind his eyes than I'd ever gave credit to.

"I like you, Lucas," I admitted.

He bowed with his head. "Likewise, your imperial majesty."

My hands went to my hips while I considered how to ask this. Thanks to Andrew, I suddenly wanted some candy to chew on. Eventually, I said, "You're still keeping secrets."

Lucas nodded sagely. "Yes. It's how I've stayed alive for so long."

"But... you're *with* us, aren't you?" I couldn't keep the emotion from my voice. I wanted him to be on our side.

"The Probabilities make it so," Lucas confessed.

I stared at him. That could mean anything. Without further preamble, I asked, "How did you make the shield?"

Like Silence, a shadow flickered in Lucas' golden eyes. "Your majesty asks the wrong questions."

A little impatient, I pressed, "What should I be asking?"

Lucas said, "Why was it pertinent I keep it secret? That's the key to all of my secrets, Xelan. Why do I keep them?"

My heart raced while I stared into the ancient intelligence inside someone I considered a brother.

Why?

For millennia, we'd known each other, and he'd lied to me the entire time. But not once did he endanger me. I breathed, "Tell me." Please, let it be good.

Alien and remote, Lucas tilted his head to one side and stared into my mind with piercing gold eyes. He said, almost curiously, "You're not ready to know yet. But soon... Yes, soon, Xelan, we will tell you."

We.

"I caught that, too."

This felt familiar.

And frustrating.

I could arrest him and force the information from him in an interrogation, but as I gazed at the monolith in front of me, I knew making an enemy of Lucas would be a mistake.

Wetting my lips, I asked the only question which mattered. "Will anyone else get hurt in the meantime?"

Lucas shook his head and assured, "We aren't interested in causing you harm."

"I suppose that will have to do."

The Icarus—if he even was an Icarus—took a step closer to me, straightened my shirt on my shoulders, and smiled in my face while he did it.

Then Lucas left.

Sagan came in next with Korac. The glowing married couple was a stark contrast to the obelisk who'd left a moment ago. For them, I could smile easily. Even facing Korac's signature smirk.

"Hello, you two."

A hug from Sagan was always welcome, especially while she's holding little Echo. She asked, "Would you like to hold her?"

This was a treat I rarely delighted in. Working all the time kept me from my god parent duties. I scooped the infant from her mother, admiring the mixture of Aegis and Lyriki qualities. Pitch-black skin with white feathers. Hard diamonds for eyes. Cute little smile.

Okay, I cooed.

Korac gave a single chuckle at the sound. "Everyone succumbs to the cuteness in the end."

Elden, my mind filled with so many questions about Echo. Like had she expressed any signs of the Siren's Gale yet? What was that like? Could she form a raging fireball because she wanted her bottle immediately? It left me snickering. "Oh, I'm so happy you're here with us, baby Echo."

She whistled at me, and I took it as a compliment. I'm sure she said I'm super cool in baby talk.

"Oh, I'm sure." Your smirk belies your humor.

I looked between the couple, saying, "The two of you see me more than anyone else here. My door is always open. How can I help you?"

Sagan glanced at Korac before saying, "Well, you know I don't need anything from you, except maybe an extension on my vacation request for my actual honeymoon." She swatted me playfully.

It hurt.

Korac, who'd leaned on the couch, nodded his agreement.

"Of course. I really am sorry for the timing," I lied.

Sagan narrowed her eyes at me, unconvinced. Still, she said, "Well, that's all I had. I'll leave you two alone before we return to the main Verse. Thanks for the session." She reached her arms out, and I was sad to let Echo go, but the beautiful smile on Sagan's face as she took her daughter lit the room.

It was worth it.

Your voice is soft as you admit, "I want to meet Echo. And Pax. I'm missing so much…"

Come home, Rayne.

"Not yet, Superman. Get back to you alone with Korac. I wish I had some popcorn." Your giggle is slightly menacing.

Alone.

Without hesitation, Korac said, "You're lying. You're not sorry."

I didn't acknowledge the accusation, and instead, changed the subject. "You were right."

That startled Korac a bit, which I enjoyed entirely too much.

I said, "About Razor and Nox. Your brother would certainly enjoy us fighting, where Nox would detest it.

But I think I stand by my earlier decision: neither of them deserve an Iona. We grant honors to those who died for us to get here, and while, technically, both Nox and Razor fit the bill, they caused too much pain along the way. My Verse has taught me that much."

I was thinking about Bethany and Pehton, the Children of Gait, the humans of Earth, Nikki—So many people. Victims of Razor and Nox.

Rayne, how do you feel about it? We're nearly at the end of my Verse. Surely you can answer now.

You're contemplative, as you say, "I think for a public institution, your final reasoning is sound. Like you said, you already honor Nox by distributing his Verse as required education—I'm sure he would never expect even that much. So... yes." You give a little nod. "You're being fair."

Korac seemed to agree. "All right. But who gets the next distinction?"

"Can I make a suggestion?" Tameka called from around the corner. We couldn't even see her.

Sagan snickered at the door, too.

Korac clicked his tongue and rolled his eyes, folding his arms to complain. "Eavesdropping is so childish."

"Come on in, since you're listening, anyway. You may as well contribute." I couldn't stop from grinning.

Tameka looked so abashed, but Sagan knew no shame.

My lover, the mother of my son, suggested, "The ten million Icari."

Both Korac and I exchanged a glance before I said, "Which specifically?"

Sagan elaborated, "The ten million who sacrificed their nacres for Rayne's Sphere, formerly Nox's Sphere, on Earth."

"Without them, we could never have evacuated Cinder," Tameka finished.

Korac nodded, getting it. "Yes. I second or third this opinion."

Anonymous Icari willing to do anything for their people—The Icarean Prerogative. "Elden would be proud," I said, beaming at Tameka.

Tameka added, "And if this debate ever resurfaces, there are plenty of people who died for the side of good before the Shadow should honor any sacrifices with potentially ambiguous or non-righteous motives."

Korac's brows went up, and he let his eyes fill with respect.

I simply kept beaming at my girl.

I am so lucky.

"Damn straight."

ENTRY FOURTEEN

HOPE IN THE LIGHT OF SHADOW

"**Welcome to the final chapter of my Verse.**"

Snacks littered my study, surrounded by pajama-clad Shadow. They looked ready for my last chapter. Eager, even, as I suppose they would be after spending an impromptu week in my stronghold.

These were the faces of the people I trust, maybe marginally for some, but still...

Here we go.

"So, as you've guessed by now, my time in exile was one long nervous breakdown. Until the day it wasn't. Occasionally, I couldn't stop myself from leaving to feed from CoN compounds and tracking the Progeny lines. Did you know that, Lucas?" When I said his name, it held a weight to it which hadn't been there before. It wasn't my intention, but after our conversation, I think differently of him.

Lucas either didn't notice or was a better actor than I am. He stood with his usual smile and said, "We knew of every move you made. Including the day you wandered into the Baptist Hospital in 1987, which is where I presume you were heading."

Tameka perked up beside me. All the current Progeny came a bit more to attention.

I said, "The day Tameka was born, all the lights within a mile of the hospital went out. Backup generators kicked on to keep life-saving machines operating. Powerhouse. Fury."

"Mom?" Pax was looking at his mother for confirmation.

"That's right, sweetie. I was awesome from the start."

Chuckles and snickers filled the room.

I rubbed the back of my neck awkwardly as I continued, vulnerable to any discussion of my mental state. "It was a sign to me. Proof positive: this line of Progeny were different. But… I couldn't focus. I couldn't maintain my mind in all its fragmented pieces. Not to mention, I wasn't fit to be in public. But I figured Lucas knew I was there because a few years later, he knocked on my door."

Kyle pointed out. "Your stronghold doesn't have a door."

"Thanks for volunteering, Kyle. Please read volume three-thousand, two-hundred and eight. Page thirty-two."

With a grumble, Story Taker did as he was told.

Rumors.

Rumors of Nox investigating this generation of Progeny.

Rumors of a girl in flames, destined to end it all. Most of what I'd heard was talk of her biorhythms in perfect synchronization with the Probability Matrix.

Primary Rem and Abresson—

They said the same thing about me once during one of Umbra's festivals. I overheard them while I pretended to play at their feet.

I'd never heard 'beautiful' said in such a creepy way.

Five years have passed since Tameka was born—

Was that right?

Had it been that long already?

I'd meant to see them all brought into this world—To search for confirmation—

It didn't matter now.

The girl in Cascading Light. The girl I could see in the black fire. She would be… four now.

I hoped for her sake—for all their sakes—the rumors weren't true.

What was her name?

Did I ever learn it—

Laughter rang through the stronghold and lights flashed all around. Was I having an epileptic fit—

No.

The alarms.

Someone was outside.

I checked the security monitors to find a face so familiar… Relief rushed through me and flooded my eyes with tears.

Lucas.

He'd flown here in a jet and covered it with a camouflage tarp. I opened the cylindrical lift and granted him entry through the Gait security measures.

Welcome to my prison.

Now that sounded too dramatic…

I scratched my head, my hair trailing behind me. Putting it up kept people from noticing me, but… It was a lot of work and when I didn't keep it clean, well… it was impossible.

"Your highness."

How bad did I smell this time? Were my teeth in good condition—

"Traitor Prince."

Maybe I could bathe before he made it down the lift—

"Xelan!" Lucas took my shoulders in his hands, stopping the circle I'd been spinning without realizing. "What has this isolation done to you?"

Wasn't it obvious?

Lucas set me down in a chair and worked to make me focus on his eyes. I couldn't because they were too warm, too concerned. It hurt to face them. To see the reflection of the monster I'd become in his eyes.

The kindness in Lucas' voice hurt my ears. "Let the Tribunal come for me. I am not leaving you like this. Xelan, can you speak?"

It had been five hundred eighty-one thousand, eighty days since I'd spoken to another soul.

I cried because I knew…

I was too far gone.

Without words, Lucas took me to my rooms and paid me his usual charity. Beyond friendship, there are no words for the kindness he paid me. All the while, he talked. The sound of another voice.

News and updates.

These Progeny were doing well, and CoN was on the rise. Lucas reported the same rumors I'd intercepted with comms devices about the Icarean Army massing to claim this girl as the salvation of their race. Our race.

"Rayne."

Lucas stopped cutting my freshly washed hair to peer at me in the mirror. "Yes. That's her name. Rayne Echo Callahan. She's Celindria's descendant. And Korac's agents are quite interested in her." He continued trimming, saying, "I thought to bring some suits which should fit you—At least you didn't starve yourself. Perhaps you could put one on, and we'll go see the Progeny. The Callahans just bought a bookstore in Little Rock. Quaint little shop. Seems like your influence on their line, in my opinion…"

Lucas told me all about the situation on both sides. It was so nice to hear from another person. A friend—

"I never should have left you in this exile. None of us felt right about it. Iuo asks after you often, and Seps went into hiding with F8—Xelan, we need you."

If you'd asked me what was happening in my head at this moment, I'd tell you there was no way for me to know. But…strategy formed on its own. Logistics and estimations. What would it take to station an installation in Little Rock? How fast could I staff it? But first—

"Let's go see the bookstore."

That's where you come in.

Little you peeks out from under the fort, smiling with a little, "Hee."

Preteen you asks, "Why 'Iona?'"

Oh. I suppose I've never explained before. Iona is the only Icarean word which defies translation. It means 'endlessness.' Not eternal or unstoppable, but something with no limit to its potential.

Both versions of you smile. "Iona Pax: Endless Peace."

Exactly.

I can't help it. When I talk about this moment, I grin—Beam even. "Most of you don't know this story, but I put on one of Lucas' suits and a fake pair of glasses for anonymity. And because they looked cool. It was night, as we still couldn't walk through the sun's rays, but the door to the bookstore was open.

Still, Kavanaugh Boulevard was a popular street with its neighborly hustle and bustle. I took notice when a crowd started gasping and pointing at the road. This little girl with dark pigtails and cute little overalls had run out into the street. Some impatient jerk was speeding through an intersection. I scooped Rayne up in the nick of time."

Sagan asked, "Did you say, 'I got you?'"

"Of course."

Tameka was smiling as she said, "Wow. Rayne's first 'I got you.' Why hadn't we heard of this?"

I spread my hands, explaining, "Well, she didn't remember. Not until later. But I took one look into those big blue eyes, and I knew...

"That same night, I bought an old airline and started recruiting to outfit the Ionas. Exile could fuck off."

That stirred the room. Cussing just wasn't my thing, and it felt weird in my mouth.

Even Korac acknowledged it with a solemn nod. "I'm an excellent influence."

You're quiet.

Both versions of you are smiling at me, but the preteen version looks deeper in thought until you say, "I never knew…I mean…This is unexpected, but I'm glad I brought you out of it."

That voice in my head was different with you. It didn't say to hide you or protect you. It said to help you. To build you up and see you soar.

"I saw it in your eyes. I remember how you looked at me. How you're looking at me now. Thank you for always saving my life. I love you, Superman."

I love you, too, Rayne Callahan.

Closer to the secret now.

"The Brethren kept tabs on me for the next ten years. While Lucas was an ally, not every member agreed with me breaking exile." I nodded at Caedes.

He stood and said, "I was among them. We believed he'd bring the wrath of the Tribunal down on our operations. The Brethren walked a fine line as a council of leadership. Some—Frullop, for example—wanted Nox and Cinder to invade. Pro-Icari only. And Pro-Humans wanted to end the Progeny lines to prevent Nox from obtaining Rayne's blood and entering Earth. Obviously, the dissenters haven't survived the actual Invasion, but it was a political time for us. And the Traitor Prince posed a threat to that balance."

Kyle, who was reading ahead, said, "Well, you certainly gave them the middle finger. I gotta say, Wingmaster, I never thought of you as cool, but wow. Molotov cocktails? Nice."

Tumu humphed. "We knew. Of course, we knew. Do you have any idea how much work it was to keep the Tribunal off of you? Although, it's likely Imminent enjoyed the Probabilities you fostered into existence." He glanced over at Lucas, Silence, and Smith. "Am I right?"

Smith simply grinned.

Silence peered at Lucas, who offered, "We enjoyed our time with the Shadow, even early on. We wanted you to thrive as the Mother would want, yes?"

That ambiguous 'we' from Lucas again.

Silence nodded, beaming.

I couldn't help but smile, looking back at my first crew in Iona-01. Colton, Cypher, Six, and Smith. I confessed, "I loved that time, too. We made one helluva team."

Andrew gasped. "'Helluva?!'" He followed it up with a burst of laughter.

Sagan and Tameka snickered along.

I sobered with a thought. A thought of you, Rayne.

"What's that, Superman?"

To reclaim everyone's attention, I said, "The day came to tell the Progeny, and I wasn't sure what to do. I'd been in and out of Rayne's life after CoN became more interested in her, so I knew where you went to school—"

"Not at all creepy, dude." There was humor and teasing in Kyle's voice, but I still winced.

"I would never have otherwise, but…"

Tameka drew from the Verses. "The cultists were after us. One attacked Rayne when she was twelve. Nox swore in his Verse he forbade any contact with the Progeny."

"I would've killed the CoN member myself when we arrived in 2002," Korac confessed. "Anyone who went against our orders was a danger, but anyone so outside of their mind to approach a Progeny… Automatic execution. And a public one at that." As the room winced at his ruthlessness, he turned those flat, white eyes on Kyle. "Give our imperial majesty a break. We—the Icarean armies and CoN—were breathing down your necks from the moment you were born. Hell, even we became paranoid about your safety and kept tabs."

Sagan added, "That's right. Imminent was around, too." She smiled warmly at me. "I'd convinced myself when I was a little girl that I had a guardian angel. I guess I just had good instincts."

I blushed. It was too sweet. The Shadow warmed with the kindness of it.

You grin. "Sagan can do that to a room."

That she can.

"Kyle, would you care to read volume three-thousand, four-hundred and fifty-five? Page one?"

"Yeah. Like I have a choice." Kyle continued the story.

{AUGUST 2002}

MORE RUMORS.

This time of the worst kind.

Standing at the top of the Arkansas State Capitol, I stared out over downtown Little Rock at night. Such a little city, so unaware of the space-scrapers only a conduit away. Cargo pants and a black tank top had become my standard issue gear since moving full time into Iona-01 with my team. We worked day and night to maintain the airline operations while negotiating The Brethren's careful political landscape.

"Your highness."

Speaking of. "Hey, Lucas. It's good to see you."

We hugged once he fully alighted in the cupola, our designated meeting space. Often, we scouted the area for potential centers in case… in case…

"Is it true? Has Nox found a way to Earth?"

Lucas shook his head and patted my shoulder reassuringly. His voice was full of confidence as he said, "It's not possible. How could they gain access to Rayne's blood this soon?"

"Did you know we did, in fact, make it to Earth?" Korac asked while painting his fingernails black. Blowing them dry, he glared with more than a little suspicion at the golden-eyed man.

Lucas dipped his head. "Yes. Smith and I knew. The Brethren did not. Well, I'm uncertain about Frullop. Andrew took his nacre before we could interrogate him."

Andrew waved sheepishly as the Shadow glanced his way.

I considered Korac's question. Did it really matter now if Lucas knew or not? It happened and now we're here. "Kyle, please continue. Skip ahead to September."

Again, he grumbled, but obeyed.

{SEPTEMBER 2002}

CELINDRIA'S VISITS TO MY DREAMS HAD INCREASED IN FREQUENCY OVER THE LAST MONTH. I couldn't wait any longer. It was time to tell Rayne. I followed her family, to keep them safe, across the southern United States. Now here I was at this beach after the sunset, and there she was, alone on the boardwalk to watch the fireworks.

Racing thoughts filled my head and accelerated my anxiety.

Just go talk to her.

She'll understand; she's Progeny.

But look at her. She's so young. And happy.

No.

Don't interrupt this moment.

The smell of the beach. Waves and sand, ice cream and sunscreen, the breeze… The last day of summer…

I blink as you take both my hands.

"Xelan."

Rayne.

You're sitting across from me, and you're not a preteen anymore, nor a little girl. You're all grown up. Although, you'll always be *my* little girl. It's in that smile, in the brightness of your eyes, and the kindness in your voice. "Hey, Superman. It's been a while."

I'm so happy to see you, but... Rayne, I don't have you programmed at this age in this Divine Booth—

"Shh. Finish your Verse, old Icarus of mine, and then we can talk." Your skin is glowing, and your hair is so long, like a thick black curtain. "Every time I think about cutting it, I remember how disappointed you were when Tameka cut it for me. Do you remember?"

The night we met with Nox. Yes. How could I forget? Come here.
We hug, and it's warm, and sort of confusing.
How are you here?

"Verse, first. Talk after. Oh, Xelan, I'm so happy to see you, too. These really are the best hugs."

Where was I...? Oh, right. The night we met.

"Rayne was still sunburnt from the day before at the beach, and Michelle..." I spared Jack a glance filled with sympathy. "Your mother was still exhausted after driving home from Florida so your dad, Ray, could work his shift. And you... well... You were a troublemaker back then."

Jack smirked. "Yeah. Chris straightened me out."

Chris held up his fist. "That's right. I'm the best. Send all your kids to me and Karter for babysitting duties."

Lynn said, "We'll take you up on that," while Pablo placed a hand on her belly. They beamed.

Tameka brought us back to the story. "So Rayne told us all about how she first met you and asked her to meet at the skating rink that Friday. We started training after school. Then the memories regressed into our dreams, for some… for others…"

"Some of us had visitors." Your smile is so sad as you say it.

I still want my answers, Callahan.

That brightened your expression a little. "Keep telling the Verse, Superman."

<hr>

I loosened my collar for this next bit. "In December of 2006, Rayne came to me about her dreams with Nox. To solve them, I stepped out of my lane to summon The Brethren. While I trusted you, Lucas, I knew there was no way Nox could invade her dreams on this scale from another planet. The nanites didn't resonate that strongly in her blood. Not without a nacre. Do you remember what you said to me?"

"'Oops.'"

Kyle barked out a laugh. "Oh, oops. 'I guess that one bad guy and his armies crossed a planetary border, after all. My bad.'"

I rewarded the shit-talking with a grin before saying, "But as punishment for breaking my exile on official channels, someone in this room locked me down in my own Iona."

I didn't look at the person responsible. I'd let him stand and identify himself if he deemed it necessary.

Honest and brave, Caedes raised his glass of Yun liquor. He said, "It was me. But only after the entire Brethren voted unanimously on it." He slid a glare in Lucas' direction.

The clandestine not-sure-if-he's-an-Icarus bowed with his head. "True. But your address was quite convincing. Not to mention, if I hadn't held you back, your imperial majesty, Nox would've murdered you in front of your Progeny. Left you broken in a burning building while all the world still needed you."

A hush fell over the study.

How could Lucas always know so much? More than the entire Brethren and CoN and—

"Colita."

Korac said her name like it was a dirty word.

Of course.

Lucas begrudgingly stood and straightened his suit to answer yet another round of questioning. He said, "Yes. She was always a reliable informant. I knew when you arrived and how you organized within the CoN compounds across the world. Colita also ranted about Nox's fascination with Rayne in her dreams. How he didn't even feed from Colita anymore. Then she told me of your plan to test the Progeny with false victories—I knew they were in no danger. So what was the harm in postponing your ultimate confrontation a little while longer?"

First, there was silence. No pun intended.

Then...

"You could've told us so I could warn my sisters! Ross could've taken Bethany to safety!"

"Imminent murdered my parents while I was skipping class and Rayne was at school! We could've saved them!"

"I think an Icarus killed my dad. It's funny. I never went to check."

"We watched all of our classmates die! Lynn's parents were murdered. Thanks to Bones, I learned mi madre survived—But no thanks to you at all!"

"I killed the band teacher..."

"Rayne's arm was decimated, and I was nearly drowned in a toilet."

"I thought I'd killed you..."

The last voice stopped them all as Sagan cupped Korac's jaw in her hand. She repeated, "You made me think I'd killed you, and I mourned you. It was only hours until you and Nox left the school together, but I didn't like the way the world felt without you in it."

Echo whistled and cooed beside them with a mighty kick in her footie jammies.

Lucas stared at them with a shocking intensity. Their love was proof of the outcome. Still gazing, he asked, "Would you undo it, Sagan? The day of Invasion for all those reasons you cited. Would you change it all?"

Sagan met Lucas' golden eyes first. Unashamed, she shook her head.

Korac kissed her palm and said, "No."

Pax climbed up on the couch, over the arm, and onto the back. The little boy accidentally kicked Jack in the head, who took it with a gracious smile, while Pax laid across the back like a cat and held out his hands to Tameka. "Mom! Can I go to the treehouse tomorrow?"

The palatial grounds sported more than a few playgrounds for children, but the tree village was Pax's favorite.

It wouldn't exist without Invasion Day.

Pax wouldn't exist.

Tameka gave him two high fives. "You got it, kiddo."

Finally, Jack answered for all of them. "It's too hard a question to answer as individuals. You can say our lives are wonderful now, and you'd be right. But it didn't come without a price. Since three billion of those lives weren't ours to represent, we can't say if we'd change it or not." He took Ross' hand and squeezed it, saying, "But I am happy. I just wish..." He shot me a glance, obviously referencing you, Rayne.

Would you change it?

Your eyes are sad again, near tears, as you say,
"My last thought when I died...I wanted a hug

from my mom. That I would trade everything for one hug from her."

It's enough to send tears to choke me.
There are no substitutes for those hugs. Not even mine.

A pretty, sad smile spreads across your lips, and you hold out your arms. "I'll take one though."

It's a good squeezer of a hug, and I feel a frailness in your arms.
Are you all right where you are? Tell me the truth.

"Soon, we'll all be okay."

Martyr.

Our laughter harmonizes until we stop hugging, and you say, "It's time to close your Verse. Tell them the truth, but tell them it's under control so I can have more time."

I will do what I can for you.

I wasn't ready to tell my secret, and I was at the same time. It maligned through me like a cancer, eating away at my thoughts, my heart, and my sleep for too long. Before much longer, it would chew through my body—And I couldn't have that while raising Pax.

With a sad smile—I couldn't muster a grin—I waded into the pallets of Shadow. Progeny, Icari, Humans, Tritans, Lamias, and Drones. My family minus a few warm faces. I met all their stares as I brought my Verse to its conclusion.

"There are still some loose-ends. I want to take a moment and say Colita's death saddens me. She was a good friend to me, but I know she was an enemy of the Shadow. Like Razor." I shot Korac a distressed glance, saying, "She deserved better for an end."

Tameka agreed. "Even *I* think killing Colita in battle was better than Nox locking her in the Martyr Complex."

Korac conceded with a nod. "Fair enough."

I took the spotlight back. "We need to continue investigating who took my birth nacre from Nox's castle and placed it in the resurrection casket below Gait's prison."

Kyle asked, "Do you think someone in the Shadow could've done it?"

I frowned, asking, "Why would they hide it?"

Kyle gave a not-so-subtle glance at Tumu and Lucas. "Well, we've had a few clandestine and ambiguous members in the past. What if some people are still keeping secrets?"

You snicker as you say, "That's rich coming from the guy who fell in love with the most important amnesiac in the galaxy."

Andrew stood with an apologetic look in my direction before saying, "I know this Verse is a sour reminder of Lucas' complicity in some of our worst moments, but we agreed. When you look at the facts, he was always on our side. Sometimes, bitterly so. Please remember he fought with us on Volcano Day when it mattered. Side-by-side. Bleeding and burnt. He just looked better than all of you while he did it."

That shameless, goofy grin.

Despite myself, I barked out a laugh, holding my ribs.

The Shadow smiled or chuckled, joining in the warmth. Sagan even stood up and hugged Andrew, then Lucas. She said, "It's okay. Although ironic after the lecture you gave me for being in love with Korac all those years ago."

Andrew chuffed. "Yeah. Yeah. Your Icarus is less evil than mine. I get it."

Evil.

What did Lucas do that was evil?
Or Korac?
Rayne, wouldn't you say the definition of that word changes with every Verse?

"Yes." You glow a little extra at the thought. "I don't think anyone is evil anymore. Well, maybe Abresson, but Lucy paid him the goodbye he deserved." Everything about you sobers a bit and somehow you are gentle and stern all at once. "Tell them."

"I let Celindria go."

All the faces were mid-laughter, smiling, and filled with the infectious warmth of this place until my words sunk in.

Smith was still smiling, but it was full of… respect.

It was the same smile on Lucas' face.

Korac also looked less surprised than I expected, but that didn't mean he looked happy. The smile wiped clean from his face and undiluted disappointment replaced it.

Eventually, Jack asked, "Wh—What did you say, Wingmaster?"

Pehton coughed, choking on something, and squeezed out, "Did you just say—"

"I let Celindria live after her fight with Remorse. She was injured, but I couldn't bring myself to kill her."

"Son of a bitch." Kyle knocked over his drink as he jumped to his feet.

Andrew followed, and, judging by the look on his face, tasted my intentions.

I let him have them. All of them.

You were right that day. I did let her go, and I lied to you about her death. I'm sorry. Please understand me. I can't bear my responsibility for her insanity. She doesn't understand. There's nothing she can do since she stepped into the source of Cascading Light. What little remained of her soul will wither, and she'll take us with her. And I deserve it—

"Stop!" Andrew was clutching his chest as if it hurt, staring at my face as he repeated, "No more."

Sagan asked, "What is it? What's in his intentions?"

Korac humphed and spoke into his glass. "Guilt."

They were getting closer to me.

Except the First Wave Progeny.

T.a.o. knew, Andrius had sensed it from me, and Devis was… the only person in the room smiling with relief.

Dizzy.

So dizzy.

"How could you let her go?"

"Please tell me you know where she is?"

"Is that who's been stealing our shipments from Pil?"

"Did my memory fix her?"

All the voices and faces were familiar, but their words exploded like firecrackers in my ears—

Deaf.

I couldn't hear.

No.

The room went silent.

Why—

I spun to find myself crouched in the center of my study, shielding myself. But everyone had backed off. Everyone but Tameka. The woman I love, the mother of my son—Her green eyes reflected concern, but… something else.

"Go to bed, Xelan." That 'something else' was in Tameka's voice, in her soft hands on my face. It was final and not to be argued with. She said, "Sleep and don't pretend this time. Come down only when you've rested for at least eight hours. We'll still be here when you're ready. *All* of us."

Korac called, "You heard our Co-Emperor, people. Go get some rest, and we'll discuss this in the morning."

They moved back, giving me room to walk out of the study. All the while, they shared the same expressions.

Hurt.
Disappointment.
And a little fear.

What have I done?

So here I am. Hiding in my shame from my family inside a Divine Booth I stole from Razor and programmed with younger versions of you to brainstorm ideas and, well, grieve. Because no matter how hard I try to convince myself, some part of me still questions.
Did you die with Enki?
Rayne, how long have I been asleep in here?

You're still holding both my hands as you bite your lip before saying, "Four hours. They don't know where to find you, and they're searching the stronghold over. It won't be long before they think to look in here."

I couldn't help but notice you've tied your dress with the same nacre rope I remember seeing in our previous encounters—It's you. It's really you.
I try to hold it together, but the tears fall, anyway.
You're alive.

You stand, pulling me up with you into a hug. I can't help but crush you in the embrace, clinging to my sanity for all these months, fearing you were gone.

Against my chest, you say, "I've tried so hard to tell you, but you wouldn't sleep..."

Your tears are warm through my shirt, and I brush my hand down your hair to apologize. My eyes squeeze shut to let the tears fall.

I was so afraid...

When I open my eyes again, the Divine Booth's simulation of my study is gone, and we're standing on the same beach as always in your visits. Except this time, I notice an island with a volcanic eruption pouring lava into the waves. It's symbolic, but of what?

"Never mind that." You separate us to stare up at my eyes with yours red from tears. "I understand everything now. You weren't training me all those years to kill Nox. You were training me to defeat Celindria because you can't do it."

I nod, unable to speak yet. Instead, I cup your cheek, letting my sorrow into my eyes.
Please forgive me.

The wind loosens your hair, and you push it from your face, so I can see how much you understand. "You don't need to ask me, Xelan. I've been with you this entire time. Tell me, what are her abilities, defenses, and weaknesses?" You lean into my hand, urging, "We have little time."

Celindria can manipulate shadows and use them to travel. I'm not entirely certain how. She doesn't have wings that I know of, but well, you were there in Umbra's Spire. She got to the window somehow. Cascading Light gives her an advantage over you, and I can't speak to the limits of it. Since Thailea, I think she can only experiences negative emotions. No more hints of love or joy. Only grief and malice. And...

"Yes?"

Once, I thought Celindria possessed a flicker of her sibling's abilities, but that can't be entirely true or she wouldn't have needed Pax for Ishkur.

Your eyes are so clear beside the water that I can see myself in them, but not me. I can see how you see me. Frock coat, pirate tricorn, and an earring. It leaves me incredulous.

Really?
You grin at me, and I'm immediately disarmed. I grin back.

You ask, "Can you give me anything else?"

What remains of Imminent will want you dead once they've learned you've survived the impossible. I've afforded you some cover by encouraging the Rayne tributes. Be careful.
A thought suddenly occurs to me.
I have safe houses across the Worlds—

"I know." You're still grinning as you say, "They're in Razor's dossier."

My mouth fell open. I closed it. Razor.
He gave it to you?

You nod and fuss with your hair again. "Yes, before we died. He uploaded it straight into my nacre memory bank."

I'm both shocked and totally unsurprised. Use any of them you like except the one on Thailea. It was too experimental, and you may get lost trying to find it.

"Thank you. I'll let you know which one I'm in when it's time. I'll bring the others in when I

need them, but please, I know it hurts, but let them think I'm dead."

I open my mouth to argue—

You shake your head. "It's okay for Jack to have hope, I guess. But anyone else will come after us. I can't have that."

Us. That reminds me...
Come collect the two strawberry milkshakes I owe you.

Your smile is sly and sad at the same time. Quite the paradox with the light in your blue eyes. Softly, you say, "I guess I owe you some answers."

I nod slow and deep.
I need to hear it, please. You've kept me on the hook long enough. How is Nox featuring in your dreams? How do you feel about him now that you've grown into this brilliant young woman capable of anything? Now that you know everything.
You cup my hand already on your face and bring the other to match, holding them both in place. A fresh tear streams from your lashes, and I prepare myself for the answer.

"I can't love Nox because you won't let me." Your voice is trembling, and the rest of your words come out on a breath. "On the same day he killed you, he hurt me. Maybe one day I can forgive the latter, but never what he did to you. The things he said as he sent you to Eternity...

"And yet..."

Now there's a fear of disappointing me in your eyes, and I kiss your forehead to assure you.
There is no way you could ever disappoint me.

On half a sob, you confess, "Nox did so much for me. More than you can ever know. But I hold it all back—gratitude, affection, forgiveness—because of you. As long as you can't forgive him, how can I let myself love him?"

Rayne, is Nox alive with you—
A knock sounded, and Tameka's voice pierced the veil. "Xelan, are you in here? Korac, can you help me open this?"
Seconds.
We have seconds, and I'm not wasting anymore of them on Nox.

I press our foreheads together, and you cling to my coat, crying.

I never told you, but that day when you ran in front of the car, you saved my world. All our worlds. I keep saving your life because you keep saving mine, and for that reason, I don't want you fighting alone.

"I'm not alone."

A shadow appears behind you, a silhouette burnished against the sun, massive and strong. Just when I assume it's Nox, gold glitters where it's painted along charcoal skin. Eyes open with Li inside them, matching your own.

"I'm not alone, Xelan, and neither are you. Hang tight for me. It's almost over."

I'm writing this entry thirty-six hours after I awakened in the Divine Booth with the others. After much conversation, I've convinced them that the matter with Celindria is being monitored, and I've already devised strategies for detaining her. They do not know you're alive, nor that Elden is aiding you. I will keep my faith in you a little while longer, but if I don't hear from you at regular intervals, I'll assume the worst and come find you, Callahan.

That means I'll be sleeping regularly. Tameka, my loving mate, is taking on the role of caretaker—One I'd never wished to burden her with, but that Korac and Tumu deemed necessary. Aria and Torch are even taking shifts to ensure I'm caring for myself. It's humiliating, and I'm ashamed, but beneath all of it is pure gratitude and love.

No one has called into question my competence to co-rule this empire, possibly because it is so reliant on others—The King Elects, Iona Councils, and my Co-Emperor. We are undergoing the search for a few psychologists to treat all of our various traumas, and I think it's past time. You know it's gotten bad when Korac's the one suggesting it.

The happy couple finally got to take off on their honeymoon, but...

I think Korac knows.

I'm almost certain Lucas knows.

Only one of them will search for you, so I'll keep an eye on Korac. Fortunately, he hasn't told Sagan. We both know that if she suspected you're alive, I would simply tell her the truth. I'm sorry.

Probabilities continue to shrink. I'm personally for it. I also think it has something to do with you and your work.

There's an air of mystery around you and your capabilities, Rayne. I'm not even certain what you can do, but I **am** certain you'll call when it's time.

Thank you for coming to see me and for convincing me I'm not a monster. I'm the Traitor Prince of Cinder, Tameka's loving mate, Razor's pet corsair, and father to a genius little boy with a mind full of potential. I'm glad someone gave me a second chance.

Now it's time to learn why.

SNEAK PEEK

CASCADING LIGHT

{Six Months Prior to Sagan and Korac's Wedding}
RAYNE WAS DEAD. As the explosion reached critical mass, her body disintegrated and scattered like phosphorous butterflies. The light blinded her for only a second, embracing its destiny—

The end of Enki.

Rayne was neither alone nor afraid. She was warm in Nox's arms. There were no tears. No pain. He shouldered that burden. In the last second of Rayne's life, she cupped Nox's jaw, clenched in agony. The pain he asked to take from her.

Then nothing.

For a little while.

Rayne first became aware of her regenerating body when a freshly grown tendon tugged on a reflex and alerted her to the presence of an arm. Two, in fact. Eyes were forthcoming. She laid on a surface, one she understood was a resurrection casket, but with no idea of how she was in it. She only knew it was taking a while.

Time was hard to measure without a watch. Or a body. Especially without knowing how it had taken to constitute the two arms and half a leg—maybe an entire brain—Growing a new body was exhausting.

And boring.

Rayne had lain there for a long time before she could twitch a finger. Then the voice came.

"Daughter."

Kindness in a familiar baritone. Nox had inherited his voice from Elden. This wasn't Rayne's first time speaking to the deity. He always came to Rayne at her darkest hour. The first time, Elden had come to Rayne heartbeats after she'd slayed Nox. The second time happened while she was dying in the heart of Enki, an hour before the Weapon fully detonated. But how...

"Elden?" No voice yet. Rayne asked the question with her consciousness, hoping to reach him. She wanted so badly to open her eyes, but maybe they still needed to form. Ew.

Light permeated Rayne's mindscape and under Elden's construct, her consciousness became an empty white expanse like on TV. Stood inside it, wearing her last outfit, Rayne checked the metal links holding the blue full-body suit together. Her hair was the same, too. Into the white, Rayne called again, "Elden?"

"Daughter."

Rayne turned to find an enormous figure behind her. Charcoal gray skin with molten gold tattoos, dancing along the striations of his corded arms. They framed his face—Elden was extremely handsome and a little bashful about Rayne's inner monologue, if the blue flush to his cheeks was any indication. His eyes... They were hers in Atramentous. Li blazed in them.

Although it was an honor to see Elden's face for the first time, Rayne was spellbound by his hair: black on the underside of each strand and white on the topside. He was an Icarus. How did he have Aegis-esque features?

A sadness competed with the kindness in his voice as Elden said, "A mystery for another time. We have much work to do, daughter."

After a reverent pause, Rayne spoke with her mind again. "How am I alive... grandfather? Dad? Throw me an endearment here."

Elden's chuckle was rich and filled Rayne like a plate of her mom's cooking: comforting and gone. He said, "'Forefather,' if you would. And I would be so honored." The deity of the Icarean race—of the entire galaxy—bowed to Rayne.

She was proud to say, "Forefather."

With strides as graceful as a jaguar—the cat for which the Shadow was named—Elden crossed the white space and held out his closed fist. Rayne stared down at it until he opened his slender fingers, revealing a nacre. A white one. His. Incomplete with one empty chink and one amber sliver from her nacre.

Elden said, "There is nothing which will stabilize the Weapon in you. Even now, it wishes to begin again. To fulfill your promise, you require instruments more advanced." He held up the nacre, pinched in his fingers so that Rayne viewed him through it. "This will see my children and Cinder safe. Will you accept it, Rayne Echo Callahan of Earth and Cinder?"

Rayne's heart said to reach for it without hesitation, but her wisdom told her to consider with caution. She wet her lips before saying, "Tell me of its composition. Its upgrade history? What about you? Will you—"

"I will be within, but apart from you." This rang with truth as Elden's eyes burned with sincerity. As much as an exploding star could look sincere. He said, "This is Quet's nacre, the Tritan Primary who created and wronged my Silence. He was the strongest and most intelligent of his kind. I am uninformed of its history before the Aegis granted it to him. Seek which Aegis created it, if this is significant to you. The upgrades are made from constructs based on my understanding of the now. Are there more questions?"

Elden gave the avian head tilt of an Icarean warrior. Thin gold rings, piercing Elden's ears and nose, moved with the gesture. His shadow, too, but it wasn't only his. Silhouettes of Elden's descendants formed the shade he cast. Massive man, massive family.

Considering Elden's proposal, Rayne tucked a strand of hair behind her ear. After a few heartbeats—and she had a heart to beat—Rayne asked, "Will I be able to communicate with you? Or will you have any influence over me?"

"Yes."

Rayne's eyes widened a little. She asked, "To what end?"

Elden straightened and his fist closed over the nacre once more. He gave Rayne the full weight of his burning stare as he said, "I want to take the life of the perversion. The woman who spurns the gift of life. Celindria."

Of course. "She's what you mean by 'seeing your children and Cinder safe.'"

In a familiar gesture which broke Rayne's heart, Elden bit his thumbnail, paced, and explained, "Yes. Celindria poses the only indomitable threat to my children's empire. To Cinder. And to Pax."

The smallest peak of a figure in Elden's shadow gave a little wave.

Rayne blinked at it and shook the odd sensation from her head before asking, "How much time will you give me? Until you decide to take my body into your own hands—Turn me into a weapon like everyone else?"

Elden's back was to her while she watched him stiffly lower his hand. His voice wasn't only in three pitches. More like a million. It was hard to even understand the words cascaded into her head.

"One year."

With her hands covering her ears, this was enough to choke Rayne. Even here in her consciousness, tears—hot and scalding—rolled down her cheeks. Pouring her heart aloud, Rayne begged... to anyone who was listening. "Will someone give me a choice? Ever? Why am I only *this*?!" Lost, she fell to her knees and let her head hang with the weight of her constant responsibility and sorrow.

Thunder rumbled all around.

Elden's voice was back to one pitch, and he let some gentleness into it as he assured, "None of my arrangement is permanent. If we kill the perversion within the year, you can return me to the nacre chamber and take a neutral nacre."

A thought occurred to Rayne, and she enthusiastically wiped the tears from her face. "Why can't you resurrect yourself like me? You can have your own body and—"

"Part of my nacre must always remain with Cinder to keep the Sphere functional. Forgive me. I want better for you, which is why I offer this. Take my nacre. Leave yours here with a sliver from mine. And you and I can defeat Celindria—A mission you already wish to undertake. Only with this arrangement can I assist you."

Alive with Elden...

"What about Nox?" Will there be two Icari in Rayne's head? She glanced around, searching for him, and frowned. "Where is he?"

Elden's eyes narrowed a touch, but enough for Rayne to notice. The Icarean deity said, "I love all my descendants, but perhaps one among them disappoints me. Nox died in an act of true selflessness, so I honor him as fitting to the son of the Icarus who ruined my daughter. Nox's nacre occupies Umbra's pedestal in the nacre chamber, shining alongside all the Coalition who'd sacrificed themselves so Cinder could survive. Appropriate, is it not?"

Nox's words came to Rayne. The words he'd said when they'd lived his greatest sin against her together. *"I'll regret it until I'm gone, until I'm dust, and long after."*

Lightning branched in an arc of kinetic energy behind Elden, striking the white space in a shower of sparks.

"Elden, I'll agree, but only if you let me resurrect Nox, as well."

So, yes. Elden's eyes reflected his view of Li, a red giant, from the nacre chamber. And, yes. Like all Icari, he was differently emotive in his facial expressions and body language. But there was no mistaking it.

Elden grinned bright enough to light his eyes. It was such a perfect echo of Xelan's signature smile that it squeezed Rayne's heart to see it. The behemoth of a god said, "Granted."

Rayne took Elden's white nacre from his hand and swallowed it.

Cheers to another year as someone's weapon, but at least this time, Rayne was given a choice.

THE VAST COLLECTIVE CHRONOLOGY

7M BCE	Enki Terminates Li, Elden's Sacrifice, Umbra Seizes Control of Cinder, Nox is born
3M BCE	Xelan is born, Nox becomes a weapon
2M BCE	Gait's children disappear, Korac joins Cinder's royal family
1.7M BCE	Umbra invades Lacceirus Capra
1M BCE	Umbra invades Monarch 3
500K BCE	Valkyries & Lyriks Revolt
250K BCE	Savis & Umbra pass into eternity, Nox becomes King of Cinder
6K BCE	First Icarean invasion of Earth, Nox invades Thailea, Xelan creates the Progeny
5.5K BCE	Celindria's uprising, Disbursement of Progeny lines, Formation of The Brethren, The Vacating
100 CE	Celindria 'dies' in Thailea incident
400 CE	Razor introduces Nox to Cascading Light, Xelan is banished to Earth, Nox & Korac plan their next invasion of Earth
1987 JAN	Tameka Phillips is born, Xelan builds Iona-oo
1993 May	Xelan saves Rayne Callahan from a fateful car accident
2002 SEP:	Xelan trains the Progeny, Icari commence 'soft' invasion of Earth
2006 APR	Full-Scale Invasion Day
2006 AUG	Volcano Day Battle
2008 JUL	Gait's destruction
2009 SEP	Enki's destruction

IONA PAX CHRONOLOGY

2009
SEP The Shadow form the Concerted Empire of Iona Pax

2010
MAR Sagan & Korac's wedding

2010
APR Find out in Cascading Light